The women were quiet. Meg felt sorry for Alissa. Something in the eyes of this aggressive little blonde now spelled sorrow. Sorrow for a life gone by. Sorrow for love relinquished. She knew the feeling only too well.

"Haven't you ever wondered about him, wondered what would have happened if you'd stayed together?" Alissa asked.

"You mean, the man I could have married?" Zoe asked.

Should have, Meg thought. Should I have? Could I have?

"Sure I've wondered about him," Zoe said. "All the time."

"What about you, Meg? What about your one and only? Don't you ever wonder how your life would have been different? How it would have been better?"

Meg silently wished she could say, *No. My life wouldn't have been better. It would have been worse. And besides, my life is just fine the way it is.* But she couldn't seem to say anything. She couldn't seem to lie.

There was silence around the table. Meg looked at Zoe, who was watching Alissa.

"I think we should find them," Alissa said. "I think we should find the men we once loved and show them what they've missed."

Also by Jean Stone

SINS OF INNOCENCE

First Loves

Jean Stone

BANTAM BOOKS
New York   Toronto   London   Sydney   Auckland

FIRST LOVES
A Bantam Fanfare Book / February 1995
FANFARE *and the portrayal of a boxed "ff" are trademarks of Bantam Books,*
a division of Bantam Doubleday Dell Publishing Group, Inc.

All rights reserved.
Copyright © 1995 by Jean Stone.
Cover art copyright © 1995 by Wendi Schneider.
No part of this book may be reproduced or transmitted in any
form or by any means, electronic or mechanical, including
photocopying, recording, or by any information storage and
retrieval system, without permission in writing from the publisher.
For information address: Bantam Books.

> If you purchased this book without a cover you should be aware
> that this book is stolen property. It was reported as "unsold and de-
> stroyed" to the publisher and neither the author nor the publisher
> has received any payment for this "stripped book."

ISBN 0-553-56343-2

Published simultaneously in the United States and Canada

Bantam Books are published by Bantam Books, a division of Bantam Doubleday
Dell Publishing Group, Inc. Its trademark, consisting of the words "Bantam Books"
and the portrayal of a rooster, is Registered in U.S. Patent and Trademark Office
and in other countries. Marca Registrada. Bantam Books, 1540 Broadway, New
York, New York 10036.

PRINTED IN THE UNITED STATES OF AMERICA

RAD   0   9   8   7   6   5   4   3   2   1

To E. J.

1

"On two counts of murder in the first degree, we find the defendant not guilty."

Meg Cooper clutched the defense table, closed her eyes, and savored the rush. It sped through her veins and poured into her heart. Victory. Again.

Holly Davidson—the twenty-one-year-old daughter of a now dead shipping magnate—threw her silver-and-gold-sequined arms around Meg. The New York State Supreme Court, Manhattan Criminal Branch, room 33, erupted in cheers.

"We did it!" Holly shouted above the noise. "Son of a bitch, we did it!"

No, Meg wanted to reply, we *didn't do anything. I did it. I defended you, and now you are free.*

"The jury is discharged with the state's thanks," the judge declared.

"Champagne at Neon City!" Holly squealed to the crowd of friends who had shoved their way toward the defense table. Through the chaos Holly's heavily mascaraed eyes met Meg's. "You'll be there, won't you, Meg?"

Meg slipped her yellow pad into her briefcase and snapped the lid shut. "I'm afraid not," she answered. She'd done her job. Her only hope now was that she'd never lay eyes on Holly Davidson again.

She took her briefcase and pushed her way through the mass, dodging the flashing bulbs and television cameras and microphones thrust into her face, as she headed for the back of the courtroom.

Outside the room another bevy of reporters stood poised for the attack.

"Congratulations, counselor!" came the shouts.

"How does it feel to win again?"

"Do you think you'll get a judgeship?"

Meg buttoned the jacket of her slender Armani suit and tucked a shock of her copper-colored hair behind one ear. The rush of victory was already fading, daunted, as always, by cold reality.

"No comment," she said.

"Ms. Cooper. Please ..."

Meg shook her head and ducked past the zealous ranks of the nation's media. Such underpaid people with so much passion, she thought. *So much passion, and so much power.*

The group clung to her as she opened the outer door. More people crowded on the stairs. Gawkers. Supporters. Fans. Protestors. Clinging together in the posttrial side show she never got used to.

She hurried down the steps, shutting out the questions, knowing the media would punish her for her aloofness with tomorrow's headlines, but not caring. For Meg Cooper had stopped letting the media push her around long ago.

The firm's limo waited among a string of tinted-window stretches by the curb, but Meg waved off her driver. She felt like walking.

She heard a voice call out, "Here's Holly!" The crowd surged *en masse* toward the victorious Holly Davidson, who had enough money and fame to get away with anything, even murder.

Meg quickly headed up Fifth Avenue, away from the

clamor, toward her Upper East Side brownstone. She had done it. She had won. She had set a murderer free.

"No jury in its right mind will convict a twenty-one-year-old girl on a defense that her father sexually abused her," had been the words of the firm's senior partner, Avery Larson. "Not in this day and age."

"She's not a 'girl,' Avery," Meg had protested. "She's a shrewd, conniving brat who used her father's money to finance her career, then killed him and her mother, too."

"She claims her mother knew of the abuse."

"Maybe she did, *if* it ever happened. But is that enough to justify murder?"

"Counselor . . ."

"Dammit, Avery, the girl killed her own parents!"

"So did the Menendez brothers," Avery had said, then scowled. "Are you worried about your client, or are you afraid that you'll lose?"

Meg stood rock still. She stared at Avery. He stared back. "I'm not going to lose," she said.

He leaned back and put his feet on his desk. "Then make the government do its job, counselor."

Meg hated the way Avery referred to the prosecutors as "the government," as though they were the almighty threat to society, to justice.

"If they don't do their job right," he'd continued, "that's not your fault. It's their incompetence. I also don't think I have to remind you that Holly Davidson has become a valued client."

A valued client, Meg knew, meant a wealthy client. Now that Holly was acquitted, the girl would inherit over two billion dollars.

And the "government" had, once again, failed at its job, because Meg was smarter, Meg was better. And because Meg craved the rush—that elation that came from winning.

Case closed. Case dismissed.

Meg tilted her head up toward the warm spring sun, squinting her cinnamon-colored eyes, eyes that were well-trained to gaze squarely at juries as she said, "My client is telling the truth." She would be thirty-nine years old this year, at the peak of an explosive career. No one would have guessed that Meg had set out—once upon a time—to become a champion of women's rights. But the world was changing, values were twisting. Fame and flash were what brought clients to the firm. Huge retainers kept her partners smiling. So Meg had become the savior of the scandalous rich, the queen of courtroom glitz, the sought-after maker of the tabloid headlines she had spent so many years trying to avoid. Now, by winning the Holly Davidson case, nothing was out of her reach. Well, almost nothing.

It had been three weeks since her relationship with Roger Barrett had ended. "I don't love you," she had announced. "I can't go on sleeping with you." They'd been together four short months. Meg knew he loved her, but she couldn't bring herself to love him, to love anyone. And she couldn't pretend.

Meg stopped walking. Home was empty, except for Raggedy Man, her three-year-old Persian. Home was where nobody cared that she was brilliant and gorgeous and had just brought off the trial of the year. There was nothing at home for her. Nothing, and no one. No one but Raggedy Man.

She stared at the sidewalk, hesitated for less than a second, then turned and walked down East Fifty-fourth, in the direction of Park Avenue, toward the offices of Larson, Bascomb, Smith, Rheinhold, Paxton, and Cooper. Toward the next challenge, and the lure of the rush.

Meg's office was not unlike the offices of many other top criminal-defense attorneys in the city: mahogany and leather, brass and books. But where her partners displayed smiling photos of their spouses and children and children's children in neat golden frames atop their credenzas, Meg had chunky pots of tired philodendrons. Her view beyond the heavy green drapes, eight floors down to the avenue, was close enough to watch the endless parade of yellow cabs and anonymous faces flooding past, yet removed enough to feel sheltered from the grit of the street, the grime of the people.

She stood by the window, looking down. Holly Davidson was now free to walk Park Avenue, Fifth Avenue, or any other avenue in the world. Holly Davidson, who had used their live-in chef's fillet knife to quietly slit the throats of her billionaire father and socialite mother while they slept. Meg knew that sexual abuse was becoming an all-too-popular defense in murder trials. It sickened her, mostly because it was so damned unfair for the ones who really suffered. *In another few years*, Meg thought, *these defenses won't hold up at all*. The judges, the juries, would have heard the arguments one too many times. Then, worse than guilty people getting off, innocent people would go to jail. It was the system. It was the American way. And they—the defenders—would be forced to create new tactics, new angles, to beat the government.

She moved from the window, sat at her desk, and tried to focus on her work. Though she almost always won, Meg was often let down after a trial. It was, she reasoned, the downside of the high. The crash.

She folded her hands on her desk and studied her fingernails. They were perfectly trimmed and glossed. Neat, but colorless. Without personality, without passion. Neutral. Like her life. A long way from the glamorous, high-profile image alluded to by the press.

She balled her fingers into fists. There was only one solution to her depression. Meg needed another case. Another case to dig into, to get lost in. She needed another case, and she needed it now. Right now.

She sat up straight and pressed the button on her intercom. "Janine? Is Avery in?"

"Nope. But Danny Gordon just walked in. He'd like to see you."

Danny Gordon was one of the investigators retained by the firm. He often worked alongside Meg on her most difficult cases: he had, in fact, worked on the Holly Davidson case. Danny was a few years older than Meg. He was slightly wild looking and slightly cocky. But unlike many of his counterparts, Danny was very bright and very tuned-in to his work. He was also, Meg knew, very gentle, vulnerable. They had almost slept together once, three years ago. But Meg had known what would happen. She would use him to curb her loneliness until he fell in love with her. Then she would leave him. So instead of being a lover, Danny became something Meg had never known: he became a friend.

"Send him in," she said now.

He blew through the door as if he'd been shot from behind. "Counselor! My congratulations on seeing justice served once more!"

"Can it, Danny." Though Danny knew the system—was *part* of the system—he always became a disgusted cynic whenever the guilty went free.

He flopped his compact, yet muscular, body onto a leather chair and brushed a hunk of flyaway dirty-blond hair from his forehead. His brown eyes sparkled. They always did, for even in his posttrial disgust, Danny's underlying strength was never jarred. He simply did not take it personally. He was, Meg knew, one of that rare breed of happy, self-contented human beings, the kind of man who exuded such confidence in himself that even his daily dressed-down attire of denim shirts and faded jeans was never challenged, not even by Avery.

"You split from the courthouse pretty fast," he said.

Meg didn't answer.

"You won the case, my dear. It should be the *Post* headline in the morning. 'Cooper Frees Holly.'" He stretched his hands to mimic the type.

She shrugged. "Jurisprudence."

"Touché." Danny leaned forward on the chair. "Maybe now you'll be able to afford a new plant," he said, motioning to a wilting philodendron.

Meg glanced behind her. "Not everyone has your talents, Danny."

"Orchids don't take talent, babe. They take love. Nurturing."

Meg had seen Danny's fabulous garden of orchids that flourished under the skylight of his rooftop apartment, where the gentle hiss of humidifiers spritzed the blossoms at timed intervals. It was more than love, she suspected. Orchids were Danny's obsession. Lavender. White. Pink. Yellow. He once told her that he grew them for their erotic vision, their soft, supple petals, their sensuous female folds and curves. It had made Meg feel naked. Exposed.

She turned back to Danny. "I know," she responded. "And I kill my plants."

"You don't kill them, Meg. Your plants commit suicide."

"Very funny. But you didn't come here to talk about my horticultural deficiencies."

He rested his elbows on the desk and folded his hands under his chin. His eyes stared into hers. Meg shifted on her chair.

"Avery is going to be pissed that you skipped out on the interviews," he said.

"He knows I like to be alone after a verdict." More than once Avery had expressed his displeasure over Meg's aversion to publicity.

"This was no ordinary verdict, Meg."

"Then I guess I'm no ordinary attorney."

He smiled, a slightly mischievous, knowing smile. "And I won't even mention the fact that you didn't have the graciousness to attend your client's victory celebration. One that will most probably make every trash tabloid and trash-tabloid TV show this side of planet Jupiter."

Meg found herself smiling, too. "I guess that makes me the fool, doesn't it?"

"Not if you agree to have dinner with me instead."

Meg frowned.

"An early dinner," Danny continued. "Nothing more. Unless, of course, you already have a date."

Meg shook her head. She hadn't told Danny about her

breakup with Roger Barrett; she'd been too embarrassed that she'd "done it again."

"Then we're on. Our own celebration. Even though this case pisses me off, I'm happy for you. I'm glad you won."

"Really?"

"Really. Now let's drown my sorrows and toast your victory with a giant bowl of spaghetti."

As the maître d' escorted them to a table in the back, Danny whispered from behind, "I hate it when you're taller than me. It's a macho thing, you know?"

He was, Meg knew, referring to the three-inch heels added to her five-foot-seven-inch frame. Danny stood only about five nine. In his boots. Meg smiled. She never knew quite how to respond to his directness. But she knew that Danny would be good medicine for her tonight. He would help ease the loneliness of the crash.

They sat down and Danny smoothed the tablecloth. "Red-and-white-checked," he said. "My favorite."

Meg laughed. "You're such a sweetheart, Danny."

"Whoa! Is that an endearment coming from the Ice Maiden?"

Meg winced. "Ice Maiden" was a label the press had given her when she'd defended a Wall Street financier accused of raping the daughter of a Mideast diplomat. The sixteen-year-old girl with the huge dark eyes had sobbed in the courtroom, effecting great sympathy. But Meg's defense had implied that Daddy's little girl was far from innocent. And she'd convinced the jury. Because "the government" hadn't done its job. So now the press called her the Ice Maiden. They didn't know how right they were.

Meg lowered her eyes. "Please don't call me that."

"Sorry," Danny said quietly. "I really am an asshole."

Meg forced a grin. "Yes," she said. "You are."

They ordered a bottle of Chianti and sat silently for a few moments. Meg stared into the candle, trying to relax.

"So what's next on the docket?" Danny asked.

Meg shook her head. "Don't know. We really didn't expect this trial to go so quickly."

"Are the partners disappointed that their fees will be less than anticipated?"

She placed a hand across his. "Let's not talk about it, okay?"

He looked down at her hand. "I'm sorry, Meg. But sometimes it bugs the shit out of me. Watching the defense of guilty people."

She pulled back her hand and took another sip. For some reason the wine burned her throat. "I've defended a lot of innocent people, too," she said. "Like Donald Haggerty." She was referring to the case of the crusty old man accused of killing his daughter-in-law because she was after the family fortune. Meg had argued that Haggerty's son, who had been the most believable witness for the prosecution, was actually the murderer. The jury had agreed.

"No offense, babe," Danny said, "but you defend anyone who's willing to pay the firm's outrageous fees."

She gripped the stem of the wineglass. Danny, of course, was right. But if Meg didn't do it, someone else would. And someone else would reap the benefits. She had faced this issue years ago. And she had made her decision. "Donald Haggerty was innocent," she said, though her tone was oddly without authority.

"And he is rich. Not to mention that the case made headlines."

Meg took another sip of wine. *Don't let him get to you,* she thought. *You did your job.* She set down her glass and stared into the shining red liquid. She knew Danny well enough to know he wasn't condemning her; he was only coming to terms with today's verdict, blowing off steam. And easing the guilt of his part in the trial, of gathering the evidence that had helped Meg get Holly off.

"Face it, Meg," Danny continued. "Do you honestly think there would have been an acquittal today if Holly wasn't so ..." He seemed to struggle for the right word.

"... so visible?" Meg asked.

"So rich."

"So sensation seeking?"

"So attention getting."

She raised her eyebrows. "So what?"

Danny curled the edge of the tablecloth. "So nothing, I guess. You're right. Let's talk about something else. Let's talk about sex."

Meg laughed. "Let's not. Let's talk about something pleasant, instead."

Danny let out a low whistle. "Sounds like you need a new man in your life."

"I just got rid of one. I don't need another."

"Roger Rabbit?"

She smiled. "Barrett. Roger Barrett."

Danny sat back in his chair. She felt his eyes studying her. "I don't get it, Meg. You have everything going for you. You're bright, you're successful, and you're absolutely beautiful." He leaned forward, smiled, and lowered his voice. "You do know how beautiful you are, don't you? With that thick auburn hair, that luscious Carly Simon smile, those long, long legs ..." He moaned softly, closed his eyes, and placed a hand over his heart. "Those incredibly long legs ..."

Meg laughed again. "Stop it, Danny."

He sat up. "But it's all true, dammit, and you know it. So I don't get it. Why can't you just let go, Meg? Let go and love someone? Let someone love you?"

She looked around the dimly lit room, at the cozy diners, smiling couples with intimate lives. How could she answer Danny's question when it was one she'd been unable to answer herself for so many years? She looked back at Danny. "I tried," she said. "I thought Roger was different. I thought this time things could be different." Each time, with every man, Meg had thought it could be different. But none of them could penetrate the cocoon she'd wrapped tightly around herself and her feelings after she and Steven Riley had split up. None of them—not in over fifteen years—could compare with Steven. The first man she'd ever loved. The only one. And now she was capable of loving only her work, her career. She swallowed back the tears before they could form in her eyes. "We're all different, Danny. You love having someone on your arm. In your bed. Someone. Anyone. As for me, I'm better off alone."

"Maybe you just haven't met the right guy."

"This may surprise you, but there are other things in life important to women besides men."

"So this is all you've wanted? Fame? Fortune?"

"What I wanted was to work hard. I hate the fame. You know that."

"Sure. You hate the pictures, you hate the headlines. But the money? That's what you want. Working for Larson, Bascomb has given it to you."

Meg didn't respond.

"Come on, babe. That brownstone of yours is your dream palace."

She pictured Raggedy Man lying in the bay window, surveying East Eighty-second Street, waiting for her return. Loyal, loving Raggedy Man. Would he know the difference if she was rich or poor? Would he care? The image of her cat quickly vanished. In its place was one of a small, dingy room. The room in which she had grown up. She quickly blinked and sat upright in her chair.

"Money makes life easier, Danny."

He raised his glass. "To money, then. Screw romance."

She cleared her throat and raised her glass to his. "To money," she echoed, and wondered in her heart exactly whom she was trying to convince.

Just then a figure appeared beside the table. "Ms. Cooper?" a voice asked.

Meg glanced up at a young man with thick dark hair and a Pentax slung around his neck.

"Jamie Holbrook. *New York Globe*. Any comment on today's verdict?"

Meg looked back at Danny. He shrugged. She shook her head. "Go away," she said. "Leave me alone."

It was after eight when Meg let herself into her brownstone. She had declined Danny's offer for a ride home. She was feeling a little too shaky, a little too vulnerable. If he asked to come inside, Meg was afraid she wouldn't be able to say no. And she was fearful of what might happen after that.

She flipped a switch, flooding the marble foyer with eager light, making the room seem less empty, less alone. Raggedy Man did not greet her; he never did. It was, Meg suspected, his way of saying "You left me alone all day. Now come and find me." She found him in her study, sprawled across a pile of books on the floor. She tossed her briefcase onto the desk and bent to nuzzle the cat.

There was a time when Meg had loved living alone. When she'd first moved to New York, there was nothing more comforting than to curl up in her tiny apartment and hear nothing but quiet. She would often sit for hours, not reading, hardly thinking, just savoring the solitude. The distant sounds of sirens wailing, horns honking, people rushing by, had provided a muted backdrop for the hint of life somewhere, outside, not there. Not in her world, her world that was finally peaceful, completely independent, totally free. Free from scandal, free from shame.

In a few years, however, her feelings had changed. As Meg had watched others around her—acquaintances, coworkers, even strangers walking hand in hand with other strangers—she had begun to wonder what was wrong with her ... why she couldn't fall in love again—this time, with the right man ... why she couldn't find someone to marry, to have children with, to share her life with. She'd watched, and she'd wondered, and slowly, what had once been blissful solitude had become a chronic ache of loneliness. Her infrequent, yet futile, attempts at relationships had perhaps, she thought now, made things worse.

She stood and slipped off her jacket, just as the doorbell

rang. Meg sighed. She wondered if Danny had followed her home.

It wasn't Danny. It was Avery.

"So," he said. "You're here."

Meg nodded. The white-haired, wide-shouldered man stepped past her and walked down the hall.

"Come in," she said, then closed the door and followed him into the study.

He removed his cashmere coat and sat, his six-foot-four-inch frame filling the sofa. Despite his sixty-plus years, Avery still exuded a commanding presence both in and out of the courtroom. "I won't bother to ask why you didn't show up at Holly's party," he said.

Meg rubbed the back of her neck and leaned against the desk. "Avery, you know I don't do well at those things."

He reached into his breast pocket, withdrew a long white envelope, and handed it to Meg without comment. She frowned. He folded his arms across his chest and nodded once. "Open it."

She peeled back the flap and pulled out a brochure. Clipped to the top was a hand-scrawled note on shocking-pink stationery: *"I've made arrangements for you to have a vacation here. Set your own dates. They're expecting your call."* It was signed, *"Thanks, Holly."* At the bottom of the page was an added note: *"P.S. My mother's friends love it here."*

Meg took off the clip and looked at the cover of the brochure. There was a full-page color photo of a castlelike building surrounded by lush green grounds. The title read: *"Golden Key Spa. Escape to Luxury in the Berkshires."* Across the bottom was a subtle addition, *"For the Discerning Woman."*

She laughed. "What the hell is this?"

Avery didn't answer.

She opened the brochure. Scattered across the pages were hazy mood photographs of women being manicured, pedicured, facialed, and massaged. One shot showed two women nibbling on salads and sipping on something that looked like mineral water with a twist of lemon, thank you, darling, and a spritz of lime. Meg laughed again and pitched the brochure into her wastebasket.

"It's not a joke," Avery said quietly.

"What is it, then? A thank-you gift?"

"From a grateful client."

"Well, it's ridiculous. To begin with, if I was ever going to take a vacation, the last place I would go would be to some snotty spa for the ultrarich."

Avery unfolded his arms and poised his fingertips together in an A-frame configuration. Again he made no comment.

An unsettled feeling crept into her. She moved behind the desk and sat down. "Her 'mother's friends love it.' Is that supposed to impress me?"

Avery stroked a cleanly shaven cheek—cleanly shaven, Meg suspected, especially for Holly Davidson's victory party. Press photos always reproduced better without a five o'clock shadow. A small knot formed in her stomach.

"Avery," she said, trying to soften her tone, "surely you understand I'd never fit in, in a place like that. Women who go to those places are pampered, snobby bitches."

He hoisted himself from the sofa and walked to the window.

Meg tapped the edge of the desk. Dead air hung in the room. The pregnant pause of intimidation. The kind of silence that forced the other person to squirm. An effective trick, an attorney's masterful ploy. Meg studied Avery's back. She sighed. "I wouldn't fit in, Avery," she said.

"You'll fit in just fine." Avery chuckled that fatherly chuckle, the one that always made Meg feel inadequate, infantile. "After all, you are a woman. And a woman's got to do what a woman's got to do."

Meg's jaw tensed. "Look, Avery, I'm good at what I do and have a little money to show for it, but these women are from the big leagues. The ones who were either born with silver spoons dangling from their siliconed lips or made damn sure they found husbands who treat them as though they were."

"Precisely."

"What do you mean?" She sensed that Avery was going to insist she go. A tight stiffness inched up the back of her neck.

"It doesn't hurt to travel in the right circles, Meg. You made a huge name for yourself today. Now's the time to capitalize on it. For your own sake, as well as for the firm's."

"Avery, I'm a working woman, not a spa-going lady. All I want to do now is get involved with another case. The sooner the better."

He turned from the window and faced her. "This could be considered working. Call it public relations. It could only benefit the firm if you learned to mingle with the right people."

Meg averted his stare. She fixed her gaze on the top of her desk, at a pile of papers brought home from the office. Work was her world. Not vacations. Not mingling. It was the way she wanted it. It was the way it was. *So this is all you've wanted?* Danny had asked. *Fame? Fortune?* She quickly moved her eyes from the desk, from the facts of her life.

"Think about it," Avery said. "It would please the partners as well as me."

The partners, she thought. It seemed that no matter what she did, they expected more. And because she was a woman—the only female attorney in the firm—Meg kept pushing herself, proving herself, justifying that she was worth keeping. But Avery was the senior man, the boss. And even though he might be upset with her for a few days, Meg knew he'd forgive her. She was good at her job, and he respected that. If she refused to go, the partners would put a mental black mark beside her name, but they'd get over it. Eventually.

She looked back at Avery. "I've thought about it. The answer is no. Now, what about my next case?"

Avery smiled. "Nothing that one of the partners can't handle for a couple of weeks."

"Avery . . ."

"You might enjoy the Golden Key Spa. It might do you some good to get away."

He wasn't backing down. Meg wondered if any of this would have happened if she'd gone to the damn party. Or spoken to the damn press.

"There's more to life than courtrooms and dockets, Meg."

"I doubt it."

He returned to the sofa and picked up his coat. His expression turned serious. "You're a maverick, Meg. That's a fine quality in the courtroom, but it could end up hurting your career. If you socialized more, you might find it easier to handle the more human niceties of the business."

Meg stood up. "Avery, I win your cases. Do me a favor and stay out of my personal life."

"As a criminal lawyer, you have no personal life. But you do have social responsibilities. And the firm expects you to live up to those responsibilities both in and out of court."

It was a blow she hadn't expected. Meg had always presumed that if she spent her life working hard, success would be inevitable. Now Avery was throwing her a curve. An uncomfortable curve. Her resolve weakened. "I'll hold a press conference tomorrow. I know the media wants comments."

"Meg," he said firmly. "Don't change the subject. I'd consider it a personal favor if you went to the spa."

Suddenly it all became clear. "You planned this, didn't you?"

He put on his coat and adjusted the silk scarf at his throat. "Holly asked if there was something special she could do for you. We talked."

"It was your idea."

"She wants to do something for you, Meg. The girl is genuinely appreciative."

"And she is worth thousands of dollars to the firm."

He nodded. "Many thousands."

You defend anyone who's willing to pay the firm's outrageous fees. Danny's words again. Meg shuddered. Avery walked to the door. "I'll think about it," she said coldly.

"Don't take too long. I understand that spring is a lovely time in the Berkshires."

Meg sat in her study for over an hour, thinking one primary thought: Why was Avery trying to make her do this? Why couldn't he accept her the way she was? Why wasn't he just grateful to have a partner—junior though she was—who was good at what she did? But no. Avery was always thinking of the firm. How things looked for the firm. How the firm looked to the outside world. He'd called her a maverick. Maybe she was. But it couldn't really hurt her career. Could it?

Danny had once told Meg that Avery got to where he was by being an intimidating ass-kisser. Danny, Meg knew, was right, although she wouldn't have admitted it to him. If nothing else, she knew the importance of loyalty. And now Avery was testing that loyalty.

She plucked the brochure from the basket. The shocking-pink note came with it. "My mother's friends love it here." Meg wondered what Holly's mother had been like. Had she really known about the alleged sexual abuse? Had she really done nothing about it? Meg thumbed through the photos of smiling women in the brochure. No matter how odd Mrs. Davidson might have been, there was one thing for certain: she had been nothing like Meg's mother. Nothing like Gladys Cooper. And Holly's dead father had been nothing like Meg's.

Meg set the brochure on the desk and closed her eyes. She envisioned Gladys Cooper, dressed in a stained housecoat, hair twisted around pink rollers. Surely there had never been a mother and daughter so unalike, so caustically different: Meg, quiet and sensitive; Gladys, boisterous and crass.

"You're just like your goddamn father," Gladys would bellow as she poured another cup of coffee, lit another cigarette.

But Meg didn't know that for fact: she had never met her father, the over-the-road-truck-driving man who had patronized the diner in Bridgeport, Connecticut, where Gladys had served him ham and eggs and apparently other treats when he passed through town on Thursday nights. Meg didn't even know his name: Gladys only referred to him as "your goddamn father."

"Your goddamn father was married," Gladys told her one night when Meg was around seven or eight and had finally found the courage to ask about him. "He'd have left his wife and married me, though, but I got knocked up with you and he took off like a scared rabbit." Then Gladys narrowed her eyes and looked at her daughter and said, "If it wasn't for you, I'd have been happy."

Later that night Meg had been awakened by a disturbing, mournful sound that seeped through the thin wall of her bedroom. It was a sound she'd never heard before, but after a moment Meg realized what it was: it was the sound of her mother softly weeping. Meg slid down in her bed, pulled the covers over her head, and vowed she would never again ask about her goddamn father.

She rubbed the back of her neck now, trying to erase the growing-up images. She'd spent her early years as "the kid with no father" in an era when that was a rarity, even in Bridgeport. She was too timid to make friends, too afraid they would uncover her secret that the reason her mother wasn't married, and wasn't happy, was all her fault. Then there had been only one escape. It had come through books. Each night Meg had retreated to her dingy, small room and read and read and read, until the grating bells and whistles and cheers of her mother's TV game shows finally ceased, until she was sure her mother was finally asleep, until she was certain there would be no more talk that day of her "goddamn father." Or no talk at all, which in some ways was even worse.

When Meg was in high school, she took a job in the library. It was there she discovered the world, as seen through grainy photographs in *Life* magazine. It was there that Meg knew there had to be more to her world than Bridgeport, Connecticut. More than a dingy, small room and a stale-smelling house that always needed something repaired.

With the help of a compassionate guidance counselor, Meg applied to college. She became the valedictorian of her class and was accepted to Wellesley on a full scholarship. Four years and magna cum laude later, Meg Cooper was at the Bridgeport laundromat one night, getting ready to pack for Harvard Law School. She paid little attention to the screaming sirens that wailed past. When the dryer finished its tumbling, Meg slowly folded her clothes, placed them in the wood wicker basket, and began to walk the five blocks home. By the time she arrived, the small clapboard house was a pile of smoldering rubble. Gladys Cooper had never known that her cigarette had fallen between the cushions of the sofa.

The only similarity, Meg thought now, between Holly Davidson's mother and Gladys Cooper was that they were both dead.

She picked up the brochure again. "The Golden Key Spa. For the Discerning Woman." Was that what Meg had become? She looked around her study, at the rich appointments, the leather-bound books, the silk damask draperies. The problem was definitely the money. She had believed that money could insulate her from pain.

Meg was still sitting at her desk at eleven-fifteen when the phone rang. She looked at the answering machine and let it connect. There was no one to whom Meg wanted to speak.

"Meg? This is Roger," she heard. She put her face in her hands. "I wanted to congratulate you on today's verdict." She reached over and turned down the volume. When the message stopped, she rewound the tape without listening.

The next morning Meg dressed in a beige linen suit. She

walked the two blocks down to Park, then turned right toward the office. She blocked out the morning-street sounds, the hurrying-people sounds, and thought about the Golden Key Spa. It wasn't fair. Aside from the fact that she didn't want to be Avery's token public-relations girl, Meg simply didn't know what to do on vacation. She'd never had one, never wanted one. There would be too much time to think about too many things she'd spent too many years trying to forget. She'd tell Avery today that she wasn't going to the spa. It wasn't as though he could fire her. She was, after all, a partner.

As she reached the corner on Sixty-third, Meg brushed against a wire rack at a newsstand. She grabbed the edge to keep it from falling. A squatty little man with brown teeth reached out to help, just as a stack of newspapers flopped to the pavement. Meg looked down at the mess. A bold black headline screamed from the front page: "ICE MAIDEN COOPER GETS ANOTHER ONE OFF."

Another damn headline, another assault by the press.

Beneath it was a picture of Meg coming down the courthouse steps, the crowd from Holly Davidson's trial in pursuit.

And there, tucked between today's headline and yesterday's picture, was a small, fuzzy photo from Meg's college days, the photo that had been frozen in her mind, returning to life over and over for so many years in her dreams. It was the photo that had started—and ended—it all.

It was of Meg ... together with *him*.

2

A putrid smell of stale semen hung in the bedroom. Alissa Page turned on her back, wondering if it was the stink or the groaning snores of her husband that had awakened her. She assumed that Robert had not been home long; she wished he'd had the decency to shower before coming to bed.

She stared at the dark ceiling, listening to the steady roar of his breathing. Tomorrow she would tell him it was time for separate bedrooms. There had to be a place in this twenty-four-room mansion where Alissa could get a decent night's sleep. It wasn't as though they needed to sleep together any longer: they hadn't had sex for years, at least not with each other. It was a situation they'd never discussed, for they were, after all, one of the finest families within their Atlanta-and-beyond elite social circle. Old money. Prominent name. Civilized.

Robert snorted and shifted onto his side. Alissa sighed and wondered what his patients would think of the director of the world-renowned Center for Infectious Disease—brilliant research physician, Dr. Robert Hamilton Page—if they could see him, hear him, or smell him now.

She squinted at the Cartier clock on the nightstand:

three-thirty. There was no use staying in bed when she had a party for twelve hundred to plan. She pulled herself up, slipped a long silk robe around her tiny, overdieted frame, then tucked her feet into white satin mules and tiptoed from the room.

As Alissa moved across the thick carpet on the balcony toward the wide, curved staircase, tears fell from her eyes. She wondered for the thousandth time who Robert's lover was. Was it someone new? A nubile, young research assistant, perhaps? Or had he been seeing the same one for years? A married woman? Alissa tried to convince herself it didn't matter: she and Robert had been married twenty years, and he hadn't left her yet, wouldn't leave her or the girls. Of that she was certain. Fairly certain.

She slowly descended the staircase, unsure why Robert's infidelity still bothered her so much. At first, of course, it had. And along with it had come an ache of fear such as Alissa had never known. The girls had been young: Michele only ten; Natalie, eight. Alissa had found a receipt from the Hyatt Atlanta in Robert's shirt pocket. It was dated November 7, the weekend he was supposed to be at a conference in Dallas. Or so he had said. For months Alissa had wondered what she'd done wrong. She was, after all, the perfect wife, the perfect mother. Her only crime, she'd decided, was that she was no longer twenty.

It was then that Alissa had begun going to the Golden Key Spa twice a year for relaxation and pampering. She'd had a few nips and tucks on her face and neck—"Catch it before it falls" had become her motto—renovated a bedroom into a closet for the hundreds of outfits and matching accessories she'd begun to purchase, and poured her energies into becoming the premier hostess of Atlanta. Now, at forty-two, Alissa Page was the one whose parties anyone-who-was-anyone craved an invitation to. Still, Robert had not stopped cheating. But Alissa was now too busy to notice. Almost. And Robert was, at least, discreet.

At the foot of the stairs Alissa wiped her tears, glad that

it was nighttime and there was no one to see her cry. She passed through the huge marble foyer to the tall double doors that led to the library. Just as she turned the heavy brass handle, she noticed a thin strip of light under the door.

"Mother!"

The sharp cry of sixteen-year-old Natalie was followed by a scrambled squeaking of flesh on the leather sofa and a frantic rustle of clothing. Alissa adjusted her vision to the light. A young man she didn't immediately recognize stood beside the sofa now, his brown hair ruffled, his cheeks flushed, his pants clutched in his hand in front of his crotch. Alissa sighed.

"Party's over, Natalie," she said. "Get to bed." Then she added, "Alone."

The young man hurried past Alissa.

"I'll see you tomorrow," Natalie called out. But the only response was the firm latch of the outside door closing behind him. Natalie pulled her cropped cashmere sweater over her firm young breasts, her nipples, Alissa noted, still stiff and expectant. Better luck next time.

"Mother," Natalie said, "you pick the damnedest time to prowl through the house."

"I wasn't prowling, Natalie." She walked to the wet bar and poured brandy into a snifter. "And besides, I'd think you'd be discreet enough not to bring your parties home."

"You make it sound like I'm some kind of whore."

Alissa shrugged and downed the brandy in a quick gulp. The liquid singed her throat. "Just be thankful I was the one who came in here, not your father."

Natalie was silent. She zipped up her skirt and straightened her mane of chestnut hair—thick, healthy hair, so unlike her mother's fragile blond wisps, so like Robert's.

"Who was he, anyway?" Alissa asked.

"John. John Wentworth."

The name stunned Alissa like a negative RSVP. *Wentworth.* Of course. He had his father's lust-filled eyes, his mother's stern mouth. "Wentworth?" she asked with applied indifference. "As in Grant and Betty Wentworth?"

"Of course. I thought it would please you to know that I'm dating someone who drives a Porsche."

Alissa felt the sarcasm of Natalie's words. But as rebellious as her daughter was, it appeared she was finally cultivating at least one positive trait. "Well, if you intend to hold on to him, you'd better think twice about having sex so easily."

"Oh, Mother. Give it a rest. We're not virgins anymore. Not like when you were sixteen." With that Natalie strolled past her and left the library.

Alissa poured another shot into the snifter. "No," she said to the empty room. "You certainly aren't." She sipped the brandy this time and wondered what she should do. Should she ground Natalie? On what charge? Fornicating on the premises? Maybe she should tell Robert. Let him deal with it. Then she remembered the way he'd flown into a rage when he'd discovered she'd taken Michele to get the pill. That was last year. Michele had been seventeen. Robert had seen the gynecologist's bill. What he didn't know was that prior to that Alissa had taken Michele to get an abortion. The pill was the least of their problems, but it was the only one Robert had found out about. And he couldn't even handle that.

Alissa took another swallow and scanned the shelves of leather-bound medical books, interspersed with classics. She wondered how he'd feel if he knew that after that escapade with Michele, Alissa had made sure that Natalie also began taking the pill. One couldn't be too careful these days. Natalie was right about one thing: they weren't virgins anymore. Alissa mused that today young girls seemed to go directly from the cradle to satin sheets. Or leather sofas. She only prayed that someone would come up with a cure for AIDS before it affected any of them. Maybe that someone would be Robert. God. If that ever happened, what a party she could plan.

She turned the small key that was kept in the lock of the desk drawer and reached behind Robert's Smith & Wesson .38-caliber "self-protection" for her silver cigarette case. Robert had long ago stopped trying to get her to quit smoking: in return she had agreed never to smoke in public, or when he was around. She took out a long, thin cigarette, and as she went to pick up a lighter, Alissa noticed the new issue of *Town & Country* on the desktop, the one she'd seen that afternoon. Her hand stopped in midair, then began to tremble as she felt the sting of reality once again. Slowly she opened the magazine; slowly she turned the pages. Past the slick, glossy ads; past the colorful photos. And then, there it was. The "Parties" section. Where only the most sociable ladies throughout the country were featured as they attended the most important charity events, dressed in their finest gowns, adorned with their showiest jewels. Alissa knew this section well, for she had graced these pages often enough: five times, last year alone.

But now it wasn't Alissa's own face that smiled back at her in black and white. For there, in the photo of the Peach Valley Gala, was Michele Page, her elder daughter, flashing her eighteen-year-old smile, elegantly flaunting her youth and beauty. It was Michele's picture there now, not hers.

As she stared at the photo, Alissa raised a hand to her throat, to the tightened skin, free of lines, free of puckers. Chicken skin that disgusting flesh that drooped in tiny folds from the chins of older, less savvy women—would never be allowed to mar Alissa's appearance. She reached up and ran her fingers lightly around the corners of her eyes. No crow's-feet, no visible webs of age. And yet ... and yet ...

The trouble with having daughters, Alissa thought, is that you feel yourself age more quickly. You look at them and are reminded too readily that it seems a hundred years since you could get away without blusher. You envy their ability to confidently go braless, or worse, sleeveless. Then they bring home boyfriends who, you have to accept, would rather be with them than with you, for no matter how flat your stomach or how well sculpted your thighs, any male in his right mind must assume that a woman, once past forty, is a lump of limp, a pile of sag, dried up, no turning back.

Alissa lit her cigarette and sucked in a deep drag of smoke. Then she realized maybe it had been this photo, not Robert's scent or sound, that had awakened her in the middle of the goddamn night.

The banquet room at Chez Luis was decorated in the requested sea-foam and forest-green tones; several round tables were properly linened and laced, adorned with fresh aqua lilies in appropriate crystal luncheon-sized vases. There were no candles: there never were in the daylight hours. Not when the gathering had been planned by someone who knew what she was doing.

Alissa checked her watch. She hoped to get this meeting over with quickly; it was, after all, Tuesday, and she had a much more important meeting after this. One which, today, she needed more than ever.

She moved to the head table and positioned herself by the clusters of potted ferns to review her notes. She had dressed in a pale-aqua silk suit to complement the decor, accented by matching silk pumps and the perfectly coordinating teardrop opals that hung demurely from her ears and around her delicate throat. The best part was that none of the ladies would know that underneath her silk suit she wore a skimpy lace teddy. Nothing else.

From the ambience of the room to the attire of the hostess, Alissa Page knew the importance of planning a perfect luncheon, even when its purpose was merely to plan yet another event. And, Alissa knew, no one in Atlanta could do any of this quite the way she could. She hoped all forty-three members of the Women's Federation for Atlanta would show. She would assign them their tasks, and the WFFA September Homeless Benefit would be under way.

Alissa smiled as she scanned the index cards filled with her notes. It amused her that she had thought of a party for the homeless. As if anyone remotely connected with the benefit could relate. The closest they'd come to homelessness was when the savings-and-loan scandal had resulted in two of their "dearest" friends losing their horse ranches and their Palm Springs retreats to cover their debt. Robert had instructed Alissa to remove their names from guest lists; it would not look good for the CID if they continued fraternizing with felons.

Of course, she wasn't completely without compassion. Or awareness. On one of her "getaways" just the week before she'd seen a group of socially conscious artists raising money for the homeless. They were selling their paintings to camera-carrying tourists in the funky shops of Atlanta's Underground. Though she'd smiled and said he could keep the painting, Alissa had given one artist a fifty-dollar bill. After all, if it hadn't been for Aunt Helma and Uncle Jack, she, too, might have been destitute, homeless, alone.

Alissa blinked. *Unthinkable.* She quickly straightened the index cards and shifted on one foot. She wished the luncheon were over.

Several women drifted into the room chattering and laughing.

"But did you read about Louise Cotton?" came one high-pitched voice.

"Oh my God! Imagine . . . finally divorcing that husband of hers."

"And his millions."

"More like billions."

"Alissa," one of them called, "did you hear?"

Alissa put down her notes. "Yes, it's quite something, isn't it? I've sometimes thought of doing it myself."

Everyone chuckled, because everyone knew there was no way Alissa would divorce Robert. Without him she would have nothing, be nothing. Without their husbands none of them would be anything.

Alissa smiled, sat down, and felt the sensuous comfort of

lace rubbing her crotch. She checked her watch again. Twelve-fifteen. Only a couple more hours to wait.

Sue Ellen Jamison, of the Rockford Jamisons, approached the head table. Somewhere on the other side of sixty, Sue Ellen had upheld Atlanta society since long before it became fashionable. Her stocky frame was always impeccably groomed, her white hair always in place.

"Darling," she said to Alissa, "what a simply gorgeous photo of your Michele in "Parties." No one ever referred to *Town & Country* by its title. After all, there was only one important section in the magazine, and to these ladies it simply *was* the magazine.

Alissa tightened her grip on her index cards. "Yes," she said clearly, "we're quite proud of her."

"Both your girls are so lovely, dear. You've done a wonderful job. Simply wonderful."

Just wonderful, Alissa wanted to say. *You should have seen my sixteen-year-old fucking on the living-room couch a few hours ago.* Instead she smiled back and said, "Thank you, Sue Ellen. Coming from you, that means a lot."

Sue Ellen laughed. "The next generation is coming of age. Looks like I'll be the grandmother of Atlanta before you know it."

"More like the Grand Lady, Sue Ellen," Alissa said convincingly. "And don't forget," she continued, wanting to change the subject, "I'll be counting on you to line up the most fabulous entertainment for the homeless benefit."

Sue Ellen nodded. "As soon as a theme is decided, you know I'll do whatever I can."

Alissa smiled, knowing Sue Ellen was dying to know who would lead the theme committee. Next to Alissa, as chairperson of the event, this would be the woman with the most power. Everyone expected her to give the job to Fran Charles, a frustrated artist whose husband sat on nearly every important board in the city. His connections had, in the past, turned numerous galas into extravaganzas at minimum cost.

The room filled; seats were taken. Alissa knew the ladies would be on time. They always were. They had busy lives, busy schedules. They knew that to make anything happen, you had to be organized.

Over sorbet, between the endive salad and the poached salmon, Alissa decided whom she would name as chairperson of the theme committee. She would have to work closely with the woman; she decided to give it to someone she must get to know better. It was something she'd thought about doing for several months; after last night it now seemed imperative.

She set down her spoon and stood. "This year," Alissa announced, her authoritative voice coated in sugar, "with the Olympics coming up, the city is putting on a new face. An exciting face, one of freshness and energy. Therefore, I've decided to follow that lead and appoint someone to head the theme committee who can bring new ideas and create new challenges for us all." People were glancing at one another from table to table. Fran Charles folded her hands in her lap.

"To head the theme committee for our homeless benefit, I appoint Betty Danforth Wentworth." She resisted the urge to add, "whose son is fucking my daughter."

Betty, for whom no amount of grooming could mask the pursed lips and perpetual scowl, stood and eagerly accepted the position. Alissa noted the beige Caché suit that Betty wore. Grant Wentworth managed his wife's fifth-generation peanut-and-cotton industry; Alissa wondered if Betty consciously dressed in beige and white to promote the family crop.

Silence filled the room, followed by polite applause. Alissa knew there would be criticism behind her back. But no member of the WFFA would challenge the selection. Not even gracious, talented, and most likely now totally pissed-off Fran Charles. Alissa smiled as she felt a sudden rush of empowerment. She checked her watch again and wondered if across town, on the thirty-second floor of the Danforth

Peanut and Cotton Properties Building, Grant Wentworth was doing the same.

Alissa let herself into the condominium with the key Grant had given her shortly after their affair had started. She knew she probably wasn't the first woman to take up Tuesday-afternoon residence there, but in the past four months she'd come to think of this as "their" place ... their haven from life.

She tossed her purse onto the ivory settee in the foyer and called out, "Grant? I'm here."

She was greeted by silence. He was late. Again. She blinked away the reality that he had been coming later and later each week, as she quickly moved past the wet bar, through the large living room, into the white-on-white garden bath. She turned on the spigots of the deep, oversize whirlpool tub, took a crystal decanter from the deck, and poured in a generous amount of foaming oil. Then Alissa went to the dressing room to change.

Grant was not the first. For three years after Alissa had discovered Robert's infidelity, she'd remained faithful. Faithful. Stupid. Then, five years ago, she'd found out how easy it was to have an affair, how free it made one feel, how desirable, how in control. She'd started with a stable boy at the club—trite, she realized now, the kind of thing usually confined to a bad paperback novel. But the sex had been great. Lustful, daring, exciting. And with the sweaty, muscular, stable boy Alissa had experienced orgasm for the first time in years. It made her want more.

She slipped out of her lace teddy, regretting that Grant wasn't there to take it off for her. It had taken a half-dozen or so other trysts before Alissa had allowed herself to graduate to sleeping with a member of her own circle. There was a certain daring in this, too, a forbidden fruit. She'd ended each affair when it had begun to get complicated—and, damn, they always did. But while they were good, they were very, very good. And they helped shut out the pain of her husband's rejection.

Rejection was a despairingly familiar feeling for Alissa. When she was six years old, her parents were killed in a plane crash. Her twin brothers, aged eleven, were sent to live with their maternal grandparents in London. But the old couple didn't want to raise a little girl, so Alissa was taken in by her father's reluctant brother and his wife, a childless, middle-aged couple who spoiled her with material things but never quite knew how to love her. It wasn't long before the little girl began equating ponies and yachts and shopping and parties with a sense of stability, a wedge of emotional security. In these later years she'd merely added sexual liaisons to her list of things to do, things to have. They were not trophies; they were life preservers.

She returned to the bath and slid beneath the warm bubbles, then heard the door slam. *Good*, she thought. *He's not too late, after all.* There'd be plenty of time before she'd have to be home at six. Robert would be home then, and there was the gallery opening to attend.

"Alissa?"

She heard him call her name. God, she loved hearing the sound of his voice. It was so strong, so commanding. "In the bath," she responded. "Come join me." She pulled a swirl of foam over her breasts, leaving the dark circles of her nipples exposed to the cool air. The thought of his leaning down to kiss them made them harden to aching points.

Grant appeared in the doorway, his large, lean frame clad in a pale-gray hand-tailored suit, his soft white hair and just-enough tan setting off his light-blue eyes. Those lust-filled eyes.

"Get out of the tub," he said. "We have to talk."

There was an edge to his voice Alissa hadn't heard before. She ignored it and licked the tip of her finger. Then she slowly touched her nipple. "We can talk in here," she said. "Take off your clothes."

He buttoned his suit jacket. "We will talk in the living

room. Dry yourself off. I'll wait for you there." He turned and started out the door.

"Grant?"

He stopped. "What?"

She slid partway out of the water and leaned her elbows against the side of the tub. "I've waited all day to suck you."

He stood still, his back toward her.

"Please?" she added. "You know how I love to suck you." Whatever it was that was on Grant's mind, Alissa was damned if he was going to cheat her out of her Tuesday fuck.

He still hadn't moved, but she could see him run his hand through his hair. She heard him sigh.

"Alissa, sex is not the answer to everything."

She swished the bubbles and said nothing. He remained in the doorway. Then, quietly, she said again, "Please."

He put his hands on his hips, hesitated a moment, then walked from the room. "I said we'll talk in the living room."

Alissa felt heat rise into her cheeks. He had no right to treat her this way. No right to treat her like a whore. Didn't he know how lucky he was to have her? She'd like to know the last time that frigid-faced wife of his had given him a blow job. Tears stung her eyes. *Damn him. Damn him. What the hell did he think he was doing?*

She pulled herself from the tub, stepped down the marble stairs, and stalked into the living room naked, foamy soap glistening on her breasts, her legs, her pubic hair.

He was standing at the wet bar, fixing himself a Scotch. He glanced at Alissa. "I want you to get dressed. Then I want you to get out of here."

Alissa put her hands on her hips. Water began to form a sad puddle beneath her on the Aubusson carpet. "Grant," she demanded, "what is going on?" She was amazed at the control in her voice. It didn't even sound as though her heart was thudding as hard as it was, as though her stomach was lurching the way that it was.

He took a sip from his glass, then held it to his chest. "On your way out please leave the key."

Alissa reached over, grabbed the glass from his hand, and hurled it against the wall. Splinters of crystal flew in all directions.

Grant glared at her. "I wouldn't have anticipated histrionics from you."

Alissa's mind raced. The words spilled out haphazardly, without prethought. "What in hell is happening here? I come here the same way I have for four months. We both come here for the same thing, in case you've forgotten. Now, what the hell is happening? I want an answer, and I want it now. And I'm not leaving until you give me one."

He calmly poured himself another drink. "If you think about it, I'm sure you know the answer, Alissa."

A chill enveloped her body. She wanted to put something on—the terry robe she'd bought at Neiman's, which hung in the dressing room, Grant's velvet Dior smoking jacket—she wanted to put something on, something, anything. But she was afraid to let Grant out of her sight, afraid that once she did, he'd be gone. "I don't know what you're talking about," she said.

He took a long sip and tipped his head back as he swallowed. Alissa could almost feel the Scotch burn his throat. "It was most inappropriate of you to name my wife to chair your little committee."

Alissa laughed. "Is that what this is all about? Come on, Grant, you don't know what you're talking about."

"No? The way I see it, you wanted to get close to her. To taunt her, perhaps? To tell her about us at some point?"

"Don't be ridiculous."

He took another swallow. "You're the one who's being ridiculous. The last thing I want is a scandal. You're a bitter woman, Alissa. Vengeful. But just because you have a, shall we say, 'bored' husband, you need to know that I'm not going to leave my wife."

Alissa resisted the urge to grab the new glass from his

hand. "I've got a news flash for you, you son of a bitch. I don't want you to leave your wife. God forbid you give up your throne as king of her family's fortune. Christ. I can't even believe how predictable you are. But I'll tell you one thing. I may not want you to leave her, but I do want you to tell your son to stop fucking my daughter. Or so help me, I'll have him up on charges for rape of a minor." She hoped Grant wouldn't realize the last part was a lie. She hoped he wouldn't know she would never subject her daughter—or her family—to the stain of scandal. Besides, she knew that in Georgia a sixteen-year-old girl was not considered a "minor" when it came to consensual sex.

Grant froze, his glass poised in midair. "Excuse me?"

"You heard what I said. Tell your pimply-faced son to stop fucking my daughter."

Grant blinked. The light-blue eyes had lost their lust. "I had no idea . . ."

"I'll bet. You probably told him how hot the Page women must be. You've probably been cheering him on."

He set down his drink and looked at Alissa. "I will speak to John," he said. "Now. Please. Get dressed and leave."

Alissa stormed into the dressing room. Tears welled in her eyes. She couldn't believe he was ending it all. She couldn't believe it was over. This was to have been the one special affair, the one that would last, the one that would give her the peaceful escape she needed.

As she pulled on her silk suit, one morose thought came into her mind: *What the hell was she going to do now on Tuesday afternoons?*

She stood in the wardrobe room, aimlessly poking through cocktail dresses, halfheartedly trying to decide what to wear to the gallery opening that night. As much as Alissa didn't feel like going, she knew she must. Not to put on a smiling face as one of the patrons of the artist, or even to be seen mingling in the right place at the right time. No, tonight Alissa must go to keep herself busy, to take her mind off the past twenty-four hours: Robert coming home reeking of sex; Michele's photo in *Town & Country*; Natalie's escapade on the library sofa. And Grant Wentworth.

Even an evening in Robert's company would help. Then maybe she would think about going to the Golden Key Spa for a couple of weeks. Maybe it was time for a vacation. A rejuvenation.

A short black faille dress caught her eye. She removed it from the rack and held it out for inspection. It was backless. *No*, she decided. *Too sexy.* She pulled out the one next to it. Red. Short. Plunging neckline. She shoved them back onto the pole and stared at the rows of dresses. Was this the way she'd been dressing lately? Like a hooker?

She moved up and down the aisles. Stopping. Looking. Rejecting. Then she spotted a chocolate dress. It was street length, with long sleeves and a high collar. The perfect outfit for someone feeling old, undesirable, depressed. Perfect for tonight. She'd bought it after she'd broken off with her last lover; she'd taken up with Grant the following week, so she never had a chance to wear it.

"Mother, are you in here?" Michele's voice called.

Alissa unzipped the protective plastic that covered the dress. "In the back."

Michele rounded the corner with her usual lightness. Michele was the mirror image of Alissa when Alissa had been young, both in looks and in personality, even though she was now dressed in saggy jeans and an oversize sweatshirt, her blond hair tossed in a careless ponytail. But Alissa knew that an hour at her vanity table would transform her daughter into a beauty queen.

"Is there anything in here I can wear tonight?" she asked.

"Where are you going?"

Michele started pushing back hangers, frowning at each dress. "To the gallery opening."

Alissa felt her temple begin to throb. "I didn't realize you were going."

Michele looked at the dress in her mother's hand. "You're wearing that? God, Mom, that's gross."

Alissa clutched it to her protectively. "When did you decide to go?"

Her daughter shrugged. "Last night. David talked me into it." David Johnston was her boyfriend—this month. "Are you and Daddy going with anyone?"

Alissa shook her head, trying to decide how long it was going to take her to get used to the idea of her daughter attending the same social events as she. Her daughter. Glamorous. Young. Not at all like her mother, after all. Not anymore. Alissa's vision blurred with envy.

"Hey, Mom, can I wear this?"

Alissa looked over at the white body dress Michele was holding up. Alissa had bought it last year when she and Robert had gone to the America's Cup. The yacht parties had been fabulous, and her photo had appeared everywhere. *God*, she thought now, *was that only last year?*

"Sure," she finally answered, "if you want your next picture to appear in *Playboy*."

"Mom . . ."

"I just think it's a little old for you."

"Mother, I'm eighteen. It's perfect for me."

And not for me, Alissa wanted to scream. *Never again for me.* She marched to the racks of shoes and rummaged through the plastic boxes. The chocolate satin pumps, she knew, had to be there somewhere. She scattered the boxes across the floor. *The shoes have gold clips.* She ripped off another lid. White leather. She tossed the box aside. *I'll wear the gold-and-topaz earrings with the matching brooch.* She jerked at another box. Black high-heeled sandals. She threw the box behind her. *I'll use the bronze eyeshadow to accentuate my amber eyes. Amber. Gold. The color of wealth. The color of power.*

"Mother, what on earth are you doing?"

Alissa dropped a box beside her. "I can't find my shoes. Did you take them?"

"No. You know your feet are smaller than mine."

"Yes. Yes, well, they must be here somewhere."

"Let me help." Michele squatted beside her and started looking through the boxes.

"I don't need your help."

Michele stopped. "Oh."

"Go get dressed. Fix yourself up. You look like hell."

Michele sat on the floor. "Mother. What's wrong?"

Alissa pulled another box from the rack, peeked inside, then threw it down. "Wrong? Nothing's wrong. I just can't find those damned shoes."

"If you really don't want me to wear the dress, I won't."

"Wear the damned dress. I don't care. Now, would you please leave me alone?"

Michele stood up. "Sure. I'll go get dressed."

"Fine. Go."

She heard Michele's footsteps fade away. Alissa slumped to the floor, put her face in her hands, and began to weep. This was so unfair. It was all so unfair. She looked around at the mess she'd made. The piles of material things. Possessions. It reminded her of when she'd been a child, playing in Aunt Helma's dressing room, showing Polly and LuAnn—Alissa's new private-school friends, her only friends—all of Aunt Helma's dresses and fur coats, giggling as they modeled the huge number of Aunt Helma's pillbox hats, like Jackie Kennedy's, with the dyed-to-match elbow-length gloves. And when the little group of girls had played this same game at each of their houses, Alissa had known they secretly envied her, because none of them had a mother with a wardrobe as big or as fun as Aunt Helma's. Somehow this seemed to compensate for the fact that her friends had mothers and she didn't. Somehow it made her feel loved.

Until, of course, one day when Polly and LuAnn had decided they were too old to play dress-up, and that they didn't like Alissa anymore, anyway. Alissa had told them to go to hell, that they were spoiled brats, and just because they had mothers and fathers didn't make them anybody special.

She'd told them off real good, and she'd even made them cry. But Alissa hadn't cried. Not until they'd left and she'd gone back into Aunt Helma's closet and closed the door behind her. Then she'd put on a pillbox hat and a pair of the elbow-length gloves and sat in the middle of the floor and cried and cried until she didn't figure she'd have any more tears to cry with for the rest of her entire life.

Aunt Helma, however, had been glad to see Polly and LuAnn go. She'd said they weren't good enough for Alissa, that their families, quite simply, were nobodies. Uncle Jack had told Alissa to ignore Aunt Helma, that she was just bitter because her life wasn't as happy as she wanted it to be. Alissa hadn't wanted to upset them, so she'd gone back to having no friends.

And now, if Grant Wentworth thought Alissa was the one who was bitter, well, maybe she had a damn good reason to be.

She picked up a peach-colored silk heel and threw it against a rack of clothes. Why was love such a big deal, anyway? No one had really ever loved her, and she seemed to be surviving just fine.

Then Alissa remembered Jay Stockwell. He had loved her. It had been long ago, in another life. But Jay Stockwell had loved her. She ran her hand across the shoes strewn about her. In place of her anger, sorrow crept in.

And Robert. He had loved her once. Hadn't he? Not the same way as Jay, no. Not passionately. Not totally. But he had loved her with a gentleness, a tolerance. Their romance had been based on the familiarity of their lives, the similarity of their values, their backgrounds. He had loved her as a partner, a comfortable mate.

When had that changed?

And why?

Alissa rubbed the soft suede of a navy flat. Was it too late for Robert and her?

She didn't hate Robert. There was nothing to hate. He was still kind to her, patient, sensitive. He was simply cheating on her. Was that something she possibly could reverse, even after all this time?

She pulled herself from the floor and studied the remaining shoes on the rack. Maybe it wasn't too late. It wouldn't be long before the girls left home; maybe it was time to get to know her husband again, to try to salvage her marriage. Just because her elder daughter had come of age didn't mean life was over for Alissa. She was still young—well, young enough—and there was still time to prove to Robert—and to the world—that Alissa Page was somebody better than any mistress Robert could find, better than all the young, clear-skinned beauties on the deb list that year.

She would win Robert back. She would start tonight.

She glanced at her watch. Four-fifteen. She would dress, then take his tuxedo to the lab for him. The employees would be gone. She could seduce him then and there. He would be able to shower and dress in plenty of time for them to make the opening.

Alissa felt a calm wash over her. She would go to Robert; she would surprise him. She would put some magic back into their marriage. They had too many years behind them, too many years ahead of them, to go on living like this. Or to throw those years away. She would be the woman he married again. She picked up the black high-heeled sandals and walked to the back of the closet to retrieve the short black faille dress. Then she reminded herself to instruct Dolores to clean up this god-awful mess tonight.

The Center for Infectious Disease wasn't far from their estate. Privately funded by a consortium of corporate sponsors and unencumbered by government budgets, the CID boasted the most superior facilities in the world. Robert had put together a team of brilliant physicians and technicians from all over the world who were now primarily concentrating on finding a cure for AIDS. The risk to Robert—and ultimately to herself—from working with AIDS patients was something that had concerned Alissa at first, but Robert had assured her that AIDS was no more contagious to a doctor than hepatitis.

"In fact," he told her, "you could have a one-night stand with someone who's infected and have a better chance of getting pregnant than of getting the virus."

Alissa didn't believe him. "If that's true," she asked, "then why all the fuss about it?"

Robert said that a fuss had to be made; AIDS was still a preventable killer; people had to realize that.

That had been over a dozen years ago. Now, as Alissa exited the highway and headed down Peachtree Road, she realized she had always trusted Robert. She knew he would never hurt his family, never expose them to the risk of AIDS or any other infectious disease with which he was working.

It wasn't as though Robert had to work. Each of their trust funds provided ample money for their family to maintain the style in which they'd been raised. But Robert loved his work. He was a physician, a healer. Beyond that he was the most intelligent man Alissa had ever known, the most self-assured. Maybe that was part of why his infidelities still hurt so much. It was as though he were telling Alissa that she wasn't pretty enough or good enough or *young* enough to totally satisfy a man. Especially him.

She wheeled her Jaguar into the lot. She immediately spotted Robert's own XJS and noted that, though it was after five, there were still several other cars there. Disease, after all, has no time clock.

As Alissa parked the car, she realized how good she felt about doing this. She thought about the tux in the backseat. All men, Alissa thought, looked good in black tie. But Robert looked great. She thought about how, at forty-six, he was still very handsome. Certainly the handsomest man in their circle; chestnut-colored, not-quite-silver hair, and dark eyes that penetrated anyone with whom he talked, showing how much he cared about what they had to say. As handsome as he was, Robert was never arrogant, never self-centered. Not like Grant Wentworth. A sick feeling rose inside her, and she wondered what in the hell she had ever seen in the bastard.

She shook her head to dispel thoughts of Grant, then shut off the engine and got out of the car. She took the garment bag from the back and carefully walked on her three-inch-heeled sandals toward the security entrance. She hoped she'd get past the guard without his alerting Robert: she didn't come there very often, so it wasn't as if he would know her. She did, however, want to surprise her husband. Tonight could mark the beginning of their return to a glorious rest of their lives together.

The guard was seated in a small brick tollboothlike structure just outside the door. He was younger than she had expected. On the pocket of his neatly pressed shirt was a nameplate that read: T. DICKSON.

"May I help you, ma'am?" he asked with a pleasant yet businesslike smile.

"Yes, Mr. Dickson," Alissa said. "I'm here to meet Dr. Page."

"Do you have an appointment?"

"An appointment? No. He's my husband." She smiled in return. "I don't think I need an appointment."

"I'll have to ring him."

"Wait." Alissa held up her hand. "Please don't. I want to surprise him."

"I can't just let you go in, ma'am. I don't know you."

"I know that. But it's really very important that I surprise him. Please."

He shrugged. "Sorry. Rules, you know. It's my job."

Alissa frowned. "Yes. I wouldn't want you to jeopardize your job. Would it help if I showed you some identification?"

He rubbed the side of his face where a beard would have been if he weren't so clean shaven.

She looked back at his name badge. "Are you married, Mr. Dickson?"

"Yes, ma'am. Six years. Two kids."

"That's nice. Dr. Page and I have two children, too. Girls.

They're teenagers now." She fished through her evening purse and withdrew her license. She passed it through the window. "See?" she asked. "That's me. Alissa Page." She fumbled in her purse once more and took out a silver key. "And see? This is the key to his office." She was glad she'd thought to take the extra key from Robert's desk drawer at home.

He studied the license, then looked at the key.

"Has your wife ever wanted to surprise you?" Alissa asked.

A small grin came across his face. "Well, ma'am . . ."

"Then you know what I'm talking about. Please. It's a very special evening."

He nodded, then gestured to the garment bag. "You'll have to show me what's inside."

"Certainly." She unzipped the bag and pulled out the tuxedo. "Like I said, we're going to have a very special evening. It's our anniversary," she lied.

He thought a moment more.

She tucked the license and key back into her purse. "Don't worry about Dr. Page," she added. "I'll tell him I threatened you."

He smiled. "Whatever happened to meek little southern women?"

Alissa shrugged. "That's only a fantasy reserved for the Yankees." She put the tux back in the bag. "I assume you're going to let me go in now?"

"Sure. Go ahead. Do you know where his office is?"

"Yes. Third floor."

He buzzed the door open and she stepped inside. "Have a nice night," he called after her.

Alissa walked down the long corridor, trying to remember where the elevators were. It had been a long time since she'd been there. Too long. She really must take more of an interest in Robert's work; maybe that was where she'd gone wrong.

She found an elevator and pushed the button for the third

floor. Her heart started racing; she realized she was excited. Surely this would please Robert. Surely he would find it all rather exciting. It had been so long since they'd made love. She hoped he'd respond eagerly, lustfully. God, she thought, she hoped she could, too.

The elevator stopped. The doors opened. Alissa took a deep breath and stepped out. There was a sign directly across from her. Robert Hamilton Page, M.D., Director, it read. Beneath the type an arrow pointed to the left.

Alissa walked down the hall, glad that it was softly carpeted. One thing Robert had insisted on was a comforting atmosphere. If people were being treated for infectious diseases, he'd reasoned, the last thing they needed was the intimidation of bright lights and tile floors. It was, Alissa thought now, evidence of Robert's deep sensitivity.

Alissa reached the door to Robert's waiting room. A few feet past that was another door, marked Private. That was the direct entrance to his office. It must be the door the key fit.

She quietly approached the door, took out the key, and slipped it into the lock. She turned the handle and pushed open the door. The first thing she saw was a magnificent aquarium that stretched across an entire wall. Bright-orange and vibrant-blue and flame-colored fish swam in lazy luxury. Then her gaze was drawn downward. There, on the floor in front of the aquarium, was a man. He was lying on his stomach. He was naked. He was on top of someone else. And he was moving up and down. Even from behind Alissa recognized Robert. Just as she shrieked, Robert groaned in ecstasy. She dropped the garment bag. He bolted upright and snapped around to face her. His penis wavered in the air. The figure beneath him rolled over and looked up at Alissa. It was a man she'd never seen before.

3

There was blood everywhere. Zoe Hartmann stood in the doorway of the study and wondered how in the world she would ever get the wall clean. She couldn't ask Marisol to do it: Marisol had a weak stomach, and besides, the blood belonged to Zoe's husband, so it seemed only right that she clean it herself.

She squinted her eyes and noticed something else. Sprayed against the wall, mingled among the splatters of blood, were flecks of tan stuff. They looked grainy, fibrous, almost like sand. And they were dripping down the wall. Somehow Zoe knew these were bits of William's brain. She leaned against the doorjamb and found it curious that she'd known right away what they were. She'd always thought the brain was gray, not tan. "Use your gray matter!" she could almost hear her third-grade teacher—what was her name?—Miss Lindstrom. That's right—Miss Lindstrom. Anyway, "Use your gray matter!" was what Miss Lindstrom always said. "Use your gray matter!" meant "Use your brain!" Zoe wondered now if Miss Lindstrom had ever learned that brains were tan, not gray.

Her gaze fell from the wall back to the floor, back to William's body. He didn't look peaceful, loving. Not as he had while curled against her in sleep last night. God. Had that been only last night?

His mouth was open. That must have been where he'd aimed the gun. He must have opened his mouth, inserted the gun, and pulled the trigger. She was amazed to think that the bullet had actually gone through his head before he'd hit the floor. That would account for the blood and stuff all over the wall behind him.

He blew his brains out. The thought jarred her. So this was what that term meant. William Hartmann, successful Hollywood agent to the stars, husband of Zoe—the has-been box-office sensation of the seventies—had blown his brains out.

There was a foul odor. It smelled like ... shit. Zoe looked down to William's crotch, at a dark stain on his pants. *He blew his brains out and it scared the shit out of him.*

She noticed the gun. What was it? A Saturday night special? She didn't even know what one was. Was it a .38-caliber, the kind they'd used on the set of *Day of Judgment*? Or was it one of those things that had catapulted Clint Eastwood to superfame? A .350-something-or-other? No, Zoe decided. This gun didn't look scary enough. It just lay there, beside William's right hand, looking kind of bluish-black and cold. Cold, like the startled look in his eyes.

She supposed she really should call the police.

But wait. Wasn't there supposed to be a note? When someone kills himself, there's always a note, isn't there? Her eyes darted around the room, first to the top of the U-shaped desk, then to the bank of computers, the sofa, the lounge chairs, the cocktail table, the thick wooden built-in bookcases. She saw no note.

She looked back to William, thinking maybe he had clutched the note in his other hand. But his hand was on the other side of him, hidden from view. She didn't really feel like walking around the body and looking for it, because, suddenly, Zoe was tired. And, besides, Marisol would be bringing Scott home from school any minute. She really must go outside and welcome him home.

If only she could get her feet to move.

Zoe felt like a character out of *Alice's Adventures in Wonderland* as she stood by the graveside listening to the rabbi. There was something surreal about the outscaled size of the group crowded around the tiny brass urn that sat on the ground, next to the small mound of dirt covered by a wee AstroTurfed tarp, beside the tiny hole in the ground. There was no large mahogany casket, no standard-sized grave, as there would have been had she been back home in Minnesota, where land was plentiful and tradition was something you didn't change, even if you were in the minority, even if you were Jewish. But this wasn't Minnesota, and Zoe hadn't been there in over twenty years, so she really had no right to call it home.

She also felt foolish to be dressed in black on such a bright, sunny California day.

The Lord is my shepherd . . .

She heard the words and felt the squeeze of Scott's hand. Through the haze of her veil Zoe looked at her son. Though only fourteen, he was already taller than she. His fine, chiseled cheekbones, blond hair, and blue eyes gave him an undeniable handsomeness, even though he bore no resemblance to Zoe—with her black eyes and dark, exotic looks, the looks that had created a larger-than-life superstar, the looks that had guaranteed Zoe's future. Once. Long ago. She briefly let herself wonder what would happen to Scott now that William was dead. She wondered what would happen to them both.

He maketh me to lie down in green pastures . . .

Beside her Zoe heard the quiet sobs of her closest friend, her surrogate mother of sorts, Marisol Perez. Marisol had been with her since the beginning, from Zoe's early days in the housing project in L.A., through her stardom, her marriage, through Scott's birth, through the aftermath. Zoe had witnessed Marisol's hair change to silver, her waist and hips thicken with time, her tawny brown skin become spotted and dry, the stoop of her gait grow more stooped with near-crippling arthritis. And through it all Zoe had drawn on the strength of her friend, had learned from her courage. Now she would need to again.

Zoe hadn't looked, but she could feel the claustrophobic presence of hundreds of mourners, could hear the occasional cough, the predictable murmurs. Had they really come to pay their last respects to William Hartmann, or had they come to steal a glance at Zoe? To mourn not the dead, but to scrutinize the living? She was forty now. Had they come to view how old she'd become, how fat, how unstarlike? She adjusted the veil so that its folds hung thickly on the left side of her face. There was no need for them to know everything.

Yea, though I walk through the valley of the shadow of death . . .

The service, she knew, was almost over. She wondered if it was safe now, safe to think about him. She studied the tiny brass urn. It didn't seem possible that a six-foot, fifty-one-year-old man was contained inside. Ashes to ashes, dust to dust. Zoe felt a small catch come into her throat. She quickly blinked. No, it wasn't safe to think about William yet. Not here. She focused on the rabbi's face. His glasses had slid down a little. Zoe wanted to reach across the small hole in the ground and push them up onto the bridge of his nose.

Surely goodness and mercy shall follow me all the days of my life . . .

All the days of my life. Zoe held tightly on to Scott's hand.

And I will dwell in the house of the Lord forever.

The crowd, even the media, at least had the decency not to flock toward them as Zoe, Scott, and Marisol walked slowly, arm in arm, toward the long black limo. Zoe kept her head bent, eyes to the ground, and tried to ignore the constant clicks and whirs of automatic cameras. They climbed inside the car, and the driver quietly closed the door behind them. Zoe sank into the backseat and stared straight ahead at the tinted privacy window. She wondered when she was going to cry. She wondered if.

There was a light tap on the side window next to Zoe. She looked across to Marisol. Her friend said nothing. There was another tap. Zoe took a deep breath and quickly touched the button. The heavily tinted window went down about two inches, enough for Zoe to recognize Phil Clifford, William's legal adviser.

"Zoe?" he asked quietly. "Are you all right?"

She nodded but kept the window in the same position.

The man nervously fingered his thin gray mustache. "Do you think we could get together later?"

Zoe stared at her close-up view of his mouth. His lower teeth, she noted, were stained with nicotine. She'd never really liked Phil Clifford. She'd never really trusted him. "Why?" she asked.

"There are some things we need to go over. William's will. His legal affairs."

"No."

Phil Clifford's white eyebrows raised.

"Not today," Zoe added. "Tomorrow if we must."

"Tomorrow will be fine. Shall I come out to Cedar Bluff?"

"Two o'clock." Zoe touched the button again, and the window raised before Phil Clifford had a chance to answer.

The limo started moving. Zoe suspected it was going so slowly because of all the people, all the cars. But she had no interest in seeing any of them.

"You don't like him, do you, Mom?"

"No, honey. Not much."

"Do you think he's going to cause problems?"

"Problems? No. I don't see how he'd do that."

"Well, with Dad's will and everything. I suppose it'll be pretty complicated." For fourteen years old, Scott worried about too many things.

"There's no need for it to be complicated, Scott."

He seemed to think about this a moment, then said, "I

thought whenever anybody with a lot of money died, things were just normally screwed up."

Zoe smiled. "Not necessarily. I'm sure your father took care of everything."

The car turned a corner and picked up speed. *Thank God,* Zoe thought, *we must finally be out of the cemetery.*

"Mom?"

"What?"

"Are you going to sell Cedar Bluff?" The sprawling, multilevel wood-and-glass house, nestled in the hills overlooking the canyon, was the only home Scott had ever known. He'd never lived in the projects. He'd never known the poverty.

Zoe looked at Marisol. Her friend's eyes were warm, supportive. Zoe patted Scott's hand. "Let's not worry about that right now, okay, honey?" But quietly Zoe berated herself for never having gotten involved in William's finances. As of now she really had no idea how much money there was, how tied up it was, or how long it could last. She folded her hands over her black purse and closed her eyes, wishing only for a hot bath, a cup of tea, and maybe, just maybe, a good cry.

"Mom?"

Zoe felt her shoulders tense. She wished to God Scott would shut up. "What, honey?"

"There's something I've been wondering about."

"What?"

"Well, it was just something that's probably stupid."

"Tell me."

"It's no big deal or anything. I mean, I don't want you to worry about it. I'm just curious, that's all."

She pulled the veil from her face and rubbed her eyes. "What is it, Scott?" She hoped her impatience didn't come across in her voice.

"Is it possible . . . I mean, is there a chance that . . ."

It wasn't like her son to stammer. "What is it, Scott?"

"Well, I was just wondering. Is suicide hereditary?"

Zoe thought her heart had stopped beating. She looked at Marisol. Her friend's dark eyes widened in surprise.

"What an awful question," Zoe managed to say.

"Well, I mean, Dad was a man, and I'm a man ... well, almost ... and I was just wondering if there was a chance that when I'm older ... I mean, I know that lots of things are hereditary. Some people say alcoholics come from alcoholics. And druggies. Stuff like that. I just wondered that if Dad committed suicide, if there was a chance ..."

His words trailed off. Zoe stared at Marisol, hoping her friend would say something, could find some words that she could not. Her friend had a knack for smoothing out a crisis, as readily and as calmly as she smoothed the wet clay on her potter's wheel.

Marisol bit her lip. "Scottie," she said, "I don't think you need to worry about it. Your father—well, he had problems we didn't know about. But you're a different person from him, with different feelings and different ways of reacting. Besides," she added with a comforting wink, "half of the stuff you're made of comes from your mother."

Zoe turned her head toward the window, as though she were watching the bright springtime California landscape passing by. But instead there was an aching, sick feeling growing in her stomach as she realized that someday, maybe someday soon, she might be faced with having to tell her son the truth.

It was a hazy afternoon, the kind of gray-veiled day that was so common in the city, yet infrequent here in the hills. Zoe stood on the deck of the dramatic cedar house and looked out over the valley. She rubbed her arms, wondering why she felt such a chill. There was no breeze in the air; in fact, it seemed as though there were no air at all.

Marisol had tried to get her to leave the house after the police took William's body away. She tried to convince Zoe to get away for a while, go to a hotel, do anything but stay there. She said she didn't think that being in the house where William had shot himself was smart. Marisol was Zoe's friend—her best friend. And though they'd been through so much together over the years, Marisol still could never know the gratitude and love—well, it had grown into a sort of love—that Zoe had felt toward William.

If Zoe's parents had been still living, she could have gone there. But her father had died a decade ago, and her mother two years ago.

Zoe had nowhere to go. But it didn't really matter, for she couldn't possibly leave Cedar Bluff. William had built it for her after Scott was born. It was where she'd spent the long years of recuperation, of rehabilitation, after the stroke—the stroke she'd had in the delivery room, the stroke that had left her partially paralyzed for years. At Cedar Bluff she'd isolated herself from the media, from her fans, from the world, preserving the secret of what had happened. At Cedar Bluff, with William's devoted encouragement, with Marisol's loyal patience, and with the hard work of a team of trusted therapists, Zoe had learned to walk again, to talk again. At Cedar Bluff she had discovered what was important in life. No, Zoe couldn't leave here. Not now, not ever. She touched the left side of her face, the corner of her mouth that still drooped a little. The scar that her fans did not, nor ever would, know existed. Let them remember her as she had been. Let them remember the beautiful, intoxicating, flawless Zoe.

She heard the doorbell chime. She was alone in the house; she'd convinced Marisol to take Scott to the beach house for the day. She hadn't wanted him there when Phil Clifford came.

As she padded across the wood floor in her bare feet, the bell chimed again. Zoe's nerves grated at the man's insistence. At the thought of the man himself. She crossed through the living room and into the foyer, where she stopped and adjusted the front of her caftan. Not used to receiving visitors, Zoe had been unsure of what to wear. She'd chosen the caftan because it was loose enough to hide most of the unwanted pounds she'd gained since stardom, and, most appropriately, it was black.

She opened the double doors. Phil Clifford stood there, eye to eye with her five-foot-three height, dressed in a polo shirt and jeans, carrying a DeVecchi briefcase that had more class in its handle than Phil had in his entire body. Someone, Zoe assumed, must have given it to him.

"Phil," she said, "come in."

"How you doing, Zo?" he asked as he stepped inside. Zoe hated it when anyone called her "Zo." It sounded too childish, almost disrespectful. William had never called her that.

"I thought we could meet in the living room," she said as he followed her obediently. "The, uh"—she hesitated, wanting to get the words out—"the cleaning people haven't finished in the study yet." Her words hung, unanswered, in the air. Zoe could almost feel him cringe, almost feel him grappling for something to say, awkwardly coming up with nothing. *Good,* she thought. *I hope he's as uncomfortable as hell. Because he has no right to intrude on my grief.*

She led him into the large, open room, the walls of which had been covered, at William's insistence, with colorful promo posters from Zoe's days of stardom. The chronology wasn't difficult to detect: posters of her early films featured the titles and a photo in which Zoe was one of two or three actors; the later ones had "Zoe" emblazoned across them and showed a photo of only her. The film's title was printed in small type, usually near the bottom. In many ways William had made Cedar Bluff a shrine to Zoe's success. But there was one element missing: Zoe had not allowed him to construct a theater. After the stroke she did not want to see herself walking, talking, whole.

As she sat on an alpaca-covered chair, Zoe decided the room must be redecorated in order to rid herself once and for all of the past that could never be resurrected.

Phil went to the matching sofa and tossed aside a woven pillow, nearly knocking over a round aubergine-colored pottery bowl, a favorite piece of Zoe's, one that Marisol had crafted. Without apology he sat down. Zoe didn't offer him a drink.

He unclasped his briefcase and took out some papers. "It's still unbelievable to me," he said, shaking his head. "It's still so unbelievable that William ..." He averted his gaze and looked at the floor. Zoe couldn't tell if he was sincerely distraught, or if he was playing it up for effect. Living in Hollywood tended to bring out the theatrics in people.

Phil rubbed his mustache. "He didn't leave a note?"

"No."

Phil nodded. "That's surprising."

"Yes. The police thought so, too."

He shrugged. "I guess it happens sometimes."

"Yes. I guess."

There was silence. Phil nodded again. He was, Zoe decided, nervous. Genuinely nervous. For all his usual brassy, big-mouthed demeanor, Phil Clifford seemed, quite simply, at a loss for words. And although they had never actually been adversaries, she suspected Phil knew she wasn't crazy about him. She had tolerated his presence when it was absolutely necessary: maybe he had felt the same about her. But he had been William's friend for many years. Perhaps, she thought now, he was suffering a loss, after all. Perhaps he was grieving, too.

"Would you like something to drink?" she asked quietly. "Some iced tea, perhaps? Lemonade? I'm afraid we don't have any alcohol."

He shook his head. "I'm fine," he said. "But thank you." He cleared his throat and fluttered through the papers on his lap as though he'd just remembered the reason he was there. "I really hated to bother you so soon," he said.

Zoe didn't respond.

"But there are a few matters that need tending to right away." He stared at the papers, not making eye contact. "I don't know how familiar you are with William's financial situation."

She folded her hands on her lap. "Not very," she responded, not wanting to sound as though William had purposely excluded her. "William always felt I had enough on my mind without worrying about those things."

"I see." Phil put the paper down. Zoe noticed that his brow was beginning to sweat. His lips tightened. "Then you don't know."

"Know what?"

He sighed and rubbed his mustache again. "William invested heavily in real estate back in the eighties."

Phil cleared his throat again, then took a deep breath. Zoe had a feeling she wasn't going to like what he was about to tell her. She wondered if she'd have to leap from her chair, grab him by his skinny shoulders, and shake it out of him.

"He bought into several condo developments, venture-capital projects, things like that," Phil finally said.

Zoe crossed her legs. She didn't know any of this, though she had assumed her husband was involved with other businesses, for he hadn't had a client since Zoe who was so successful, such a guaranteed moneymaker. He had a smattering of stars, though no megastars, no one who could have brought enough income into William's agency to provide them with the lavish lifestyle, and the constant medical care for Zoe, that William provided. Not one singular career whose 15 percent could have maintained Cedar Bluff.

Phil had stopped talking. Zoe blinked and turned her attention back to him. "I think I'll have some lemonade, after all," he said.

So she was gong to have to shake it out of him. That would probably be what he wanted: a little confrontation to regain his control. Zoe wasn't about to give him the satisfaction. She stood up. "Of course," she said calmly, steadily. "I'll just be a minute."

She went down the hall to the kitchen, walking carefully, yet assuredly. Part of the reason Zoe liked to go barefoot was that it allowed her to feel certain that her left foot was connected with the floor. Her left foot—the one that for several years had been virtually lifeless, unworkable.

Zoe took two glasses from the cabinet and opened the refrigerator door just as Phil appeared beside her.

"Never mind," he said. "I don't want any lemonade."

Zoe closed the refrigerator door.

"Zoe," he said, "you've got some problems."

She looked at him cautiously. "Problems?"

"William took some heavy losses in his real-estate deals."

She stood squarely on the floor, wishing she were sitting down, realizing that the foreboding she'd sensed earlier hadn't been her imagination. It now stood between them like a heavy black cloud, a seemingly impenetrable barrier, one that Zoe feared she did not want to pass through. "How heavy?" she asked.

"Very heavy," Phil rubbed his mustache. "He lost everything."

Zoe thought she had misunderstood. "Everything? That's not possible."

"It is. He did."

The cloud between them now surrounded her, enveloped her. "No," she said.

"Yes," he answered.

She leaned against the refrigerator and hugged her arms around her thick waist, uncaring that her stomach protruded, indifferent as to whether Phil noticed. "You're wrong," she said. "Cedar Bluff is still here. He didn't lose everything."

"I'm afraid he did."

"No."

Phil stepped forward and placed his arm on Zoe's shoulder. "William mortgaged and remortgaged Cedar Bluff to help cover his losses in other deals. The house is in your name alone. You must have signed the refinancing papers."

Zoe struggled to pull her memory to the surface. There had been papers, yes. Once. Twice. Three times? She couldn't remember. Nor could she recall that William had told her what they were. She didn't think the word "refinancing" had ever been mentioned, but, then again, she'd always trusted William, and she probably hadn't paid too much attention.

Phil removed his hand from her shoulder and stepped back. "To put it simply, there's a balloon payment of half a million dollars due on this place in less than sixty days. William didn't have the money."

Zoe looked into Phil's eyes. They were small and they were sad, and they told her he was not lying. "I think I need to sit down," she said.

Somehow Zoe endured the rest of the day. There were tacos and burritos for dinner—delivered, of course, for Zoe didn't cook, had never learned how. She acted out her role as though it had been an ordinary day, as though nothing were wrong. Any more wrong than the fact that William had killed himself just a few days earlier.

It was after eleven now. Scott had gone to bed; Zoe sat with Marisol in the family room, sipping tea. She had explained to Marisol what Phil had reported. As she watched her friend try to digest the information, Zoe felt as though she must be in a dream, that soon she would awaken and this entire nightmare would have been just that. But as she looked around the room at the southwestern-style furniture, the aqua and salmon and beige appointments, Zoe knew this was no dream. The images were too crystal clear, the edges too defined.

"It must be why he killed himself." Marisol said suddenly. Her words were exactly what Zoe had been thinking.

Zoe wasn't convinced of that, but neither was she strong enough to contradict. "There is insurance," she said. "He'd taken a half-million-dollar policy out on each of us. It's enough to cover the balloon payment, but after that there's nothing."

Marisol stirred a spoon in her thick mug.

"I guess I'll have to sell the house," Zoe continued, but

even as she spoke, she heard disbelief in her mechanical words. "After the other debts are paid off, there should be enough to buy another place. A smaller place. For the three of us." Marisol had been a part of their family for so many years, Zoe wanted to reassure her that wouldn't change. Or maybe it was herself she needed to reassure.

"Where?" Marisol asked. "Back in the projects?"

Zoe gripped the handle of her mug.

Marisol put her hand on Zoe's. "Listen to me. I can go back there. Living in this house was always a fantasy for someone like me. But you? No. You cannot go back, Zoe. This is where you belong. You and Scott."

Zoe felt the tears come. She had waited so long to cry; now the tears flooded down her cheeks. Days of tears. Maybe months. Maybe years.

"I have no choice," she sobbed.

"You always have a choice. Look at you. You're beautiful. You're a star."

Anger rose in Zoe's cheeks. She scraped her chair against the tile floor and stood up. "Don't be a fool, Marisol. Of all people I thought I could count on you."

"You can."

"Not when you talk like that! Look at me!" She skimmed her hands over the front of her body. "I'm old. I'm dumpy. And my freaking mouth still hangs down like it's made of Silly Putty."

"No, it doesn't."

"Yes, it does. It's all I see when I look in the mirror. That, and the fact I seem to have lost my cheekbones under about a hundred layers of fat cells."

"You look in the mirror too closely. You don't see the Zoe I see."

"God, Marisol," she ranted, ignoring her friend's comments. "It's not only the way I look. For godsake, I haven't worked in fifteen years. I'm a has-been. Over the hill." She scooped her mug off the table. It caught on the edge. Tea spilled all over the floor. "Damn you!" she screamed.

Marisol calmly got up, took her napkin, and began mopping up the mess. "Sit down," she commanded.

Zoe sat.

Marisol returned to her chair. "Listen to me. A lot of people, they still think of you as Zoe the star. But I know you better. I know you as Zoe, my friend."

Zoe choked back more tears.

"You came up from nothing. Nobody knows that better than me. And you never forgot me. Even when you were sick. You gave me this job. You told me I would always be part of your life. Sure, I took care of you. But you took better care of me. You saved me."

Zoe remembered the loud nights, the frightening sounds of the beatings in the next apartment. She remembered hearing the shouts through the walls, the cries; she remembered seeing the bruises for days on Marisol's face and arms and legs. Marisol had been unable to have children, something for which she was very sad, yet very glad. It had made leaving her man so much easier, once Zoe had convinced her it was the right thing, the only thing, to do.

"You want to sell Cedar Bluff?" Marisol asked. "I don't think so. Maybe someday. Not now. It's too soon."

Zoe put her face in her hands. "You're the one who didn't want me to come back here after William died."

"Sure. For a few days. A week maybe. But you belong here, Zoe. Cedar Bluff is part of you. At least for now." Marisol pulled Zoe's hands from her face. "I'll tell you what you're going to do. You're going to go back to work. You said the insurance will give you enough money for this big balloon thing. But you're going to go back to work. Then if you decide to sell this place, it will be because you want to, not because you've got no choice."

"Marisol, I can't . . ."

"Don't give me no shit. You're going to do as I tell you."

Zoe remembered those words. She'd heard them often enough from her friend while she was recuperating from the stroke. At times when she was afraid to try walking. At times when she'd go for days without trying to talk. "Don't give me no shit." Marisol certainly had a way with words. But it had worked. Then.

"It's different now, Marisol. We're not talking about keeping up my spirits or trying to get me back on my emotional feet. There are debts here. Bills. Big ones. I simply don't have what it takes to overcome this."

Marisol leaned across the table and took her friend's face in her hands. She looked squarely into her eyes and said, "Yes, you do. You got guts, honey. You got Scottie. And you got me. And I'm gonna help."

Marisol stood up and began to pace the floor. "And here's where we're going to start. First, you're going to get yourself fixed up. Because if you look like a star, you'll feel like a star again."

Zoe sighed.

"We're going to get you to one of those fat-farm places."

"A spa?"

"Yeah. A spa."

"And within ten minutes of check-in every tabloid in the country will know about it."

Marisol circled the table again. "Well, then we'll find a real private place. Somewhere far away."

"Marisol. I appreciate what you're trying to do here. Honest, I do. But you have to be realistic. First of all, I can't go to any spa. They're expensive. I have no money."

"Yes, you do."

"Right. I think I have a few thousand in a checking account with my name on it. Money I'm going to need. Not money to blow on losing a few pounds." She stood up and went to the window. "What I need to do is sell this place. Move. Find a new life. One without dreams."

"I got money."

Zoe turned and faced her friend. "What?"

"I said I got money. Plenty of money. You've paid me a lot of money over the years. I saved up."

Zoe shook her head. "No. Whatever you have is yours.

You took care of me. Of Scott. You never let me hire a housekeeper. You protected me from strangers, from the media, from the snooping eyes of people who would have loved to know how far and how low I'd fallen. No, Marisol, what you have is yours. You earned it."

"No. I want you to have it."

Zoe waved her hands. "Absolutely not. I won't have you spending your money on me."

"So what've you been doing all these years? You've been spending yours on me. Now it's my turn. Besides, you and Scottie, you're my family. You know that."

"Marisol ..."

"Here's what we'll do. We'll find you a place to go. A spa. I'll pay for it. Then we'll see where we go from there."

"Marisol, I love you more than I would my own sister if I had one, or my own mother if she were still living. But the truth is, I don't think I can be an actress again."

"That's your first mistake."

"What?"

"You don't call yourself an 'actress' anymore. You're an 'actor' now. The men won that round."

Zoe laughed. It felt good to laugh.

"And you're going to start tomorrow. Tomorrow you're going to meet that agent William used to work with. What was his name?"

"Tim? Tim Danahy?"

"Yeah. Him. You're going to meet him and tell him you want to act again. You've got nothing to lose."

"Marisol," Zoe said quietly as she walked back to the table. "There's one thing you haven't considered. I don't think I even want to be an actress again."

Marisol shook her head. "Yes, you do."

"What makes you so sure?"

"Because, honey, you got no choice."

She wore a short blond wig, large-framed sunglasses, black leggings, and an oversize black-and-white tunic. Zoe didn't know if she was really camouflaging her face or her fat; then again, if no one was expecting her, they probably wouldn't recognize her. It had been so long. So many years.

She took a deep breath and stepped beyond the door that was lettered The Timothy Danahy Agency, remembering when it read Hartmann and Danahy. That was before William and Tim had split, just before William made Zoe a star.

Inside the small waiting room everything looked surprisingly the same. Same earth-tones decor, same understated furniture, same lackluster oil paintings purchased at some no-name street fair. Tim Danahy, Zoe suspected, was surviving. Barely.

Zoe walked to the middle-aged receptionist, who peered at her suspiciously over half glasses. "Yes?"

"Is Tim available?" Zoe asked. She'd not phoned ahead; she hadn't wanted to make an appointment in case she changed her mind.

"Is he expecting you?"

Zoe tucked a flyaway blond curl behind her ear. She wondered if her black hair had crept out. It had been so long since she'd had to disguise herself to go out; it had been so long since she'd gone out, period. "No."

The woman chewed the side of a pencil. "You'll have to make an appointment," she said dryly.

Zoe took another deep breath. "If he's available, I think he'll see me."

The woman's eyebrows raised.

"Please," Zoe said.

"What's your name?" the woman asked.

"Tell him it's a friend from long ago," she said. "Tell him it's Zoe."

The woman laughed. "Sure, miss. And I'm Cindy Crawford."

Zoe took off her sunglasses and looked around. The door had closed behind her; there were no other people in the room. She pulled off the wig and shook out her long black hair.

The woman gasped. "My God. It really is you."

Zoe smiled. "Yes."

The woman simply stared. "I can't believe it's you." Then she paused. "Oh, my, I'm so sorry about your husband."

"Thank you. Now, do you think Tim is available?"

The woman sprang from her chair. "Oh, my, yes. Follow me." She crossed the room, then opened the door to an inner office. "Tim ...," she began to say.

"I know," came a deep voice beyond. A voice that was so familiar to Zoe. "Send her in."

Zoe went inside and the woman discreetly disappeared, probably in a hurry to get on the phone and tell her friends who was there. Tim Danahy sat with his back to Zoe. "You knew I was here?" she asked.

He swiveled around in the chair and faced Zoe. He pointed to a small box on his desk. "I monitor everything that goes on out front."

Zoe smiled. Same old Tim. Same old paranoid Tim.

He stood up and came around the desk. He reached out and hugged her. His arms felt good. Comforting. "How are you, Zoe?"

"Fine, Tim. Honestly."

He pulled back and motioned to a chair. "Have a seat. I was there, you know. At William's funeral."

"I didn't know." As she sat on a worn leather chair, Zoe noticed that one thing had changed: the pungent stench of Tim's trademark cigars no longer clung to the air and everything in the room. Sometime over the past fifteen years Tim must have quit smoking. She wondered if he'd changed in other ways as well.

He returned to his desk chair, shaking his head. "I still can't believe it. That William is gone."

"I know."

He put his elbows on the desk and propped his face in his hands. "And now you're here."

Zoe shifted uncomfortably on the chair. "Now I'm here."

"I don't think I have to guess why."

Zoe let her gaze drop to her lap.

"It wasn't a secret, Zoe. About the hard times that had fallen on William."

"It was to me," she said quietly.

"And now you want my help."

She raised her head. "I want to act again. I need to." God, why did she feel as though she were begging? It wasn't as though she had to prove herself to him. It had, after all, actually been Tim Danahy—not William—who'd first spotted Zoe. Who'd *discovered* her. She'd been Zoe Naddlemeyer then. Small town, small potatoes, Zoe Naddlemeyer. It had been Tim's idea to drop her last name. It had been Tim—not William—who had created "Zoe."

He laughed, though not unkindly. "Zoe, darling, if you'd asked me for money, that would be easier. And believe me, I don't have much of that myself these days."

Zoe sat silently.

"Of course," he went on, "I would have had more money—lots of money—if William hadn't stolen you out from under me."

Zoe realized that Tim might have changed his cigar-smoking habit, but part of him was still angry. She didn't blame him. "Tim ..."

He waved his hand. "Sorry. That wasn't fair. But he did steal you. In more ways than one. I was in love with you, you know."

Zoe had known. But back then it seemed everyone was in love with her. Her face, her body, her ability to stun the camera.

"William lied to me. He told me you were taken by some boy from back home."

An image of Eric Matthews rushed into her mind. *The boy from back home.* The boy who had forever altered the course of her life. "That wasn't a lie."

"No? Then William told me our partnership was over, and the next thing I knew the boy was out of the picture and you and William were married."

"It didn't happen quite that quickly."

"No, it didn't. First William split off from me. Then you became a star."

Then Eric left me, Zoe thought, with a tug at her heart that had never quite gone away, not even after all the hurt he'd caused. The emotional hurt, the physical. She touched the loosened muscle at the corner of her mouth.

"Then," Tim continued, "William married you."

"You remember it well."

"I told you. I was in love with you. When you love someone, you remember the pain as well as the pleasure."

Zoe sighed. She'd never as much as had dinner with Tim Danahy, let alone given him "pleasure." She folded her hands in her lap. "Tim, it's all ancient history now."

"You're right." He neither apologized nor appeared to be embarrassed.

"I need a job," Zoe said quickly. "That's all I'm here for. I need to get back to work."

"So why come here? Look around, Zoe. I haven't exactly been successful."

"I'm here because I trust you, Tim."

"Ahh. The trust factor."

"And I need you. I need your help."

Tim stood and walked to a wall of bookcases, which were filled not with books, but with videotapes. "How old are you now, Zoe?"

She swallowed. "Forty."

"Forty years old and trying to start over in a world of twenty-year-olds."

"I was hoping that had changed."

He shrugged. "It has somewhat. Streep. Glenn Close. God, even MacLaine. They've proved you don't have to be twenty to be a star." He shook his head and turned back to her. "But they've had a hard fight, Zoe. Are you sure you're up to it?"

She wasn't sure at all. "Yes," she said.

"It could take some time to find you the right part."

"I don't have time, Tim."

He returned to his desk and began rifling through a drawer. He pulled out a thick manuscript. "This is something one of my writers came up with."

"You just happened to have a script in your desk?"

Tim smiled. "Let's say I thought you might be dropping by."

Zoe didn't know if he was patronizing her, but she decided she was in no position to play prima donna.

"It's a decent script," Tim continued. "I've been talking with Cal Baker about production."

"Cal Baker?"

"He's a director, Zoe. A top-notch one. God. You *have* been out of circulation."

She took the manuscript. *Close Ties*, the title page read.

"It'll be a miniseries," Tim said. "Made for TV."

Zoe pushed the manuscript aside. "I don't do TV, Tim. I'm an actress."

He leaned back in his chair. "Then don't plan on getting any work," he said.

She looked at him. The steady gaze of his eyes told her he was serious. She picked up the manuscript again.

"The part of Jan Wexler calls for a thirty-five-year-old. Do you think you could pass?"

"How much time would I have?"

"A month. Six weeks."

She stared at the manuscript. She was grateful that Tim hadn't mentioned her weight. Or, if he'd noticed, the telltale droopy lip, the remains of her stroke. Zoe thought about Marisol's offer of the spa. "Yes," she answered. "Sure."

"You'd have to test."

"What? A screen test?"

"Yep."

"God, Tim, you're not going to make this easy, are you?"

He looked into her eyes with the same intensity that he had long ago. The same intensity, the same concern. "It's been a long time, Zoe. The camera could look at you differently now."

She touched the corner of her mouth once again. Had he noticed, after all?

"Take the script, Zoe. Study it. We'll see what happens."

She stood up and tucked the script into her large bag. "I knew I could count on you, Tim."

He stood and put his hands on his hips. "Give me a call when you're ready. Oh, and Zoe . . ."

She turned as she walked toward the door.

"Would you answer one question for me?"

She held her breath a moment.

"Your son. What's his name?"

"Scott?"

"Yes. Scott. He really isn't William's is he?"

She clinched the strap of her bag. "I'll be in touch, Tim," she said, and went out the door.

On the drive back to Cedar Bluff, Zoe stopped at a 7-Eleven. With her blond wig and sunglasses firmly back in place, she entered the store and headed for the junk-food aisle. Tomorrow would be soon enough to start her diet.

4

Meg closed her eyes and breathed in deeply. With all the walking she did in the city, it was hard to believe that the insides of her thighs were so tight with pain as she sat cross-legged on the small mat.

"Okay, ladies, breathe in ... slowly ..." A *whissh* of sucking filled the room. "And ... out ..." A *whoosh* of air was expelled. With it came the sour scents of female body odor, seeping through cirrus clouds of invisible French perfume.

This was ridiculous. Meg opened her eyes and looked around the walnut-lined conservatory of the Golden Key Spa. At one end of the room stood a silent, lace-draped grand piano; at the other, a small grouping of stiff, velvet-covered Victorian chairs. In between, scattered across the handworked needlepoint carpet, two-dozen leotarded ladies with varying layers of cellulite and divergent degrees of cosmetic surgery sat, entranced, at the afternoon seminar entitled "Stress and Self." These were the women Avery Larson expected Meg to relate to. Schmooze with. And bring into the firm one day, as clients.

"Find your center, ladies. Now, slowly ... in ... out."

She closed her eyes again and wondered how one went about finding one's "center." It was an issue that had never arisen for her in nearly thirty-nine years. Maybe it was a technique developed at birth, or maybe it was a genetic thing. It certainly wasn't anything she'd learned at Harvard Law School. An icy chill ran up Meg's uncentered spine.

"ICE MAIDEN COOPER GETS ANOTHER ONE OFF." As if the headline wasn't bad enough, there had been that picture, taken sixteen years ago, of Meg and the "professor." They were sitting under a tree in Harvard Square. And they were holding hands.

She tried to take a deep breath, but the air stopped somewhere between the memories of yesterday and the reality of today. The article had paralleled the questionable morals of Meg—the prominent, yet elusive, criminal attorney—with those of the notorious clients she served. But it was seeing that old photo that had upset her the most. Though back then it had altered the course of Meg's life, the scandal that followed had been relatively minor. At the time they had been lucky. It was an era that was pre–Gary Hart, pre–Donna Rice, and the picture had appeared in the campus newspaper as only one of a montage of photos depicting "students cavorting with faculty." Fortunately, even the tabloid reporter of the nineties had apparently not discovered that the man holding Meg's hand was married. And that he had gone on to become a United States senator.

Still, Avery had exploded. "This is *not* the type of publicity we want for the firm," he'd shouted, while his white eyebrows danced up and down and his face grew redder by the second.

Meg had withdrawn. With a new need to get out of town and a halfhearted desire to appease Avery, she quickly made reservations and ducked out to the Golden Key Spa. There was no point in confronting the libelous tabloid: doing that, Meg knew, would only have triggered their interest, risked the truth coming out, and would have accomplished nothing—exactly what this simpleminded exercise was accomplishing now. Meg straightened her shoulders and wondered when her life had become so complicated. And she wondered why.

She opened her eyes again. Beside her breathed a pale-faced, birdlike creature. The diamonds on the woman's bony fingers were larger than Meg's own two-carat earrings—the ones she'd bought herself for her last birthday. On the other side sat a portly pink woman whose flesh reverberated with each in ... and ... out. She, too, was heavily bejeweled, in a display of sparkle incongruous with her straining spandex. Meg would have bet that these women hadn't bought—or at least hadn't paid for—those baubles themselves. These were women who were "materialized" by husbands, indulged with limitless checkbooks and multiple homes in multiple places, and chauffeurs and servants and unfathomable wardrobes and getaway trips to luxurious health spas. Women with no need to inspect their pasts or doubt their futures. Women with obviously nothing to do but sit and breathe. And perhaps worry if their heirs would slaughter them in their sleep.

Anger swelled in Meg's chest. No one had the right to glide through life without contributing, without being productive at something more than traveling or shopping or doing lunch. She rubbed a spot below her throat, trying to ease the pressure, longing for the calming high of total immersion in her work, instead of this pathetic farce of reality. Then, from the corner of one eye, Meg saw a sharp movement. She flicked her gaze to the front of the room, where the picture-of-health instructor stood, wagging a reprimanding finger in Meg's direction. Meg smiled and shrugged. Then she quietly stood, reached down, picked up her straw mat, and left the room.

Alissa walked into her suite. It was, she noted, a carbon copy of the California Golden Key: all peachy and forest-green, the right blend of lightness and elegance. She tossed her purse onto the overstuffed lounger in the sitting room and went into the bedroom. Her suitcases had been placed in front of the wall of brass-accented, mirrored closet doors. Alissa sighed. In Beverly Hills they would have unpacked her things and put them away. But, then, Beverly Hills was the last place she wanted to be right now. She knew too many people there. The Berkshires were safer; anonymity was what she needed. Anonymity, and a little peace and quiet.

She returned to the sitting room, unbuttoning her silk blouse as she went, trying not to think about Robert, Grant Wentworth, and her beautiful, youthful daughters.

She picked up the welcome packet from the table next to the lounger, then sat down and began thumbing through the contents. Same old stuff. The daily listing of spa happenings, including everything from aerobics classes to body shaping to wellness seminars. God, Alissa noted, there was even a roundtable on menopause. She smirked, Maybe she should attend that one. Maybe that was part of her problem. Her hormones were beginning to go into overdrive, or underdrive, or whatever the hell they did on the dark side of forty.

She turned to the other sheets in the folder: the standard directory of services—biofeedback, massage, aquatherapy, salt treatments. There was a brochure detailing each day's menu, including the total calories and fat grams in everything from whole-wheat granola waffles to paillard of mallard duck. The names of the foods, Alissa knew from experience, sounded much more exotic than their taste. But, then, food didn't interest Alissa. Why would it? There was nothing more revolting to Alissa than fat on the body. Anywhere on the body. It showed such a lack of discipline, and almost always indicated a person who was not in control.

Control.

She threw down the packet. None of this mattered. None of it meant shit. Because suddenly Alissa's whole life was out of control. She tapped her foot, wrung her hands, then rummaged through her purse for a cigarette. She quickly lit one and inhaled deeply. There had to be a way to get her life back together. There had to be something to live for.

Her thoughts kept returning to the homeless benefit. If she could somehow turn it into a premier showcase, a gala to end all galas ... God, that would show them all. Grant Wentworth and his dowdy wife, Betty. Sue Ellen Jamison. All of them. She took another quick drag, stubbed out her cigarette in an alabaster candy dish, and began pacing the room.

All she needed was an idea. The right idea.

She moved to the French doors, pushed back the silk drapes, and stared out onto the private terrace.

Then she turned from the doors and moved toward the bathroom, unclasping her jewels as she went. Her thoughts began to spin. She leaned into the glass-enclosed steam shower and turned the faucets. *Think big,* she commanded herself. *Think bigger.* She shed her clothes and let them fall into a puffy pile on the floor. She tested the water. Warm.

Atlanta wasn't New York. Or Washington. Still, maybe it was time to show the country—no, the world—that Atlanta was the new cosmopolitan city in the nation. A place that existed for more reasons than changing planes. So what if it wasn't true? Alissa was no fool. She knew that if enough people were told enough lies, sooner or later everyone would believe them. The hell with the Olympics. Alissa Page would put Atlanta on the map.

She rifled through the wicker basket of powders and gels on the long vanity and popped open the top of a bottle of all-natural body cleanser, thankful that they had glass bottles here, none of that plastic, private-label-hotel-chain crap.

She set down the bottle and stared into the mirror. She could start with Ted Turner. And Jane. She could try to enlist their names, if not their support. Turner was, after all, the prince of Atlanta. Some had even called him the savior. And Jane. There was no arguing that a Hollywood connection would boost exposure.

She scrubbed the lotion onto her body. A Hollywood connection would do more than make the "Parties" pages of *T & C.* It would make the tabloids. Robin Leach's show.

Maybe more. Her mind swirled with images of ball gowns and twinkling lights and flashlit photos of herself.

Just as Alissa was about to step into the shower, the telephone rang. She stopped and looked around. She spotted the phone on the peach-marble deck of the sunken tub.

It rang again.

Wow, she thought with a laugh. *Maybe that's Ted and Jane now.*

She skipped to the tub and answered the phone. It wasn't the Turners. It was Robert.

"The girls told me where I could reach you," he said.

"Remind me to thank them," she replied.

"Alissa, we need to talk."

She held the phone to her ear and slowly rubbed more cleansing gel into her skin. What right did Robert have to call her now? To interrupt the most wonderful dream she'd had in a long, long time?

She heard his sigh through the phone. "Are you coming back?" he asked.

"To Atlanta? Or to you?"

"Either. Both."

"I really don't think you need me to come back to you, Robert." She felt a small, closing sensation in her throat. "You see, as it turns out, I'm not your type."

"Alissa . . . please. Let me explain."

She said nothing.

"This is very difficult for me," he continued.

And it's not for me?

"It's something I've been living with for a very long time."

She looked around the bathroom, at the pale-peach fixtures, the gold-plated faucets. She focused on the bidet and was pleased, once again, that she'd finally had one installed in her master bath at home. Home.

"Alissa, I need you."

"I doubt it," she managed to say. "I'm forty-two years old, Robert. There's little chance I'll grow a penis between my legs."

It was Robert's turn to be silent, but through the phone Alissa could almost see him wither.

"Robert, I have to go. I'm meeting some people for dinner," she lied, then hung up the phone.

She went back to the shower, stepped inside, and closed the glass door behind her. Then she leaned against the wall, warm water spraying over her body, salt tears creeping down her cheeks, soaking into her pores, seeping through her skin, touching all those lost, lonely, little-girl places beneath the surface, within her soul. The glamorous vision of ball gowns and twinkling lights and mass-media coverage was gone—replaced by an image of Robert on the floor of his office having sex with that man.

She ran her hands across her naked body and thought of all the times—long ago—he'd touched her here, here, and here. How he'd touched her with those sensitive, healing hands—passionless touches, perhaps. Touches more of caring than of lust. But had it meant nothing to Robert? Had her body revolted him? Had making love to her been only an act, a performance?

Now those hands were touching a man, feeling those taut, masculine chest muscles, rubbing a soft, furry spot below the waist, grasping and rocking, back and forth, the firm, pink flesh of a penis.

She wondered if—when they had still been making love—Robert had, even then, been having sex with men.

She pulled her hands from herself and sobbed into them. Why had he done this to her? Why wasn't she good enough for him? *Why in the hell did he want a man?*

She cried for the loss of a bond she now knew she'd never had, for the aching emptiness within her heart, and for the white-hot flash of reality that told her she would gladly relinquish her parties, her photo spreads, her "Who's Who" name in society, if only she could feel she was loved. She took her breasts in her hands once again, slowly caressing them, gently massaging them until the tips of her nipples tightened at her touch and a flush of warmth moved between her legs. And, then, for the first time in a long, long time, Alissa found herself yearning for the touch of the man who had once truly loved her, the touch of Jay Stockwell.

Zoe was lonely without Scott and Marisol. And William. William. She pushed aside the tray of wilted vegetables. They had been bright green and crisp when they'd arrived at lunchtime. But that had been hours ago. For the past two days Zoe had barely eaten, yet she still felt fat, full. Maybe it was because she'd had no exercise, for she was still afraid to leave her suite. Leaving her suite would mean having to face the world. Leaving her suite would mean that someone might recognize her.

She rose from the Duncan Fife dining table and crossed to the sitting area. On the cocktail table was the script Tim Danahy had given her. It lay there, as yet unopened. She'd left L.A. with such high hopes, such renewed energy. But since arriving at the spa it was as though Zoe had frozen. Her mind was immobile, unable to focus on her future, unable to care. Unable to come to terms with what this minute, this hour, this day, could possibly matter. Never mind tomorrow.

She walked to the glass doors that led onto the terrace and gazed out across the magnificent grounds of the Golden Key Spa, at the explosive colors of springtime azaleas, at the dogwoods, the cherry trees. In the distance Zoe could see the enormous Federal-period main house, its grand, porticoed entrance, its sweeping circular drive. She'd read in the promotional literature that the dining room was there, the library, the conservatory, the seminar salons. She wondered if she'd ever have the nerve to go there.

Beyond the main house were what had been the stables, which, according to the brochure, had been converted into a "total fitness center." She supposed that was where she should be right now, bending and stretching and swimming and jogging ... anything to get rid of twenty pounds of excess flesh. *Not today,* she thought. *Maybe tomorrow.*

She walked back into the room and flopped onto the overstuffed love seat. She draped her legs over the arm, the hem of her fleecy robe sneaking up to midthigh. Zoe looked at her legs. The once shapely calves, the once narrow ankles, now seemed puffed and bloated, with threadlines of spidery veins now scattered indiscriminately.

With the tip of a finger Zoe traced the fine purple lines. She wondered if William had ever noticed them. She closed her eyes. *Damn him,* she thought. *Damn him for leaving us. Damn him. Damn him. Damn him.*

A moment later she heard someone wail—a low, sobbing, moaning wail. Then Zoe realized the sound had come from herself. From her gut. From her twenty-pounds-too-heavy gut. From her heart.

She lay back against the armrest and placed her hand below her chest. Around her stomach the skin was stretched too tightly, as though her pain were pressing against it from within, pushing to burst through. Suddenly tears poured from her eyes. She raised a fist and clenched it between her teeth to muffle the noise, to cushion the pain. With all the things that had happened to her over the years, Zoe knew she never would have done what William had done. Even now, to kill herself was not an option. She would never do that to her son. She would never put him through the hurt. William had not thought of that. Maybe he would have if Scott had really been his.

Her sobbing eased. But Scott had been William's son, hadn't he? Not biologically, no. But only Zoe and William and Marisol had known that. At least that's what Zoe had thought. Now she knew that Tim Danahy had never been convinced.

But it had been William who had raised Scott. William who had held his hands when Scott took his first wobbly steps, while Zoe was still bedridden, still uncommunicative, still traumatized by the stroke. It had been William who had bought him his first catcher's mitt, his first bicycle. It had been William who had raised him as though he were his own. Just as it had been William who had taken away Zoe's pain when she had been left alone, pregnant. William who had adored her. Who had protected her, who had saved her from scandal. And now William had left her, too. Alone.

He had probably killed himself because of her. He had probably known she'd never really loved him as a woman should love a man; he'd probably kept buying her things, squandering his money, because he'd thought it might make Zoe love him. And when he'd lost everything, he'd probably been afraid he would lose her, too.

How could I have made him feel that way?

What could I have done to change things?

My God, this man never would have hurt me. And now he's dead. Because of me.

The ache in her stomach clawed through to her spine. Zoe put her hand to her mouth and bit into it. William was gone. And now she was alone, with no one to blame but herself for the problems that lay ahead. Problems she was neither emotionally nor physically equipped to handle.

"Don't give me no shit." Marisol's words suddenly sprang to her mind.

Zoe's eyes were dry now. She stared at the ceiling and thought about her friend. How loyal Marisol had been all these years. How much gratitude she had apparently felt toward Zoe, when it was Zoe who should have been grateful. First, for Marisol's friendship. Now, for what she was doing, for giving her the money. But it wasn't, Zoe knew, the money alone. What Marisol was doing now was believing in her. Maybe, Zoe realized, it was time for her to start believing in herself.

It was obvious that Marisol didn't think Zoe was to blame for William's death, and whether or not she was, Zoe couldn't let herself get tangled in the guilt. She had appeared in too many films where guilt was a destructive force; she couldn't let it consume her own life now, for there was nothing to gain by it, and everything to lose—everything, that is, that may not have already been lost.

She swung her legs off the arm of the sofa and sat up. It was time to face the world. She would shower, then go to the dining room and eat dinner like a normal human being. Afterward she would begin studying the damn script once and for all. It might be her only chance to keep Cedar Bluff, and Zoe knew she had to try. For Scott. For Marisol. For herself—most important, for herself. But first, dinner. She hauled herself up and headed for the bathroom, wondering what the chances were that they'd be serving Twinkies for dessert.

A lean, fair-haired male with a tanning-booth glow and sinewy buttocks that strained the seams of his sleek pleated pants greeted Meg at the entrance to the dining room.

"Good evening, Ms. Cooper. Did you have a good day?"

For all the sex that oozed from his tightly cleansed pores, Meg suspected that the maître d', like most of the staff, was instructed to look but not touch, flirt with but not fuck, the revered guests. She smiled without answering, embarrassed that even she—upright, sophisticated woman of the world—had a momentary yearning to feel his naked, hard body beside her in bed.

"I have a nice table for you tonight," he said as he gestured her to follow him. "By the window."

She kept her eyes off his ass and on the ivory carpet as he led her to a table where a plump woman in a soft yellow caftan sat, a matching silk turban around her head, her gaze fixed on the centerpiece of fresh calla lilies.

The maître d' pulled out a chair for Meg.

"Enjoy your dinner," he said, then left.

Meg took the linen napkin from her plate and smoothed it self-consciously on her lap.

"Do you suppose they imported him from California?" the woman in yellow asked.

"Excuse me?"

The woman nodded toward the entrance. "Richard. The maître d'. Every woman's fantasy."

"Oh," Meg answered. "I didn't notice."

The woman looked at her and smiled. "I'm sure the management will be disappointed. I expect Richard is part of the ambience."

The woman had the darkest eyes Meg had ever seen. But as dark as they were, they glowed with warmth, a kind of open friendliness. They reminded Meg of something, someone, but Meg wasn't sure who. Certainly she hadn't seen her in any of the seminars. She would have remembered those eyes.

"At least he's not eighteen," Meg said.

"Ah," the woman responded, and held up a hand, which Meg noticed was devoid of baubles and bangles. "That's part of it, too. They don't want the guests to feel they're fantasizing about a man young enough to be their son. Or grandson."

Meg smiled but decided not to respond. For all she knew, this woman could be a journalist who had paid Richard to seat them together. Maybe that was why she looked so familiar.

"Tonight they're serving steamed sea bass," the woman said, then laughed at Meg's look of horror. "That was my reaction." She held out her ringless hand. "My name's Zoe."

Meg shook her hand. "Meg," she said. "Do you come here often?"

"I'll tell you one thing," Zoe said. "I don't come here for the sea bass."

A waiter placed nearly translucent gold rimmed bowls in front of them. The bowls were filled with a pale liquid on which a sprig of basil floated.

"Eggplant consommé," Zoe said. "Dig in."

Meg picked up her sterling-silver soup spoon and sipped the consommé. Someone, apparently, had forgotten the salt.

"Actually, it's my first time here," Zoe was saying. She leaned across the table and lowered her voice. "Tell me," she whispered. "Do the women here keep their jewelry on even when they sweat?"

Meg couldn't help laughing. "You sound as though you don't feel you fit in," she said, and wondered if this woman with the radiant dark eyes had any idea that Meg, too, didn't belong there.

Zoe smiled and raised her glass of mineral water. "Believe me," she said, "I don't."

Just then a small blond woman with a choker of marquis-cut diamonds at her throat appeared beside them. "This is fine, Richard," she said in a sweet southern drawl, the kind Meg equated with pure insincerity. The woman quickly sat between Zoe and Meg. "Alissa Page," she said, introducing herself. "From Atlanta." She draped her napkin in her lap, propped her elbows on the table, and rested her chin on her jewel-covered fingers. "What are ya'll having for dinner?"

Meg shot a quick glance at Zoe and noticed the fine lines around Zoe's eyes tighten, the soft parentheses that framed her mouth grow taut.

The waiter arrived with Meg and Zoe's entrées. Meg studied the small portion of colorless fish before her. Next to it lay three stalks of asparagus. A circle of Chinese red cabbage decorated with a thin slice of orange was curled around a rose-carved radish. She'd give anything for a frozen dinner. Lasagna, perhaps. Stouffer's.

"Unfortunately, I don't know anyone here." Alissa Page flitted a hand around the room, which had begun to fill. "In Beverly Hills I always know just about everyone."

Zoe pushed back her chair. "Excuse me, it's time for me to place a phone call."

Alissa reached out and placed a hand on Zoe's forearm. "*Now* I know," she said. "You're Zoe. The actress."

Zoe stood still. Meg's napkin slid to the floor. She looked up at Zoe. Zoe? Zoe, the actress?

"My God," Alissa said quietly, "I thought you were dead."

Zoe pulled out the chair and sat back down. "I might as well have been." She quickly gave Meg a tentative glance.

Of course, she is Zoe, the actress, Meg thought. *That's where I've seen those dark eyes before.* Meg wanted to disappear under the table. Zoe, the actress. Not a tabloid reporter on a Meg Cooper hunt. Only Zoe, the actress. One of the most famous women in the world.

"I never thought I'd meet Zoe in Massachusetts, of all places," Alissa said.

"I'm on vacation. And trying, without success, I'm afraid, to remain incognito."

Alissa put a hand to her mouth. "That's right. Your husband just died."

Meg was too surprised to speak. She watched the dark eyes coat with tears, the dark eyes of Zoe, once the actress, now, apparently, the widow. She wondered who this Alissa Page woman was, and how she knew so damn much.

"William died a couple of weeks ago," Zoe answered.

"I am so sorry," Alissa said. Her voice almost sounded sincere. "I saw the obituary on your husband. It mentioned you, of course. But ... it's been so long ..."

"Since my last film," Zoe said, finishing Alissa's thought.

"Yes. Well, yes," Alissa said, then flashed her diamonds again. "But don't worry about me. I won't tell anyone who you are."

Meg tried to read Alissa's eyes as though she were a client, but the woman was inscrutable. She looked back to Zoe. "I'm sorry, too," Meg murmured, then added, "I didn't know ..." She didn't know what else to say. She felt, to say the least, ridiculous.

"I worked with your husband," Alissa continued.

Zoe's eyebrows raised. "You worked with William?"

"Over the years," Alissa was saying, "your husband generously arranged for more than one of his clients to be guests at some of the charity events I support."

"William was very generous," Zoe replied. She turned to Meg. "I'm sorry I didn't tell you. I guess I assumed you knew who I was."

Meg picked up her fork and pushed some flakes of fish around her plate. "I should have," she said. "I've seen all your films. I admire your work tremendously."

Zoe's smile returned. She patted Meg's hand. "You must have a good memory."

The waiter appeared with the consommé for Alissa. "I'm not terribly hungry tonight," the lady from Atlanta protested.

Zoe leaned toward her. "Please. Take the soup. And the breadsticks. If you don't eat them," she said as she pointed to Meg, "My friend here will. I think she's starving."

Alissa turned back to the waiter. "Forget the breadsticks. Bring your famous sourdough dill rolls. Three. With butter." Meg noticed that the syrup in Alissa's voice was gone, replaced by a tone of take-charge firmness.

"Yes, ma'am," the waiter replied, and walked away.

Meg laughed. "I didn't think you could do that here!"

"I know the ropes at these spas," Alissa said with a grin. "You've been to one, you've been to them all." To Zoe she said, "I'll never forget the time your husband arranged for Dawn Michaels to sing at our Peachtree Festival. It was the year she'd won three Grammys, and that movie she starred in—what was the name of it? *Glory Days?* Something trite like that . . ."

"Yes. *Glory Days.*"

"Well, unbelievably, it was number one at the box office, so the timing was incredible. We had a phenomenal turnout.

"I'll bet you're thinking about making a comeback."

Alissa's abrupt comment seemed to catch Zoe off guard. "Yes I am," Zoe admitted. "After I've taken off a few pounds and got myself back into shape. *If* I can."

Alissa stared at Zoe, her expression again unreadable. "Of course you can. And you will. We'll make sure that you do." She turned to Meg. "Won't we . . . oh," she said, a slight scowl on her face. "I didn't get your name."

Meg hesitated. She didn't want visibility. She didn't want notoriety. But then again, who would care who she was, with Zoe—God, *Zoe*—sitting at her table? "I'm Meg," she answered. "Meg Cooper."

"Well, then, Meg Cooper, we have a job to do. We're going to get the famous Zoe back into shape." She waved a gold-bangled wrist. "We'll start with step aerobics. Seven A.M. I've been to enough of these places to know what works and what doesn't." She scanned her gaze over Meg. "From the looks of things, you have too."

Meg laughed again. "Not really, this is my first time."

Alissa pressed her fingers to her temples. "Ah," she moaned. "Amateurs. I'm surrounded by amateurs. Well, we'll manage." She pushed the gold bangles up her arm. "If you don't come to spas, Meg Cooper, what on earth do you do to look so good?"

"I walk a lot. I live in New York City."

"Oh, good heavens," Alissa said. "Your feet must be flat. No offense, it just makes me feel better to think you have a flaw."

Meg smiled and shook her head.

Zoe laughed. "What do you do in New York, Meg?"

"I'm an attorney."

"A lawyer?" Zoe asked.

"Corporate lawyer, no doubt," Alissa said.

"No," Meg replied. "I'm afraid I'm the worst kind. I'm a criminal lawyer."

"That's hardly the worst kind," Alissa said. "I'd say the worst kind is the bunch who push fradulent malpractice ... hey. Wait a minute. You're that lawyer who's always on the news."

Meg stared into the centerpiece.

"You defended that ... that Holly Davidson."

Meg swallowed air. "I'm afraid so."

"It seems I'm not the only celebrity in the group," Zoe said as she placed a hand on Meg's arm. "Good. Believe it or not, I hate being the center of attention."

"So," Meg said quietly, "do I."

Alissa couldn't believe her luck. She let herself into her suite, kicked off her shoes, and lit a cigarette. Then she flopped onto the lounger and started to laugh. She couldn't believe she'd landed at the table with Zoe, for godsake, and that high-voltage lawyer. Of all the people she could use right now, these two were perfect. And use them she would. For Alissa Page knew how to seize opportunity. She flicked her ashes at the marble candy dish. Starting at seven tomorrow morning, Alissa would take the first step toward creating the gala of the century, after all. And the best part was she wouldn't have to worry about getting Ted Turner and Jane, for her connections had—amazingly, incredibly—just fallen into her deserving lap.

5

She'd been here a week and a half, and for the first time in more years than she could remember, Meg was having fun. She stood in her bra and panties, sifting through the warm-up suits in the closet, humming a long-forgotten Carole King song, her feet tapping to the beat. She found what she was looking for: the pearl-gray silk shirt-dress that she'd worn on the plane. She held it up: it was, like all her clothes, conservative, screaming "Park Avenue attorney" in an understated, exceedingly dull way. But Meg wasn't going to put on preworkout, or workout, or after-workout attire later that night: a few moments ago at breakfast Alissa had announced it was time for a much-deserved escape. Meg, Zoe, and Alissa would have dinner in town, complete with plenty of calories and a bottle of wine. She hung the dress on the shower rod in hopes that the wrinkles would fall by evening and decided that no matter where they wound up, she'd order a cheeseburger, cole slaw, and a pound of fries. She was starved.

She pulled the rubber band from her ponytail, sat on the vanity stool, and began brushing her hair. Then her hand stopped, and Meg smiled into the mirror, remembering what Alissa had said the night before. "You need to let your hair down, kid. You're as tight as a spinster who's never been laid."

And though Meg was far from a virgin, she supposed she was, in reality, a "spinster." Over thirty—hell, nearly forty—and single, with no hot, or even lukewarm, prospects. Maybe tonight she'd meet a silver-haired, dashing Prince Charming who would sweep her off her non-flat feet and they would live happily ever after. Maybe not. But she was, at least, letting her hair down now. She resumed brushing the thick coppery mass and wondered why she so readily did everything Alissa suggested.

Because, she thought, *Alissa Page makes me laugh. And for years no one but Danny Gordon has made me laugh.*

Last night before dinner Alissa had found Meg reading *Law Practice Management*—a publication of the Bar Association. She'd put her hands on her hips and groaned. "You're hopeless, Meg Cooper. You're supposed to be on vacation."

Meg had quickly closed the magazine, embarrassed that she'd been caught. "I was just reading one article...."

"Article, schmarticle," Alissa had said as she'd grabbed the magazine from Meg's hand. "There'll be no more of this. 'Just one article. I promise I won't do it again,'" she had whined. "You act like you're in withdrawal."

Meg had giggled. "I'm a lawyer, Alissa. Not a junkie."

"No difference. Power is power, whether you're powerful, or powerless. Either way, it sucks."

Yes, Meg thought as she braided her hair in a single plait that fell past her shoulders. *Alissa Page, with all her bold, caustic honesty, makes me laugh.* As for Zoe—well, Zoe was wonderful. Warm, loving, funny. And as determined as Meg and Alissa were to help Zoe reclaim her star's appearance, Zoe had sided with Alissa to help Meg see there was more to life than the law, courtrooms, and careers.

"Don't ever think your career can replace the really important things in life," Zoe had told her one afternoon by the pool. "Or you'll wake up one day and find your life isn't what you meant it to be."

Meg didn't understand how Zoe could know that. Zoe, after all, had relinquished her career years ago, a step that Meg assumed she'd taken to devote herself to her family. Still, Zoe's words of caution seemed, as Zoe herself, genuine.

Meg checked her watch. She sighed and went to the closet to get out another pair of sweats. It was time to meet Zoe in the pedicure salon—for yet another appointment that had been "Alissa-arranged." As she slid the soft pants up to her waist, Meg remembered that she'd soon be returning to the city. She realized she would miss Zoe and Alissa. And she would miss the Golden Key Spa. But no matter if she never saw them again, she'd have to thank Avery for forcing her to come. Then again, if she met Prince Charming later that night, maybe he would thank him for her.

Zoe lay back on the recliner, letting the soothing, steamy moisture of the herbal wrap soak into her pores. For nine days now she had been oiled and scrubbed and massaged and creamed. Pampered. Even better, she had begun to drop weight. Somehow Alissa had arranged for private aerobics classes for the three of them—Zoe, Alissa, and Meg. "Money, influence, and balls will get you anything," Alissa had said with a wink. "But, of course, you two already knew that."

Zoe did know that. She also knew she no longer had money and, therefore, probably little influence, and she had never been one to have "balls." And Zoe suspected that Meg, for all Meg's cool facade of control, was also lacking those qualities contained in that missing link, that symbol of maleness, that gender-driven pair of rocks that did, so often it seemed, get one anything.

She shifted slightly under the menthol-scented wrap and realized that what was making the Golden Key fun was that Alissa had balls enough for them all.

The three women had been taking their meals together in Alissa's suite. In the evenings Alissa made sure that Zoe retreated to her room to study her script. Zoe didn't question why Alissa was putting herself out for them. She didn't want to think beyond the present toward screen tests and bankers and balloon payments due. For now Alissa was a godsend—Zoe needed to be bossed around. Perhaps Meg did, too.

The attendant adjusted another herb-soaked sheet around Zoe's thighs, which were no longer as puffy as they had been. Between the three quarts of mineral water she was consuming each day, and the grueling workouts, Zoe could feel her body trimming, toning, and tightening. And with every day that passed, she felt her confidence slowly returning.

"Zoe, are you under there?" It was Meg's voice.

"Sort of," Zoe mumbled.

"How much longer will you be? Alissa made pedicure appointments for us in ten minutes."

Zoe smiled. In Alissa's frenetic quest to recreate Zoe's body and soul, she was leaving little time to waste on self-doubt.

Alissa went into the bathroom of her suite, popped a Fiorinal, rubbed her pounding temples, and wondered why in the hell she felt guilty. It wasn't as though Zoe or Meg could figure out that the only reason she wanted to get them away from the spa that night was to solidify their friendship, to further her plans for the greatest, grandest gala on the globe. So what if they laughed at her jokes and did positively everything she suggested, without question? So what if they were ... nice? So what? It wasn't as though she owed them shit.

Still ... there was something in that look of thanks in Zoe's eyes this morning at breakfast that made Alissa want to vomit. It was just so damn ... *real*. Not like the "thank-you-darlings" of the Betty Wentworth and Sue Ellen Jamison types. Not like what Alissa was used to, what Alissa could handle.

"You'll never know what you've done for me." It was all Zoe

had said. But it was enough. Because those huge, dark cow eyes had filled in the rest.

She went into the living room and stretched out on the sofa, covering her too-tight forehead, shielding the light from her eyes.

A flash of Polly and LuAnn sprang to her mind. They had used Alissa, they had used her for Aunt Helma's clothes. People always used people, didn't they? Always did, always would.

Robert had been using her for years. The gracious hostess, the charming wife. The perfect cover.

Now Alissa was using Zoe and Meg. So what? Didn't she deserve a little happiness? A little subtle revenge?

She took a deep breath, sat up, and lit a cigarette. *So nothing.* She and Zoe and Meg would go out that evening. They would have a few laughs. She would win their trust and their friendship, and, come autumn, her ultimate prize—the gala of the century, an event extraordinaire.

Alissa took a drag on her cigarette and prayed her headache would subside.

The European chairs in the pedicure salon were complete with lumbar massage and a tiny, sudsy whirlpool at the base to therapeutically bathe the feet from, in Alissa's words, "the bottoms of your heels to the tips of your little toes." But Meg's toes had barely had a chance to tingle when the girl she recognized from the front desk burst in.

"Ms. Cooper?" she asked. "There's a phone call for you. He said it's urgent."

Meg stiffened in the chair. "He." It must be Avery. "Just checking in," he'd say. More like checking "up" than "in."

"He said to say it's Danny. From New York."

Danny? She stared into the soapy water. Why was Danny calling? A flush of heat crept into her neck. If Danny was calling, he must need her for something. Something important.

"Would you like a cordless phone?" the girl asked.

Meg quickly scanned the female-filled room. Too many bodies, too many pairs of ears. "No," she said as she pulled her feet from the whirlpool. "Transfer it to my suite."

"Is everything okay?" Zoe asked from the chair beside her.

Meg shrugged. "We'll see," she answered with a steadiness she did not feel.

Once outside the salon, Meg raced toward the west wing. If Danny was calling, something was probably wrong. A case must have come in that he thought she should know about. But it must be a big one. And it must be something Avery was dragging his heels on or he would have called her himself. She would, after all, be back in the city in two days.

She jammed the key card into her door and ran into the room, conscious that her adrenaline was pumping. No matter how hard Zoe and Alissa tried to convince her otherwise, her career *was* important. It defined her; it gave her reason to live.

The phone was ringing. Meg dashed to the table and grabbed the receiver.

"Danny?"

"Meg. I'm glad I got you."

"What's up?" She was breathless, panting.

"Bad news."

"What, for godsake?"

"It's Avery."

"What's he done?"

There was a pause. "Take a deep breath, babe."

She did. "Okay," she said, then took another. "What has Avery done?'

"Avery," he said, "is dead."

She held the phone to her ear. She stared at the floor. She did not move. She must have heard Danny wrong. "What did you say?" she asked.

Danny cleared his throat. "Avery's dead. Heart attack. This morning."

She slumped onto the sofa. "Shit."

There was a silence a moment, then Danny said, "I knew you'd want to know right away."

She pictured her boss, senior partner of the firm, peering at her over half glasses, a fatherly look on his face. "Yeah. Yeah, thanks. Where'd it happen?"

"At home."

"Shit." Avery, like herself, lived alone. His wife had died many years ago; he'd turned all his time and energy into the firm, working by day, socializing with clients by night. Being visible but, still, alone. "Who found him?"

"The housekeeper."

It could have been worse. If he'd dropped dead at a party, a cocktail in one hand, a group of impressionable people surrounding him, Avery would have been humiliated. In the throes of death his mask would have been gone. He would have appeared human.

"When are you coming back?" Danny was asking.

"The day after tomorrow."

"Make it tomorrow night, okay? The funeral's set for the next morning. At St. Patrick's."

Meg was silent. It was so hard to believe this was happening. It was so hard to believe he'd never coach her or praise her or scold her again. She would never again hear the wisdom of his experience.

"The limo will pick you up at nine-thirty, okay? At your place?"

The limo. God. The partners. Avery had served as a buffer between Meg and the others—the ones who resented Meg as a woman, who fought with Avery when he made her a partner in the Park Avenue good-old-boys firm. "No, Danny," she said. "I don't want to go in the limo. I want to go with you."

"I'm just a hired hand, honey. You need to go with the other partners."

He was right and she knew it. She rubbed the back of her neck. "It'll be a huge funeral."

"Yeah. A big event. For the richest and the most powerful."

"And they'll all be there," Meg said.

"Not to mention the politicians. From the DA's office to the White House. The place will be crawling with them."

Meg sighed. "Avery told me once that his dream was to be appointed to the Supreme Court."

"He might have made it. If the Republicans had stayed in office."

They talked for a few more minutes. After she hung up, Meg paced around the suite. Avery. Dead. She stopped at the window and stared outside. Her hands began to tremble. Her legs began to ache. Avery. Dead.

Then something else Danny had said came back to Meg's mind, and a slow, sickening feeling spread through her.

The politicians, he'd said. *The place will be crawling with them.*

They were on their second bottle of wine. Meg had reluctantly joined Zoe and Alissa: she'd wanted to rush home to New York to mourn Avery, the mentor–advisor–father figure she'd now lost. But Alissa had insisted Meg stay until the following day. "You're in no condition to travel," Alissa had said when Meg had tearfully told them the news. "You're far too upset. You need to be with your friends tonight."

And so she had stayed.

She looked around the restaurant, a dark publike room filled with thick square pine tables set with red paper place mats. There were only a few patrons: Prince Charming didn't appear to be among them. Beside her, Zoe and Alissa were talking; Meg was feeling oddly comforted by their presence, as though the sound of their voices alone was easing her grief. She wondered why she had never let herself have any close friends until then. And how was it possible that she felt close to these women? She had, after all, known them only a few days.

After tomorrow they would go their separate ways: Meg

back to New York, Alissa to Atlanta, and Zoe, eventually, back to L.A. But something inside Meg hoped they'd stay in touch. In the last couple of weeks she'd learned that female friends—not just male lovers—were missing from her life.

Through the haze of the wine Meg actually convinced herself that Avery's funeral might not be so bad: maybe Senator Steven Riley wouldn't be there, after all.

She took another sip as a waiter appeared beside their table.

"What'll it be, ladies? Ready to order?"

All eyes turned to Meg. In the past few hours her appetite had dwindled. But Zoe and Alissa were trying so hard to help, it didn't seem fair to let them think their efforts were in vain. "I'm ready," she said as she sat up straight in her chair. "I'll have a big, juicy cheeseburger." And, she promised herself, she would stop thinking of Avery, she would stop anticipating the funeral. She would have a good time now, here, tonight with her friends. The way Avery would have wanted her to.

"Fries?"

"Sure. Why not?"

Zoe smiled.

"Make mine the same," Alissa said.

Meg would believe Alissa could eat that much when she saw it.

"Not me," Zoe said. "I'll have the scallops. Broiled. No butter. And salad. No dressing."

"What a good girl," Alissa said. Her words, Meg noted, were a little slurred. She wouldn't have thought Alissa was the type to drink too much, to let down her guard.

Zoe smiled. "Got to look good enough to be with a leading man."

Alissa slammed down her glass. "Don't do this for any man, honey. Leading or otherwise. You make yourself look good for you. Nobody else. 'Cuz nobody else matters. Besides, the last thing a woman can depend on is a man."

Meg knew that Alissa was right, yet she was surprised at the hostility in her voice.

"Sometimes," Zoe said as she ran her finger around the rim of her wineglass, "I wonder if I had paid more attention to my appearance, well, maybe William would have been happier."

"And then what?" Alissa asked. "Maybe he wouldn't have killed himself?"

Meg was startled. "Alissa, that's not a very nice thing to say."

"No. You're right. I'm sorry, Zoe. But what you've got to understand is that you can never really understand what goes on inside a man's head."

"That's an understatement," Zoe said, and seemed unruffled at Alissa's cruel remark. Meg wondered where Zoe got her strength.

"Men," Alissa continued. "They really are scum, you know."

"Maybe it's partly our fault," Meg said quietly. She wondered if Avery's late wife had thought he was scum. She wondered if Steven Riley was scum. She'd never given herself the chance to find out.

"Are you nuts?" Alissa asked. "Besides, what do you know about men? You're not even married." She took another sip of wine. "Bet you have a boyfriend, though. Some equally successful power attorney, perhaps? Or maybe that private investigator? What was his name?"

"His name is Danny. And no, he's only a friend. A good friend. But right now there's no one special in my life."

Alissa set down her glass. "See? If someone as beautiful and clever and smart as you doesn't have a boyfriend, it proves they're all scum. I rest my case."

Though she knew Alissa's words could be considered a compliment, Meg suddenly found old feelings resurfacing, the feelings of being the kid with no father, the one who was different, inadequate. "I've had a lot of boyfriends—men friends," she stuttered.

"But how about relationships?" Alissa pressed. "*Real* relationships?"

In her mind Meg saw his face, his eyes, his lips. She felt his touch. "Once," she replied quietly, "a long time ago."

Alissa leaned back in her chair. "Yeah, I guess you could say I had one once, too. But it sure as shit wasn't with my husband. It was before him." She drained her glass and poured another. "God, it was good."

Meg was relieved to have the focus of the conversation off herself. "What happened?"

"His name was Jay. Jay Stockwell. Our parents had summer homes next to each other."

"You were childhood sweethearts?" Zoe asked, then added wistfully, "I think they're the best. Everyone involved is so innocent."

Alissa shook her head. "This wasn't innocence. It was love. Real love."

They grew quiet. Meg thought of Steven Riley, about their affair. That was real love. But it had been years ago. A lifetime ago.

The waiter arrived and set their dinners on the red paper place mats. Meg stared at the cheeseburger. Again she had no appetite.

After he left, Zoe spoke. "What is real love, anyway? How do you know? William took good care of me and of Scott. But I can't honestly say I loved him. Not like I'd loved the boy back home."

"Ah," Alissa said, "the boy back home. For me that was Jay. The trouble was, he didn't want to stay home. He had things to do, a world to save."

"Where did he go?"

Meg was glad Zoe was encouraging Alissa to talk. Her sad thoughts of Avery were sliding into lonely, depressive thoughts of Steven. She could feel her walls closing around her, her need to escape into herself. For some reason she thought about the cat she'd had when she and Steven had been together—a gray tiger named Socrates. For the longest time after Steven was gone, she'd closed Socrates out of her bedroom. She'd not been able to stand hearing him purr; the sound was too close to the soft snores of Steven beside her, at peace in his slumber after their lovemaking.

"First, Jay went to San Francisco," Alissa was saying, and Meg snapped back to the present. "It was in the early seventies. He'd been deferred from the draft. From Vietnam."

"Was he sick?" Zoe asked.

"No," Alissa said. "He was rich. Rich boys didn't have to go. Jay's family owned—and still do—a megabroadcast conglomerate. TV stations. Radio stations. All over the country. Jay loved broadcasting, but not business. He was a born journalist." She pushed the plate with her untouched cheeseburger and fries aside. "When he went to San Francisco, he gave his family the finger."

"And you never saw him again?" Zoe asked.

Alissa laughed. "Never saw him again? Honey," she said, as she took another sip of wine, "I went with him."

"You went with him?" Even Meg was surprised at this. She couldn't picture Alissa following anyone, anywhere.

"I was eighteen. Love seemed more important than trust funds or appearances or social standing."

"So what happened?" Zoe asked.

She shrugged. "I realized I was wrong."

The women were quiet again. Meg felt sorry for Alissa. Something in the eyes of this aggressive little blonde now spelled sorrow. Sorrow for a life gone by. Sorrow for love relinquished. She knew the feeling only too well.

"God, he was handsome," Alissa said. "He still is."

"Still is?" Zoe asked. "You mean you still see him?"

Alissa shook her head. "I left him standing on the corner of Haight-Ashbury. It seemed appropriate at the time. He was working for one of those liberal underground newspapers. I went home to Atlanta, married Robert, had the kids. Then one day I turned on the TV and there he was. Reporting from Cairo."

"So he went back into broadcasting," Zoe said.

"Full steam ahead apparently. Delivering stories on the oppressed people of the world. Over the years I've seen him standing against backdrops in Lebanon, Ethiopia, Iraq, you name it. He was on the air for days during that Tiananmen Square thing in China or wherever that is."

"Oh," Zoe said, "Jay Stockwell. Sure. I've seen him, too. His stories have real sensitivity."

Alissa shrugged. "I never paid much attention to his stories. I was too busy looking at him. Wondering."

Zoe picked at her scallops, then set down her fork. "Wondering what would have happened if you'd stayed together?"

"Sure. Haven't you ever done that? Wondered about your boy back home?"

"You mean, the man I could have married?" Zoe asked.

"Or should have," Alissa said.

Should have, Meg thought. *Should I have? Could I have?*

"Sure I've wondered about him," Zoe said. "All the time."

"What about you, Meg? What about your one and only? Don't you ever wonder how your life would have been different? How it would have been better?"

Meg silently wished she could say, *No. My life wouldn't have been better. It would have been worse. And besides, my life is just fine the way it is.* But she couldn't seem to say anything. She couldn't seem to lie.

There was silence around the table. Meg looked at Zoe, who was watching Alissa. Meg turned to Alissa, just in time to see her surreptitiously wipe a lone tear from her cheek. Alissa caught Meg's eye and quickly cleared her throat. Then she raised her glass toward them both. "I think we should find them," Alissa said. "I think we should find the men we once loved and show them what they've missed."

Meg wished she'd brought along something to help her sleep. She lay on her back, staring up at the dark ceiling, with one primary thought: Steven Riley. She felt a little guilty—she should have been thinking about Avery, doing some kind of grieving, detached or otherwise. But now she could think only of the past.

She rolled onto her side and tried to shut out the memories. That first day she'd met him, that first class in criminal law. He was the instructor, the charismatic, powerful attorney from New York City, guest lecturing at Harvard for the semester.

Their first cup of coffee, in the coffee shop across the square. Talking with passion about the law, waving his hands as he spoke. It was then that he'd first touched her. A light touch on her hand. A gesture of speech. Yet his hand had stayed there a beat too long. Their eyes had met.

She turned onto her stomach, fluffed the pillow, and could almost feel his touch again, this time on her back, in the little hollow at the base of her spine. She could feel his lips there. Kissing softly.

It hadn't bothered Meg that Steven was already married. The fact that he had three small children had helped. For Meg knew—long before she'd left home for college, long before her mother had died in their small, smoke-filled house—Meg knew that she would never marry. Marriage was for other people, not for her. She was not worthy of being loved.

"If it hadn't been for you," she could still hear her mother cry, still envision her sitting at the metal kitchen table in her stained bathrobe, though it was the middle of the day, drinking black coffee and coughing that cigarette cough, "if it hadn't been for you, your goddamn father would have never left. If it hadn't been for you, he would have divorced his wife and married me. He will never come back to me now. And it's all your fault."

Meg turned onto her other side.

Steven had loved her. And worse, she had loved Steven. For thirteen weeks they had held hands, touched, looked into each other's eyes, made love. For thirteen weeks Meg Cooper had been happy. Thirteen weeks. A semester that would last a lifetime. And end another.

He had bought them matching sweatshirts: crimson and gray. Meg had washed them when he went home on weekends, then snuggled against his for hours after it came out, warm and cozy, from the dryer.

He had bought her a bouquet of bright paper flowers. "Like our love," he'd said, "these will never die."

He had taught her how to make clam chowder; how to play backgammon; how to make love.

Then came the photo. "Students cavorting with faculty." And suddenly the risk had become too great, the stakes too high. And Meg knew what she had to do.

The night of the final exam they had met in the coffee shop.

"I cannot go back to New York," Steven had said. "I want to stay in Boston with you. I want to divorce my wife. I want to marry you."

Meg had stared into his eyes. "No," she'd answered. It was not supposed to have come to this. She couldn't let him leave his wife. She couldn't let him leave his children. She could not let him risk the political career he was being so carefully groomed for. It was not going to be her fault.

Meg got out of bed now and went into the sitting room. She curled up on the sofa and hugged her knees tightly to her chest. Loneliness squeezed around her. She wondered if Alissa was sitting, sleepless, on the sofa of her suite, thinking about Jay Stockwell. She wondered if Zoe was thinking about her boy back home.

She glanced at the clock. One forty-five. She got up and went into the bathroom, where she found a couple of aspirin, quickly downed them, and returned to bed. All this nonsense was getting her nowhere. She pulled the comforter around her and clenched her eyes shut, forcing herself to think of something else. How Raggedy Man would survive being cared for by the neighbor. When to leave tomorrow. What to wear to Avery's funeral. She did, after all, want to look her best. Not because Steven might be there. No, that had nothing to do with it.

We should show them what they've missed. Alissa's words echoed, an unwanted ghost in her mind.

Finally Meg drifted off to sleep.

And then he was there. Standing on a podium. Red, white, and blue balloons floated above him, around him. Giant balloons. The size of beach balls. Music blared. Trumpets. Saxophones. She could not see them, but Meg could hear the crowd. Shouting. Cheering. Steven waved both hands to them. His smile was huge. Bigger than Meg had ever seen it. His teeth were straighter, whiter that she'd ever known. *He must have had them capped,* she thought. *Sometime, over the last fifteen years, he must have had them capped.*

He brought his arms down and stepped closer to the microphone. "I, Senator Steven Riley, accept your nomination for the candidacy of the office of President of the United States." His words reverberated. The shouts, the cheers, grew louder. He reached his left arm out to his side. Meg stepped forward, into it. She was dressed in a tailored bright-red suit. He encircled her waist, leaned down, and kissed her. A long, slow, sensual kiss. For all the world to see.

He broke away and waved back at the crowd again. The roars were deafening. Meg spotted the two of them as they were projected on the huge video screen. They were gorgeous together, perfect. The next President. The next First Lady. Then, on the screen, she watched as he outstretched his other arm. His wife stepped forward, into it. She was dressed in a tailored bright-red suit. Just like Meg's. He encircled his wife's waist, leaned down, and kissed her. A long, slow, sensual kiss. For all the world to see.

He put his other arm around Meg again. Meg was smiling, watching the video screen. The three of them stood there, proudly, arm in arm.

"But where are your children?" Meg shouted into his ear.

"They didn't come," he answered.

"Why not?"

His wife leaned across him. "You know why." She smiled. "They didn't come because it's all your fault."

Meg nodded and looked back to the faceless crowd. *Of course*, she thought to herself. *I knew that.*

The lights of the television cameras were warm. Meg was beginning to sweat. She started to wipe her brow. Her heart started to pound.

She awoke. Her hand was on her forehead. It was damp. Her heart was thumping wildly. She sat up in bed, then buried her face in her hands. It had been years since she'd dreamed of Steven. It had been years since she'd let herself even think of him. It had been years. Hadn't it?

"What time are you flying out?" Zoe asked Meg as they lay by the indoor pool the next morning. They were the only ones there. Mornings were active for seminars, group workouts, and those activities whose participants did not have the advantage of a personal-fitness guru named Alissa.

"I'm catching the four-thirty shuttle," Meg answered.

Zoe adjusted the limp tea bags on her eyelids and wondered what on earth had prompted her to drink so much wine the night before. What had begun as an evening meant to offer solace to Meg had turned into a night of obsessing over Eric, obsessing as she hadn't done in years. If only Alissa hadn't started talking about her old flame, her long-ago lover. If only Alissa hadn't made her remember. Her head throbbed. If only she hadn't had so much wine.

"I'm glad I'm not flying today," she said quietly. "I can't remember when I've been so hungover."

"I'm sure if you asked, the staff could come up with some surefire cure for a hangover. Something a little more nineties than tea bags."

Zoe laughed. "I'm an old-fashioned girl. I keep telling you that. What I really need is a little tomato juice and a raw egg, but God knows, they probably don't have eggs around here. Cholesterol, you know." Zoe folded her hands across her diminishing stomach, trying to let the atmosphere soothe her. A faint sound of Debussy was blanketed by a warm, closed-in sensation and the hypnotic drone of a water filter.

"Alissa was in fine form last night," Meg said.

"Mmm. I get the feeling she's not too happy in her marriage."

"It was curious, though, what she said about that man. Jay Stockwell. It's hard to picture her with someone like that."

"Only because of the way she is now. My guess is he really is the only guy she ever loved. And that maybe she was too scared to stay with him." Even as Zoe spoke the words, she wondered if she was speaking of Alissa or of herself. Had she been afraid of her love for Eric? He had, after all, been the one who'd left her. But how hard had she tried to find him? She'd made one phone call, nothing more. Had she been so caught up in her stardom that she was afraid if Eric returned she'd lose all that had so miraculously come her way? Zoe squeezed her eyes more tightly. She hated to think she had been that shallow, that self-serving. But if that had been the case, she'd paid dearly, had been paying dearly for her mistake all these years.

"Speaking of our social director," Meg said, "I wonder where she is this morning."

"Probably sleeping it off. Which is what I should be doing."

"It was her idea to come to the pool—a celebratory last farewell before I go back to the city and 'desert' you two, I think was her word."

"But that was after her how-many-eth glass of wine, Meg? She probably forgot."

"I didn't forget." It was Alissa's voice.

Zoe plucked the tea bags from her eyes. Alissa stood, dressed in an oversize T-shirt of beige cotton, the color which, this morning, emphasized the sallowness of her skin.

"Good morning," Zoe said. "You don't look like you're ready for a swim."

Alissa sat on the end of Zoe's lounge chair. "I'm not staying."

Zoe glanced at Meg. Meg closed her eyes and lay back on her chair. "Why not?" Zoe asked.

"The worst thing about drinking too much isn't the way you feel the next day. It's when you remember all the asinine things you said the night before."

Zoe knew what she meant. She, too, felt foolish for having mentioned Eric. The boy back home. Had she called him by name? Had she let on that her life had been anything but perfect with William?

"Don't be silly, Alissa. We all have memories we don't want to forget. Personally, I think those memories are good. Sometimes they're what keep us going." Zoe surprised herself when she said that. Surprised herself that she could admit inwardly that it had been Eric, and the way she'd loved him, that had kept her going so many times throughout the difficult days of the past years. That even through her resentment and her anger, it was the memory of Eric that had sustained her so many times. Especially when she looked at Scott, the very image of Eric when they were young and dreaming of their future together.

"Talking about the past is a waste of time."

"It doesn't have to be," Zoe said. "It can be cathartic."

Alissa fumbled in her large bag and withdrew a nail buffer. She quickly began buffing her nails. "Then why don't you tell us?" she asked.

"Tell you what?"

"About your boy next door."

Zoe was silent. She pressed her fingertips to her temples and lay back on the lounge. Beside her Meg spoke. "Maybe she doesn't want to."

Alissa threw the buffer back into her bag. "See what I mean? It's embarrassing to talk about the past. It's humiliating."

Humiliating? Zoe wondered. Is that what love had to wind up being? Eric's leaving her. William's shooting himself. Humiliating? No. More like devastating. "His name was Eric Matthews," Zoe said. "We grew up together in a small town in northern Minnesota. He was Nordic, like most of the people around there. I was Jewish. As a kid I always felt out of place around all the fair-hairs. Eric made me feel special."

Alissa had bared her soul to them the night before. She had trusted them with her secrets. And if it weren't for Alissa, Zoe knew she'd probably still be locked away in her west-wing suite, waiting for the days to pass, succumbing to the fear that she would never be able to face the world again, that she had no choice but to return to L.A. and sell Cedar Bluff before she went into default, that a comeback was a ridiculous hope. She would live out the rest of her life fat, unrecognized, and eventually broke. She could tell them about Eric now. Not everything, but some things. Maybe she owed Alissa this much.

She took a deep breath and began. "Eric encouraged my acting. But it was easy for me. See, there was more to being Jewish in Minnesota than being dark-haired. I never felt I belonged. I always felt the other kids looked at me like I was strange. As though they were afraid of me. Anyway"—she sat up in the chair and hugged her arms around her knees—"I guess that's why acting came so natural to me. I'd been doing it all my life.

"After high school Eric convinced me to head for Hollywood. He wanted to act, too. And he was handsome. God. He had those chiseled cheekbones and those drop-dead blue eyes and that tall, sturdy Nordic build. We spent a few years in L.A., living on macaroni and cheese." She paused, then laughed. "He cooked. Even back then I was spoiled. Anyway, that's where I met my friend, Marisol. She lived in the apartment next door. I guess I haven't told you about Marisol." Saying her name brought her friend's image into Zoe's mind. She realized how much she missed her.

"Then I was discovered. Not by William, but by his partner, Tim Danahy. Things happened so quickly. Before I knew it, I was thrust into the spotlight. I was signed to a three-year contract, while Eric was still standing in cattle calls trying for bit parts. William took over my representation. I started going to parties with him, being seen. He didn't think it was wise for Eric to come along. He said it would look better to the public if it appeared that I was unattached."

"I'm sure that didn't thrill Eric," Alissa said.

Zoe shook her head. "I was too busy to notice. My wildest dreams were coming true. Anyway, one night I came home and Eric was gone."

"Ah. Sweet tragedy."

Zoe stared off across the calm aqua water of the pool. That seemed to be all she needed to say. She didn't have to tell them the rest.

"Where did he go?"

Zoe shrugged. "I've no idea."

"You never tried to find him?"

Zoe leaned back. A small catch came into her throat as she realized the words she was about to say were the truth. "I guess I didn't feel he wanted me anymore."

"At least it wasn't your choice," Alissa added.

"What do you mean?"

"It was my choice to leave Jay. It's a choice I've had to live with. It would have been easier if he'd been the one to leave me. Or if he was dead." Alissa stood, avoiding Zoe's eyes. "I'm going to take a sauna."

They didn't have a clue how hard it was. Meg, with those gorgeous looks she'd been born with, that she never had to work at. And her brains. God. Looks and brains and independence. She'd never have to depend on any man. She'd never have to worry about getting older, becoming less desirable.

And Zoe. A full-fledged Hollywood star, who never had to try to get her photo in magazines. It had been there. Everywhere. And it would be again. The American people loved nothing more than one of their idols making a comeback.

They didn't have a clue.

Alissa tugged her T-shirt over her head and wrapped a thick terry towel around herself. She pulled open the heavy door to the sauna and stepped inside. Her eyes stung. She wasn't sure if it was from the wine, the heat, or unleashed tears.

She climbed onto a bench and stretched out. She knew she'd blown her chance—there would be no Zoe in her corner, no grand gala to plan. Alissa had made a fool of herself in front of them. God. She couldn't believe she'd cried. She'd been so busy trying to act like "one of the girls" that her defenses must have slipped. But *crying*? In front of them? In front of *anyone*?

She covered her face with her hands. Maybe it was just as well. Maybe she shouldn't even bother to go home. Her whole life was nothing more than a farce, anyway. Had been nothing but a farce since the day she'd walked away from Jay Stockwell.

She heard the door open.

"Alissa?" It was Zoe. "Alissa, you can't desert us."

Meg's voice came next. "I'm not leaving until this afternoon. I need you to tell me what I'm supposed to be doing until then."

"Besides," Zoe continued, "I have a terrible craving for chocolate. I need you to talk me out of it."

Without removing her hands from her face, Alissa said, "Distract yourself, Zoe. You're a big girl. Take a walk. Have a cigarette."

She heard their footsteps move into the sauna, then stop. She assumed they sat down on the bench facing her.

"I can't smoke," Zoe said. "Right after Scott was born, I had a stroke."

The only sound in the sauna was of the slow steam from the coals.

Alissa sat up. Zoe and Meg faced her, toweled just as she was. Three women, so very different, such unlikely friends. But here, in their towels, they were stripped of their differences.

Zoe walked slowly toward a cedar bench and sat down.

"It's a secret that's been kept under wraps for almost fifteen years."

Secrets. Thoughts of Robert flashed through Alissa's mind.

Meg took a seat and crossed her legs. "For a lot of people," she said, "secrets are a way of life."

The coals hissed, the women were silent. Then Zoe shook her head. "Some secrets are worth keeping. But one about having a stroke? That was selfish. Today more and more women—famous women who have much more to lose than I ever did—are going public with horrendous stories of cancer, abuse, and all kinds of life-threatening problems that they've overcome." She let out a low, short laugh. "But me? I couldn't even admit I'd had a stroke. It wasn't that I was afraid of losing my career. I was afraid people would laugh at me, that they'd think I was weak. Then I wouldn't fit in. And I'd wind up feeling like the same out-of-place kid who grew up as a Jew in northern Minnesota."

Alissa swallowed. She suddenly thought of her little-girl friends, preening in mirrors, adorned in Aunt Helma's fabulous furs. "None of us like to admit our weaknesses," Alissa said. "Especially to ourselves." But even as she heard her words, Alissa couldn't believe they were coming from her. A leftover tear from the night before—the month, the year, before—found its way to the surface. Alissa let it fall.

"My selfishness hurt a lot of people," Zoe continued. "I pressured William to keep the news of my stroke from the media. He told them I'd gone into seclusion to raise my baby. What they didn't know was that I was paralyzed on my left side. I couldn't walk. I couldn't talk. After a couple of years the press finally gave up on me." She raised her eyes to the dark cedar ceiling. "I'm sure it was awfully hard on William. Not only my illness, but my selfishness. It was hard on Marisol, too. And especially on my baby."

Alissa couldn't believe what she was hearing. Was Zoe making this up to pacify her, to convince her that everyone had problems? That no one was perfect, or led a perfect life?

Zoe didn't seem to be making it up, but still ... Alissa studied Zoe's face. The woman's skin was flawless, with that dark, creamy texture that God seemed to have saved for the Jewish princesses of the world. It was hard to believe that no words had been uttered from Zoe's pouty, full lips for two years. Alissa cleared her throat. "You look all right to me."

"She's right," Meg said. "You look fine."

Zoe shook her head. "I am now. In fact, I have been for about ten years. William hired the most trustworthy, the best, therapists. Marisol was there for me. But for the first two years I refused even to try. I was happier hiding from the world, feeling sorry for myself, I guess."

"I know what it's like to hide from the world," Meg said as she raised her chin and turned her face away—a gesture Alissa recognized as one meant to deflect the pain within. "First," Meg continued in her deliberate, guarded voice, "you do it because it seems safer."

"Then," Zoe interjected, "you do it because it's a habit you don't know how to break."

Closing her eyes, Alissa let the heat envelop her, soothe her. "Or you do what I do," she said. "You rise to the challenge and show the world who's boss." She rested her aching head against the wall, conscious that for once, she didn't feel like being the boss. She felt defeated, deflated. And replete with the sudden knowledge that, in reality, like Meg and like Zoe, Alissa was alone. After a moment she said softly, "I never should have left him. My happiest days were spent with Jay."

A silence fell. Meg cleared her throat. "At least the two of you have your children. Families. Friends."

Alissa opened her eyes. "So you feel the same way—that you shouldn't have left that man you once loved."

"The only man I ever loved."

"And I," Zoe said, "should never have let Eric go."

Alissa tightened the towel around her bustline. "What are we saying here, ladies? That we're all sisters in regret?"

"It's too late now," Meg said. "We have to keep on doing

what we've been doing all these years. We have to get on with our lives."

Alissa snorted. "Get on with my life? I have no life! My life sucks the big one right now. I get the feeling both of yours do, too. Maybe we ought to do something about it."

"Like what?" Zoe asked.

"Like I said last night. Let's find them."

"What!" Meg exclaimed. "Why? To show them what they missed?"

"Maybe," Alissa answered quietly, "or to see if the flame is still there."

"You're crazy," Zoe said. "And it's too hot in here for me. I'm leaving." She stood up and moved toward the door.

Alissa reached out and put a hand on Zoe's arm. "Think about it. Say we all go home. Back to our lives. But we have a secret. We won't tell anyone else. We'll look for our men, and we'll find out what kind of lives we might have had. Then we'll be able to close the book on those memories once and for all."

"You seem to be forgetting one thing," Zoe said. "You still have a husband."

"Believe me," Alissa said, "he wouldn't care."

"And my 'lost love' *is* someone's husband. He's not interested in seeing me again," Meg said as she, too, stood.

"You don't know that."

The three women studied each other.

"We'll never know if we don't try," Alissa said. "What have we got to lose?"

6

They sat in the front pew, for the partners were, after all, the closest thing Avery had to family.

Meg knew a hundred pairs of eyes were boring into the back of her head; she'd have given anything to know if one pair belonged to Steven Riley. She looked to either side of her and noticed that everyone's head was bowed. She quickly lowered hers.

In the hollowness of the stone cathedral, the drone of the priest's words was interrupted only by an occasional cough, a foot scuffing the floor, a gentle, sincere-sounding blow of a nose. Most of the people were there only to be seen, Meg knew, but they were there. She briefly wondered how many would be there if the funeral were for her. The partners, of course. Well, maybe the partners; now that Avery was gone, even that was doubtful. Danny Gordon would be there. Janine, the receptionist. Perhaps a few from the clerical pool.

She peeked around at the still-bowed heads. There would hardly be enough mourners to fill two pews if the funeral were for her. She closed her eyes again. Well, maybe the neighbor who took care of Raggedy Man when she was away. That made one more. She wondered if the neighbor would keep Raggedy Man for good.

There was a faint sound of bells, and Meg felt movement stir around her. She raised her head. The priest was sprinkling something over the orchid-draped coffin. *Orchids,* Meg thought. *Danny must have provided them.*

Why couldn't she have fallen in love with Danny? Why couldn't she have fallen in love with *anyone*? Had Steven ruined her ability ever to love again? Had he stolen so much of her heart, taken so much of her soul, that nothing was left? What had been so different, so special, about Steven Riley? Meg had told Danny that she was better off alone. But did she really believe that?

The bells sounded again. Meg stiffened. In a moment she would be expected to face people, talk to them, be sociable. In a moment she would know if Steven was there.

A small pool of perspiration formed between her breasts. *Damn Alissa Page,* Meg thought. *And damn Zoe Hartmann.* If it hadn't been for the two of them, she wouldn't be sitting there dwelling on Steven, or trying her damnedest not to dwell on Steven. She should be mourning Avery. For all their differences, Avery had done something for Meg: he had given her a chance. She folded her arms across her stomach. Those foolish women had stirred up emotions that were best left alone. Then she half smiled. Well, maybe that would be two more to add to the guest list for her funeral.

The partners rose. Meg quickly stood and smoothed her taupe-colored skirt. Not exactly funeral attire. But she knew the elegant shade brought out the toffee-colored flecks in her eyes. If she had to see Steven Riley, she might as well look her best.

As they filed from the pew, Meg tried to think about Avery. He would have chastised her for not wearing black. Or navy, at the least. *Sorry, boss,* Meg said silently as she watched the casket being wheeled by. *A woman's got to do what a woman's got to do.*

She took a deep breath and followed the partners down the telescoping aisle. Slowly, they walked. On either side people stood, solemn-faced. Meg didn't have to look at them.

She knew their eyes were on her. *She's the one who defended Holly Davidson,* she could sense their whispers. *She's the one who got her off.* She wondered if Steven knew about the trial. She wondered if he knew about all the guilty people she'd defended, that money had become what made Meg Cooper tick. She wondered if she would be able to feel which pair of eyes was his. Alissa's words again echoed in her mind.

"You don't know that he's happy."

Meg kept her eyes fixed on the navy-suited back of one of the partners. Would it be so wrong for Steven and her to love again? The navy suit continued to move stiffly in front of her. She wasn't sure who it belonged to; from this view the partners all looked the same.

At last there was sunlight. They moved onto the front steps. Meg drank in the fresh air, relished the commotion of Fifth Avenue, the rush of footsteps, the impatience of cars. She ignored the converging media as a small disappointment rose within her. She had not felt Steven's eyes. He must not have been there.

George Bascomb, next in command at the law firm, leaned toward Meg. "Smile for the cameras," he said sarcastically. "I'm sure they're only here to see you."

Meg ignored him, too, and walked toward the limo. Just as she bent to step inside, she heard the shout of a reporter:

"Senator Riley! Would you care to comment on the defense cuts?"

Meg stumbled into the car. She pulled the door closed before the chauffeur had a chance. She stared straight ahead. She would not look. She would not turn her head. But as the car pulled from the curb, she could not stop herself. Something—magnetism, chemistry, curiosity, or pure stupidity—made Meg turn her head. Just a little. But through the crowd of people on the stairs, she could not see Senator Steven Riley.

He did not go to the cemetery. From behind large sunglasses Meg had studied every dark-suited man who stood over six feet. But Steven had not been among them. After the graveside service, she had skipped the formal luncheon at Le Cirque. Avery would not have been surprised.

Now she unlocked the door of her brownstone and immediately sensed something was wrong. She stepped inside and glanced around the foyer. The huge Steuben vase stood in its place on the table, filled with delicate silk lilies. A stack of mail sat neatly beside it, exactly where Meg had left it the night before when she'd returned from the spa. But still, something wasn't right.

"It's about time you got home," came a voice from the living room.

Meg smiled. "I'd ask how you got in, but you'd probably lie to me." She went into the living room. There, on the white-on-white sofa, sat Danny. He was still dressed in his funeral outfit—pale-blue shirt, red tie, navy sport coat, and jeans. A smug grin was on his face.

"I wouldn't lie," he said. "I'd say it's a professional secret."

"And I'd say it's breaking and entering," she said as she flopped beside him and kicked off her shoes. "But I'm glad you're here."

"I'm not staying."

"No?"

"Neither are you." He loosened his tie, then took it off and unbuttoned the top button of his shirt. "Put on some walking shoes. We're going to the zoo."

They bought pretzels at the entrance to Central Park—his with mustard, hers with no salt. They walked through the entrance, past the life all around them—the people, the pigeons. Danny broke off a piece of his pretzel and threw it. The birds converged; the birds fought. The winner took all.

"Life is a skirmish, Meg," Danny said. "Avery got what he wanted out of it."

Meg tucked her hands into her pockets and silently walked beside him along the winding path. Suddenly she became aware of the zoo sounds, the zoo smells. She went to the massive seal cage and looked inside. The animals were sunning on the rocks, peaceful, quiet. She leaned against the rail.

"Avery died alone," she said.

Danny nodded.

"That scares me, Danny. Dying alone."

Danny brushed the hair from his forehead.

Meg gave a short laugh. "The trouble is, in order not to die alone, you have to live with someone. I don't know which scares me more." She stared at the seals, at their immobility. She wondered if they were sleeping. She wondered if they were dead.

Danny took her arm and led her across the walk, toward a small arched bridge. "There's more to life than worrying about dying, Meg," he said. "It's living you should be thinking about. You haven't done a whole lot of that, you know."

She stopped and stared at him. "What are you talking about?"

"You work, Meg. That's it. Oh, sure," he said with a wave of one hand, "once in a while you have a boyfriend. But you're just going through the motions."

She looked out over the water that lay idly beneath the bridge. It was too early in the season for small boys with their sailboats; it was too early for lovers lounging on the grassy banks.

"I'm worried about you, Meg," Danny went on. "Work is one thing, but it's going to be different with Avery gone."

Meg shrugged.

"Isn't there anything you're passionate about, Meg? Isn't there something that excites you more than anything in the world?"

"I love the law," she said quietly. "Sure, the phoniness of our clients bothers me. And the sensationalism. God." She shuddered.

"It is going to be tougher, now that the partners will be in control."

"They don't like me very much. They tolerated me because Avery believed in me."

"That's where you're wrong. Avery was the big name in that firm. After him it's you."

"What are you talking about?"

"I'm talking about you, Meg. The reputation you've developed. In your own enigmatic way you're the most visible part of the firm. Don't sell the partners short. They may be envious of you, but they need you. I think you'll be able to call the shots now. Choose your cases. Handle only the ones you're comfortable with. They need you, Meg," he repeated. "You're their drawing card now."

The trembling seemed to start in her knees. Quickly it spread to her thighs, her breasts, her shoulders. Meg sank her teeth into her lower lip so hard she thought it might bleed. And then the tears erupted. Danny stepped forward and took her in his arms. She sobbed deep, racking sobs, onto his neck, into the strands of his flyaway hair. He rubbed her back, he smoothed her hair. He kissed her lightly on her head.

"I don't want to be anyone's drawing card," she cried. "I just want to do my work. I just want to be left alone."

He held her more tightly. "I don't think so, babe," he said quietly. "I don't think that's what you want at all."

She tipped her head back and looked into his eyes. Suddenly his mouth was on hers. She clung to him, to his kiss. His tender touch eased her tears; his loving taste warmed her heart. But as her senses calmed, Meg remembered that this was Danny. Danny, her friend.

She pulled away and turned back to the bridge, back to the pond below.

He walked up behind her and put a hand on her shoulder. "Jesus, I'm sorry, Meg. I didn't mean to do that."

Meg smiled and wiped the last tears from her face. "It's okay, Danny. It was actually kind of nice."

"I guess I was feeling as scared as you. As lonely."

"Do you think we'll always be alone, Danny? You and me?"

He rubbed her arm. "I'm forty-three years old, Meg. But I haven't given up my dreams that somewhere out there is the right woman for me. As long as I keep the dream, I don't worry about being alone. But you have to dream, Meg. You have to dream."

"Sometimes that's hard."

He squeezed her gently. "A lot of people might wonder why in the hell we've never gotten together, you know."

"I know. But what they don't know is we have something so much stronger, so much better."

"We're friends."

She rested her head against his cheek. "The best kind of friends."

He kissed her hair. "I love you, my friend," he said. And Meg knew that he meant it, in the way that only a friend can love another friend, without obstacles, without conditions.

The partners had scheduled a review meeting for the next morning. Meg stood at the reception desk, looking through her mail. She would have to deal only with Bascomb, Smith, and Paxton now. The other partner, Josh Rheinhold, was dying a slow lung-cancer death and had retired to his summer home in the Hamptons. Out of professional courtesy his name remained stenciled on the door, imprinted in Park Avenue conservative gray on the letterhead. Meg wondered how long it would be before the partners deleted Avery's name from the firm. She guessed they would hold off. No matter what kind of "drawing card" Danny thought she was, Avery's name and reputation would continue to bring in the big bucks. Avery or no Avery.

Janine had separated the condolence cards from the rest of the mail. "Everyone should see them," she said.

Meg picked up the stack of cards and quickly flipped through them. One caught her eye. She stopped and stared at the envelope. "United States Senate," the return address read. *This could be from anyone,* she reasoned. *There were several Senators at the funeral yesterday. This could be from any one of them.* She hesitated. *But it could be from him.* If she took out the card, she could see his signature. She glanced around to see if anyone was watching. Janine was by the coffee machine. Meg slipped the card from the envelope. It was a standard white card engraved in gold. "Deepest sympathy from the office and staff of Senator Howard Levine." She shoved the card back into the envelope and continued flipping through the cards. There was another one. "United States Senate." She pulled out the card. It was identical to the other, except that this one read, "Deepest sympathy from the office and staff of Senator Steven Riley." Beneath the type was his signature. "Steven K. Riley." Meg wondered what the *K* stood for. Was it possible she'd never even known his middle name?

"Are you ready for the meeting, Meg?" The voice startled her. She looked up to see Lloyd Paxton standing in the doorway of the conference room. "We have a lot to go over."

Meg quickly tucked the card from Steven's office into her own pile of mail. "Right away," she said, then took her mail, her briefcase, and went into the conference room.

They were seated at the long oval table in their usual spots. Except for George Bascomb. He sat at the head of the table. Avery's place. Meg felt a twinge of resentment as she took her own chair. Maybe they'd leave his name on the door for a while, she thought, but inside, where there was no one to impress, Avery Larson was history.

"All right, people, let's get started." George Bascomb's voice commanded attention. Meg shifted uneasily in her chair. She'd never worked on a case with George; she hardly knew him. He was as short as Avery had been tall. He was younger than Avery had been, fifty, perhaps. He was round, going bald. He also had an eighty-foot yacht moored off the Bahamas and a well-connected wife with old money.

He began to review the caseload in progress. Tax litigation. Insurance fraud. Embezzlement. In turn the partners gave updates, but it was clearly George who was in control. Meg sat quietly and doodled on her yellow lined pad.

"Arnold Banks," George finally said. "Murder one."

Meg sat up straight. Arnold Banks was a sixty-five-year-old museum curator accused of strangling his elderly mother after years of abusing her. Of the domestic staff of five at the Banks's three-generations-old stately Park Avenue home, two said he did it, two said he didn't. One wasn't talking. It was rumored that Dominic Dunne had already received a hefty advance from *Vanity Fair* to cover the story. And one witness had already signed an exclusive with a TV "news" show. The case was primed for sensationalism. Weary of tales of sexual, spousal, and child abuse, America's tastebuds were now whetted for elder abuse. Meg wanted no part of it.

George shuffled some papers. He peered over his glasses. "As you know, this was Avery's case."

No one spoke.

George set down his papers. "The Banks's account has been handled by this firm for a number of years. He'd prefer one of the senior partners to take over the case."

Meg felt her spine relax. She needn't have worried about George insisting she defend Arnold Banks: clearly, Banks was a good old boy, and the good old boys must stick together, without interference from a young, dynamic female.

"However," George continued, "I disagree." His tiny eyes focused on Meg. "It's your case, Meg."

She dropped her pen. "What?"

"You're going to defend Arnold Banks."

She gazed around the silent room. Then she looked back at George. "I don't want it."

One of the other partners stirred in his chair. Another coughed.

"This isn't a question of what you want, counselor. It's a question of what's good for the firm. For some reason the media has taken a liking to you. If we play our cards right, this case will become more sensational than Holly Davidson. The more press the firm receives, the better."

If we play our cards right. Meg sucked in her cheeks and moved her gaze to the top of the table, to the montage of indiscernible doodles on her yellow lined pad. *You're their drawing card,* Danny had said. God, Meg thought, the practice of law really had become nothing more than a game—and she'd been as great an offender as any of them.

"And if I refuse?" she asked.

George slammed his fist onto the table. She flinched, then hated herself for it, for allowing George Bascomb to strike a cord of visible fear.

"This is your case. Period. This transition is not the time to be a prima donna. You've got to think of the firm. Do it for Avery's memory. He would have expected nothing less from you."

She picked up her pen and formed a string of neat triangles on her pad. *The greater the challenge,* she thought, *the bigger the rush.* But would deferring to George Bascomb be worth it? She connected the triangles. She could get up, she could leave right now. Leave the office, leave the firm. She could easily find another job. She filled in the spaces, wiped out the triangles. She knew it would be no better anywhere else. Another firm would only expect her to maintain the image she'd already created. She pushed the tip of her pen into the paper.

"The trial is scheduled a few weeks from now, so you'd better get started today," George continued. "I've had Avery's files transferred to your office."

"I think that Avery at least would have listened to my argument," Meg said.

George bent his head and straightened his papers. He stood up. "Avery is dead, Meg. I'm in charge now." He took his briefcase and left the room.

The files on the *State of New York* v. *Arnold Banks* sat in the middle of Meg's desk. She pushed them aside and sat down, tossing her briefcase onto the floor, and her mail where the files had been.

She sighed and picked up the stack of mail. From between the envelopes slid the engraved condolence card from Steven's office. Meg picked it up and ran her finger across his signature. *Steven K. Riley.* He hadn't prefaced it with "Senator" or "The Honorable," or any of those pretenses he could have used. Perhaps that meant he hadn't changed. Perhaps that meant he was still the unaffected, sensitive man who had taught her about the law, and about love.

She opened her top drawer and put the card inside. She stared at the card. Did she have the nerve to actually face him again? To be close enough to feel his magnetism, his warmth?

"I cannot bear the thought that you will never touch me again." Those had been Steven's words the last time they were together. The time when she lied and told him she no longer cared for him. The time that he cried.

The phone on her desk buzzed, startling her. "What is it, Janine?" she barked.

"Mr. Bascomb wanted you to know that Mr. Banks is scheduled to come in at three this afternoon. He said you'll take the meeting. Is that okay?"

Meg gently closed the desk drawer. No matter what she thought of George Bascomb, he was still a senior partner.

"Yes, Janine," she answered. "Three o'clock is fine."

She pushed all thoughts of Steven Riley from her mind and carried the stack of the *State of New York* v. *Arnold Banks* files to the sofa. It was time to get back to work. Time to rise to the challenge. She slipped out of her heels, sat on one end of the sofa, and put her feet up on the other end. Then she began to read. Page after page of double-talk, page after page of boredom. Arnold Banks, Meg deduced after less than one hour, was, indeed, guilty. No doubt about it.

She skipped lunch. Shortly after one o'clock her phone buzzed again. Maybe it was Banks canceling. Maybe it was George saying he'd changed his mind.

"Yes, Janine?" she shouted from the sofa.

"A woman on the phone for you. Someone named Alissa Page."

Her first thought was that something was wrong with Zoe. She jumped from the sofa, darted to her desk, grabbed the phone receiver, and pushed in the red flashing light. "Alissa?" she asked. "Is everything all right?"

The laugh was unmistakably Alissa's. Meg felt a strange comfort of familiarity.

"Everything's fine. We just wanted to be sure you got home safe and sound. How was yesterday?"

Meg sank into her desk chair. "Horrible."

"Well, we were thinking of you."

Alissa and Zoe were thinking of her? Had anyone ever thought of Meg before?

"What about the media?" Alissa went on. "Did they pounce on you with their flashbulbs?"

"I didn't give them a chance."

Alissa laughed. "Oh, Meg. And I always have to work so hard to get the media's attention! Listen, I'm calling to ask you a favor. That fellow who called you to tell you about your boss? Did you say he's a private investigator?"

"Danny? Yes. He's on retainer here at the firm."

"Does he freelance?"

"What do you mean?" Meg wasn't sure she liked the sound of this. Alissa as a long-distance friend was one thing; Alissa involved in her day-to-day life was quite another.

"Well, I need to hire someone to look for Jay. I wouldn't know where to start."

Meg stretched the phone cord. "You said you last saw him on cable. Why don't you start there?"

"I don't have patience for that. Besides, I can't take the chance of anyone finding out what I'm doing. I'm a married woman, remember? So here's what I've decided. Before I go back to Atlanta, I'll take the shuttle into the city. We can meet for dinner tomorrow night at the Russian Tea Room. I really want to hire your private investigator friend to find Jay.

I would at least feel as though I could trust him if he was a friend of yours. Besides, if he's a professional, I'm sure he's discreet."

She nodded. "Yes. Yes, Danny is discreet."

"Great. Then I'll see you tomorrow. The Russian Tea Room, eight-thirty."

Meg hung up the phone, wondering what on earth she had just agreed to. She opened her desk drawer again and looked at the card. *Steven K. Riley.* Did she really have the nerve?

7

Alissa settled into the narrow seat in the low one-seat-per-side cabin and rejected the flight attendant's offer of honey-roasted peanuts and a cold drink. As she hooked the buckle of her seat belt and tightened the strap, Alissa congratulated herself on remembering to give the staff at the Golden Key an extra tip so that Zoe's special needs were met after Alissa was gone. She'd also promised to call Zoe and make sure she was sticking to her diet and adhering to the workout schedule Alissa devised. She was satisfied with Zoe's progress so far, and prayed her new friend would be able to accomplish a major comeback. What that would mean for Alissa was almost too wonderful to consider.

If Zoe got that part in the TV movie, it would be aired less than two weeks before the gala. Fans would come out of hiding. The press would go wild. Zoe would quickly become the hottest thing in the news, the most sought-after personality since Princess Di retreated from the limelight. And then it would be time for Alissa to call in a few favors. After all, what were friends for?

As the plane taxied down the runway, Alissa closed her eyes and smiled. Meanwhile she would consolidate her endship with the celebrated Meg Cooper—another social up. *I'm brilliant,* Alissa thought.

The plane revved its engines and Alissa braced herself for takeoff. In front of her she could see two hands holding across the aisle. Terrified passengers. One hand belonged to a young man seated on the opposite side, just one seat up from Alissa. The other hand was delicate and had a tiny diamond set in gold on the ring finger. *Young lovers,* Alissa thought. Probably their first time off the farm.

The plane rattled and rumbled. As she felt the thrust as it left the ground, Alissa saw the hands clasp more tightly together.

She closed her eyes again and wondered how long it had been since anyone had held her hand. Had Robert? Ever? Had any of her lovers? Holding hands was such an intimate thing to do, more intimate in its way than kissing, more intimate than making love.

Jay Stockwell had held her hand.

An uneasiness rose within her as she felt the small plane level off at cruising altitude.

The first time, they had been at a polo match. She had been fourteen. Jay, two years older. They'd gone out to the stables to see Jay's father's new horse. Alissa had had to stand on a bale of hay to peek into the stall. Jay had taken her hand to help her keep her balance. But he'd held it longer than he had to.

They had first made love when she was fifteen. A fact, Alissa mused now, that would probably shock her daughters. They'd done it in the back of his father's limo on the chauffeur's day off, safe from all eyes, in the garage on the Stockwell estate. They'd been innocent and awkward, but, still, it had been wonderful. And afterward he'd held her hand.

And now where was he?

"I'm going to help save the people of the world," he'd said in their last conversation in San Francisco. "I'm going to work for peace."

"But don't you want to make a name for yourself?" Alissa remembered the long fringed tunic she'd worn, and the beads around her neck. Jay had actually made her that bead necklace, and she'd sworn never to take it off. She wondered what had ever become of it.

Their apartment in San Francisco had been squalid. At the time it had seemed perfect. The walls were covered with neon posters where plaster had once been; the kitchen had a huge yellowed-porcelain sink where they'd drained spaghetti in an old tin colander. They'd eaten no meat. They'd had a lot of friends, though she could not remember their names. They'd drunk a lot of wine, smoked a lot of hashish, and occasionally Alissa had watched Jay drop acid. She had been terrified of LSD and had never taken any herself. She hadn't wanted to probe the dark corners of her psyche; she hadn't wanted to expand her mind beyond the here and the now. She hadn't wanted to lose control.

In the daytime Jay had written poetry and read to her while she plucked flowers from the gardens at MacArthur Park. At night they'd slept on a thin, worn mattress, wrapped in each other's arms. Alissa had often been awakened by the gentle push of his eager penis against her; it was the time she had loved most of all, to feel his hardness, and his need, while she slept.

Looking back, Alissa realized that San Francisco had been the most memorable time of her life. It was a shame it had lasted only two months. Two months was all it had taken for Alissa to realize that, for Jay, this was no game. No phase. He had meant everything he'd said, about saving the world, about spreading the peace. To Alissa it had all seemed like such hard work, such a waste of time.

"If you make a name for yourself, you'll be able to help the people more," she'd tried to reason with him on that last day.

"You think I could do that by going home and working in my father's business?"

She had looked at him. His hair was longer than before

they'd left home. His clothes were starting to get worn. And they smelled. His mother, she remembered thinking, would be appalled.

As would the members of the WFFA if they ever knew I'd lived that way, Alissa thought now.

She looked out the tiny round window at the puffy white clouds below. Why was she even considering trying to find him again? *Because,* Alissa realized, *I never stopped loving him.* She thought of all the nights, all those years when she'd secretly flipped through the channels, desperately hoping to catch a glimpse of him, to hear his words, his voice. The words that had once been poetry written for her, the voice that had once read to her. It was the only time in her life that Alissa had felt special. Loved.

If she'd stayed with him, yes, her life would have been different. She'd have had a world beyond Atlanta; she'd have had a life filled with excitement and culture and challenges.

But she would never have had the courage.

She wondered if she had the courage now.

Alissa stepped inside the main level of the Russian Tea Room at eight fifty-five and glanced quickly around the deep, narrow room at the patrons clustered around small, cozy tables. She spotted Meg off to the side and realized it was the first time Alissa had seen her in a suit. As she waved and walked toward the table, Alissa wondered why this beautiful woman insisted on looking the part of the stereotypical attorney. Some color, some jewelry, and something other than "sensible clothes"—something more like the short-cropped light wool jacket and car-wash pleated skirt that Alissa had on—would certainly win Meg more recognition.

"Sorry I'm a bit late," Alissa said as she slid onto the leather banquette. "It always takes longer than I think to get anywhere in this city."

"Where are you staying?"

"At the Plaza. I love looking out over Fifth Avenue. It's so Manhattan. Of course, I mush prefer the Helmsley—poor

Leona—but the location gives me claustrophobia." She hailed a waiter and ordered wine. Then she fumbled in her purse and took out a cigarette and her gold Cartier lighter.

Meg raised her eyebrows.

Alissa glanced around. "Don't tell me. No smoking."

"Sorry."

"God, that pisses me off." She jammed the cigarette and lighter back into her purse and folded her hands on the table. "The more I need to smoke, the fewer places I can do it in. I'll bet if I was one of your notorious clients, they'd rush over here with an ashtray. Probably two."

"My clients aren't all notorious."

"They are once the tabloids get ahold of them. What are you working on now? Incest? Murder? I want to hear all the juicy details."

"Sorry. Client confidentiality."

"Oh, pooh. You're no fun at all. And here I thought I'd actually found a friend I could talk to about something more than charity balls and fund-raisers." There. She'd gotten the words out. Charity balls and fund-raisers. She'd planted the seed.

"Tell me about them," Meg said. "It sounds much more glamorous than what I do."

Alissa waved her hand. "It's nothing. Really. Though every fall I do put on an enormous gala. This year it will benefit the homeless." She sighed. "Homelessness is becoming such a problem. Even in Atlanta." She tried to pose her face in an expression of concern and caring. "I haven't figured out the details yet, but I've decided to make it an ever extraordinary. One that will be talked about all over the globe."

"Well, if anyone can pull it off, you can."

Alissa smiled. There was no need to go on about the gala. She'd made her point. "Speaking of memorable events, did you talk to your friend about helping me?"

"Danny? Yes. He said he'll be glad to meet you tomorrow

ut he wants you to know looking for lost loves isn't really is field of expertise."

"Money is money," Alissa said with a shrug. "I'll pay him well enough, I'm sure. Tell him to be at my suite at ten 'clock. I'm on the second floor, overlooking the Avenue."

Meg jotted down the information in a small notebook.

The waiter arrived and placed a glass of wine in front of lissa.

"Is Danny going to help you find your guy?" Alissa asked fter the waiter had left.

Meg laughed. "I don't think that's a good idea."

"Why not?"

"Let's just say this is something I have to do myself."

"Hey—this is just for laughs, remember? To see how our ves could have turned out. You're not chickening out, are ou? So what if he's married. It's not stopping me."

Meg fingered the rim of her glass. "I'm afraid there's ore to it than that."

"Well, for heaven's sake, Meg, what is it? It can't be all at bad."

"Let's just say he's in the public eye and leave it at that."

Alissa gasped. This was simply too good to be true. "Ah," he murmured, "the plot thickens."

Sensing that Meg would not divulge anything further for e moment, she opened her menu and scanned the offer- gs, wondering who on earth Meg's man really was and ow on earth she was going to find out. She could hardly and not knowing a good bit of gossip. After all, you never new when it would come in handy.

leg hadn't warned her that Danny Gordon looked as if he'd st gotten out of bed. With a woman. Alissa stood in the pen doorway of her Plaza suite, wishing she'd worn some- ing sexier than her aqua linen pants and jacket. At least e ivory camisole was silk.

"I could probably talk better inside than here in the hall,"

Danny said, with a slightly crooked grin that showed his even white teeth and made his dark eyes sparkle.

Alissa couldn't remember when she'd seen such long thick lashes on a man. She stepped aside. "Of course. I'm sorry. Come in." Maybe this was the reason Meg didn't want Danny to help her. Maybe Meg was sleeping with this guy. If not, she was a fool.

He crossed the room and helped himself to a seat by the window. Alissa didn't miss the tight movement of his ass through his jeans. "Nice place you have here."

Alissa laughed. "Thanks." She fluffed her wispy blond curls. She'd give anything to be running her fingers through his unruly black hair. "I love it here." She walked to the window and stared out. "It makes the city seem almost civilized." She put a hand on her hip, brushing away her jacket, hoping he would notice the tiny lace cup of her half bra through her sheer blouse. She wondered if her nipples were hard.

God, she thought. *What the hell am I doing? Didn't I learn anything from Grant Wentworth?* She cleared her throat, closed her jacket, and sat on a chair facing Danny. "I don't know how much Meg has told you."

Danny shrugged. She tried not to notice that the muscles strained against his polo shirt; she tried not to imagine how they looked beneath his casual sport coat. "Only that there's someone you want me to find. I hope she told you this isn't my usual way of making a living."

Alissa crossed her legs. "Yes. She also told me how good you are at what you do."

"Sure I'm good. At criminal cases."

"Even with criminal cases, I'm sure you've needed to locate missing people once or twice."

Danny looked into her eyes. God, she wished he didn't have those eyes. "Once or twice," he said.

Alissa stood again and walked to the fireplace. She leaned against the mantel and turned back to Danny. "I need someone I can trust, Danny." She slipped a hand into her pocket forcing her jacket to fall away from her breast once again. "May I call you Danny?" Under normal circumstances Alissa wouldn't have bothered to ask. But under normal circumstances she wouldn't have been so bothered. If she were a man, Alissa bet she'd have a hard-on.

He laughed. "Call me whatever you like."

She straightened and folded her hands in front of her. "I need ultimate discretion. Which is why I'd like you to handle it. Meg trusts you. I trust Meg." *And I need Meg on my side,* she reminded herself, *so that I can pull off the greatest gala of the year.*

"Sounds like you have it all figured out."

"Whatever your going rate, I'll double it."

He let out a low whistle. "An offer too good to refuse."

And before I'm through with you, Danny Gordon, she thought, *it may not be the only one.* "That's the idea."

He raised his foot and rested it against his other knee. She noticed that he wore boots. Quality leather boots. Rugged. Masculine. A tingle moved between her thighs. Jeans, boots, and a sport coat. A man with a mind of his own.

"Looking for lost people has always seemed to me to be right up there with spying on husbands and wives. About as respectable as ambulance-chasing attorneys."

"Oh. I see. It's beneath you." *Which,* she wanted to add, *is exactly where I'd like to be.*

Danny laughed. "Let's just say it's not my specialty."

"I assure you, this has nothing to do with spying on anyone. This person is someone I knew years ago, and I must find him."

"But you don't want anyone to know you're doing this."

"Right."

"Sounds a bit nefarious to me. No offense."

"I should think you'd be accustomed to that in your line of work."

Danny narrowed his eyes. "Look, lady, I'm long past an age when I want to be looking over my shoulder."

"Why don't you let me worry about that?"

"Because I need to know what I'm getting into before I agree to anything. I like life. Especially mine. And I'm not big on having jealous husbands or scorned wives decide that I'm the bad guy. Double my rate or not."

So, Alissa thought, *money alone isn't enough to lure him. Maybe his pride is what matters to him, or his need for a squeaky-clean reputation. If that's the case, he's in the wrong business.* She walked back to the window and looked down onto the street. The limos were lined up in front of the Plaza, the doormen jockeyed people, the bellmen juggled bags. If it was integrity that Danny Gordon valued, Alissa knew how to handle him. She was, after all, a pro at that, or at the very least, at making things appear that way. If that's what he wanted, she'd slap him with an overabundance of integrity—right between those bedroom eyes.

"Look, Mr. Gordon, this isn't easy for me. I've never done anything like this before. But I have my reputation to protect. My husband is a very well-respected physician. He heads one of the most prestigious medical facilities in the world. I cannot take the chance of anyone doing this for me who I cannot trust implicitly. Meg recommended you. This is something I've wanted to do for many years. But I'll be perfectly honest with you. If you won't agree to help, I won't go elsewhere. I simply won't be able to bring myself to risk doing it."

Danny stood up. "The trouble is," he said, "even if I wanted to help you, I'm on a big case right now with Meg's firm."

"I've waited this long, I suppose I can wait a little longer."

Danny shrugged. "They're my bread and butter. After this case there will probably be another."

Alissa's annoyance peaked. Who the hell did this guy think he was? "Then work me in. I really don't think it would take someone of your expertise terribly long."

Danny smiled. "Why don't you let me be the judge of that? When was the last time you knew where this person was? Give me some details."

She held up her hand. "Not so fast. Not until you agree you'll do it."

"Double my rate?"

Alissa nodded.

"Plus first-class expenses?"

"You drive a hard bargain, Mr. Gordon. But I suspect money isn't your bottom line."

He smiled again. "First-class expenses?"

"Yes. Yes. All right."

"Okay. You've got a deal. But only because you're a friend of Meg's."

So that was it. It was Meg. The buttoned-up attorney had this hunk of a guy by his emotional balls. "Then let's get started," Alissa said. "I've got a family waiting for me in Atlanta, and I can't spend the rest of my life in New York."

Later that night, back home in Atlanta, Alissa sat, her feet tucked beneath her, on the leather sofa in her library, wondering if she would need any more charity balls if Jay was in her life again. Still, it would be nice to have both. Then the issue of getting rid of Robert would take care of itself. She could get on with her life, and Robert would fade into the sunset. There would be no humiliation of people discovering he was gay, for she would be the one to make the break, she would be the one to be reunited with her one true love, and who could argue with that?

She heard the door slam. She heard footsteps in the foyer. Robert's footsteps. Alissa felt nauseous.

"Oh," he said. "You're home." He stood at the French doors leading into the library. His face was pale, sheepish.

"The last time I checked, I still lived here."

He hesitated in the doorway, as though he was unsure if he would be welcome to join her. "How was the spa?"

She swung her legs onto the floor and sat up. "Robert, we have to talk."

"I know."

He stayed where he was. Alissa sighed. "Then for

chrissakes, come in and talk. I'm not going to shout at you from across the room."

"You want to do this now?"

"As opposed to when? Next month? Next year?"

He walked slowly into the library. Robert wasn't a tall man, he wasn't a big man. But he was compact and muscular, and his dark hair and even darker eyes gave him a rugged, outdoorsman look, a look that sharply contrasted with the white lab coat he wore. *He really is quite handsome,* Alissa reminded herself. *He doesn't even look gay.* He set his briefcase on the desk, then sat in the chair behind it, as though trying to act professional, trying to don his doctor mask to conceal his feelings.

"This is difficult," he said.

His statement required no comment.

"Do you want a divorce?" he asked.

"No," she answered. *Not yet,* she wanted to add. *Not until I can be sure I can get out of this the way I want: without tongues wagging about poor Alissa.*

"Good," he said. "Because I wouldn't want to have to go public on this."

She stared at him. So. He was going on the defensive. "What the hell do you mean by that?"

"I mean, I'm sorry if this hurts you, Alissa. But I've been suffering with it for years. To be perfectly honest, there's nothing I'd love more than to come out of the closet." His tone of defense had now changed to one of sadness. "There's nothing I'd love more than to finally be free."

Alissa tried to repel the compassion that stirred within her. "Free of me?"

"No. Free to be myself."

She fluffed her hair, then touched an index finger to the corner of her mouth. "You'd have to give up medicine. A lot of people wouldn't go to a doctor who's an admitted homosexual."

"I have AIDS patients, Alissa. They'd still come."

"I thought you were working on a cure. Or would you conveniently prolong that to keep yourself in business?"

"Alissa, that's uncalled for. You know me better than that."

"I've suddenly discovered I don't know you at all."

The room was silent. Alissa wished she had the guts to get up and walk out, to leave this all behind. But leaving Robert would mean leaving her entire life and everything in it. And she couldn't bring herself to do that yet. Not unless, or until, she found Jay.

"We have the girls to think about," he said.

"Don't you think I haven't considered that?" She realized then that she really hadn't. Would they be irreversibly marred by the disclosure that their father was gay? Michele would. She'd rant and rave and flee into exile in New York or L.A. or somewhere far from Atlanta. But Natalie? Probably not. Knowing her younger daughter, Alissa figured she'd probably feel it was something that would give her some sort of elevated status among her peers. She could go on *Donahue. Sally Jesse.* She could make a name for herself. She'd love it.

"I love them, Alissa. I love you."

She reached into her pocket and took out a cigarette. She lit it and blew out a frustrated stream of smoke. Robert winced.

"Explain to me, please, why I find that so hard to believe."

He didn't answer.

"And while you're at it, explain to me why you would rather have your prick shoved up some man's filthy asshole than inside the woman you supposedly love."

He remained silent.

Alissa studied the red glow on the tip of her cigarette. She'd never wasted time pondering the lovemaking habits of homosexuals—it had simply never mattered: it had been something that never infringed on her world. But it wasn't as though she didn't know any gay men. Artists. Hairdressers.

But not doctors. And not husbands. "What do you want, Robert?"

"I want us to be a family. I want us to stay together."

"So you can go on having your little dalliances on the side?"

"And so can you."

"Touché. But, my dear, we aren't exactly talking apples and apples. Although I suppose we could create a new relationship. One where we could compare lovers. You know, the size of their dicks, things like that."

In the silence that followed Alissa could hear her heartbeat.

"I guess I deserve that," Robert finally said.

"You deserve more than that. You deserve to have your balls cut off."

Alissa sat and smoked, wishing she could fast-forward to a year from now. Two years. Then she would know how she'd handled this, how everything had turned out. Would she be somewhere safe and warm with Jay? Would she still be someone to whose parties everyone wanted to go? Would she still be here, stuck in a gutless marriage?

"I don't need you, you know. I get plenty of money from my trust fund to support myself nicely. Add that to the enormous alimony you'd have to pay me, and I'd be better off than I am now."

Robert leaned back in his chair. "Just think. You could spend every month you're not planning a party at a health spa." His attempt at sarcasm was diluted by a crack in his voice, an underlying hint of fear.

"I could do that. Couldn't I?" Alissa said coolly, but her insides churned. The thought of having nothing to do, no home that was grounded by a traditional wife-husband-children structure, was something she couldn't imagine. The girls wouldn't need her around much longer as it was. Without Robert, what would she do? Where would she go? What would she do after she got up in the morning? What would be the point?

All the more reason to find Jay.

"Can we give this some time?" Robert asked.

"Why? So you'll change?"

"I can't change, Alissa. I told you. I've been wanting you to know about this for years. I've tried to change. I can't. But that doesn't mean we can't have a full life together. I do love you, you know. But maybe it's not the kind of love you want."

"I don't have a clue what love is anymore."

"What are you going to do?"

She ground out her cigarette. "I guess you'll just have to wait and see."

"Did you and Daddy have a fight?" Michele barged into the dressing room where Alissa sat quietly, staring into the mirrored wall.

Alissa adjusted the sash of her silk robe. Sooner or later, she thought, one of the girls was bound to ask. "Who wants to know?" she asked.

Michele plopped onto the long counter. "Mother, don't patronize me."

"Such a big word coming from a blond."

"Mother ..."

"Sorry, darling, I'm just not ready to talk about it, that's all."

"You always told me it's best to talk about things. Get them out in the open."

"That only works for daughters."

"Well, Daddy sure is acting weird. All the time you were gone, he came home early every night. He just sat in the library, not doing anything. When David brought me home after our dates, Daddy was still sitting there."

Alissa saw the opportunity to change the subject. "You're still seeing David? Isn't this some kind of a record?"

Michele slid off the counter and picked up a sable brush. She swirled it around an open jar of loose bronzer and dusted her face. "He asked me to marry him," she said.

Alissa laughed. "You're eighteen years old. Your life is just beginning. Why the hell would you want to get married?"

Before Michele could answer, the telephone rang. It was Alissa's private line, the one reserved for her close friends and lovers. But her close friends were few and far between, and God knew there were no lovers pining after her right now. Alissa took her time as she reached across the vanity and picked up the receiver.

"Alissa? It's Zoe."

Alissa caught her breath. She smiled widely. "Zoe! Darling, how are you?"

"I'm late for aquatics so I can't talk. But get yourself to TV and turn it on."

"Why? Oh, hold on a second." She put the receiver to her chest and looked at Michele. "Private call," she said, "Disappear, okay?"

"Does it have anything to do with you and Daddy?"

Alissa gave her a nasty look. "Out," she said, and pointed to the doorway.

Michele gave a disgusted grunt and sashayed from the room.

"Sorry, Zoe," Alissa said into the phone. "One of my daughters was here. Now, what's this about TV?"

"Turn on the Global News Network. Hurry. Jay's on."

Alissa's pulse raced. "Jay?"

"Hurry, Alissa."

Alissa threw down the receiver and ran into the bedroom. With trembling hands she tried to work the remote. Her mind spun. She couldn't remember the channel number for Global News. "Damn!" she screamed. "Damn!" She flipped through the channels. Too many channels. *Too many goddamn channels.* And then he was there. The remote flipped past him. She flipped it back. And held her breath.

His face was there. It was older. It was tanned. He was standing in front of a cluster of makeshift tents, saying something about emergency food supplies. Alissa paid no attenon to his words, only his voice—his deep, strong voice, deeper than she remembered, still ingrained with traces of prep-school breeding, but resonant with that damn liberal note of concern.

She slowly let out her breath and studied the man on the screen. He seemed softer somehow. Not his body, really. Not his face. But something about Jay was different, as though the quick, eager edge of youth had been leveled off, smoothed over, polished.

She wished she knew how she felt. Maybe if the camera moved in closer, maybe if she could see his eyes ...

"This is Jay Stockwell for Global News."

Suddenly the anchor appeared. And Jay was gone.

Alissa stared at the television. It had been him. It had really been him. How long had it been since she'd rapidly changed channels, hoping to catch a glimpse, hoping to hear his voice? He was here. And now he was gone. Again.

She sat on the bed, realizing, through her numbness, that she hadn't seen him long enough to know if she still cared. But the picture was frozen in her mind, his voice engraved in her thoughts. "This is Jay Stockwell for Global News."

She stared at the screen, at the moving lips of the anchor. She had seen Jay. Jay Stockwell for Global News.

In the distance a small voice dangled from the phone. "Alissa?" it called. "Alissa, are you there?"

8

Zoe packed her suitcases with bittersweet satisfaction. True, all the clothes she had brought with her to the Golden Key Spa six weeks and twenty-two pounds ago were now too big; but equally true was the fact that she had no money to waste buying new ones.

She zipped the last suitcase closed and glanced at her watch. She still had half an hour before the driver would take her to the airport. Then the long flight home to L.A., home to who-knows-what lay ahead.

She sat on the edge of the bed and folded her hands. She knew she was prepared for the screen test. At the end of each exhausting day she'd studied the script, over and over, until she knew it cold, until she had become Jan Wexler, the spitfire single mother fighting to keep the gangs from infiltrating her urban neighborhood. She had studied hard, but whether or not she was any good, Zoe simply didn't know. Any more than she knew if she'd be forced into selling Cedar Bluff.

One thing she did know, she was going to find Eric.

Zoe stretched on her back, enjoying the fact that her hip bones protruded once again, not caring if she wrinkled the cotton jumpsuit she'd bought that morning in the Golden

-y boutique. Alissa had "rattled her cage," as Scott would -y, when she'd challenged each of them to find the man of -r past. It was something Zoe had longed to do for years, -t never had, because of William.

"You are the most beautiful, most talented woman in the -rld," Eric had told her that night after the last perform- -ce of their high-school class play. They had done *West Side -ory*. Zoe had played Maria; Eric, Tony. It still been -ld, that Minnesota night in the middle of May, but some- -w he had managed to pluck her daisies from someone's -suspecting garden. "I want to be with you forever," he'd -id.

That was the night they'd decided to go to Hollywood.

Eric had saved a little money working in his father's -re, and they'd pooled their graduation money. Together -ere had been enough to get them there by bus and pay a -posit and the first two months' rent on a seedy apartment - a seedy building. To them it had been a palace, for they'd -en together, in love, and were following their dreams.

What had gone wrong?

Zoe sat up on the bed. She knew what she had to do. -aching for the phone, her heart began to pound. She -ked for an outside line, then directory assistance for Min- -sota.

"Operator. What city, please?"

Zoe paused, afraid the operator would recognize her -ice, afraid she would be found out.

"What city, please?"

Zoe took a deep breath. "In Hibbing, please. The number - Roland Matthews." There was a chance his parents were -l in the same town. There was a chance, Zoe supposed, -y were still living.

A digitized voice clicked on and spewed out a phone -mber. Zoe was so stunned she didn't write it down. Eric's -rents were still in Hibbing. Eric's parents were still alive. She hung up the phone and stared at it.

Was she out of her mind? What was she planning to do?

Call his parents and say "Hi. You probably don't remember me, but I ran away with your son over twenty years ago..." How absurd. To begin with, of course they would know who she was. She was Zoe. And everyone in the world over twenty-five knew who Zoe was.

Did that mean she'd have to remain in hiding forever?

She pushed a suitcase aside and got off the bed. She went into the living room and flopped onto the sofa. There was another phone there, on the end table. Beside it was a small pad and a pen. She picked up the receiver, asked for an outside line, then information in Minnesota. This time she wrote down the number.

Quickly Zoe pressed her finger on the button and requested another outside line. Then she dialed the number direct.

"Hello?"

It was a voice she didn't recognize. An old voice. A woman's. Zoe's heart sped in her chest.

"Hello," she said in a thin, tinny voice that sounded as though it belonged to someone else. "I'm trying to reach Eric Matthews. Is he still at this address?"

There was a pause, then the old voice asked, "Who's calling?"

Zoe's hand began to tremble. "I ... I used to work with him," she stammered.

"He doesn't live here, but I can give him a message. Who's calling?"

Zoe stared at the notepad, edged in gold, embossed with the Golden Key logo. She hung up.

She ripped off the sheet with the phone number and wadded it into an angry ball. What the hell did she think she was doing? Didn't she have enough problems? She pushed herself off the sofa, walked to the wastebasket, and dropped the ball of paper into it. *Fool,* she thought. *Damn fool.*

But as she stared at the rumpled paper in the bottom of the basket, Zoe knew in her heart that she wouldn't give up. They were supposed to have been together. Forever. Soon-

or later she would find Eric. Sooner or later she would confront him.

The phone rang. Zoe jumped. Her heart raced again. Could it be him? She stared at the phone. It rang again. Maybe his mother had recognized her voice. Maybe the call had been traced. She shook her head. Don't be a jerk.

It rang again. She crossed the room and picked it up.

"Ms. Hartmann?" a voice asked. "Your driver is here."

Zoe hung up again and smoothed her jumpsuit. *Time to get back to reality, girl. Time to get back to your life.*

She saw Marisol right away, even through the crowded concourse. Zoe raced toward her, arms open. Marisol's jaw dropped in surprise.

"My God, I hardly recognized you," her friend cried as she swooped her into her motherly arms. "You look fabulous. You look like a star again."

Zoe laughed. "I decided to pack the wig and the sunglasses. Now get me out of here before someone recognizes me."

They walked arm in arm down the concourse.

"Scott's mad as hell that I wouldn't let him skip school to come meet you," Marisol said.

"How is my baby?"

"Ornery as ever. Takes after his mother."

"More like his godmother."

Marisol hugged her. "I'll ignore that and just say he's missed you a lot."

"I'm dying to see him, too. I've never been away from him for so long."

"Honey, you've never been away from him at all. It was good for both of you."

"Thanks a lot." Zoe laughed as they made their way to the baggage level.

Just then a middle-aged woman dressed in khaki shorts and a multipocketed shirt stepped forward.

"You're Zoe, aren't you?" the woman asked.

Zoe was startled. "Why. Yes."

"I can't believe it. Colleen!" she shouted across the room. "Get over here, quick!" She turned back to Zoe. "Could I have your autograph, please?" She thrust the envelope of her airline ticket at Zoe. "Just sign anywhere."

Zoe took the envelope. The woman quickly produced a pen. "Write 'To Martha.' Oh, God, I can't believe this. Colleen!"

Zoe quickly signed "To Martha—Best Wishes, Zoe," and dated it. She smiled at the woman.

"Thank you, thank you," the woman twittered. "Oh, this is so exciting. I can't believe my friend has disappeared."

"Well, good luck to you, Martha," Zoe said, and turned with a bewildered look back to Marisol.

"Zoe?" On the other side stood a teenage boy, not much older than Scott. He had red hair, a severe case of acne, and a wide, friendly grin on his face. A camera hung around his neck. "You really are Zoe, aren't you? Wow. Wait till I tell the guys back home. Geez. Wait till I tell my dad!" He held up his camera. "Can I have a picture of you. Please?"

"Sure," Zoe said, wondering how this kid who could only have been a baby when she'd made her last film could possibly be a fan. "I guess a picture would be all right."

Marisol stepped in. "How about if I take one of the two of you together?"

"Wow. You mean it?"

Marisol nodded and reached for his camera. He quickly pulled it from his neck and handed it to her, then stood beside Zoe. Not, Zoe noted, too close. She moved closer and put her arm around him. He was trembling.

"Say cheese," Marisol directed.

"Cheese," said the boy.

Marisol snapped the shutter.

The boy looked at Zoe again. "Geez. I can't believe this. Thanks, Zoe. Thanks a lot." He retrieved his camera from Marisol and backed away, still watching Zoe as though this was the most incredible thing that had ever happened to him.

Poor boy, Zoe thought. *He has no idea he's just done more for me than I did for him.*

Marisol was smiling. She dug into her purse and produced a set of keys. "Why don't you get out of here before we're swarmed? The car's in Lot C, Green. I'll wait here and get a porter for your bags."

Zoe took the keys. She was filled with excitement, anticipation. It had been fifteen years since she'd felt this way. Fifteen years since she'd felt like a star. "I can't believe they recognized me."

"Honey, if your talent has come back as well as your looks, you've got nothing to worry about."

"Well, I guess it won't be long before we know, will it?"

Marisol grinned. "Less time than you might think."

"What do you mean?"

"I mean just what I said. I talked to Tim Danahy this morning. Your screen test is scheduled for the day after tomorrow."

Zoe stopped abruptly. "What?"

"You heard me. Now get out of here and get the car. In case you forgot, you had to let the chauffeur go."

"Well, that's one way to bring me back down to earth," Zoe said, but as she headed for the outside doors, there was lightness, happiness, in her heart. Someone had recognized her. Two people! Her screen test was the day after tomorrow, and in a little while she'd see Scott again. She stepped on the automatic door opener, then went through the open glass into the warm sunshine.

She crossed the parking lot and tried not to let her excitement turn to anguish. The day after tomorrow the truth would come out. The day after tomorrow she'd know for certain if this was really going to work. She'd find out if she could play a convincing role of Jan Wexler, braving a tough exterior, yet, inside, alone and scared. She certainly had enough inner turmoil from which to draw. The day after tomorrow she'd know if this was really happening. If she was really going to be a star again.

The day after tomorrow seemed an eternity away.

She scanned the sea of parked cars, then walked in the direction of the sign for Lot C, Green. She knew Marisol was as excited as she was about what lay ahead. And probably just as anxious. For no matter what Marisol said, she had as much at stake as Zoe. She'd invested her savings in Zoe; she'd invested her faith. Without Zoe, Marisol's future was bleak. Marisol was too old to go back to work in the fields, she was too crippled with arthritis to clean people's houses. She'd have to go back to living in the projects, hoping to earn enough money working the clay of her pottery to get by.

Yes, Marisol had as much at stake as Zoe. Which was why Zoe had decided she wouldn't tell Marisol about her plans to find Eric yet. She didn't want to spoil their much-needed optimism.

Later that evening Zoe and Scott were in the study. While Zoe had been away, Marisol had had the room entirely redone. Fresh paint, pale green this time, a cushy celery carpet, bookcases stained in dark mahogany. There were a new desk and chair to replace William's old one, and the sofa and lounge chairs had been recovered in cheerful stripes and a floral print. The money to do it, Zoe was certain, had come from Marisol's dwindling savings.

Because of her friend's compassion, Zoe was determined to use this room, to enjoy it. And not to stare at the wall where William's blood and brains had been.

She thumbed through the mail of the past six weeks. Ads. Catalogs. Bills. Lots of bills. Scott sat on the floor, surrounded by piles of old photographs and news clips from Zoe's era of fame.

"You haven't looked in those old boxes for years," Zoe said.

"I know. But I figured I'd better get used to seeing my

mother as a star. Besides, I like this stuff, even though it's all BS."

Zoe's eyebrows raised. "BS? Just what are they teaching you in school?"

Scott laughed. "BS. As in 'Before Scott.'"

Zoe rolled her eyes.

"Gotcha, Mom."

Zoe smiled and slit open the next envelope. The contents offered her an opportunity to save 35 percent on long-distance charges to the area code she called most often. She wondered if that would include L.A. to Hibbing, Minnesota.

"Hey, Mom. Here's the time you got the Oscar." Scott held up a yellowed newspaper article. With it was a picture of Zoe, smiling, standing beside William, holding the golden statue high.

"It says, 'Zoe received both a standing ovation and the Best Actress Award for her exemplary work in *Muldoon*.'"

What the caption didn't reveal, Zoe knew, was that at the time of the photo she was two months pregnant, alone, terrified out of her mind, and completely unaware that her problems hadn't even begun.

She nodded and went back to her mail. The next envelope was from Home Life Insurance. Her heart started to pound. This was the company that held the policy on William. Could it be the check? So soon? Would they simply send a check for half a million dollars by regular mail? She tore open the flap and pulled out the contents.

There were several pages. *They probably need more information,* she reasoned. Of course, they wouldn't send a check for that amount without more information. She opened the cover letter.

"Dear Ms. Hartmann:" the form letter began. "Regarding your claim on policy #BAS73239908–4927, please note that we have been unable to process settlement due to the following." There was a list of items, each preceded by a small box. Her eyes quickly scanned to the item checked in red felt marker. "Claim denied." She blinked. Surely there was some mistake. Next to the words was the type: "See Section __." With the red marker someone had penned in "14-D." In parentheses it read "See reverse side for details."

Zoe's hand began to shake as she turned over the sheet.

"Hey, Mom," Scott said.

Zoe held her breath.

"Who's this guy standing between you and Dad?"

"Not now, Scott," she snapped. "I'm reading my mail."

Scott mumbled something like, "Well, excuse me," while Zoe's eyes ran down the small print of the back side of the letter. She saw Section 14. A. B. C. D. She squinted her eyes, hoping she was reading wrong. But though tiny, the words were clear: "Cause of Death—Suicide. Exempt from coverage."

Zoe stared at the paper. This wasn't right. It couldn't be right. She pulled out the other sheets that had been included with the letter. There must be another explanation. There must be. But the other sheets were applications for more life insurance. Suicide, no doubt, exempt from coverage.

She turned back to the letter and read it again. There was no mistake. The claim had been denied. The air in the room grew heavy. Zoe couldn't catch her breath. She would not get the half million dollars. She would not be able to make the balloon payment on Cedar Bluff.

She'd had less than an hour's sleep. First thing in the morning Zoe sat on the bed in her magnificent white bedroom with the two walls of windows that drew the overpowering redwoods and the breathtaking cliffs into the room, and, in privacy, she placed a call to Tim Danahy. She had to find out if there was any hope that she could still make things work.

"Your friend told me you were getting back yesterday," he said. "So, tell me, are you beautiful?"

A twinge of shame ran through her until Zoe reminded herself that Tim's question wasn't necessarily triggered by her unattractiveness six weeks ago, but by the simple fact that beauty was Hollywood packaging. And without a glamorous package, the contents mattered little.

Still, an appealing image of a Twinkie flashed through her mind.

"I've lost weight, if that's what you mean."

Tim laughed. "Good girl. And I expect you're all set for tomorrow?"

Tomorrow. Right. In her angst over her financial problems, Zoe had nearly forgotten that she'd have to land the part first, before she'd need to worry if it would pay her enough money to keep Cedar Bluff.

"Yes. A couple of questions, though. What scene will I be doing?"

Tim told her. Zoe was pleased. It was a scene she was especially comfortable with.

"And another thing." She closed her eyes to shield her embarrassment. "Do you know how much I'd get?"

"As in money?"

Zoe opened her eyes. God, why was this so difficult to talk about? "Yes."

"I'll try for two hundred thousand. Two-fifty, tops."

Two hundred thousand dollars. Zoe had made five times that on her last film, fifteen years ago. "That's all?" she asked meekly.

Tim laughed. "This is TV, Zoe. And comebacks, well, I think you know it'll be a while before we can get you back into the big-money league."

Zoe's throat swelled with suppressed tears. Tears, she realized then, don't start in the eyes. They start in the heart.

Tim told her where to be tomorrow, and when.

"I'll see you there," he said, and, as if with a last-minute thought that she might need some encouragement, he added, "I know you'll be great."

After Zoe hung up the phone, she stared out the windows at the peaceful, majestic landscape. Cedar Bluff was home to her. It was familiar. This was the view she'd watched, mesmerized, for hours, days, weeks, months, years, while she was recuperating, while she was hiding. She'd studied each tree, each bough. She'd learned each rock, each jagged edge. And now it could all be gone.

If Tim was able to get only two hundred thousand, Zoe would see only one-seventy. After his commission. Before taxes. It was not nearly enough to cover the balloon payment. It was not nearly enough to save Cedar Bluff, or her life.

She lay back on the bed and stared at the ceiling. Maybe she could convince the bank to refinance Cedar Bluff. She could give them a hundred thousand dollars instead of five. Maybe, just maybe, they'd agree to it. Then all she would have to do was get the part. And she'd be able to hang on a little longer.

Until when? Zoe thought as she rolled onto her side and picked at the thick down comforter. Until she was able to go through another screen test? Pray for another part?

She pulled a pillow toward her and rested her forehead against it. Would it really work? And was it really worth it?

Don't give me no shit. Marisol's words once again.

Zoe sat up. One thing was for certain—the only way it could possibly work was if she tried. She went to her dressing room and took out a short black silk dress, which, though fifteen years old, was thankfully back in style. She slipped it over her head. It fit. She stepped out of the dress, quickly showered, then applied her makeup and did her hair in true star-quality fashion.

Less than an hour after she'd talked to Tim Danahy, Zoe drove into the parking lot at First Pacific Savings and Loan.

The inside of the bank was so quiet it could have been a library. Zoe stood by the counter and glanced around. She spotted the customer-service desk.

As she walked toward the desk, Zoe felt the discreet stares of bank customers, tellers. They were not tourists; they belonged there. To them another star walking into the bank should be just that. Another star. No big deal.

So why were they staring?

I thought you were dead, Alissa had said. *Maybe that's why everyone's staring now. Maybe they think they're seeing a ghost,* Zoe thought.

A young man seated at the desk looked up at her and, with only the briefest double take, asked, "May I help you?"

Zoe sat down in the chair facing him. "I'd like to speak with someone about my mortgage."

"I can help you."

He can't help me, Zoe thought. *He doesn't look old enough to be a cashier in a supermarket, never mind someone knowledgeable enough to deal with the finances for Cedar Bluff.*

"It's a complicated matter," Zoe said with a genuine smile meant not to injure his feelings. "I believe I should speak with a bank officer."

He tapped the nameplate that sat on the desk. "John Burns. Assistant Vice President, Consumer Lending," he said proudly.

Zoe's smile vanished. She was in trouble. "I need to talk about refinancing."

He asked for her name as though he didn't know it, and her street address. Then said he'd be back in a moment.

The moment took fifteen minutes. After the first five Zoe wanted to stand up and scream. She'd never thought she'd be the type to shout a goddammit-don't-you-know-who-I-am command. That kind of behavior was reserved for the Alissa Pages of the world. Right now, though, Zoe wished she had that ability, those guts, that self-confidence—or whatever it took. But she quickly reminded herself that she was there to ask a favor—a big one. She had to accept that she was at the bank's mercy, because for the time being Zoe was the underdog, the subservient one. The beggar.

He finally returned with a file, sat down at his desk, and entered some data into a computer. Then he sat back and frowned at the screen. "You have a payment due in two weeks," he announced, as though this must be news to her.

"Yes. I know. That's why I'm here," she said.

He swiveled his chair around to face her. "Will you be able to make the payment?"

Zoe cleared her throat. "My husband has recently passed away. There has been a problem with the life insurance."

"I see," he said, knitting his youthful, unwrinkled brow. "Well, we do understand that crises arise, and we try to accommodate our customers. How long do you think it will be before you can make payment?"

Probably never, Zoe wanted to say. "I was wondering if we could negotiate. If I could come up with, say, one hundred thousand dollars, that would leave a balance of only four."

"We'd have to refinance completely," he said.

"What would that entail?"

"It would be as though you were applying for a new mortgage. We'd have to go through the same kind of paperwork."

"What about the equity I have in the house?"

He opened the file. "The property has been evaluated at two million six. That, however, was a few years ago. It's probably less today."

"The five hundred thousand that's due in two weeks would pay off the mortgage, wouldn't it?"

"Yes."

"With over two million dollars in equity, it seems as though I shouldn't have a problem refinancing." Even Zoe was impressed with the authoritative, confident sound of her voice.

"Refinancing all depends," he said.

"On what?"

"On your present income."

Her confidence burst like a soap bubble in the air, dissolving into bits of worthless matter, disintegrating into nothingness all over his desk. "I don't have an income," she said quietly, then added, "at the present time."

"None?"

Zoe stared at the open file in front of him. "I don't understand," she said. "I have over two million dollars in equity. If I pay you a hundred thousand, then refinance the balance of four hundred thousand and can't pay it, the bank would end up with property worth six times what I owe."

John Burns smiled. "Ms. Hartmann, the bank doesn't want to own your property. They want you to own it. They want you to be able to pay for it." He folded his hands across the papers. "Surely there must be something you could put up as collateral. Stocks? Bonds?"

Zoe felt humiliation seep into her. She shook her head.

"Where do you plan to get the one hundred thousand?"

"I'm an actress, Mr. Burns. I am up for a part in a movie. The one hundred thousand would come from my paycheck."

John Burns smiled as though he'd heard this story before. "Are you under contract yet?"

"No."

He leaned across the desk in a fatherly fashion. Zoe wanted to slap him across his peach-fuzzed face. "You still have two weeks before the balloon payment is due. Why don't you wait and see what happens with the contract, then get back to me?"

Pain throbbed behind her eyes. "What difference would it make? Even if I can come up with a hundred thousand, you've just about told me I couldn't refinance because I don't have an income."

"If you can guarantee the hundred thousand, we could take another look at it. But right now it seems as though you can't really guarantee it."

Zoe couldn't disagree.

He pulled some papers off his desk and handed them to her. "In the meantime you might as well look this over in case there's a possibility we can work something out. It's an application for refinancing."

Zoe took the papers and stood up.

"I wish this could be easier, Zoe," he said, apparently now feeling as though having the upper hand gave him credence to call her by her first name. "But rules are rules. And these days the banking industry is governed very strictly. I'm sure you understand."

Zoe nodded and started to walk away.

"We look forward to doing business with you," John Burns, Assistant Vice President, Consumer Lending, called after her.

On the way home Zoe stopped at a convenience store and bought three packages of Twinkies and two Ring-Dings. She ripped off the cellophane in the car and devoured the sugar and the fat and the empty calories. While she was savoring the buzz, she decided she wouldn't tell Scott about her trip to the bank. She wouldn't tell Marisol. She wouldn't tell them until the last possible moment that they were going to lose Cedar Bluff. She had two weeks. She could pray for the role in *Close Ties*. She could pray for a miracle. She licked the last of the sweet stickiness from her fingers and headed toward the canyon.

The next morning Zoe stood in the wings at the studio sound stage. She had been coiffed and made-up and costumed in sweatpants and an NYU T-shirt. The ideal attire for an activist Mom of the nineties.

She was nervous. Marisol had wanted to come—"Girl, you might need some good old moral support," she'd said last night—but at the time, Zoe wanted to do this alone. She wanted to prove how far she'd come, she wanted to prove her strength. Now she wished she'd let Marisol come.

"Zoe, darling." Tim Danahy had approached from the side. "You look positively superb. I knew you could do it."

"Looks are one thing, Tim. It's what I can do out there that will matter." She pointed to the stage with a finger that, surprisingly, did not tremble.

"And there," he added as he motioned to the massive cameras that stood on the stage peering at an empty set of gray seamless paper.

"No backdrop?" Zoe asked. "No props?"

Tim shrugged. "Guess not."

Zoe didn't need to ask why. She knew the producers weren't interested in how she could act in the right setting.

They knew she could act. What they didn't know was how she'd look to the camera. This screen test, without a doubt, was going to focus primarily on one thing: Zoe's face. She said silent thanks to Alissa Page for forcing her to try salt scrubs and mud packs, for flushing her with gallons of mineral water until the excess fluid drained her puffiness, until her cheekbones had returned to their prominent position beneath her blue-black eyes. She hoped that yesterday's binge on Twinkies and Ring-Dings hadn't obliterated Alissa's hard work.

"Danahy?"

Zoe and Tim turned around. A tall, lean man with a silvery mustache and brown freckles on the top of his balding head approached them.

"Cal. Nice to see you again." Tim extended his hand to the man's large, long-fingered one.

"And you must be Zoe," the man said as he pulled his hand from Tim's and gave it to her. "Cal Baker."

"The director," Zoe heard herself say.

He smiled. His teeth were large and narrow, like his fingers; his green eyes were pleasant, unmenacing. But Zoe knew that the biggest directors rarely—if ever—came to a screen test. Cal Baker's appearance could mean only one thing: they were going to be tough on her, they weren't going to take any chances. Zoe wondered if her quivering insides were noticeable.

"Shall we get started?" Cal asked.

She started to follow his long gait when Tim put his hand on her arm. "Listen, kiddo, I'm going to disappear. I'm no good at these things. I get too nervous."

Zoe stopped. "You're leaving me?"

"I'll be back. That's a promise."

She watched him leave. She felt like a child abandoned by her parent on the first day of school.

Suddenly, from out of nowhere, people appeared. Lights flooded the studio. Voices shouted questions, barked orders. Zoe took a deep breath, held it, then let the air slowly escape. "Relaxation breathing" they'd called it at the spa. She wondered how many times she'd have to do it before it worked.

"Okay, Zoe," came Cal Baker's voice. "Let's get you onstage for lighting."

Zoe stepped forward, trying not to think of the years it had been since she'd been in front of a camera. She found her mark and stood patiently, while lights and shadows swooped around her. It was not, she remembered, unlike her very first screen test.

Except that Eric had been there.

They had gone out for breakfast but ordered only coffee and juice in order to save their money for a post-screen-test celebration. He'd received a hefty check the day before—$387.23 for a razor-blade commercial—and he planned to take her to the Brown Derby for lunch, if they could get in.

The studio wasn't unlike this one. The set had been bare. The commotion had seemed ludicrous. She'd been nervous then, too, but not really scared, for back then Zoe had had nothing to lose. And when she had looked to the wings, Eric had stood there, smiling, holding in his hand the rabbit's foot he'd brought from back home in Minnesota, squeezing it tightly, praying maybe even harder than she that she'd get the part. It had been like that with them. She'd wanted only good things for him, he for her. They'd taken on each other's pleasures and pains as though they'd been one body, one soul.

Now, when Zoe looked to the wings, no one was there.

"Sound check," a voice called from somewhere in the rafters.

Zoe cleared her throat. "Testing," she said. "Testing for sound level." She hoped that didn't sound stupid; she didn't know what else to say. She couldn't remember how it was done.

No one said anything else. Zoe stood and waited. And waited.

She tried to recall the lines of the scene. It opened with Jan Wexler standing alone in her cluttered kitchen, gazing out the window into the alley below, wondering why only a handful of her neighbors had shown up for her meeting. She was to speak only a few lines, but they needed to be powerful.

Zoe closed her eyes and decided to run through the script again in her mind. She was Jan Wexler. By the window. Looking out at her neighborhood. Wistful, pensive, sad. And frightened.

Zoe's eyes flew open. She couldn't remember her first line.

She stared at the camera. The red light wasn't yet on. She flicked her gaze around the studio. No one was paying attention to her.

Help me! she wanted to scream. *Someone help! What is my first line?*

She looked to the wings. Still, no one was there. Panic surged through her. She thought of Scott. Of Cedar Bluff. Of that patronizing John Burns at First Pacific Savings and Loan.

"Okay, Zoe, let's give it a run-through." It was Cal Baker's voice. "Whenever you're ready."

She took a deep breath, held it, then let it out slowly. *What was her line? What was her damn line?*

She thought about Eric's grin. She thought about his squeezing the rabbit's foot. And then Zoe became a young woman again, eager, confident, with nothing to lose.

She looked up to the camera. "Ready," she said, then began to recite. "They don't want to get involved. It's their own damn neighborhood, their own damn families, but they don't want to get involved." She raised her fists and shook them. Heat rose in her cheeks. "Close your eyes! It'll go away! Ha! Not until they murder one of your kids. Or maybe two." The words exploded from her mouth. She raved when she should have raved. She stuttered when she should have stuttered. Then, finally, she broke down in sobs so real they shook her soul. Zoe became Jan Wexler, inside, where it mattered. How she looked to the camera no longer concerned her, for Zoe was in character now. She was Jan Wexler.

"Bravo!" came applause from the wings as Zoe concluded the scene. It was Tim Danahy. He marched onto the stage.

Zoe blinked a moment, fighting her way back to reality, the same way she had to whenever she'd performed such an engrossing scene, whenever she'd been able to become someone else, someone who existed not only in the writer's mind, but also in hers.

"You were marvelous," Tim said as he hugged her tightly. "Simply marvelous."

"Thank you, Zoe," Cal Baker called. "We'll be in touch with Tim."

Tim kept one arm around her and escorted her off the stage. "Fantastic, Zoe. Utterly fantastic."

"I thought you were going to disappear," she said. "I thought you were no good at these things."

Tim laughed. "I only said that so you wouldn't know I was here. I didn't want to make you nervous. And you weren't at all, were you?"

Zoe suppressed a grin. "No. It was easy," she said.

"That's because you're a star. And now you're my star."

They threaded their way through the backstage maze of cables and props.

"I was really okay?" Zoe asked, but knew that she had been. She had been more than okay. She had been great.

"I think it's a shoo-in. As long as the camera agrees."

Zoe tried to stop the feeling of elation that surged through her. Maybe this was going to happen, after all. Maybe she really could be a star again. Maybe she could keep Cedar Bluff. Maybe she could have it all. Again.

"How soon will we know?" she asked, hoping that Tim would say, "This afternoon." She didn't think she'd be able to wait until tomorrow. She didn't think she'd be able to sleep.

"It won't be long," he said as he guided her toward the dressing rooms.

"How long?"

"Ten days. Maybe two weeks."

Zoe stopped. Ten days? Two weeks? Didn't anyone know she had only two weeks? "Why so long?" she managed to say.

Tim shrugged. "Who knows? Maybe they're auditioning others. Not to worry, though, you were great. Trust me."

Zoe felt sick.

"Now, get in that dressing room, take off that makeup, and change your clothes. Then I'll treat you to lunch in the commissary."

The commissary? Well, it wasn't exactly the Brown Derby, but, then again, Tim Danahy wasn't exactly Eric. And Zoe, maybe, wasn't still Zoe after all.

9

It was the most disturbing case Meg had worked on in her twelve-year career. Arnold Banks, unlike the staid, neurotic little man his name suggested, was six feet two inches of good looks, charisma, and arrogance. He referred to Meg as "his girl," and had a habit of touching her on the arm, shoulder, or hand while he spoke. She wondered if he'd ever heard the term "sexual harassment."

She sat in her office, pondering the evidence. Clearly, the man had done it. According to the deposition given by his mother's companion and personal secretary of thirty years, "No one but Arnold was allowed to see his mother for the last two years of her life." The companion had been fired at that time but sneaked back twice to see Mrs. Banks. "Her room smelled of feces, and there were bruises on her face," the deposition read.

One thing the Banks staff agreed was that, in recent years, Arnold's mother had grown unpleasant and demanding. Meg wondered if her own mother would have become that way, had she lived past fifty. She wondered if Gladys Cooper could ever have driven Meg to strangle her. It was a technique Avery had taught Meg: *Put yourself in your client's shoes.* It was supposed to make defending the guilty more palatable.

Janine entered Meg's office. "Not much mail today," she said, placing a small pile on the desk. "Once this trial gets under way, that'll change quickly."

It seemed as though the world had finally forgotten Holly Davidson. But Janine was right. The Arnold Banks fiasco would turn the spotlight back onto the firm. And onto Meg. "Thanks, Janine," Meg said as the receptionist left the room.

Meg picked up the mail, eager for a distraction. Tucked among the number-ten envelopes was a small linen one, hand-addressed to her, and marked "Personal & Confidential." It was postmarked Los Angeles. Meg frowned for a moment, then smiled. Zoe. She ripped it open and began to read:

"Dear Meg,

It's hard to believe it's been over a month since we were together at the Golden Key...."

The letter went on to relate her success at losing weight, her on-again-off-again bouts with sugar and fat, and her screen test. *Yes!* Meg wanted to say out loud. *I knew you could do it.* But when she turned to the second page, Meg's elation dissolved.

"I have at least ten days, maybe two weeks, before I'll know if I have the part," the letter continued. "Rather than sit around here and drive myself crazy, I've decided to start my search for Eric. I guess I'll go to Minnesota—it seems like the best place to start.

"Have you made any progress yet?"

Meg set the letter down and leaned back in her chair. Zoe was right. It had been over a month. What was Meg waiting for? It's not as though she was so engrossed in her case that she was too busy. Maybe now was the time. If Zoe had the courage, why couldn't Meg? She did want to see Steven. She did want to know if she still had feelings for him.

She slid open the desk drawer. The card lay flat, opened. His name. His signature.

Was she afraid? And if so, was she afraid she still loved him—or was she afraid that she didn't? Would it be worse to know that the feelings she thought she still had were, in reality, long gone—that she no longer had an excuse for not loving another man?

There was a rap on her door. She quickly closed the drawer.

"Come in."

It was Danny.

"Turkey in a pocket?" he asked.

"What?"

"An invitation to lunch. You available?" He produced a paper bag from which the pungent aroma of Santo's Deli escaped. "I've got pastrami for myself. Lots of nitrates and nitrites. The turkey was supposed to be for your boss, but he bailed out on me."

"You two have been spending a lot of time together," Meg said.

"Big case." He rolled his eyes as he walked in. "Insider trading. So are you having lunch with me or not?"

"Sure. Have a seat." She touched the drawer to be sure it was closed tightly. "How's the case going?"

"It's going. Wish I was working on Banks with you, though." He dug into the bag and pulled out two waxed-paper bundles, then inspected the contents, pushed the turkey across the desk toward Meg, and sat in the chair facing her.

"Tea?" she asked.

"I'd prefer a beer."

"Sorry," she said as she stood up and walked to the microwave. "I'm fresh out." She wished she could talk to Danny about Steven. She wished she could ask for his advice, for a male perspective. He was her friend, and she should be able to confide in him, shouldn't she?

She popped two mugs of water into the microwave. Maybe she couldn't tell him because she was afraid he'd discourage her.

"So how are things with Banks?" he asked.

Meg laughed. "Oh, God. I feel like he's all over me. He can't open his mouth without touching my arm." Why was it so easy to talk to Danny about men who didn't matter?

"Maybe you need a flyswatter."

"Or maybe I should wear Mace instead of perfume." She listened to the hum of the microwave. Maybe she could just tell Danny that, like Alissa, she too had decided to seek out a man from her past, a man she had loved. Danny might be pleased to know there had been someone she'd once been capable of loving. It wasn't as though she'd have to tell him who it was. It wasn't as though she'd have to get specific.

She dipped the herb tea bags into the hot water and returned to the desk. "Have you made any headway for my friend?" She sat down and tried to act indifferent.

Danny bit into his sandwich and shook his head. "Not much," he mumbled through the pastrami. "Haven't had the time."

"Oh."

"What's with her, anyway? Is she some kind of kook?"

Meg swallowed a bite of her sandwich. "No. Not really."

"Is she going through her change of life or something?"

"I don't think so."

Danny chewed slowly, thoughtfully, then shook his head. "It kills me, it really does. These socialite ladies who are nothing more than overglorified housewives. They've got nothing productive to do. They're bored. So they look for the most bizarre ways to put some excitement into their lives."

Meg sipped her tea and wondered how it happened that she and Danny so often thought alike. But now part of her needed to come to Alissa's defense, maybe because part of her understood. "We don't really know Alissa's motivation," she said quietly. "I don't think it's fair to judge her."

Danny laughed. "Motivation aside, it just seems a little stupid to me that she's trying to find someone from her past. I mean, past is past. Who cares?"

Meg took another bite of her sandwich. Suddenly the turkey tasted awfully dry. *Past is past, so who cares? I care, Danny. I care about finding the one man in my life I was able to love. And maybe Alissa does, too.* She pushed the sandwich away.

"Hey," he said as he gulped his tea. "I've got to drive up to New Haven tomorrow to check something out on the case. Got time for a ride?"

"I can't. I'll be out of town tomorrow." Meg said the words before she realized she'd made the decision.

He cocked an eyebrow. "Business?"

She folded her hands. "Yes."

Danny checked his watch, drained his mug, crumpled the empty waxed paper, and stood up. "Gotta run. But thanks for the company."

Meg nodded. "Thanks for the lunch."

He pitched the paper into her basket and, with a flourish and a wave, left her office.

Meg smiled. Maybe after tomorrow she'd be able to tell Danny about Steven, something positive. Maybe she'd be able to share some good news about the man she'd once loved. Maybe after tomorrow. When she returned from Washington.

Meg had seen his name on the directory: Senator Steven K. Riley's office was on the third floor of the Russell Building. She knew she was taking a chance by going directly there without calling first: he could be in a meeting or he could be out of the country, for all she knew. But she'd been afraid that if she didn't come spontaneously, she wouldn't come at all.

The glass door panel was stenciled Please Enter. In her hand Meg clutched her business card. It was poised, ready to show whomever she'd need to get past to see Steven. She stared at the card and thought of a torn corner of lined paper he'd once handed her after class. "Meet me at the coffee shop? Four-thirty?" it had read. There were other small notes secretly slipped between them over their thirteen weeks of bliss. She had saved them for years, love tucked away, sealed in a shoe box, safely hidden where it could not hurt. But when she'd moved to her brownstone, she'd trashed the shoe box without cutting the tape that held it fast, without reopening the wounds. The wounds that, Meg realized now, had never really healed at all.

She looked back to the sign, drew in a deep breath, turned the brass handle, and opened the door.

It was a surprisingly small office. A gray-haired woman sat at one desk, a dark-haired college-age boy at another. They both glanced up at Meg.

"Good morning," Meg said nervously. She passed her card to the woman, who seemed to be the one in charge. "I am Attorney Cooper. I'm wondering if the senator is available."

The woman studied the card. The young man returned to his work.

"Do you have an appointment?" the woman asked.

"No. I'm in Washington on business, and I have some free time. There are some matters I'd like to discuss with Senator Riley."

The woman looked at the card again, then up at the large round clock on the wall over a filing cabinet. "He's due on the floor for a vote in twenty minutes. But I'll give him your card. Have a seat."

Meg was too nervous to move. She tried to smile, but the muscles in her face were glued together with fear. He was there. Steven was actually there.

The woman took Meg's card, got up, and walked to another door. She knocked twice, opened it, then disappeared inside. Steven was actually there. Behind that door.

Her hands grew cold. She wrung them together. She wanted to run, but her feet seemed bolted to the floor. Her thoughts raced so fast she couldn't focus on them.

She scanned the room. The young man quietly worked. He looked up at her, she caught his eye. She tried to smile again. This time it seemed to work. Sort of. Suddenly a thought gelled in her mind. One thought, and only one:

Am I nuts?

She snapped her gaze back to the woman's desk. Meg stared at a stack of papers and wished she'd learned how to find her damned center at the spa, wished she'd never gone there, wished she'd never come here, and wondered what the hell she was supposed to do now.

This had been too easy. Steven was a United States senator, for godsake. He traveled all over the world. He had meetings, luncheons, responsibilities, *commitments*. It was unbelievable that he was here, in his office, at the very moment she had come to him after fifteen years. Unbelievable. Or destiny.

She flicked her gaze around the neat, well-organized room, at the rows of wooden filing cabinets, at the portrait of the President on the wall. She wondered if it was mandatory for every senator to display a photo of the President, even if they weren't in the same political party. She was glad she wasn't required to have a portrait of her boss in her office. Looking at an image of George Bascomb every day would be nauseating.

God, she thought, *what am I thinking?* This man was the President. This was a United States Senate office building. *This is Steven Riley's office.*

The door to the inner office opened again. The woman stepped out and closed it behind her. She no longer had Meg's card in her hand.

"Have a seat," she repeated, and motioned to a wooden chair against the wall. "He'll be a few minutes."

The gods intervened, unbolted her legs, and made it possible for Meg to walk to the chair. She sat. *He's holding my card right now,* she thought. *He's holding my card and he knows I'm out here.* It was too late to run. Or was it?

She crossed her legs and tried to act professionally. What was he thinking right this minute? Was he in shock? Was he angry? Was he pleased? Or was he merely amused? Once he'd told her she should be more spontaneous. Would he consider this spontaneity? Even though it had taken her fifteen years? Or worse, would he even remember he'd told her that?

She looked at the clock. Only fourteen minutes until he was due on the Senate floor.

She should have called first. But that would have been too risky. If she was going to talk to Steven Riley at all, Meg had known it had to be somewhere public where she could see him face-to-face. Where she could feel her reaction, where she could sense his. Then she would know if this was the right thing to do. Then she would know if she still loved him.

She also knew she had to see him in public. If she was alone when she talked to him for the first time in all those years, she knew her emotions wouldn't stand a chance. There would be no need to put on her courtroom demeanor, her career-carved aloofness, her mask. No, it was better to see him in public, where others might overhear, where she'd have to keep her words, and her feelings, under control.

The woman glanced over at Meg. Meg realized she must have been staring at her. *God, who must this woman think I am? Does my nervousness show? Would I act this way if this truly were a professional visit?*

She studied her feet. She wished she'd taken the time to polish her taupe-colored shoes. She closed her eyes, and without expecting to, without wanting to, she felt the lightness of his touch on her breasts. Softly, gently, as though his fingers were still there, had still been there, even after all this time. She wondered if he touched his wife's breasts. She wondered if he made them ache with longing the way he'd always done with hers.

She opened her eyes. Candace. That was her name. As if Meg would ever, could ever, forget. And his sons. Michael. Kevin. Sean. She'd known their names as if they'd been her own.

The kids were grown now. Probably all out of college.

They'd been spared the scars of being raised in a broken home. At least she'd done one thing right.

She looked back at the clock. Nine minutes until he had to leave. Was there another door in his office? Hadn't she seen a movie once in which the senator dodged reporters by sneaking out a back door? And isn't that what she had wanted to do in her own office so many times?

"The senator is a very busy man."

The woman's voice startled Meg. She tried to smile again. "Perhaps I should come back another time."

"It's best to make an appointment."

"Oh. Of course." The woman's tone was pleasant, but her intent was clear. Meg was being dismissed.

She stood and went to the woman's desk.

"You must understand that even with an appointment," the woman said, "he's often called away at the last minute."

The brush-off, Meg thought. *I'm getting the brush-off.* Steven had probably told her to have me wait a few minutes, then get rid of me. Steven probably had sneaked through the back door to get to the Senate. Or maybe there never was a vote at all. Maybe that was a standard excuse used for all unexpected visitors. For all unwanted ones.

An odd numbness swept through her, as though she had lost someone, as though someone had died. There was no pain, no hurt, no ache. Only numbness. She mechanically reached into her purse and took out another card. "I'm leaving to return to New York now," she said. "If you'll just give him my card . . ."

"I already gave him one."

Meg hesitated, then put her card back in her purse. "That's right," she said. "You did."

She snapped her purse closed. Fifteen years was such a long time. Alissa had suggested that maybe Steven wasn't happy. Alissa suggested it, and Meg foolishly wanted to believe it. But there were so many things she didn't know about Steven's life now, she tried to reason. There were so many things she didn't know about him.

And there were so many things that Steven didn't know about her. He didn't know how much she'd loved him, that she'd never loved him more than on that day she told him to leave. He didn't know that she had never loved another. Not in all these years.

He didn't know about the abortion.

As she started to leave, the door to the inner office opened.

"Meg?"

Though nearly fifty, Steven Riley was handsomer now than when she'd been in law school. Not that she needed to see him face-to-face to know that. She knew from the frequent photos in the *Times, Newsweek,* and other reputable journals—never the tabloids, for he apparently now led a model life above reproach. They had never connected him to the scandalous photo at Harvard.

"Hello, Steven," she said. The sound of her voice surprised her. She hadn't been sure she'd be able to speak. She studied him slowly. His dark hair was graying at the temples. His beautiful smile was perfect and white. *He's had his teeth capped,* she thought. *Just like in my dream.*

She realized he was holding out his hand. She hesitated, then reached out to shake it. Their palms touched. The heat of his flesh on hers sent a wave of contentment through Meg. *This is the man I still love,* she thought. *This man is my center.*

Their eyes locked. His were still so blue. A deep ink-blue, the color of cobalt, of the sea at dusk in winter. They looked happy, and yet they looked sad.

"Senator, you don't want to be late." It was the woman's voice.

Steven released his grasp and straightened his tie. "On my way, Edith," he said, without taking his eyes from Meg. "I'm afraid I'm pressed for time, but would you like to walk over to the Capitol? We could talk on the way."

Meg nodded. Steven started toward the door.

"Senator? Aren't you forgetting something?"

Steven turned. The woman held out a file folder.

"Right," he said, and took the folder. "I'll be back who knows when." He turned back to Meg and placed his hand on her elbow. "Let's go."

They took many steps down the long, hollow hall before either of them spoke. Finally, it was Steven.

"I saw you at Avery's funeral."

Meg felt a lump in her throat. "We got your card."

"It's a shame about him."

"Yes."

"He would have made a great politician."

"Yes."

They walked quickly, Meg's heels echoing in the corridor. She grasped her purse tightly, afraid it would slip from her hand. She clutched it—her anchor—as though it were keeping her upright, the only tangible thing preventing her from sliding to the floor. She couldn't believe she was there. She couldn't believe Steven was beside her.

"You look wonderful, Meg."

"So do you." She stared straight ahead, afraid to look at him again, afraid to look into his eyes. But his eyes were on her, steady, staring, transfixed.

He coughed a little. Meg was jolted by the sound. Steven had always coughed that little cough just before he started class, just before he gave a speech, whenever he was nervous. He had coughed it just before he'd told her he wanted to divorce his wife and marry her.

"Should I ask why you've come?" he asked now.

She gripped her purse more tightly. "No special reason. To see you, I guess."

"It's been a long time."

"Yes."

She felt as though she were in a trance. Her body was weightless, her senses dulled. She couldn't think of anything to say. And yet how many times throughout the years had she played this scene over and over in her thoughts? How many times had she written clever dialogue in her mind, as if it were an opening argument at the most important trial of her life? *If I ever see Steven again, I'm going to say* . . . what? But Meg didn't know the words now. She only knew she felt so right, so comfortable, walking next to him.

"You've made quite a name for yourself," he said.

"You, too."

"I was surprised you went into criminal law. I thought your passion was with family law. Women's rights."

Meg swallowed. He was right. Back when she was young and idealistic, she had wanted to help people. She had wanted to do something meaningful. After they had broken up, that had changed. There was no money in being anyone's savior. "I changed my mind," she said.

"That's too bad. You really cared. You would have been great. Still, you've made quite a career for yourself."

Meg walked silently, wondering if Steven was disappointed in her. She had never intended to serve only those whose checkbooks were fat with retainers. Had she screwed things up? Instead of dealing with people and problems and feelings, she had turned to the rich, the famous, the ones it was easy to walk away from at the end of the trial, and then not to look back. She felt her chest tighten. She had sold out for the money. And he had noticed. Because it was something Steven never would have done.

"I also noticed you still go by the name Cooper."

Meg pushed a strand of hair from her face and risked a glance at Steven. His eyes told her this wasn't small talk or mere curiosity. She looked straight ahead again. "I never married," she said.

People filtered into the corridor, talking, laughing, walking quickly. They approached the elevator, then stepped inside. Others joined them. On the slow descent Meg kept her eyes focused on the elevator doors. Steven was beside her, yet they did not look at one another, they did not speak. They did not touch.

The doors opened. She followed Steven's lead past a sign

that directed them to a tunnel. Steven slowed his pace to let the others pass. Then he took a deep breath.

"I never thought I'd see you again," he said in a low voice.

Meg nodded. "It's a surprise to me, too."

They walked a few more steps.

"You hurt me, you know," he said.

"I know." She didn't add that she'd been hurting, too. More than he'd ever know.

"I never got over you," he said.

She didn't reply.

The tunnel was crowded. Several motorized carts transported gray-suited men and navy-suited women, while, along with other walkers, Meg and Steven moved through the tunnel with the rapid pace of brokers moving down Wall Street at nine-fifteen. Meg's calves were beginning to ache.

They reached the other side and the crowd spread out. At the doors of another elevator Steven took Meg aside.

"I have to go now," he said as he looked deeply into her eyes once again. "Will you be in town long?"

Meg wanted to throw her arms around him. She wanted to feel him hold her, hug her, never let go. "That depends," she said.

"On what?"

"On if we can get together, I guess."

Those cobalt eyes scanned her face, her eyes, her nose, her lips. "I was hoping you'd say that."

He reached into his jacket pocket and withdrew a business card. "This is the name of a small inn just outside the city. It's discreet." He smiled, as if to take the edge off the word, as if to soften the reason he needed to use it. "We can talk there. In the lounge. Would that be okay?"

Meg took the card. She glanced at the address. She looked back at him with a warmer heart, a quicker pulse, and a more hopeful, joyous feeling about life than she'd known in a long, long time.

"Seven o'clock?" Steven asked.

A bell sounded. Meg instinctively knew Steven had to leave.

"Seven it is," she said.

Their eyes held a moment longer. "Steven?" she asked. "Your middle initial. *K*. What does it stand for?"

He smiled. "Kenefick. My mother's maiden name." *Of course,* Meg thought. That was something that rich people did. Not people from Bridgeport. He reached up and brushed his fingers over her cheek, then turned and disappeared. She leaned against the wall, clasping the card in her hand, nearly oblivious to the people who rushed past her.

When she stood alone at the mouth of the tunnel, Meg looked at the card again. "The Bridge of Flowers Inn," he had written. *What a lovely name,* Meg thought. *What a lovely name for a place to fall in love again.*

She turned the card over. Her name and address were printed on the other side. She stared at it. Steven had given her back her card. Nausea washed over her. Of course he'd had to return it. He wouldn't have wanted his wife to find it tucked in the pocket of his suit.

It was only three o'clock. Meg sat on the concrete bench in front of the Lincoln Memorial. She had walked around Washington, been to the Smithsonian, visited the Vietnam Memorial. Nothing could take her mind off meeting Steven that night; nothing could make the hands of her watch move any more slowly.

She wished she had a hotel room. She wished she could shower, change her clothes. A beige linen suit was hardly what she wanted to wear for what could become a romantic evening with the man she'd once loved. Still loved.

Fool, she thought. *For once in your life, go with your emotions.*

She picked up her purse. There were plenty of credit cards inside. She'd get a hotel room, buy a new dress, fix herself up. She winced at the reminder that she couldn't have afforded this if she'd become the lawyer of the needy, as she'd once intended. She forced the thought away and tried to focus on Steven. She'd go back to New York tomorrow. Then the evening with Steven could last as long as he wanted. Maybe it could last until breakfast. A shiver rushed up her spine. A tingle of adrenaline kicked in.

Before Meg knew what was happening, she jumped from the bench and started to cross the street toward a hotel. She stepped off the curb. Horns blared at her. She dodged between cars, her pace quickened by her impulsiveness.

"Hey, lady! What the fuck are you doing?" a cabbie shouted. She gave him the finger and kept going.

Could she do this? Could she really do something so unpredictable, so irresponsible, so un-Meg-like? Could she? Yes. Could she? No.

She reached the other side and stood on the sidewalk. Why couldn't she?

Outside the hotel Meg hesitated. She suddenly realized she had no luggage. *They'll think I'm planning a secret rendezvous,* she thought, then laughed when she reminded herself that was exactly what she was doing. And not only could she do this, she *would* do this.

She marched inside and stood at the registration desk. The clerk smiled but seemed neither to notice nor care that she was without a suitcase.

"You're in luck," he said, "there's a room available."

Everything's going too perfectly, Meg thought as she handed him a credit card. Something is bound to go wrong. She glanced at her watch. Three-fifteen. Suddenly seven o'clock no longer seemed days away. The minutes were ticking by rapidly. She'd have to act fast. Finally the clerk handed her a key.

She decided to shop before going to her room. She scanned the hotel lobby and quickly spotted an expensive-looking boutique. Within minutes Meg stood in a dressing room, a dozen "possibly perfect" dresses scattered around her. She peeled off her suit and pulled one on, ripped it off, pulled on another. She didn't look at the price tags: She didn't care. The right dress would be worth it.

The taupe silk was it: three inches over the knee and a wrap front that formed a drop-dead neckline. Plus, her shoes matched. On her way to the register Meg grabbed a pair of gold-and-clustered-pearl earrings and a necklace and tossed them onto the counter with her credit card. The salesperson took forever to ring up her purchases.

She snatched her bags and darted from the boutique and into the gift shop. She loaded her hands with toothpaste, a toothbrush, mouthwash, deodorant, a razor, shaving cream. She'd shaved her legs this morning, but they needed to be as smooth as possible, in case she got close to Steven, in case he touched her, caressed her. The thought made the shiver return.

She headed for the checkout when a display of aqua-colored bottles caught her eye. Shalimar. Steven's favorite. He'd once told her the scent gave him an erection that lasted for days. It had been so out of character for him to say anything lustful, anything lewd. They laughed at the time, but Meg began wearing the fragrance. She wore it until the end of the semester. Until the end.

She picked up the cologne, the dusting powder, the body lotion. If she was going to do this, she was going to do it right.

Why did she feel like a hooker preparing for a high-priced date?

She quickly signed for the items. Then she left the store, located the elevators, and started the agonizingly slow ascent to the twenty-sixth floor. She juggled her bags and checked her watch again. Four-twelve. Two more hours. And forty-eight minutes.

Meg let herself into her room and closed the door. The inside was dim; heavy drapes were tightly closed, and the air was flat and vacant, unlived in, with the transient odor of people only passing through, not pausing long enough to leave a trace of their presence, their warmth, behind. She stood, holding her purse, a shopping bag in each hand. Silence enveloped her, as her feet, once again, seemed planted to the floor. She gripped the thin rope handles of the bags, wondering what she was supposed to do now, how she would pass the next two hours and forty-eight—she checked her watch—forty-six minutes. Once Meg welcomed the anonymity of hotel rooms. Now she wished someone were there.

She finally moved. She set down the bags, flicked the wall switch, took the silk dress from the bag, and examined it. It didn't need pressing. She hung it in the closet, then stood back and stared at it, as though its fibers could foresee, and would foretell, what would happen tonight.

She went to the bed and sat down. The mattress was hard.

It was too soon to get ready. Meg folded her hands in her lap. She thought about turning on the television but didn't want the distraction. What she wanted was to think about Steven. To talk about him to someone. To share with someone the excitement within her, the anticipation, the anxiety.

It had to be someone she could trust. But not Danny.

She took the small address book from her purse and quickly flipped the pages—most of which were blank—until she reached the phone number of the one woman she could call, the one who was her friend: Zoe.

Moments later Zoe was on the line.

"Meg? God, I can't believe it's you. How are you? Where are you?"

Meg laughed. "You wouldn't believe me if I told you. I got your note. I was afraid you'd left for Minnesota."

There was a pause; then Zoe said, "I'm going the day after tomorrow. I'm terrified."

"I know what you mean." Meg twirled the phone cord. "But things might turn out better than you think."

"That sounds very positive coming from you."

"Maybe I'm changing my tune."

Zoe gave a little gasp. "Is there something you're not telling me?"

Meg smiled into the phone. She wanted to tell her—really, she did. If for no other reason than to taste the sound of his name on her lips.

"Come on, girl," Zoe said, "spit it out. What's going on?"

Meg took a deep breath. "I found him."

"What?"

"I found him, Zoe. I saw him. I talked with him."

"Oh, Meg . . ."

Meg stood up and walked as far as the phone cord would take her, then back again. "I'm meeting him tonight."

"Oh, my God. How did it go?"

"Like I said, I'm meeting him tonight."

There was silence; then Zoe said, "Wow."

Meg laughed and slumped onto the bed. "Yeah. Wow."

"Is he there? In New York?"

She sat up. Now was the time to tell her. All she would have to do was say she was in Washington. Then she could tell her. Then she could say his name. And then—finally—someone would know.

"Meg?"

Meg cleared her throat. "I'm not in New York," she began. "I'm out of town." *Say his name, dammit.* What was stopping her?

"Oh," Zoe said. But she didn't ask where Meg was, she didn't pry. It had been one of Zoe's qualities that had first appealed to Meg, but now she could have used a little help, a little nudge.

Oh, for godsake, grow up.

Just as she opened her mouth for form the words "I'm in Washington," Zoe spoke again.

"Meg, I understand that you don't want to say more. And I respect that. You're not ready. If you were, you wouldn't hesitate. Maybe after you've seen him tonight, but not now, Meg. Tell me later."

Meg closed her eyes. "Maybe you're right. Maybe after

I've been with him, maybe if things progress . . ." Her words trailed off as she startled herself with their implication. *If things progress.* It was almost as though she were planning a future with Steven. A future beyond seven o'clock tonight.

"And you know," Zoe continued, "sometimes things are best left unsaid."

"I suppose." She wondered if Zoe would be shocked to learn Steven's identity. Probably not. After all, if anyone knew how tough it was to have a real life in the midst of fame, Zoe did.

"Anyway," Zoe said, "I'll be thinking of you tonight." What time are you meeting him?"

"Seven o'clock," Meg answered. "Four, your time." Well, she'd at least admitted she was still on the East Coast.

"I'll be thinking of you. And be thinking of me in Minnesota."

"Day after tomorrow. I will. Alissa was right about one thing."

"What?"

"This is turning out to be fun."

But after they said their good-byes and Meg headed into the bath, she wondered how long the fun would last, and when the reality of what she was doing would come crashing down upon her.

As she sat in the lounge of the Bridge of Flowers Inn, she glanced around the room, wondering if the other patrons were meeting clandestinely, too. It was a cozy atmosphere. Wide dark boards lined the walls, soft prints framed in colonial blue were scattered across them, candles in pewter sconces cast a soft, romantic glow. The tables and chairs were all of dark woods; the floor was rustic and uneven. It was a perfect atmosphere to fall in love. Again.

Meg looked at her watch. Seven-fifteen. From where she sat she could see the front door. Steven was late. As she slowly sipped from her wineglass, she caught the aroma of

Shalimar on her wrist. Maybe he would never know that she'd remembered. Maybe he'd changed his mind.

The door opened. A dark figure stood silhouetted against the outside light. It was Steven. She'd know his stance, his outline, anywhere. He paused a moment, as though adjusting his vision to the darkness. Then he stepped forward, toward her. Meg started to perspire. A lump found its way into her throat.

"Meg," he said as he leaned over and lightly kissed her cheek. The tingle of his lips remained, even after they'd left her skin, even after he sat across from her. "I'm sorry I'm late. I got tied up in a meeting."

He ordered wine. He put his elbows on the table and set his chin in his hands. "You look wonderful," he said.

Meg laughed a nervous little laugh, which made her sound like a schoolgirl. A college student. She wondered if it was true that when people reunite, they revert back to the way they acted when they had once been together—the way adults act like children when with their parents. "You said that this morning," she said.

"Then it must be true."

She sipped her wine again.

"You look different than you did in Harvard Square," he said.

"You, too. Your hair's shorter."

"So's yours." He laughed. "And I must say that dress is more becoming than jeans and tie-dyed shirts."

"You wouldn't have thought so then."

"Maybe not."

There was silence. Meg felt enveloped with comfort, as though time had never passed, as though they were sitting in the coffee shop, safe in the knowledge of their love. "I wonder if the old coffee shop is still there," she said.

Steven smiled. "Probably not. I'm sure it couldn't have survived without our business."

She lowered her eyes, pulling up the memories she'd thought were buried so deeply, so long ago.

"God, Meg, it's been such a long time."

She looked back at Steven.

"Tell me about your life," he said.

"It's not nearly as exciting as yours." *But don't tell me about yours,* she wanted to add. *I don't want to know about your wife. I don't want to know about your children. I want to pretend that you and I are the only two people in the world. At least for now.*

The waiter arrived with his glass. Steven leaned back in his chair and studied Meg. "The life of a senator isn't as exciting as you might think," he said after the waiter had left. "It's tedious and intense and, actually, rather confusing. I want to hear about your life. About all the exciting cases you try. About the real world I've missed out on."

Meg tried to smile. What did she know about the real world? Her life revolved not just around the small percentage of people with real money—not just around the small percentage of them who got into trouble—but around the even smaller percentage of them who got caught. Here, with Steven, she felt embarrassed about her career, about it's superficiality. But talking would give her something to do. It would force her to think. It would keep her in control. She began by telling him about the Holly Davidson case. She talked; he listened. He nodded; he smiled. Meg wondered what had taken her so long to do this. She wondered why she'd ever let him go.

"Even though I never pictured you as a celebrity lawyer," Steven said when she'd finished, "it seems to agree with you."

Agree with me? Meg moved her eyes from him, down to the wide-board floor. *No,* she wanted to say. *It doesn't agree with me. It's phony and empty and I hate it.* What surprised Meg was that this revelation of her feelings came as no surprise.

They had three glasses of wine and a plate of fruits and cheeses and some kind of crackers. Meg was too nervous to eat. Finally Steven folded his hands and looked squarely into her eyes. "If I have to wait one more minute to touch you," he said, "I think I'll lose my mind."

Upstairs at the Bridge of Flowers Inn were a few rooms for overnight guests. Meg followed Steven up the steps as if it were something she'd been doing for years, something she did every night.

Like the lounge, the room was a picture of early America. A four-poster bed was covered with a patchwork quilt; the walls were papered with a small floral design; lace doilies adorned the nightstand. It was quaint and cramped, but as far as Meg was concerned, somewhere larger, grander, more magnificent wouldn't have made this night any closer to perfect. She was with Steven again. It was all that mattered.

Once the door was closed behind them, Steven took her into his arms. They embraced for a long, slow moment; then he pulled back and kissed her, with a tenderness Meg hadn't remembered. With longing, with love. Tears spilled from her eyes.

"My God," he said, "you smell wonderful."

He noticed.

He took her hand and crossed the room. He sat on the edge of the bed and drew her toward him. He put his arms around her waist and nestled his face against her. She held his head and sank her hands into his hair. They didn't speak.

Slowly Steven began to caress her back. He dropped his hands. He moved them down her legs. Then up, underneath her new silk dress. She felt the warmth of his touch against her panties.

"After you left me," he whispered, "I thought I was going to die."

She moaned a tiny moan.

He gently pulled her onto the bed. Meg released her feelings with a rush of love that had been pent up inside her for years. She gave herself over to his caresses; in turn, she caressed him. She was aware that he was taking off his jacket, unbuttoning his shirt. She was aware, but more interested in feeling his body, in touching his skin. There was more hair on his chest than she'd remembered: it was now soft and thick and flecked with gray. She curled her fingers around it.

He raised her dress over her head, then lightly touched the tops of her breasts, which rose over her French-cut bra. He reached behind her and unclasped the hook, then slid the straps down her arms. He studied her breasts. She lay still, watching him watch her, the same way he'd watched her so many times, so long ago, with those same cobalt eyes, so filled with longing, so radiant with love.

He lowered his mouth and gently, wetly, sweetly, slowly encircled her nipples with his tongue. A flush of heat raced through her. She whimpered.

With his hands Steven slipped off her panty hose and rested his long, thick fingers low on her stomach, massaging her lightly, barely touching the skin. She reached around him and felt the taut muscles of his back, the lean, strong firmness of his legs. She pulled him closer. She felt his hardness.

Instinct guided her hand to him. She gently clasped his shaft and held it. Her head was dizzied by its throbbing; her mind grew manic with her need.

And then his fingers were inside her.

She raised her hips to meet his touch, as he probed her wetness, explored her smoldering fire. Those were his fingers. He was there. Steven was there. That was his touch. The touch she'd ached for. The touch she'd longed to feel again.

He smiled down at her. Her orgasm exploded into ecstasy, her hand still clinging to his penis, her eyes fixed upon his own, her heart flooding with joy.

He stroked her face. He kissed her hair until her soft sobs eased, until she shivered for more. And then he was inside her, and it was as if the years apart had never been. He opened his mouth and bent his face to hers. She parted her lips. The tips of their outstretched tongues touched once, twice, three times. Passionate kisses. Like the ones Meg had tried so hard to forget.

They moved in frenzy, rocking, arcing, calling out to one

another. And then his body tightened. She saw his face twist with want. She saw his eyes grow wide, the corners of his mouth curve up in pleasure. She felt the wave within her rise again, and together they cried out. And at last Meg was at peace. At last Meg felt at home. Here in his arms, safe in his bed. Safe. Loved. Complete.

He sagged upon her, then moved his weight aside. Meg lay quietly. Inside she felt his stickiness; inside she felt his love as it soaked into her still-trembling flesh. She stroked his chest and tried to stop the tears from coming. For it had been this same stickiness, this same love, that had once created life within her, that had once formed the child that could have been theirs. Their child. The one she had aborted. The child she had killed. She turned her head away, so he would not see her tears, so he would not know her pain.

"I'm not happy, you know," Steven said quietly, breaking the silence within the room, within her heart. "With Candace. I never was."

Meg heard his words but tried to shut them out. She pulled the white muslin sheet to her neck. She stared across the room, at the shadows that hung in the darkness. She made out a bureau, a mirror, a luggage rack. She wondered if her new silk dress lay in a twisted pile on the floor.

"I want us to be together again," he said.

Together? How could she? How could she ever again face this man—the man she loved? How could she ever face him without telling him the truth about their baby? She had been wrong to find him again. She had been wrong. All wrong. She closed her eyes. "That's not possible."

"Isn't it?" He raised himself up on one elbow and touched her cheeks, her mouth, her nose. "It's almost the twenty-first century, Meg. It's not as though a divorce would ruin my career now."

She shook her head. "I can't." She turned away again.

He lay back and sighed. "After all this time, I still love you," he said.

She blinked back tears.

"I can't believe you don't still love me, too."

She turned on her side and faced the wall. She drew up her knees and wrapped her arms around herself.

"Why did you come back, Meg? If you didn't still love me, why did you come back into my life?"

"I don't know," she answered, and at that moment she almost believed it. Had the prospect of seeing him again clouded her judgment? Had she actually believed she could pretend the abortion had never happened, that it no longer mattered? She thought about her empty brownstone, her empty years. Steven was offering her the chance to reclaim what she'd once given up. But would he feel the same if he knew what she had done to their unborn child?

"Will you think about it?" he asked.

She remained quiet, wishing she had never met Alissa Page, wishing she had never let herself be talked into this charade, wishing she had kept the pain buried deep, where it belonged.

She sensed him get out of bed. She heard the sounds of clothes rustling, of a zipper being zipped, a buckle being buckled. He walked to her side of the bed, leaned down, and kissed her forehead.

"I will never stop loving you," he said.

She saw his shadow walk toward the door. He turned the handle; the door opened. A catch came into her throat. If he loved her, maybe he could forgive her. Maybe she could find the courage to tell him.

"Steven?" Meg whispered.

The shadow stopped.

"Call me," she said. "I want to see you again."

He paused in the doorway. "I will," he answered, and then he was gone.

Meg lay quietly a moment. Then she turned over, reached out, and pulled his pillow against her. It wasn't long before she was asleep, the scent, the touch, the taste of Steven lingering on her lips.

10

Cristal champagne seemed rather absurd at a gala to benefit the homeless. But when Alissa mentioned her misgivings to Betty Wentworth, Betty smiled and said, "What would you prefer, my dear? To serve our guests cheap wine in bottles hidden by brown paper bags?"

The half-dozen other ladies seated around Sue Ellen Jamison's formal dining-room table giggled.

Alissa seethed. "Well, it is completely inappropriate. And if I'm going to continue to chair this gala, I suggest we change it. Now."

No one spoke. Finally Betty Wentworth stood up. Her matronly beige twill coatdress was creased across her thick middle. "I don't think I have to remind you, Alissa, that you put me in charge of the theme for the gala," she said with decided authority.

I did it because your son was fucking my daughter, Alissa wanted to say. *And,* she at last admitted to herself, *maybe because I wanted to shake up Grant, your sleazeball husband.*

"The theme I've selected," Betty continued, "is 'Another Day in Paradise,' like the song. If we make people realize how lucky they are to be a part of the society that matters, they will dig deeper into their pockets. We will raise more money."

"By making them feel uncomfortable?" Alissa asked.

"They won't feel uncomfortable, darling," Betty went on. "They'll feel at home. Then they'll know how lucky they are. She walked around the table and stood behind Sue Ellen, posed as the matriarch at the head of the table, beneath one of the three prismed chandeliers that hung above. "We've even decided to rent Baccarat flutes."

"Baccarat crystal? At an event for twelve hundred?"

Betty smiled. Sue Ellen smiled. The others around the table smiled. "Danforth properties is underwriting the cost," Sue Ellen said.

Alissa boiled. She knew how to plan parties, and she was damn successful at it. And one thing she knew was where to draw the line. It didn't matter if Betty Wentworth told that asshole husabnd of hers that their company would underwrite every last dime, Cristal champagne out of Baccarat flutes would make a mockery out of the homeless.

"And since our theme 'Paradise' triggers thoughts of the Garden of Eden," Betty jabbered, "our goody bags will have tiny silver apples, with a bite taken out. Those perfume bottles in drawstring pouches have become so overdone."

Alissa said nothing. The goody bags were, of course, one of the highlights of the evening for every female in attendance. But sterling apples? The media would be certain to pick up on the fact that while the homeless soup kitchens had little fresh fruit, the fruits of the rich were handcrafted of silver.

"Isn't she brilliant?" Sue Ellen asked.

Alissa stood. "No," she said as she gathered the notes and index cards in front of her. "Betty isn't brilliant at all. She's a complete idiot. And so are the rest of you if you go along with this." She tucked her papers into her bag and marched from the room, across the huge marble foyer, and straight out Sue Ellen Jamison's double teakwood front doors.

She jumped into her car, gunned the engine, and roared out the circular drive. It wasn't until she was a mile down the road that Alissa pulled over, stopped the car, and began to shake.

She knew that ever since she'd come home from the spa, she'd been distracted. Zoe's phone call hadn't helped. Seeing Jay—or, rather, a flash of Jay—hearing his voice, had jarred her in a way she hadn't expected. She'd spent these past days trying to avoid Robert. And making phone calls. She'd started with Global News. It had taken two weeks and about two-dozen calls to uncover that Jay didn't work for Global, that he was hired as a stringer to cover a specific story. No one seemed to know where he worked. She'd put in calls to Danny Gordon: he was out, he was tied up, he'd get back to her.

She lit a cigarette and rested her head against the car window. The search to find Jay had become an obsession. Until today she'd skipped the WFFA committee meetings. But when she'd awakened this morning, Alissa knew she was in trouble. She'd dreamed about Jay—a sensual, erotic dream. They were making love on desert sand, somewhere far away. She clung to the buttons on his khaki jacket while he moved above her, the sharp sun burning over his head, the needlelike grains of earth digging into her wet, naked ass. And when she cried out in orgasm, Alissa awoke. She was crying, her arms were outstretched, grasping the air, and her clitoris was thumping from the touch that wasn't there, hadn't been there, might never be there again.

She had to do something to get him out of her mind. The gala was her only escape. She'd showered and dressed in her finest silk ladies'-luncheon attire and put on her hostess-of-Atlanta face. Maybe today she would hint that someone delectably famous would headline the gala; maybe she'd whet their appetites just a little. She knew they'd been making plans in her absence, but she'd had no idea how incredibly bad they were fucking things up. She blew out a stream of smoke and tapped her fingernails on the steering wheel.

They were turning the gala into a three-ring circus, one that the media would cover only if they layered it with sarcasm. And Alissa Page—the chairperson—would be the laughingstock of the social pages.

She rolled down her window and flung her cigarette into the street. *Screw them,* she thought as she jammed her car into gear and spun back onto the street, tires squealing, gravel spitting behind her wheels.

Back at her house Alissa went into the library and picked up the phone. She punched in the numbers. The phone rang twice; then a machine clicked on: "Hi, this is Danny Gordon. You know what to do." The machine beeped. *Arrogant bastard,* Alissa thought, then said, "Danny, this is Alissa Page. I haven't heard from you. I assume that means you're working diligently to resolve my case, so call me, goddamit." She slammed the receiver back into the cradle.

She crossed the room and snapped on the television. She sat on the leather sofa and looked at the screen. Several lower-middle-class people were lined up in chairs on a stage, talking about incest. Phil Donahue appeared. Alissa picked up the remote and muted the volume. She stared at the mouths, opening and closing, opening and closing. Wasting time, wasting time.

One of my daughters will be on this show one day, she thought. *One of my daughters will be on this show talking about her homosexual father.* She wondered what it would be like to be Meg Cooper, completely independent, totally free, unencumbered by daughters or a husband, or the need to be constantly "on." How glorious it msut feel not to have the pressure of having to be places, having to be seen, having always, always, to keep up appearances.

The words of Aunt Helma, once emblazoned into her little-girl mind, echoed now in her thoughts:

"That dress is ugly."

"Your friend is beneath us."

"If you really want us to be proud of you, make something of yourself."

Make something of herself? Had Alissa accomplished that by obsessing over her looks, marrying the "right" man, keeping her social calendar filled? And why in hell was she still trying to make her aunt proud of her? She had been dead for nearly a decade. And how proud would Aunt Helma be if she knew what was really going on in her life?

She clicked off the television and closed her eyes. She was forty-two years old: her choices had been made. Even her fantasy of seeing Jay again was probably only that—a fantasy. For now she would do what she'd been doing: she would go on. And once again she'd have to prove her importance. She would swallow her pride and continue with the gala, try to undo the mess the others had made. She'd call Zoe and convince her to be part of the gala. Then the world would know Alissa Page wasn't just another peon, another nameless nobody.

Her gaze caught the copy of *Town & Country* as it lay in the brass magazine bin—the issue with Michele's beaming photo. She thought of Betty Wentworth, of Sue Ellen Jamison, of the smirks that would tighten on their wrinkled faces when Alissa Page came crawling back.

She slapped the sofa with an open palm. She smiled at the sting in her hand. "Not on your life," she said aloud. "Alissa Page isn't out of the picture yet."

She went to the desk and took out a mahogany box of fine linen paper. The proverbial ball was now in their court. And if they wanted to win, they'd have to play the game. It was a risk, but it would be worth it. Could be worth it. She sat down, picked up her Mont Blanc pen, and wrote her letter of resignation to the WFFA.

The next morning the phone rang. It was Danny Gordon, making excuses. "I don't give a shit about your schedule," Alissa shouted, "I gave you a hefty retainer. I expected results before this." God, she was sick of being pushed around.

"I told you," Danny said, his impatience apparent, "I've been checking with my sources."

"And I'm telling you, I think if you're seriously going to do this, you'd better get your butt down to Atlanta and start here. This is where what's left of his family is. Didn't you think for one minute they might know where he was?"

"Frankly, I thought it would be best to track him through the IRS. His W-twos."

"I told you. Jay moves around. Global News said he was hired as a stringer. Who the hell cares where he worked last year? It's today that's important." She wondered if Danny had been too busy banging Meg to have even started searching.

"Now you're telling me how to do my job?"

"I'm telling you to get down to Atlanta and get down here fast. At this rate I could have done it myself. I'd have found him by now."

"I'm sure you would have, Alissa. But remember, this was your choice. I tried to warn you how busy I am."

"Just get your ass down here, Danny. Tomorrow. I want you to find Jay Stockwell once and for all." She slammed down the receiver before he could answer. She reached in the desk drawer and pulled out a cigarette. *Arrogant bastard,* she thought as she flicked her lighter with a quivering hand.

"Problems?" Alissa looked up. Robert stood in the doorway.

"None that are any of your business. And I don't appreciate your sneaking up on me."

"I was hardly sneaking up on you, Alissa. Though I do admit, hearing the name Jay Stockwell made me stop and listen."

She took a drag and exhaled a steady stream of smoke in Robert's direction. He walked through it and sat on the sofa.

"Why are you looking for Jay?" Robert asked. "Do you think life would be better with your long-lost lover? Or have you forgotten that he denounced the one thing that holds importance for you in this world—money?"

"Jay Stockwell has become successful in his own right," Alissa said. "He didn't need his daddy's fortune to make a name for himself."

Robert shrugged. "I didn't realize you thought that was so immoral. Besides," he went on, "I wouldn't exactly say that reporting from Baghdad earmarks one as successful."

Alissa was stunned. She'd had no idea Robert was still aware of Jay. "I see you've been keeping up with world news," she said. "How impressive." She took another drag but this time blew the smoke off to the side.

"What's your game, Alissa?

"What makes you think I'm playing a game?"

"What is it, then? Are you planning to try to revive your relationship with Jay, then give me the old heave-ho?"

Alissa flinched. The problem with being married to someone for twenty years was that they knew you well. Too well. "I told you I wasn't interested in a divorce, Robert."

He laughed. "Then surely it can't be that you're looking for a good lay. You certainly wouldn't have to track down an old lover for that, now, would you?"

"Frankly, no. But you already know that."

He shifted on the leather sofa. The fabric squeaked beneath him, reminding Alissa of the night she'd caught Natalie with Grant Wentworth's son. *Grant,* she thought. *Men are such scum.* So why was she looking for Jay? Because he hadn't been. Had he?

"Surely you don't think he's still in love with you?" Robert laughed again. "No, forget I said that. You don't have *that* much self-confidence."

Alissa felt tears sting her eyes. "Why are you doing this to me?" she asked. "Is it giving you some kind of perverse pleasure?"

Robert put his elbows on his knees and leaned his face against his hands. "No, Alissa, this isn't giving me any kind of pleasure at all." He rubbed his forehead. "I find it all rather sad."

Alissa said nothing.

"It doesn't please me to know that I've let down my family."

"Let us down? Is that what you call this? Oh, please, Robert. You make it sound as though you've just lost your job and we won't be able to go to Disney World. I think the situation here is a little more serious."

"I wish it could be any other way," he said. "I wish you'd never found out."

Alissa ground out her cigarette. "How long, Robert?"

" 'How long' what?"

"How long have you been gay?"

He looked thoughtful for a moment. He studied the floor. "I thought I was bisexual. I mean, I'm sure our sex life was never very passionate for you, but I enjoyed it enough."

Enjoyed it enough? When they were young and supposedly in love, he'd "enjoyed it enough"? What the hell did that mean? She thought back to the silk peignoirs she'd had especially hand-sewn for her trousseau. The ones that hugged her perfect body, the ones guaranteed to produce an erection. The blatant, naive, bridal anticipation of lust bordered on embarrassment now.

"About ten years ago," Robert continued, "I realized I really did prefer men. Maybe I'd just been denying that to myself all those years."

Or maybe I was just never enough of a turn-on. Enough of a woman. Alissa choked out her next question, wondering why she was going to ask it, wondering what compelled her need to know. "When were you first with a man?"

Robert shook his head. "It wasn't a man. It was a boy. So was I. It was at summer camp. I was fourteen."

"Oh, God."

"Yeah. Oh, God." He cleared his throat, stood up, and walked to the bookcase. He began thumbing over the spines of leather-bound volumes. "I know you feel betrayed, Alissa. But I do need you. I sincerely hope we can work out some kind of solution."

"I'm doing the best I can," she said.

"By tracking down your long-lost lover?"

"Don't grovel, Robert. One might think you're jealous."

"Maybe I am," he said. "Maybe, in a way, I am."

At twelve-fifteen the doorbell rang. Alissa was in bed, reading Robin Leach's latest volume, digging for ideas that might trigger the most original, most magnificent concept that she could incorporate into the gala once the WFFA came to its senses and realized how much they needed her. But even Robin's luscious tidbits couldn't compare with the show-stopping coup of having Zoe attend. Even if Zoe's comeback fizzled, having her here—in Atlanta, in *public*—after so many years of self-exile was bound to attract worldwide attention. There was something to be said for the mystique of the recluse. God knew it had worked for Garbo.

The bell rang again. Alissa waited to hear if Dolores would answer it. But Dolores and Howard were heavy sleepers, and chances were neither of them would awaken. She wondered who it could be at this hour. And why. It was a little late for Betty Wentworth or Sue Ellen Jamison to come begging forgiveness.

Silence was followed by another sharp chime. One of the girls had probably lost her key. Alissa slapped down the book, pulled herself from bed, and slipped a robe over her lace chemise, the one with the hem that barely skimmed her now vacant, now unappreciated, soft mound. She padded out of her lavish bedroom, thankful that Robert had been the one to move to another room. She really detested disruption.

Alissa made her way down the stairs as the bell rang again. "Jesus Christ," she snarled. "I'm coming."

"Alissa?" She looked back to the balcony. Robert stood, dressed in those god-awful lavender silk pajamas he special-ordered by the dozen from that dotty little shop in SoHo. Lavender silk. She realized now. It probably should have given her a clue about his sexual orientation. In his hand Robert held his eye mask. "Is everything all right?"

"Go back to bed, Robert. I'm sure one of the girls has

locked herself out." But he remained in place. Chivalrous Robert. The perfect husband.

Without peering through the frosted glass, Alissa pulled open the door. It wasn't one of the girls. It was Danny Gordon. She caught her breath.

"What the hell are you doing here?" she demanded.

Danny shrugged. "I believe I was summoned."

"Alissa?" Robert again, from the balcony.

She waved a hand at him. "It's all right, Robert. Go back to bed." Robert hesitated a moment, then walked back to his room, the look of a rejected lover on his face.

"Are you going to make me stand outside?" Danny asked.

Alissa glared at him. "How did you get my address?"

Danny stepped past her into the foyer. "I'm a private investigator, remember?"

She'd have slapped him across the face if he weren't so damned sexy looking in his rumpled denim shirt and tight jeans. He wore, she noticed, custom-made cowboy boots. She wondered if he owned any sexless shoes.

"Do come in, Mr. Gordon," she said coldly, and motioned him into the study.

He tossed his briefcase onto the sofa and sat down, folding his arms across his chest, a smug grin on his face.

"By all means, make yourself at home," Alissa said. "Then tell me what the hell you're doing here in the middle of the night."

"I told you. I was summoned."

"A more civilized person would have waited until morning."

He smiled that slightly crooked smile. "I suppose."

Alissa sighed and sat beside him on the sofa. She was aware of her flesh tingling beneath her nightgown. *Too bad this man is off-limits,* she thought. *Too bad he's not interested in me. Too bad he's hot for Meg.* Well, she certainly wasn't going to give him the satisfaction of knowing that being this close to him made her crazy with lust. She wasn't going to give him the satisfaction of anything, even of guessing that having him show up unannounced, at this time of night, had taken her completely off guard.

"Well, the fact of the matter is you're here, and it's about time. Let's get started, shall we?"

Danny took a small notebook from his briefcase. "You said you felt I should go to his family."

"Yes. Jay's aunt sits on several boards with me. I'm sure she must know where he is."

Danny raised an eyebrow. "You never thought to ask her?"

"One doesn't ask questions like that of the Stockwells."

"I see. So how do you suggest I go about it?"

"You're the damned investigator. You figure it out."

"Well, you seem to be pretty good at telling me how you think I should do my job."

Alissa stood up and walked to the bar. "Would you care for a brandy, Mr. Gordon?" She pulled out the stopper of the Waterford decanter and poured the dark amber liquid into a small snifter, pleased with herself that she kept her robe tightly closed, her inclination to seduce him in check.

"What happened to 'Danny'?" He was standing behind her now, so close she could feel his warm breath on the back of her neck. Alissa hadn't heard him approach. She froze.

"Would you care for a brandy, Danny?" she whispered, feeling her self-imposed shield begin to crumble, savoring the scent of foreplay in the room.

"No, thanks," he said.

She turned around. He was strolling back to the sofa. Was he driving her crazy on purpose? She leaned against the bar and swirled the brandy in the glass. She wasn't going to fall for his bullshit.

"His family's offices are downtown," Alissa said. "But you won't get past the receptionist. Especially looking like that." She nodded toward his body.

"Stockwell Media Group has a dress code?"

"Stockwell Media Group has principles," she retorted.

"It would probably be better for me to start with the aunt, anyway. I seem to have better luck with women."

Alissa took a sip of her brandy. It burned her throat. "I'm sure you're right," she said.

They stared at each other a moment. Suddenly the doors to the study opened. "Oh, Mother, you're . . ." Michele stood in the doorway, looking at Danny. "Oh. Sorry."

Alissa frowned. "Michele. This is Mr. Gordon. We're working on a project together."

Michele didn't look convinced. "Oh. Hello. Well, good night, Mother." She closed the door.

"A lovely girl," Danny said.

"My oldest."

"She looks like her mother."

"She's only eighteen."

"She looks older."

"Don't get any ideas."

Danny smiled. "I think you have a distorted image of me, Alissa."

"I doubt it. Now, where were we?"

He crossed one leg; the hem of his jeans crawled up his boots. *God,* Alissa thought. *What is it about those boots that makes me so crazy?* He moved his ankle. The leather creaked.

"I believe we decided I must start with Jay's aunt."

She took another swallow of brandy. "Yes. I can give you her address."

"No need. I already have it."

"Oh."

"It's my job, remember?" He flashed that slightly crooked smile and ran a hand through his loosely tangled, so-goddamn-sexy-looking hair.

Alissa set down her glass. If she had to stand there another minute, naked beneath her robe with only the coolness of satin and lace kissing her flesh—if she had to stand there another minute, sensing his teeming testosterone, breathing his animal scent—if she had to stand there another minute, she would lose her fucking mind. She resecured the sash of her robe.

"What I remember," she said, "is that I hired you to find Jay Stockwell. I expect an update by tomorrow evening. Now, good night, Mr. Gordon. Shall I see you to the door, or can you let yourself out?"

They met at a bar in the Underground the following evening. It was a dark, lively place, tucked in the back of Kenny's Alley, where Alissa often came when she didn't want to be seen by anyone she knew. Her crowd rarely came to the Underground: it was too trendy, too touristy, too cluttered with artsy-fartsy types who got off on the push carts and street musicians and the overpriced boutiques and antique shops, and who munched on New Orleans–style beignets as they sipped café au lait and wondered why they didn't have such a campy shopping district underneath the streets of their hometowns. They were the same people who bought the wares to support Atlanta's homeless.

When Danny had phoned late that afternoon to tell her he had some information, Alissa had quickly suggested this place. She didn't want Robert spying on her; she didn't want Danny eyeing her daughter again.

"So what do you have?" Alissa asked as she slid into the booth and faced him.

"An interesting place you picked," Danny said as he ignored her question and waved his hand toward the sepia prints of the old-time saloons and livery stables that lined the walls—places that had stood on this spot in the late nineteenth century, long before old Atlanta it was relegated, then preserved, beneath the pavement.

"I didn't ask you to meet me here to expand your cultural horizons," Alissa said. "Why don't you just tell me what you found out."

He drank slowly from a beer mug, then wiped the corners of his mouth. "Not a lot. His aunt hasn't heard from him in two years."

"You brought me down here to tell me this? You call this information?"

Danny held up his hand. She noticed he wore the same shirt he'd had on last night. She wondered if he'd slept in it. A vision of Danny sleeping, naked, suddenly crept into her mind. She pushed it away.

"I do have information," he said. "As of two years ago Jay Stockwell was in Shanghai."

"China?"

"That's the only one I know of."

"Very funny. How did you find out?"

He shook his head. "Sorry. Professional secrets cannot be revealed."

"You're a pain in the ass, do you know that?"

He smiled. She felt herself melt a little. Damn him. "Yeah," he said. "So I'm told."

She wished she'd worn something other than the black turtleneck and jeans. With her black heels on, Alissa feared she looked too sexy. She feared Danny would get the wrong idea. Or would it be the right one? Even if Meg was sleeping with him, what the hell, it's not as though Meg was an old friend. It's not as though Meg had ever done anything for Alissa. Except introduce her to Danny.

She looked past his thick lashes into those incredible eyes. With no Grant Wentworth in her life, Alissa was beginning to feel horny. She needed a good lay. She suspected Danny would be a great one. Better than a dream, anyway.

She lit a cigarette. "What do you do next?"

"Next, I go back to New York."

A flutter bobbed in her stomach. "Why New York? Why not Shanghai?"

Danny laughed. "I've told you, I don't know how many times, that I'm a busy man. I've got responsibilities back in the city."

Alissa sat back. "So that's it? This is all I get for my money? Christ. I should have hired a real detective."

Danny put the mug to his lips again. "You did. One you

can trust, remember? Hey, do you want a glass of wine or something?"

"No. I don't think I'll be staying."

He took a drink. "Suit yourself. But I tried to warn you. This is going to take a little time."

Alissa felt tears well in her eyes. "I don't have much time," she said quietly.

Danny set down his mug and gazed at her. "What's the rush?"

She couldn't believe a tear was running down her cheek. Alissa quickly brushed it away with her hand, hoping he hadn't noticed it. "I want to find him so I can get on with things," she said. "Believe it or not, I do have a life to live."

"I noticed. I assume that was your husband standing on the balcony last night."

"Yes." She couldn't say more. She was afraid another tear would fall.

"Does he know you're looking for Jay Stockwell?"

"Not that it's any of your business, but, yes, he does."

Danny nodded. "Now, that's interesting."

An odd desire to defend Robert—or maybe to defend herself—crept into her. "Robert and I lead rather separate lives."

"I would have expected that was frowned upon in your social circle." His words, she knew, were meant to mock her. But that crooked smile of his precluded offense. That crooked little smile. The one that defied manipulation. The one she'd give anything to see while his hands caressed her body.

She took a long drag on her cigarette and fingered a napkin on the table. "Maybe I will have that glass of wine."

Danny motioned to the waiter. "Wine," he said. "Chardonnay."

The waiter left. "How do you know if that's what I wanted?"

"I didn't figure you for the Chablis type. Or the burgundy. And those are probably the only choices here."

She looked past those thick lashes again, deep into those eyes. "We don't have to stay here," she said.

He palmed the outside of his mug. "What did you have in mind?"

She smiled. "That depends."

He smiled. "On what?"

She put out her cigarette. "On where you're staying."

Danny drained the beer. "Actually," he said, "I've got a reservation on the eleven o'clock flight back to New York."

"Tonight?"

"Tonight."

Alissa refused to allow her expression to falter. "I see."

"Besides," Danny added, "I never mix business with pleasure."

Her face flamed. *Bastard,* she thought. *God. He really is a bastard.* "And just what did you think I was suggesting, Mr. Gordon?"

He shrugged. "Nothing in particular. But I didn't want you to think I take advantage of my clients."

"Does that go for Meg Cooper, as well?"

He twirled his empty mug. So. She had struck a nerve.

"You know, Danny," Alissa said smugly, "Meg hasn't exactly been up front with me. Now I think I understand why."

"What are you talking about?"

"I think that maybe her past obsession—her long-lost lover—isn't anyone famous at all. I think the man she thinks she should have married may very well be you."

His voice grew soft. "I didn't realize Meg was looking for someone, too."

"Of course you did. You're not a fool."

Danny remained silent.

The waiter delivered her wine. Alissa looked at the glass, picked up her purse, and stood up. "Call me when you find Jay Stockwell," she said. "And not before."

11

"Why won't you tell me where you're going?" Scott's words resounded with a mixture of concern and whine.

Zoe tried not to look at him as she folded a sweatshirt and placed it in her suitcase. It was the end of May, but she knew it could still be cold in Minnesota.

"I told you," she said, trying to minimize her irritation, "it doesn't matter. I'll be back in a few days."

"You just got home."

"That was different. I was at that spa."

"Why was it different? Gone is gone."

She tucked a flannel nightgown in under the sweatshirt. "You'd better get used to this. If I'm going to work again, I might have to take off now and then."

"I want to come, too."

Zoe sighed and zipped the suitcase closed. She turned to Scott, still not used to the fact that he was now a full two inches taller than she and she now had to look up at him. And the fact that, with his fair complexion, light eyes, and maturing physique, he resembled Eric more and more every day. She wondered if he would break some girl's heart, the way Eric had broken hers. "Can't you simply trust me? I'll be back before you know it. I promise. Besides, you should be studying for final exams."

Scott frowned. "I'm smart enough. I don't need to study. Please, Mom. I want to come."

Zoe tugged the suitcase off the bed and set it on the floor. "No."

He paced the room. "Then at least tell me where you're going. I have a right to know."

Fourteen was such a difficult year. Too old to be treated as a child; too young to be considered grown-up. And yet, with all Scott had been through—a mother who had barely nurtured him the first two years of his life, and now the loss of the man he'd called Father—he was perhaps more of an adult than Zoe chose to admit. She knotted the silk scarf at her neck. "You're right, Scott. You do have a right to know where I'm going. But I'm not ready to tell you."

He shuffled his feet and stared at the floor. "Then let me go with you to the airport."

"No. Marisol is going to drop me off at the door."

He threw up his hands. "Mom! What's with all this cloak-and-dagger stuff? Let me at least go to the airport!"

Zoe smiled. "So you can follow me inside to see what flight I take? Really, Scott, you're making far too much of this. You're the one who's turning it into 'cloak-and-dagger stuff.' Now, please," she said, motioning to the large suitcase on the floor. "Take this out to the car. I'll get my carry-on." It was her carry-on bag that was important: that was the one that held the blond wig and the large round sunglasses.

He leaned down and picked up the suitcase. "You know something, Mom? I don't think I'm going to like your being a star."

Zoe felt a pang of guilt. Why was she leading Scott to believe this sudden trip had something to do with her career? Why couldn't she just tell him about Eric once and for all? *Not yet,* she commanded herself. *Wait until you get home.* After all, Eric might choose to ignore her. There might be no need for Scott ever to know about his real father.

She reached up and ruffled his hair. "You're going to love my being a star. We're going to have a wonderful life again."

Scott started out the bedroom door. "I don't know how it can ever be wonderful again without Dad."

Zoe watched him go, and for the first time she wondered if perhaps it would be best to leave things alone, to forget about trying to find Eric, to avoid upsetting Scott, Marisol—and herself—any more than they already were. *But things aren't the same anymore,* she reminded herself. *They can never be the same again. William is gone, and you're on your own. It's time to put the pieces of your life back together. And fast.*

"When was the last time we kept a secret from each other?" Marisol asked as she wheeled the car off the exit ramp toward the airport.

"Please, not you, too. I've already been through this with Scott."

"I'm not your son. I'm your best friend. The one you tell everything to, remember?"

"Then you should know me well enough to leave me alone on this." She wished she could be as manipulative as Alissa. Zoe was sure that when it came time to find Jay Stockwell, Alissa would find a way to go through the motions deftly, with no one the wiser. Or Meg. Lucky Meg. She had no one to answer to, no one to be accountable to for her whereabouts. She wondered how Meg's evening with her man had turned out. Perhaps Zoe hadn't heard from her again because Meg hadn't wanted to gloat. Or to tell Zoe anything that would discourage her from doing what she was about to do.

"Does it have to do with the movie?" Marisol asked.

"No. Other than the fact that I'm going stir-crazy waiting for an answer and I need to get out of this town."

"Does it have to do with raising money?"

"Marisol, please . . ."

"I told you, I have some money left. If this has to do with money . . ."

"It doesn't have to do with money."

"You're worried about Scottie's school, aren't you?"

"What?"

"You're worried that you won't be able to afford to send him to private school in the fall. You're worried he'll have to go to public school."

Zoe looked out the car window. "The thought has crossed my mind, yes."

Marisol steered under the ramp marked Departures. She wedged the car between a valet van and a limo. "So that's it, then."

"What's it?"

"You're going to look at another school for Scott. A cheap one, maybe. You're thinking of sending him far away."

Zoe opened the door. "Marisol, please. I'm not going to send my son away."

"Not even to that one back east where William went? I'll bet you could get them to give you some kind of discount."

Zoe picked up her carry-on bag. "I'm not going to look at any school for Scott. I'm going away for a few days. Period. End of discussion."

She opened the car door.

"Will you call me?" Marisol asked.

"Yes. Of course I'll call."

Zoe got out of the car and stood by the curb, waiting for assistance with her bags. A porter came. She showed him her ticket and he wheeled her bags away. She leaned back into the car. "Well, I guess I'm off."

Marisol put her hand on Zoe's arm. Zoe looked down at the tired brown fingers, the swollen knuckles, the closely trimmed nails rimmed with gray traces of clay. All that Marisol had in her life was her pottery, Zoe, and Scott. Upsetting that balance for Marisol would be devastating to her friend, and yet Zoe had to take that chance.

"Zoe, can you stand it if I ask just one more question?"

Zoe looked into her friend's dark eyes. "As long as it has nothing to do with where I'm going."

Marisol turned her head and stared out the windshield. "Does this have anything to do with Eric Matthews?"

Zoe felt a chill envelop her. Marisol knew her too well. But this wasn't fair. Zoe needed to do this alone, and she deserved her privacy, her right to think and act things through on her own. She stood quietly a moment, then straightened up. "I'll call you tomorrow," she said. "Take care of Scott." She slammed the car door and walked with anger, determination, and more than a little guilt, toward the terminal.

Once inside LAX, Zoe ducked into the ladies' room and put on her disguise. This was not the time for adoring fans to surround her; this was not the time to answer questions of any kind. This time was for Zoe. Not for Scott, not for Marisol. Certainly not for her fans.

She stopped at the newsstand and picked up a copy of the latest *New Yorker*, then located the gate of the flight departing for Minneapolis. There were no available seats on the commuter to Hibbing; she'd have to rent a car and drive the long drive. But it would be worth it. She hoped.

She boarded the plane, found her seat without being recognized, and settled in, the magazine spread open, close to her face, a position she maintained throughout the three-hour flight, except for a halfhearted attempt to eat the tasteless lunch and a brief trip to the rest room. She had decided not to think about Eric until the plane landed in Minneapolis: there would be enough hours on the drive north to plan what she would do, what she would say, if she found his parents, if she found him.

But as the plane banked for its final descent, Zoe's mind drifted, drifted to Eric, and couldn't find its way back. She set down the magazine and gazed out the window at the murky sky. She thought about the way he had loved her, about the way she had loved him. Young love, perhaps, but it had seemed so right at the time. It wasn't as though they weren't together long, didn't know each other well. Seven years. Seven years of setting up housekeeping, seven years of living as man and wife. Looking back, Zoe knew that the first two years had been the best, when neither of them could get jobs, when meals consisted of leftovers Eric brought home from the restaurant where he bused tables, when all they could depend on was each other, and their love.

Then Tin Danahy discovered Zoe. And slowly, as her career escalated, Eric retreated. The night she got pregnant with Scott, Eric had come home drunk, a situation that had become more and more frequent as Zoe's name became more and more visible. Caught up in her growing fame—busy, exhilarated, and heady with optimism—Zoe hadn't felt his love diminish. She'd thought she was doing everything for them.

The rivers and streets and houses and buildings grew larger now as the plane tipped, then leveled toward the runway. And as she felt the wheels thump down beneath her, Zoe suddenly knew why she needed to find Eric so badly, and why she needed to do it now: she couldn't get on with her future until she came to terms with her past. Alissa Page had simply stirred up what had been meandering through Zoe's veins for years. Sooner or later, with or without Alissa, Zoe knew she would have tried to find Eric. If not for the sake of love, then for revenge. For as much as she deserved privacy from Marisol, privacy from Scott, Zoe deserved to know why Eric had left her. Why he had left her virtually to die.

As she traipsed through the terminal searching for the least expensive car-rental agency, Zoe did a quick mental review of her finances: not the overall picture—God, that would be too much to bear—but the current cash on hand, in purse, right now. She'd allowed herself only six hundred dollars for the trip, and thanks to the latest round of airfare wars, she'd been able to buy a round-trip coach ticket for only four hundred dollars. That left two hundred—for a car, a room, and food. One ninety-seven, she corrected herself, because she'd already given a three-dollar tip to the porter. Zoe had been out of touch with the real world for so long, she wasn't even sure if $197 would be enough. She stopped at a counter marked Discount Rent-A-Car, and wondered if her fans would ever believe that Zoe had been reduced to counting single dollar bills.

A few minutes later Zoe climbed into the cheapest car she could get: a four-passenger tin box that had roll-down windows and an AM radio. But it was only sixty-nine dollars for four days, including insurance. Things were looking up.

She pulled out the road map the car-rental clerk had provided, started the tinny, pathetic little engine, maneuvered the car through the maze of on-off-arrival-departure ramps, and, propelled by a heart filled with fear, headed north, to Hibbing, birthplace of the famed folk-turned-pop singer, Bob Dylan, and of the Hollywood film-sensation-turned-legend, Zoe. She wondered what it would feel like to be home.

The countryside didn't look familiar. As she made her way up Highway 35, only the names of some of the towns brought back filtered memories: North Branch, Pine City, Sandstone. She remembered not the towns, but the signs, from her family's twice-a-year trips into Minneapolis for clothes and shoes and a taste of civilization. Zoe checked her watch. She should make it to Hibbing by nightfall.

She stopped in Cloquet for a sandwich and a cup of coffee, then turned off to join Route 53, which would take her into Virginia. She remembered buying a pair of jeans in Virginia at the Woolworth store. They'd been light blue with rust-colored top stitching. Eric had told her they made her look sexy, so they had become her favorite pair. She'd taken them to L.A.; she'd worn them long after she could afford new ones. She'd worn them for him. After he'd left, she'd thrown them away, along with his high-school picture, the program book from *West Side Story*, the rabbit's foot he left behind. She'd thrown it all away, as he had done with her.

Virginia was the first town that looked familiar. It was also the first time Zoe saw a sign that read: Hibbing. The arrow pointed west, on Route 169. Her heart began to pound as she turned left at the sign and, for the first time in twenty years, headed home.

The forests were still there. She traveled for miles, seeing nothing but enormous trees, taller than she remembered, more dense, interrupted only by an occasional house. She smiled when she saw the first Forest Fire Danger indicator standing at the side of the road. The dial was pointed to Moderate. It was a familiar, comfortable sight. She sighed and tried to relax on the stiff, cheap car seat.

And suddenly there was the gas station. The landmark on the edge of town. But something was different, Zoe noted. It was cleaner, newer. The three-bay garage was gone. In its place was some sort of convenience store. And the gas pumps all read Self-Service.

She checked the gauge and decided to pull in. She parked beside a pump and got out. No one was around.

She went into the store. A lone female clerk was behind the counter, watching television.

"Good evening," Zoe said. The girl looked up and half smiled, then returned to her program. Zoe noticed that she wasn't a Nordic blond. She had red hair and freckles. *Integration,* Zoe thought. *Integration finally arrives in the Midwest.* But it had arrived too late for the dark-eyed Jewish girl who had run away to California before she was swallowed by prejudice.

She poked around the aisles, then decided on a bottle of iced tea and a package of fat-free cinnamon cookies. They probably tasted like cardboard, but it was better than Twinkies or Ring-Dings, although that was certainly what she'd prefer.

She went to the cash register and placed the items on the counter. "I'll need some gas, too," she said as the clerk rang up her purchases. "How can I get it?"

"What pump you at?"

"What pump?"

The girl sighed and came out from behind the counter. She peeked out the window. "Number Three," she said.

"Number Three?" Zoe didn't understand. All the pumps looked the same to her.

"I'll turn it on for you. Just pop your cap and pump it in. How much you want?"

"I don't know. Fill it, I guess."

"Then you've got to give me fifteen dollars now."

"Why?"

" 'Cuz I can't have you running off, now, can I? My boss would have my hide."

Zoe gave her the fifteen dollars.

"Come back when you're done. We'll square up then."

Somehow Zoe managed to pump her own gas. She splashed some on her hands, spilled some on the fender. She wondered how much money she had wasted. A dime's worth maybe? A quarter's? She jammed the nozzle back into the pump and told herself she was being ridiculous. A quarter or a dime wasted would not put her on skid row.

Would it?

The girl owed her $2.35. While she was taking it from the register, Zoe saw an opportunity. She took a deep breath and braced herself to sound casual—interested, but not too interested—for she remembered that northern midwesterners guarded their own.

"Do you know if the Matthewses still live around here?" she asked, although her phone call from the spa already had given her the answer.

"The old people? Sure. Pop and Mrs. Matthews live over on the State Road. Where they always did, I expect. You from around here?"

"No," Zoe said a little too quickly. "My father used to do business with Pop Matthews. Does he still own his general store?"

The girl shook her head. "Nope. That's been gone a long

time. Most folks go to the shopping centers now. Or stop in here."

The girl was surprisingly free with information. Zoe decided the new generation played with their own set of rules, even in Hibbing. She took a step closer. "I remember the Matthewses had a son. Do you know if he still lives around here?"

"Eric? Sure. Not in Hibbing, though. He owns the luncheonette over in Chisholm. My sister's a waitress there."

Zoe tried to hold back her excitement, tried not to alter the expression on her face. Eric was there. Close by. He had come back to Minnesota, after all. And now she knew where to find him. "Oh," she said, brushing back a strand of blond wig and trying to sound unfazed. "Well, is there anywhere around here I can spend the night?"

"Back in Virginia, maybe. There's a motel on the highway. Nothin' around here."

"Well," Zoe said as she scooped her change from the counter and dropped it in her oversize bag. "Thanks."

Outside, the sun was setting. But even though Zoe knew she'd have to drive all the way back to Virginia to get a room, there was something she had to do first. She got back into the car and, instead of heading back east, drove on into Hibbing. The Matthewses still lived there. On the State Road. Zoe hadn't had to ask the address: it was half a mile from the house where she grew up.

She drove slowly through the center of town. The buildings, though older and grayer in the north-country twilight, seemed the same; the businesses were different. There was still a barbershop, still a library, which appeared to have the same dirt encrusted on its windows from two decades ago. But where Eric's father's store had been—where Eric worked and saved their run-away money—there was now a True Value hardware store. And the movie theater where they'd once held hands and kissed in the dark was now a discount drugstore.

Zoe took a right, past the old high school. She tried to recall the feeling of being there. She couldn't. *It is too painful,* she thought. Living in Hibbing had been too painful for a dark-haired Jewish girl who had never fit in. That was when Zoe wondered if this quest to find Eric was more than she'd thought. Maybe there were more ghosts than Eric she needed to dispel. Maybe she needed to put all the pain behind her once and for all.

She slowed the car when she came to her old house, the place where Zoe Naddlemeyer had been raised. She looked to the left. It was still there, though badly in need of paint, sadly in need of repair. She wondered if the people who'd bought it from her parents still lived there. She studied it in the dim dusk. The house seemed smaller than she remembered. Or maybe the trees were bigger. Whatever it was, something was out of sync. Something told her she didn't belong. Any more than she ever had.

Zoe drove on. And suddenly, there was Eric's house. The porch on the side, which had been made into a bedroom for him, where Zoe had sneaked in many nights, where they had quietly made love until dawn. There was an old pickup truck in the yard. Zoe would have sworn it was the same truck his father had owned twenty years ago. Only now it was rusted, and it had no license plates.

A soft light glowed behind the lace curtains at the living-room window and illuminated the front porch. The familiar glider was still there. Where she and Eric had sipped lemonade and touched each other in secret places when no one had been looking. But there were other things in the front yard now. A child's bicycle. A toddler's jungle gym.

Zoe studied the scene. Surely Pop and Mrs. Matthews didn't have young children. She glanced at the mailbox at the side of the road. "Matthews," it read. Then an eerie thought crept into Zoe's mind: *They must have grandchildren. Eric's children.*

This is what I gave up, she thought. *This is the life I turned my back on the day Eric and I left for California.* And for the first time in many years, Zoe felt grateful to Eric for giving her freedom. Grateful, and yet a little sad for the roots and the hometown she'd never really had.

She sat a moment longer, then put the car in gear and made a U-turn in the direction of Virginia, and a night's sleep. Tomorrow she would decide what to do next. If anything.

She hardly slept. In the morning Zoe walked to a doughnut shop across the street from the run-down motel and bought a corn muffin and a cup of coffee. She carried another cup back to her room.

As she peeled the lid from the plastic container, Zoe wondered if she would even recognize Eric. Fifteen years was a long time. Surely, if he'd seen her before she'd gone to the Golden Key, he wouldn't have recognized her. Maybe he looked different, too. Maybe he was fat, as she had been. Maybe he was bald.

Maybe he'd had a stroke and was paralyzed on one side. But the part of her that wished that was true was scolded by the part of her that didn't.

She blamed him. She still did. If he hadn't left her, she probably wouldn't have had the stroke on the day Scott was born. But, then, she'd never asked the doctors if that could be true because the doctors weren't aware—no one but William and Marisol were—of what had really happened in her life, or that Scott was not William's son.

Yes, she blamed Eric. It had to have been his fault. It certainly couldn't have been hers.

She sipped the steamy coffee. It tasted like plastic.

And now she needed to see him. To have him see her, to show him she'd survived. Physically. Emotionally. She set the coffee down on the laminated nightstand. But now, as much as she had wanted revenge, Zoe wanted to thank him. For enabling her to have the wonderful years she'd had with William. For giving her life beyond Hibbing.

But first, she wanted to call Marisol.

As she dialed the numbers, she hoped Marisol wasn't angry with her. She hoped she wouldn't be angry once she knew where Zoe was. Something told her that wouldn't happen, but Marisol had been right: they were best friends, confidants. She needed to share what she was doing with her—not with Meg Cooper, not with Alissa Page, but with Marisol. The one who had been there for her when no one else had.

"I knew you were up to something stupid like that," Marisol shouted into the phone. "He left you, honey. Have you forgotten?"

"Marisol, wait." Zoe tried to get a word in edgewise. "I needed to come here. I know why now. It's not because I want to get back together with Eric. It's because I have to thank him . . ."

Her friend laughed. "Thank him! For what? For dumping you? For making you cry every day and every night for how many nights, I can't remember, though God knows I should because I was there for every one of them, and don't you ever forget it."

"Marisol . . ." Zoe stared at the torn vinyl chair that sat in front of faded plastic drapes. She shuddered to think that her home might have been decorated that way if she'd stayed in Hibbing.

"And what about Scottie? Have you thought what this is going to do to him? He worshiped William and you know it. After all these years why drag this up now? It's only going to hurt him, Zoe, it's only going to hurt him big-time, and he doesn't need to be hurt anymore. He may be taller than the both of us now, but he's still a little boy deep down inside where it counts, where the hurt always comes from."

Zoe let her friend ramble until she needed to catch her breath. Then she quickly said, "Marisol, I'm not going to tell Scott. I wasn't sure what I'd do when I left to come here, but now I know. There's no need to tell him. Not now. Not ever. It's just like we decided a long time ago. Me. You. And William."

"At least you haven't totally lost your mind."

"No. I feel more in control than I have in years."

"So why bother to see Eric at all? Get your skinny little ass back to Minneapolis and get yourself home. Today. Get out of there before you change your mind again."

"You think seeing him will make me change my mind?"

"Honey, he had you over a barrel once, he can do it again. Men, they got a way of doing that. It's chemistry or something. But you gotta remember, he treated you no better than Luis did me. Oh, sure, Eric didn't beat you with his fists, but he did it to your heart. If you never take another piece of advice from me, take this one. Get yourself home. Now."

Zoe picked up the coffee cup again and noticed thick sludge in the bottom. She set it back on the stand. "I can't, Marisol. I've come this far, I'm not going to run away from my feelings any more."

"It ain't running from your feelings, honey. It's running from what's over and done with. And there's nothing wrong with that."

"No. I've got to do this. All these years I've spent hiding from the world. I was scared. I thought I was scared for people to see me after the stroke. But now I realize I was just scared, period. I didn't want to hurt anymore. Shutting myself off from the world was the only way I could avoid the pain of living."

An image came into her mind. In it she sat alone in her room, tearing into a bag of potato chips, biting the cellophane off a package of Twinkies, stuffing the salty, fat calories into her mouth with rhythmic precision: four chips, one bite of Twinkie. Again and again. Salt then sweet. It hadn't mattered that her body already bulged with fat.

She closed her eyes now. "There's something else, Marisol. I think it's all part of why I let myself gain so much weight. The fat gave me an added layer of protection. Because if I wasn't beautiful, no one would bother with me. No one would love me, so no one would hurt me."

She opened her eyes. Tears fell from them.

"I've stopped running, Marisol. Right here, where it all started. I'm going to face Eric, and I'm going to get rid of my ghosts once and for all. I'm doing this for me. Too many years I spent secretly wanting to kill him. Now I'm going to face him, and I'm going to thank him."

Marisol was silent a moment, then said, "Honey, I had no idea you had so much pain."

Zoe wiped her tears and laughed. "You know something? Neither did I. And it's amazing how much better I feel now that I do."

"You gonna be okay?"

"Yup. I may even try to catch a late flight back to L.A. tonight. I don't think I can stand another night in this fleabag motel. I was right about one thing all along: I don't belong here. I never did. I belong in a place with clean sheets and houses that aren't dumps, and around people who have better things to talk about than the weather and who-said-what-to-whom."

"That sounds like my star talking."

"I don't know if I'll ever be a star again, Marisol. But one thing I do know—I'm never going to pump my own gas again."

"What?"

"Never mind. I'll call you later tonight."

The luncheonette in Chisholm didn't appear to have a name. An orange neon sign stood atop the roof of the shiny railroad-car structure and proclaimed "Lunch." It was already eleven forty-five: there were several cars in the parking lot, and even more pickups. A popular place, Zoe thought. A local hot spot.

She parked the car and checked her wig in the rearview mirror, praying that no one would recognize her. No one but Eric. And not Eric—not until she was ready.

She took a deep breath and got out of the car, wondering why her knees were trembling, wishing she could kick off her shoes so she could feel the pavement beneath her feet and be assured of her footing.

The stroke is long behind you, she reminded herself. *Your foot is fine, your leg is fine, and he'll never notice the droop of your lip.* Still, she grasped the wrought-iron railing tightly and mounted the concrete steps with trepidation, and a thudding sensation that warned her that her heart was about to fly out of her chest.

Inside, the place sparkled. It smelled of cinnamon rolls and freshly baked bread. Cozy wooden booths lined one wall; across from them was a long, gleaming chrome-edged counter with soft padded stools. There were several customers, mostly men, talking loudly.

Behind the counter stood a young girl dressed in a pink uniform. She leaned against the wall, her arms folded across her middle. She was smiling, listening to the banter of the customers, bobbing her head up and down to the beat of a country song playing on the radio. Zoe wondered as she made her way to an empty stool if this was the convenience-store clerk's sister.

The girl stepped toward Zoe. "Coffee?" she asked. She was pretty and pleasant. Still, Zoe felt sorry for her, for she was most likely doomed to life in a small northern Minnesota town.

"Yes. Please."

The girl poured from a glass carafe and set a white mug in front of Zoe. "Anything to eat?"

"Yes," Zoe said. She wasn't hungry, but she felt obligated to order something. That is, after all, what one does in a restaurant at lunchtime, when one isn't spying on people, looking for a long-lost lover. "Do you have turkey sandwiches?"

The girl nodded. "Whole wheat or white?"

"Whole wheat, please."

The girl turned and spoke into a small opening in the wall behind her. Zoe looked around. She wondered if Eric was behind the wall, in the kitchen. She wondered if the others in the restaurant could hear her heart pounding.

The girl returned. "Fresh whole wheat this morning," she said, smiling.

"Great," Zoe said. She realized the girl hadn't asked what she wanted on her sandwich. But, then, this wasn't exactly the spa, and custom orders probably weren't encouraged.

Another pink-uniformed woman appeared from the back. She was older than the other girl, and blond. A leftover Nordic, no doubt. Maybe even someone Zoe would know. She studied her closely, then decided the woman was much younger than she was. Maybe as young as thirty. She wondered how it had happened that she'd turned forty yet still envisioned herself to be young.

The woman did something at the cash register, then headed for the back room. On her way she shouted, "Eric? Hey, honey, where are this morning's receipts?"

Zoe nearly dropped her coffee mug. So he was here. He was in the back. *Honey.* She'd called him honey. Was that Eric's wife? Her stomach knotted just as the young girl set a plate in front of her.

Zoe remembered the first time Eric had called her "Honey." They had been holding hands, walking along the path that encircled the lake behind her parent's house. He bent to pick two wildflowers. The blossoms were purple and white and shaped like tiny stars. "When we get to Hollywood, honey," he said, "we're going to be like these flowers. We're going to be stars." The flowers were lovely, the thought so filled with hope, and yet, at the time, what mattered most to Zoe was that Eric had called her honey. Honey. It was what her father called her mother; what her mother called her father. It was what people who belonged together called each other. And it was the first time Zoe felt that Eric truly, deeply, forever-and-ever, really loved her.

She stared down now at the thick turkey sandwich on fresh whole-wheat bread. Creamy-white mayonnaise oozed from the sides. Beside it a mound of potato chips was heaped, next to that a huge wedge of dill pickle. A hearty meal in a lumberjack town, where "hope" didn't mean that all dreams came true, and where calling someone "honey" wasn't always for keeps.

"Anything else?" the girl asked her. "We've got some great pies today. Coconut custard . . ."

"No. No." Zoe clutched her hand to her stomach. The air seemed to have been sucked from the room, the way it had been . . . the way it had been the night she'd come home and discovered that Eric was gone. She stared at her plate. It reminded her of the school cafeteria—the same basic food on the same basic plate, day after day, year after year, never changing, never ending, like life in a small town. *Predictability.* She struggled to think of L.A., of the new life that awaited her, with all its ups and downs, and all its unknowns. She focused on Scott, on the growing and changing he had done and had yet to do. She thought of the opportunities that lay ahead for them both, of the risks, of the challenges, of the excitement of something beyond the mundane. And suddenly Zoe knew she could no longer pretend that seeing Eric was going to fix her problems or mend her life. Marisol was right. Eric was over and done with.

"Excuse me," she called to the waitress. "I'm running a little late. Could you wrap this up for me? I'll take it to go." She had no intention of eating it, not now, not ever. Not unless she wanted to regain twenty-two pounds in a hurry.

The girl smiled and snatched a foil container from beneath the counter. She plucked the sandwich off Zoe's plate, dropped it into the container, then snapped on a lid and added up the check. "Pay at the register," she said.

Zoe fished in her purse for some change. She set it next to the plate. It could have been quarters or dimes or nickels for all she knew. The hell with waste. She only knew she no longer wanted to see Eric, and that she needed to get out of there before she was recognized.

She took the sandwich and slid off the stool. She walked to the cash register, hoping the woman—Eric's woman—would come out quickly and take her money.

The door to the back room opened. A man stepped

through it and walked toward the register. He was tall. She'd forgotten how tall Eric was. A memory flashed: Zoe was at a cocktail party soon after Eric had left her. A man had brushed past her—a man as tall as Eric. For one brief second her heart had stopped. She'd felt the comfort, the familiarity, of Eric's physical presence. Then she realized it wasn't him. And pain had ripped through her.

Yes, Eric was tall. And he was still blond. He was not fat. He wasn't bald. And he didn't appear to have suffered a stroke. In his crisp white apron, he looked wonderful. Fuller, more mature, but wonderful.

"Eric." His name fell from her mouth too late for her to catch it, swallow it, and walk away.

He walked closer. He stopped. He stared. "God," he said. "What are you doing here?"

Zoe laughed, a shrill, nervous laugh. "You recognized me."

He ran a hand through his hair. She couldn't tell if it was out of frustration or if he was trying to smooth it down, trying to look the best he could. He'd always been handsome, and he'd always been vain. Then she saw a hint of a smile tug the corners of his mouth. *He's glad to see me*, Zoe thought quickly; then, just as quickly, the smile vanished. Thin, wavy frown lines appeared on his brow.

"I can't believe you're here," he said, his voice so low she wasn't sure if he was pleased or merely perplexed. He smiled again. "God," was all he said.

Zoe's heart stopped pounding. In fact, it seemed to have stopped beating altogether. He was smiling at her. The way he'd smiled when he'd picked those wildflowers, the way he'd smiled as he stood in the wings at her first screen test. The years melted into nothingness, all with one smile.

From behind the counter came the clang of a dish clattering to the floor. Eric looked away from Zoe, then back again. She blinked. *Remember why you're here*, she said to herself. *Remember, remember. You're going to thank him.*

You're going to thank him for having spared you a life in a go-nowhere town at a diner called Lunch.

"I guess you wouldn't believe me if I said I was just in the neighborhood," she finally said.

"No." His smile, she noticed, was gone again.

She put her check and three dollars on the cash register. "I came to see you, Eric. I wanted to know how you are."

He stood on one foot, then the other. A heavyset man in a plaid flannel shirt walked up behind Zoe.

"Take this, will ya, Eric? Gotta get back to work."

"Sure, Jake," Eric said as he reached around Zoe and took a five-dollar bill from the man. He studied the check, then rang something into the register. Zoe stepped aside so Eric could hand the man change. Eric looked at her again. "Maybe we should talk out back. I'll have Marilyn take care of the orders."

"Marilyn?" Zoe asked, even though she was sure of the answer, even though she felt a stab of jealousy she couldn't quite explain.

"My wife," Eric confirmed.

The next few moments passed in a blur. Before she knew it, Zoe was standing outside at the back of the diner, next to a newly polished four-wheel vehicle. *It must be Eric's,* she thought. A material show of pride in his apparent success in a small-town sort of way.

"So what are you really doing here?" he asked, one hand on his hip, one on the vehicle, and a tone in his voice that sounded—what was it—defensive?

"I told you. I came to see you."

He tapped his finger against the fender. He looked at the ground. "About what?"

She didn't know how to answer. "About nothing special, I guess. Just to see you."

"Well, now you have." He looked off in the distance, then quickly glanced at Zoe. He blinked and looked away.

Zoe reached out and brushed his arm. "It's been so many years," she said.

"Yeah," he said, staring back at the ground. "A few hundred." His tone was no longer defensive. It was quieter, slower.

"You're married," Zoe said.

"Yeah." He raised his eyebrows, still looking off toward nothing, it seemed, in particular. "Are you?"

She shook her head. "I was married. My husband died."

Eric spoke quietly. "It was William, wasn't it?"

"Yes."

He didn't respond.

Her next question was hard to ask, but she wanted to know. She needed to know. "Do you have children?"

"Yeah. Three."

A small lump swelled in her throat. "That's nice."

He attempted another glance at her. "You?"

"One. A boy."

"I'm surprised. I always wanted kids. I never thought you did."

Why had he ever thought that? Hadn't they talked about having a family one day? Hadn't they talked about buying a big house by the sea with lots of room for their kids and their kids' kids? They had talked about it. She knew that they had. She remembered sitting on the beach, their thin bedspread beneath them, talking between bites of bologna-and-cheese sandwiches, kissing between sips of cheap wine. They had talked about it. But it was, of course, before her stardom. It was, of course, before he no longer loved her.

"How old is he?" Eric interrupted her thoughts. "How old is your boy?"

Zoe paused. "Fourteen," she answered vaguely.

Eric didn't respond. He shifted on one foot again.

Zoe tried to clear her head, to bring herself back to the present, back to reality. "Your wife seems nice," she said.

Eric nodded.

"And your parents. They're still living in Hibbing?"

He folded his arms across his chest. "Why are you here, Zoe? Is the media doing some story on 'Zoe's past'?"

"Eric, please. I haven't acted in years." She had no intention of mentioning her recent screen test. She had no intention of mentioning her work, the saber that had severed their love. "The media couldn't care less about me." Now it was Zoe's turn to stare at the ground. "I've thought about you a lot over the years."

He turned his back to her. "What are you doing here, Zoe? Why did you come? To gloat? Well, look around." He waved his arms at the diner. "This is what became of Eric Matthews. This is what became of Eric Matthews when Zoe Naddlemeyer got to be too good for him."

"I think it's a nice restaurant, Eric." She moved in front of him and looked into his face. It was red. Tears coated his eyes. "It reminds me of the diner over in Hibbing. The one we always went to...." Her words trailed off. There was no need to remind him of Charlie's Place, where they'd shared burgers and fries and cherry Cokes ... and so many dreams. Two kids, determined to beat the odds. "Eric," she said now, "you seem to have forgotten that you're the one who left me."

"Only because you were getting ready to leave me," he said.

"I was doing no such thing."

"Think back, Zoe. The last thing you needed was me tagging on your heels. And the last thing I wanted to be was 'Mr. Zoe,'" He turned away from her again.

Zoe nodded. She had been right. It was because of her fame that Eric had stopped loving her. "That wouldn't have happened," she said, though she knew she was wrong.

"It was already happening."

She leaned against the building. "Where did you go when you left? You didn't come back here. I tried to find you."

"I went to Florida for a while. Then I came back. Once I could face everyone here."

"Face them?"

He picked up a piece of litter from the ground and studied it. It was a broken plastic lid from an order to go. A broken plastic lid. Not a wildflower, in the shape of a star. "It was humiliating, Zoe. You being such a star. Me such a failure."

She felt her heart begin to break all over again. Eric had never understood. She had done it all for them. She'd thought that was what he had wanted. And yet for all the dreams that they had had, for all the love that they had shared, this town, this place was where Eric was at home—it was where he belonged. Zoe hadn't belonged here then and didn't now. Perhaps that was what he hadn't understood. "I loved you, Eric."

He cracked the plastic lid in his hand. "What you loved was being famous."

"Eric, I was scared."

"Scared? I don't think so. I think you loved every minute of it." He turned again and headed for the door. "And now I think you'd better go."

Tears spilled down her cheeks. "Eric, don't walk away from me, please. Not again."

With his back still toward her, Eric Matthews whispered, "I walked away once because I loved you too much," he said. "Now why don't you just go back to your millionaire life and leave us poor folks alone to flip our hamburgs and slug our beers? I'm sure that's what you're thinking right about now."

"You always had a bad habit of trying to tell me what I was thinking."

"Maybe that's because deep down I knew you better than you knew yourself."

"Eric. Please. Look at me."

He turned. His face was ashen, and suddenly she noticed his blond hair was streaked with gray, his once-square shoulders now slumped a little. But he was still Eric, the man she'd once loved. The man she'd both loved and hated at the same time, all these years. The emotion had surfaced now, from deep in her heart. And she could see his too, there in his eyes. Two worlds of pain; two worlds apart.

"Are you as angry as you seem?" she asked.

"At seeing you?"

"No. At life."

"My life is just fine, thank you. At least it's a lot more than yours. At least it's honest."

Zoe wasn't sure what he meant, but she knew their meeting was over. She watched as he went into the back door of the diner. She didn't try to stop him. All she wanted to do now was get home to Scott, to Marisol, and to Cedar Bluff, and put her guilt and her pain away. Because Zoe was, at last, safe in the knowledge that Eric Matthews and her past were, indeed, over and done with.

She found her way around to the front of the building, to her cheap rental car. As Zoe pulled out of the parking lot and headed toward Minneapolis, toward her life, toward her future and whatever it held, she realized she'd left the turkey sandwich with the thick coat of mayonnaise sitting on the cash register. Where it belonged.

12

Meg and Steven were going to meet in Bermuda for a long weekend, where Steven had a friend with a yacht. The friend was discreet; the friend owed him a favor. Meg was to fly in Thursday evening; Steven had arranged a room for her at the Southampton Princess. He was going to arrive Friday morning; he would meet her there; they would go to the yacht. They would have until Sunday night together; they would be lovers for three days. And she would tell him about the abortion.

On Monday morning jury selection would begin for the state of *New York* v. *Arnold Banks*.

On the two-hour flight to the island, Meg's excitement kept getting interrupted by thoughts of the upcoming trial. She should be home reviewing her opening argument; she should be finalizing her defense. But all she could focus on was Steven, and the three days that lay ahead. Beyond Sunday seemed outside of reality.

The limo pulled up the long, steep drive to the Southampton Princess. Even in the darkness Meg could see that the building was pink—Bermuda-pink, she thought, soft and lovely and romantic.

She went to the registration desk: there was a suite waiting for her, she was told. Their finest.

Their finest suite? Just for her? A spark of hope skipped through her. Was it possible that Steven was there? Was it possible he had come early to surprise her?

The bellman led the way around the curved, sweeping staircase, to the elevators. He was an older gentleman with a warm, friendly smile. *Bermuda,* Meg thought as the elevator lifted her to paradise, *will be forever etched in my memory.*

Inside the suite she was stunned by its lavishness. It was decorated in soft yellows and white, with thick butter-colored carpeting and elegant mahogany furnishings. In the center of the living room, on a large glass cocktail table, sat an abundant arrangement of fresh white flowers—lilies, orchids, delphiniums. She quickly snatched the card and read: "To love at its purest. Until tomorrow. Steven."

She felt a twinge of disappointment—he wasn't there—then she glanced at the card again: "love at its purest." She smiled.

She tipped the bellman and said good night, eager to be alone, eager to savor her happiness. She walked over to a huge glass wall of windows and stared out into the night. Beyond the hotel the sea was black, illuminated by the glow of the quarter-moon, dotted with strings of golden lights that climbed the masts of sleeping cruise ships. Tomorrow night she would be out there, somewhere, with Steven. She hugged herself and smiled. He had not come early, and yet his presence was there. And tomorrow night his arms would be around her.

Weary from her long day of waiting, Meg decided to take a leisurely shower. After she was dried and powdered, she slipped into one of her new lace nightgowns, then slid between the cool sheets on the king-size bed. She reached out her arms and tried to feel Steven's touch. *Tomorrow,* she thought. *Tomorrow I will touch him.*

The early sun awakened her. Meg stretched and luxuriated in the warmth of the bed. She checked the clock. Six thirty. Steven's flight was due at ten.

She showered again, did her hair and makeup, applied a layer of "instant tan" to restore the tanning-lamp-bronze of the spa, and dressed in a short cotton tangerine sundress. When she looked in the mirror, even she could see her own radiance. *It's love,* she thought. *Only love can do this.*

But it was only eight-twenty. She went to the wall of windows in the living area and tried to decide what to do. She could see the magnificent beach from there, down a sloping grassed hill, past lush greens and yellow hibiscus trees. She could go for a walk to the beach.

But what if he'd caught an earlier flight?

She decided to call room service. She picked up the phone and ordered coffee and croissants. She hung up the phone, then picked it up again and called back. "Make that order for two," she said. Just in case.

She packed her toiletries in her vanity case while waiting for room service, so she'd be ready to leave for the yacht once he arrived. She went back to the window and watched as tourists on little red motorbikes made a wobbly descent down the hill. Off to one side a string of horses, laden with stiff-sitting, straw-hatted riders, clip-clopped along the beach. The island was awakening. *Tourism,* Meg thought, *is such a happy industry. So unlike politics. So unlike criminal law.*

Breakfast arrived. Meg took it to the window and sat, looking out, wondering if the other tourists were as happy as she. No, she decided, they couldn't be. No one could be.

She drank two cups of coffee, nibbled on half a croissant, and thought about Steven.

Finally, it was ten o'clock.

Her gaze now moved to the driveway. Maybe she could see the limo when he arrived. She wished she'd made a note of how long it had taken her to get there from the airport: Was it twenty minutes? Half an hour?

Suddenly Meg realized that waiting for Steven resonated with familiarity. When they'd been together in Boston so long ago, waiting had become part of her life. Though Steven had been married, his wife and children had remained in New York, ensconced in grandeur at the home of his wife's affluent, politically powerful parents. Steven had left Boston every Friday afternoon and returned on Sunday nights. On weekends Meg had waited for Monday in her tiny room filled with books. Weekdays she waited in the coffee shop.

Now she waited in hotel rooms.

She'd forgotten how lonely the waiting could be.

Zoe. In Washington, in another hotel room, Meg had phoned Zoe to pass the time. It was early in L.A., but Meg recalled that at the spa Zoe had been an early riser. Meg went to her bag and took out her small book of phone numbers. She wondered if Zoe had returned yet from Minnesota. She wondered if she had found Eric. She wondered if she would dare tell Zoe about Steven.

An answering machine clicked on. Zoe wasn't home. Meg hung up. No use leaving a message; she wouldn't be there much longer.

Alissa. She could call Alissa. But did she want to? Well, she wouldn't have to mention where she was, what she was doing. She could ask if Alissa had heard from Danny about Jay. She could pretend she was at home, just calling to say hi.

She couldn't do that. Alissa would ask if she'd "made any progress" in looking for her man. When it came to something personal—something that mattered—Meg knew she was a lousy liar. Reshaping the truth for the benefit of a client was one thing, but she couldn't lie about this. Besides, Alissa would keep her on the phone too long. And she didn't want to be talking when Steven arrived.

Ten-fifteen.

She went back to her seat by the window and poured another cup of coffee.

From there Meg could see several boats moored. She wondered which was the one she and Steven would be on.

The long white one with the tall mast? The sleek one with the black windows and aqua trim? She wondered if there would be a crew, or if Steven would operate the boat. Did he know how? She shuddered at all the things she didn't know about Steven, about all the unshared details of his life. Still, she doubted that captaining a yacht was one of them. He probably had never had time to learn. Yes, she thought, there would have to be a crew. A crew, she assumed, that would be very discreet. Even though this was the nineties, adultery was still adultery. And politics was still politics.

By eleven o'clock Meg wished she hadn't dressed so early. Her freshness was fading, and the front of her sundress was getting wrinkled from sitting, from waiting.

Had it taken an hour to get in from the airport?

His plane must have been late.

She waited.

At noon the telephone rang. She bounced from the chair and grabbed the receiver.

"Ms. Cooper?" a female voice asked. "This is the desk. We were wondering what time you plan to check out."

"Check out?"

"Checkout time is twelve noon. Will you be leaving soon?"

"Soon? Well, yes, I expect to ..."

"Fine. Housekeeping needs to know when they can get in to do the room for our next reservation."

Meg hung up the phone. Of course. Steven had booked this suite for only one night. Tonight they would be on the yacht. Soon, they would be on the yacht. Until then she might as well wait in the lobby.

She collected her things and rang for the bellman. But as she was leaving the room, Meg turned back and plucked a white orchid from the arrangement. She tucked it behind one ear. Danny would have been pleased she'd selected the orchid. She smiled. Danny would have been pleased if he'd known nothing more than where she was, what she was doing. She took a last look around the suite, sorry to have to leave. It would have been wonderful to have been there with Steven.

In the lobby Meg sat, her suitcases at her feet. She checked with the airline: the ten o'clock flight from Washington had arrived on time. Two others had arrived since then. But Steven had not come, and there was no message from him.

The waiting grew lonelier. The minutes bled into hours.

At six o'clock Meg dropped the wilting orchid from her ear into a wastebasket, then asked the valet to get her a cab. All she could do then was try to trade her Sunday-evening return ticket for another that night. There was, apparently, no longer any reason to wait.

Raggedy Man was glad to see her. For once he wasn't aloof. It was almost as if he knew what had happened. It was almost as if he cared. She dropped her suitcases in the foyer, then went into the study: there was no flashing red light on her answering machine. He hadn't phoned. Steven hadn't even phoned. She fed the cat and went upstairs. Then Meg went to bed and crawled beneath the safety of covers, the warm cocoon of solitude, where no one could disturb her thoughts, where pain could not creep in.

She wished that she could fall asleep. She wished that it was tomorrow, so that she could begin the waiting again—waiting for his phone call, which would surely come tomorrow. Or the next day.

It did not.

On Sunday afternoon, as she turned onto her side for the thousandth time since Friday night, Meg thought about calling Zoe. She wondered again if Zoe was back from Minnesota, if she'd found Eric, what that had been like.

She pulled the comforter around her chin, bitterness swelling up in her at the thought of Zoe and Eric happily reunited.

Then again, Meg thought, maybe it hadn't gone well with

Eric. Maybe Zoe was in pain now, too, huddled in her bed, wishing she would die.

Meg glanced at the clock. Four-thirty. Then she realized that she was luckier than Zoe, because it was only one-thirty in L.A. And there were three fewer hours for Meg to wait until the day came to an end.

Still, she didn't call, for the chance her friend was happy was a risk Meg couldn't take.

She rolled onto her other side and stared at the telephone. She wondered if she stared at it long enough, studied it hard enough, would it ring? If she didn't take her eyes from it, would Steven finally call?

Maybe it was out of order. She pulled an arm from under the covers and plucked the receiver. The dial tone droned loudly, mockingly. Meg quickly replaced it in its cradle in case Steven was at last trying to get through. She wouldn't want him to get a busy signal.

She pulled the comforter higher, tighter, this time over her head. She lay there trying to suffocate her pain. Instead the tears began again. Suddenly she knew that Steven wasn't going to call. He'd had cold feet. Second thoughts. End of story.

She pushed back the bedclothes, covered her eyes, and chastised herself for being surprised. Of course Steven wasn't going to call. Why would he? She wasn't the kind of person who had normal, happy relationships with men.

She brushed her tears away and waited, once again, for sleep to come.

Monday morning was even worse. She had to shower. She had to dress. She had to be in court at nine o'clock and become Counselor-at-Law, Meg Cooper. She had to be ready to grill prospective jurors, to select those most likely to find Arnold Banks not guilty. She had to act as though she gave a shit.

But first she had to get out of bed.

Somehow, she did. She drank half a cup of tea and ate

three tablespoons of cornflakes. She pulled a dress from her closet, not caring which. She did not bother with jewelry.

Before leaving Meg checked herself in the mirror. She leaned close to it, appalled at the dark circles beneath her eyes, at the flesh around them that had seemed to loosen in the night. *I cannot cry,* she thought. *I cannot cry right now, because I have to go out and act as though nothing is wrong. I have to think, I have to work, I have to go on.*

I cannot cry.

An ache formed behind her eyes, the ache of tears dammed up. She quickly turned and headed toward the door, past the suitcases that stood there still, waiting, and unopened.

Outside her brownstone the bright sun assaulted her. She hailed a cab. This was no morning to walk to the courthouse: her legs would never hold her upright that long.

She rode to the courthouse, paid the driver, got out of the cab, crossed the sidewalk, and walked up the stairs, moving hypnotically, propelled by pain. At last she stood in the large rotunda, staring at the directory, examining the courtroom assignments. Her hearing was scheduled for the third floor, room 8.

"Yo, counselor!" The familiar voice snapped her out of her trance. Meg spun around. The movement made her dizzy.

Danny held out an arm and steadied her. "Hey, you okay?"

Meg nodded. "Fine. Hi, Danny." She adjusted the shoulder strap of her briefcase and tossed back her hair with a small surprise that she hadn't put it up this morning. "What are you doing here?"

Danny half smiled. "I hang out around these parts, remember?"

"Oh. Right."

"Pretrial motion today on the insider case."

"Oh. How's that going?"

He looked at Meg. "What the hell's the matter with you?" he asked.

"Nothing. I asked, 'How's that going?' "

"That's not what I mean. You look like shit."

"Thank you. I know I can always count on you to make my day."

He leaned closer to her. "What's wrong, Meg? You sure you're all right?"

She stepped back. "I'm fine. Really."

He smiled. "PMS?"

Meg turned away from him. She wanted to say "Grow up," but decided silence would be more effective.

He put his arm on her shoulder. "Hey. Sorry. It was a joke. It's just that you seem a million miles away."

A million miles away. She stared across the rotunda. How far was it to Bermuda? Five hundred miles? A thousand? A lifetime?

"I'm fine, Danny. I have a headache this morning, that's all."

He slipped his arm around her waist. "Well, come on, then, counselor. Let me escort you to your room. And how, by the way, is your friend Mr. Banks doing these days?"

She smiled through her pain, through the growing sickness in her stomach. Why couldn't she have fallen in love with Danny? Why couldn't she have fallen in love with an available man?

"Jury selection this morning."

Danny whistled. "If there are any blind-and-deaf candidates, pick them. They might be the only ones to believe his story."

Meg's insides churned.

"Sorry," Danny said quickly. "That wasn't fair."

Meg shook her head. "It's okay. Now, are you going to escort me or what?"

"Lead the way."

They crossed the marble rotunda to the elevators. Meg was glad to have Danny's company. Maybe his chatter would help take her mind off the fact that her body felt as if it had been run over by a truck. A big one. A semi. A tandem.

They stepped out on the third floor. As they walked down the hall toward room 8, Danny suggested they have lunch.

"We can celebrate your victory," he said.

"It hasn't happened yet."

"It will. I know you."

Meg smiled again.

"Hey, look at it this way, once this is done, you'll be free for the Riley case. No doubt Larson, Bascomb, and friends will get it."

Meg stopped walking.

"The *what* case?"

"The Riley case. Assuming it makes the docket before anyone gets paid off. Although," he continued with a shudder, "it'll be pretty gruesome, I'm sure. The tabloids ought to love it. What with the senator . . ."

Meg grabbed Danny's arm. "What are you talking about? What about Senator Riley?"

He brushed her hand from his arm. "Jesus, Meg, take it easy. Didn't you hear about it? Have you been out of the country all weekend?"

Meg's head started to pound. Her senses flew from neutral into overdrive. "Just tell me, Danny." She tried to sound in control. It wasn't working.

The door to room 8 opened. A bailiff stepped out. "There you are, Ms. Cooper," he said. "The judge is ready for you."

Meg snapped her head around. "I'll be right in." She turned back to Danny. "Tell me, Danny. Please."

Danny shrugged. "Happened Thursday or Friday. Thursday, I guess. Thursday night."

"Never mind when. What happened?"

His wife was driving somewhere at night. In her shiny new XJS. Anyway, some guy had the rotten luck to be coming the other way. He was on his side of the road. So was she. It was a head-on collision."

Her heart pounded along with her head.

"The guy was killed." He snapped his fingers. "Just like that."

"Was she hurt?"

"The senator's wife?" Danny laughed. "You could say that. She ran up an embankment, hit a tree, and a limb came crashing through the windshield."

Meg started to see black.

"I believe the word is 'impaled.' The branch went right through her shoulder. Stuck her to the seat like plaster to a wall."

Meg leaned against the wall. "Is she ... ?" She was afraid of the question, afraid of the answer.

"Dead? Nah. Not yet. Not the last I heard. She probably would have been except for that one little condition that saves so many lives."

Meg scowled.

"She was drunk. As a skunk."

The door opened again. "Ms. Cooper?" The bailiff's tone was harsh.

"Yes. Yes. Coming."

"I'll stop back and see if you're free in time for lunch, right?"

"Sure, Danny," she said as she headed numbly into the courtroom. "Sure."

She stood at the defense table, her knees weak, her head sick. All she could picture was the way she had tucked the white orchid behind her ear, the way she had waited for Steven. The way she had waited for Steven while he waited in a hospital emergency room, knowing that his wife had just killed a man, wondering if his wife was going to die.

If she died, our problems would be over. She gripped the edge of the table and squeezed her eyes shut. *My God,* Meg thought, *I can't believe I would even think such a thing. What's happening to me?*

The first candidate from the jury panel was seated in the witness box. Meg stared at him—a man perhaps in his early fifties. She had no idea what to ask him. She thought about asking the judge for a continuance, but that was hardly warranted, especially when she'd requested as early a date as possible.

Arnold Banks sat at her right, looking smug. Meg wished she had warned him to change his expression. The last thing the judge would want to see was the defendant looking as though he'd already won.

She envisioned the expression Candace Riley must have worn, while stuck to the seat like plaster to a wall, the limb of a tree going in one side, out the other. Her stomach turned. She quickly put a hand to her mouth.

"Ms. Cooper? We're waiting." The judge was in a snarly mood this morning.

She shuffled through her papers, trying to find some notes. *Any* notes. Something to buy her some time until she could collect her thoughts. Her mind raced.

She coughed a little and looked at the potential juror. "Mr. . . ." Her mind went blank.

The man leaned into the microphone. "Donaldson," he said "Harry Donaldson."

Meg coughed again. The way Steven always did. A tremor ran from her heart to her head. She tried to catch her breath. Suddenly a picture of Avery sprung to her mind. If he were looking down on her now, he would be frowning. A client sat next to her. He deserved her best effort. She took a deep breath and spoke quickly.

"Yes. Mr. Donaldson. Tell me, Mr. Donaldson. Are your parents still living?"

"No, ma'am."

"Oh," Meg said. She looked down at her notes, then back to the witness box. "I'm sorry to hear that. How old were they when they died?"

"My father was killed in World War Two. I never knew him. My mother last year, God rest her soul. She was seventy-eight."

"How did your mother die?"

Donaldson shrugged. "Heart failure. She was in a nursing home in upstate. Linda and I—Linda's my wife—we couldn't have her come live with us. We only have three bedrooms—"

"Thank you, Mr. Donaldson," Meg interrupted. "Your Honor, the defense rejects this candidate." She slumped into her chair. She was limp, drained, as though she had just tried the entire case. And lost.

While the judge called for the next person from the pool, Arnold Banks jabbed Meg with his elbow. "Wake up, honey," he whispered hoarsely. "You almost blew it." Meg turned away.

Next came a woman. Fortyish. Well dressed. Well preserved. Meg stared at her, wondering if Candace Riley looked anything like this.

She blinked.

"Ms. Cooper?" the judge demanded.

Meg glanced at him. For a moment she again forgot why she was there, what she was supposed to do. She looked back at the woman. The woman leaned to one side.

She was drunk. As a skunk. Maybe Candace had found out where Steven was going. Maybe she'd found out about them. Maybe this was all Meg's fault.

"Ms. Cooper. Please," the judge said sternly.

Beside her Arnold Banks sighed loudly.

Meg stood. Then, mechanically, she began to ask questions, all too aware that she was barely listening to the answers. In a dark corner of her mind Meg was, instead, trying to determine if Steven's compassion, guilt, or politics would stop him from divorcing Candace if she went to jail. If she survived.

One by one jury candidates filed into the courtroom, answered questions, were accepted or dismissed. By noon only two jurors had been selected. The judge called for a lunch recess. As Meg stood to leave, Arnold Banks grabbed her arm. "You'd better be sharper this afternoon, honey," he warned. "We both have a lot riding on this, right?"

Meg shook off his hand. "Go to hell," she said, and

stalked from the courtroom, not knowing if she or Banks had been more stunned by her answer.

Danny was waiting in the hall.

"How'd it go, counselor?"

Meg waved him off. "Let's not talk about it, okay?"

"No problem. As long as we're still on for lunch."

She pushed a lock of hair from her face. God, she must really be a mess today. "I'm not hungry, Danny."

He shook his head. "Tough. You're going to lunch with me."

"I should go to the office. I haven't been in since Thursday." *I should muster up my courage and see if Steven has called,* she wanted to add. But now she was more afraid than before that he hadn't.

"You really have been out of the country, then."

She looked at him. "Danny . . ."

"None of my business, okay? But I'm taking you to lunch. Like I said this morning, you look like shit."

They went to Schneider's Deli on East Fifty-third, Danny's favorite downtown haunt. Meg got a bagel with jelly. Danny ordered a Reuben with the works.

The restaurant was crowded and noisy, but they found a small table in the rear. He bit into his sandwich with gusto. "Tell me what happened," he said.

She couldn't tell him. She couldn't tell him about Bermuda, about Steven. She just couldn't. She picked up half her bagel, then set it down, untouched. "I'd rather not talk about it."

"Come on, Meg. How bad could it be? It was only jury selection."

Oh. He was referring to court. He wasn't referring to Steven.

She picked at her bagel again. "I had a bad morning," she said. "It happens to everyone. Even on the best of days."

She toyed with her napkin but felt Danny's eyes bore into her.

"My experience tells me that this isn't exactly one of your best days."

She picked up her bagel again. "I couldn't concentrate. That's all."

He chewed for a while, then took a long drink of iced tea. "Talk to me, Meg."

"I can't, Danny." She was too confused. She was too tired. And she couldn't erase the image from her mind of Candace Riley stuck to her seat, *"like plaster to a wall."*

"Hey," Danny said, so suddenly that she jumped. "I have good news. It's about your friend Alissa. That guy she's been looking for? I found him. He lives in Los Angeles."

A shock of pain tore through her heart and raced through her body. The room started spinning. The voices around her echoed against one another; the smells of pastrami and garlic and pickled cabbage made her reel. Meg jumped up and bolted, banging into other tables, chairs, people, as she escaped to the front door. Once on the street, she collapsed against the brick building, shaking, panting, sobbing.

"Jesus, Meg. What's wrong?" It was Danny. He put his arm around her. He pulled her close to him. She wept into his chest.

The next thing she knew, he was helping her into a cab. He told the driver her home address.

"I have to be back in court," she protested.

"I'll go," Danny said. "I'll tell the judge you collapsed. But please, Meg. Talk to me."

In the back of the cab she stared at the plastic divider that separated them from the driver. It was scratched and cloudy. And it was closed. And so she told him. She told Danny about the scheme they had planned at the spa—she, Alissa, and their other friend, Zoe. Then she told him about looking for her "lost love," about finding him, meeting him again, after all those years. She quietly told him he was Senator Steven Riley. She did not tell him about the abortion.

"Jesus," was all Danny managed to say.

And then she told him about the weekend. Bermuda. How Steven had never arrived.

"Jesus," he said again.

"What do I do now, Danny?"

"Jesus," he said. "I'm afraid you're the only one who can answer that, babe."

Meg covered her eyes with her arm. She was weary. So very weary.

"Do you want me to check on his wife?" he asked. "I could contact the hospital. . . ."

"No," she said. "I don't want to know. I have to believe that sooner or later Steven will get in touch with me."

Danny said nothing.

Meg closed her eyes and drifted into a semisleep. A sleep of the unsettled, the pain riddled.

"You were really in love with the guy, weren't you?"

She pulled herself from her dreamlike state. "Yes."

"Are you still?"

She didn't answer.

"That would answer a lot of questions," Danny said. "About you. About why you've never stayed with any one man . . ."

She turned sideways and looked at him. "Please, Danny, you must promise me one thing."

"Sure, babe. Anything."

"You must promise never to tell anyone about this. No one. Not now. Not ever."

"Does your friend Alissa know?"

"Oh, God, Danny, No. They know there's someone—they don't know who. Please, Danny. Promise me."

He held up two fingers. "Scout's honor," he said. "But I am going to do one thing."

"What?"

"I'm going to find out what hospital his wife is in, and I'm going to check it out for myself. That way, if and when you want to know, I can tell you myself. Unless, of course, you read it in the papers first."

"I try not to read the newspaper."

The cab pulled up at Meg's front door.

"I'll go plead to the judge," Danny said. "Then I'll be back later. With dinner."

"You're a pal, Danny," she said, and meant it.

He winked as she got out. And as she slowly walked up the stairs of her lonely brownstone, Meg wondered why Danny had not yet found the right woman—one who was deserving of his kindness, open to his love.

13

She hadn't ordered a glass of chardonnay. She'd ordered a bottle. Alissa had escaped to the same dark bar in the Underground where she'd met with Danny. But that had been over a week ago, and there had been no word from him since. Nor had there been word from Betty Wentworth or Sue Ellen Jamison. But Alissa was holding her ground. The problem was, so were they. She wondered who would be the first to cry uncle.

At least she had Jay to think about, and the dim hope that life may be worth living after all. Unless, of course, Danny Gordon took much longer, in which case she would probably go out of her mind first.

Somewhere between the third and fourth glass of wine, Alissa started talking to a young guy on the next stool. Thirty, maybe. Tall, long-haired, skinny-assed in torn jeans. She didn't catch his name. Somewhere between the fourth glass and the end of the bottle, she agreed to accompany him to his loft.

It seemed like a good idea at the time.

Half an hour later Alissa lay on the rumpled sheets, aware by the damp ooze from her crotch that they had had sex, though she hardly remembered the act. The mattress was a thin futon, and she could feel the slats of the frame push at her spine. There was a musky odor in the room. Maybe it was the brick walls, maybe it was the old paint cans strewn in the corner, maybe it was the dirty sheets.

"Wine?" he asked.

"Sure," Alissa replied, and took a thick-rimmed glass from his hand. He unscrewed the cap from a nondescript bottle and poured. Alissa put it to her lips and immediately wished she hadn't. The wine was bitter, cheap. Her esophagus burned, her stomach turned. She set the glass on the floor. He crawled back into bed and stretched out beside her.

She lit a cigarette and looked around the room. It wasn't the first time she'd been in bed in an artist's studio, but the others had been real artists, whose works sported six-figure price tags and were shown in the finest galleries all over the world.

He painted sailboats and sunsets and sold his wares from a cart in the mall of the Underground. She wondered if he'd been among the group who raised money for the homeless.

He rolled over and encircled her waist with his arm. She threaded her fingers through his large, overpowering ones. Such strong, confident fingers. But even in the dim light Alissa cold see paint residue beneath the nails.

"You're quite a lady, you know that?" he asked.

"Mmm," she replied.

He moved his hand between her legs and rested it there. Then he began to snore.

Alissa thought about leaving. But to do what? Go home? She had thought she needed a change. She'd read about women reaching their forties and suddenly coming out of their shell, taking charge. But Alissa had spent the last twenty-plus years taking charge. Is this what was left? Meaningless sex and one-night stands? And galas that no one wanted you to be part of?

Soon things would get even worse. No matter how hard Alissa tried to talk her out of it, Michele was insistent on getting married, complete with a huge wedding, southern-belle style. It was not going to be easy to explain that there could be no such wedding, that Alissa could no longer bring herself to pretend that she and Robert were the happy couple, the toast of Atlanta, or that every time she had to look at him now, all she could see was his thin white ass, pumping up and down on top of, inside of, that man. No, there couldn't be a huge wedding.

But it would have been magnificent. There would have been fountains on every table, champagne—probably, she thought with a wince, *Cristal* champagne—a flock of white doves to sail over the bride and groom when they were introduced at the reception. It would have been a fairy-tale wedding, certain to be covered by *Town & Country*. It would have been magnificent if Robert hadn't fucked everything up.

Alissa took a deep drag on her cigarette. She wished she had another glass of wine. Real wine.

She closed her eyes and tried to deny the small lump in her throat, the welling need to cry. Her family was interested only in themselves. Michele. Robert. Natalie. Selfish, selfish, selfish. Didn't they care about her life, about her feelings? The answer, she knew, was no. They didn't care, any more than the women of the WFFA cared.

The snoring beside Alissa stopped. His hand began to move. As though unconnected to her brain, unmindful of her thoughts, her legs parted. She raised her arm and covered her eyes. He moved on top of her, into her. She arched her hips in response, ready to perform again—the way she had performed all her life—ready to do what was expected of her.

She tuned out his gasps; she denied his hot breath on her neck. She thought about Robert. She thought of how she had been doing exactly what he expected of her. She had been handling the problems with him in her usual manner: caustic behind the scenes, smiling and steady among their friends.

She knew that Michele expected the same pattern from

her mother, that she expected Alissa would bitch about the wedding, then turn it into the most glamorous affair that had ever been witnessed east of the Mississippi. She knew that the women of the WFFA would expect her to withdraw her resignation, once she was out of her "mood."

She also knew that Natalie expected Alissa to ignore her antics.

They expected her to do these things, because she always had. She had been, if nothing else, predictable. It was, after all, the way she'd been trained by her aunt and uncle: trained to perform, trained to live on the surface and to disavow those time-wasting fantasies of things like feelings and love.

Even when she'd run away to San Francisco with Jay, Alissa had done what was expected of her. She'd come home.

An animal moan came from the man on top of her. He collapsed against her chest. His wet hair clung to her face.

"God, you're beautiful," he groaned.

Alissa started to cry.

She padded down the hall toward her room, enveloped with the disgust of having been used, of having let herself be used. Alissa clutched her stomach as she walked, trying to quiet the pain deep within.

She opened the doors to the bedroom—hers alone now, hers alone probably forever. She knew she'd never return to the bar in the Underground; she hoped she'd never go to any bar alone, ever again.

Natalie sat in the middle of Alissa's bed, clicking the remote control of the television.

"What are you doing in here?" Alissa snapped. "Do you know what time it is?"

"I think the question should be 'Do *you* know what time it is?'" Natalie answered, not shifting her eyes from the flipping screen. "It's four o'clock in the morning, Mother."

Alissa tossed her bag on the brocade chaise and pulled her sweater off over her head. The sooner she got rid of the musky smell of that loft, the better. "And are you just getting home?"

"Are you?"

Alissa resisted the urge to cross the room and slap her daughter's face. *Maybe another night,* she thought. *Tonight I'm too tired.* She walked instead to her dressing room, where she stripped from her clothes and wrapped a robe around herself.

When she returned to the bedroom, Natalie was still there.

"What are you doing in here, Natalie?" she sighed.

"Waiting for you. I was afraid I'd be here till Thursday."

Alissa went to the chaise and picked up the sweater. She tossed it into the dressing room. "You've got a pretty bad attitude for a sixteen-year-old, young lady. Haven't you ever learned the meaning of the word 'respect'?"

"I'm not here to talk about the fact that you and I don't get along," Natalie said. "I'm here to talk about Dad."

Alissa stiffened. First Michele had wanted to know what the problem was between her parents. Now Natalie. Her daughters were too smart for their own good. Maybe it was time she told them both: "Your father's gay. He prefers men to me." But something inside her warned Alissa that Natalie probably would accuse her of lying. Besides, Alissa had decided that if the girls were to be told, Robert had to be the one to do the telling. Let them hate him, not her. Natalie hated her mother enough as it was.

Alissa remained standing, hands on her hips, in the middle of the room. Then a frightening thought entered her mind: Had Natalie already found out? Was that why she was here?

"What about your father?" Alissa asked.

"He's at the hospital," Natalie said.

"So?" She really didn't need to hear about Robert's middle-of-the-night rounds. She didn't want to think about all the years he'd been telling her he had to tend to a patient with one sort of crisis or another. She didn't want to think about what he had really been doing all those nights. Right now all Alissa wanted was to take a shower. She wanted to purge her body—and her mind—of the last remnants of a night gone bad.

"He's had a heart attack."

"What?"

"I think Daddy's had a heart attack." Natalie's thin, narrow shoulders rose, then fell, in a listless shrug. "Not that you care."

Alissa marched to the bed and grabbed her daughter's arm. "What are you saying?" Natalie's gaze remained fixed on the screen. Alissa shook her. "What's going on?"

Natalie's face reddened. Her eyes narrowed. She angrily pried Alissa's fingers open and pushed her hand away. "Don't take it out on me," Natalie hissed. "I didn't do a fucking thing."

Alissa slapped her. "Don't use that kind of language around me."

"Oh, pardon me. Only you can say that, right? Only you can say fuck, fuck, fuck, when you're fucking every ripe dick in town."

Alissa stepped back so she wouldn't choke her daughter. She snatched the remote and turned off the television.

"Where is your father?"

Natalie got off the bed on the other side. "Memorial."

"Is he all right?"

"How do I know? Do I look like a doctor?"

Her father's daughter, Alissa thought. *She never liked me, never. She was always her father's daughter, her father's pet.*

Alissa stomped toward the phone.

"What are you doing?" Natalie asked.

"I'm going to call the hospital. Not that it's any of your business."

Natalie smirked. "Don't you think it would look better if you showed up? Bad enough I've been calling all over town trying to find you all night."

Alissa twirled around. "Who did you call? You had no right . . ."

"Well, excuse me for giving a shit about my father. And excuse me for thinking you might give a shit. My mistake."

Alissa shook her finger. "You, young lady, are in for a rude awakening one of these days."

Natalie tossed back her hair. "Are you going to see him or not?"

"Of course I'm going to see him!" Alissa's mind raced. Of course, of course, that's what she should do. She should go see him. Make sure that he was all right. But she couldn't let Natalie think that she'd won. She picked up the receiver. "But first I'm going to call. I want to let them know I'm coming."

"Why? So they can bring out the brass band?"

Alissa glared at her daughter. Suddenly Natalie burst into tears.

Alissa stood still, the receiver in her hand, the numbers untouched. *Christ,* she thought. *This is all I need.* Natalie in tears. When was the last time she'd seen Natalie cry? And how had she handled it? Michele was the teary child, the dramatic one. Natalie was too tough to cry, too controlled. Then a memory of Natalie falling off her pony surfaced. The little girl was crying. Alissa had tried to approach her, but Natalie had been firm. "Daddy," she'd wept. "I want my Daddy." Alissa tried to remember what it was like to want a daddy. Or a mommy. But for Alissa there had been only an aunt and uncle, who didn't care.

She set the receiver back in its cradle and went to Natalie. She hesitated, not knowing quite what to do. Then she put her arms around her, fully expecting her daughter to recoil. Instead the girl sobbed into her mother's breast.

"Mom," she cried, "I'm so scared."

Alissa stroked the mass of dark hair, so unlike her own, so like Robert's. "I know, I know. Now tell me what happened."

Natalie sniffed and pulled her head back. They were face-to-face, mother and adversary child. But the child no longer looked sixteen. Her frightened dark eyes blinked, her cheeks were flushed and blotched. She looked no older than ten. "He was in the library," she began. "I was in the hall. I was waiting for Ed to pick me up."

"Ed?" Alissa asked. "What happened to John Wentworth?" Grant's son. Grant's child-fucking son.

"He's a jerk," Natalie said.

Alissa nodded.

"I heard a noise come from the library," Natalie went on. "I went in. I thought he was ... I thought he was ..."

Alissa pulled her daughter to her again and patted her back. "I know, I know." She hated the fact that she was uncomfortable holding her own daughter. She hated the fact that they were so different, so very different. "What did they say at the hospital?"

"The doctor in the emergency room said they were going to run some tests. Something called an EKG. And some blood tests. That's all they told me."

"Was he conscious when you left?"

"Yes. I guess."

"Well, that's a good sign." Alissa didn't know if it was or it wasn't. She only knew she needed to say something to get her daughter back in control.

"Mom, I want to go back to the hospital with you. In case Daddy needs me."

In case Daddy needs me. The words stung Alissa, because she knew they were true. Robert would need Natalie long before he'd need Alissa. He would need the comfort of someone who he knew truly loved him. Unconditionally.

"Let me get dressed," she told Natalie. "I'll only take a minute."

Natalie wiped her nose while Alissa opened her wardrobe and pulled out a Dior warm-up suit. "They don't know if he's going to be okay, Mom. The doctor said he doesn't know if he's going to make it. I don't understand. Daddy always has taken such good care of himself."

Alissa nodded and quickly dressed. *Such good care of himself,* Alissa thought. She wondered if he hadn't had a heart attack at all. She wondered if he had AIDS.

"Where's Michele?"

Natalie folded her arms. "Sleeping. She said to wake her if anything happened." Tears returned to her eyes. "Wouldn't you think she'd want to be there, too?"

No, Alissa should have said. *In the past few years Michele hasn't been too partial to your father. It's been as though she sensed what was going on, as though she sensed the infidelities.* "It's her decision," Alissa said as she tucked her feet into her sneakers.

Alissa put her arm on Natalie's elbow. "Let's go."

They started out the door when Natalie stopped. "Oh, Mom, I almost forgot."

"What?"

"There was a call on your private line. I thought it was Daddy, or the hospital or something. Don't be mad, but I answered it."

Alissa decided not to react. "Who was it?"

"Some guy from New York. Named Danny. He said he has the information you wanted."

Robert was lying on the bed. Wires and cords snaked from his body to beeping monitors. Fluid from an IV bag dripped down the plastic tubing into his arm. From the glass window in the hallway, Alissa could see that his eyes were closed.

"He looks dead, Mom," Natalie said.

"He's not."

A nurse pushed past them and went into the room. She checked the IV and adjusted some buttons and knobs. On her way out Alissa stopped her. "Where's his doctor?" she demanded.

"Dr. Harrington knows you're here," the nurse said briskly. "He's with another patient." She strode away.

Alissa unzipped her jacket. Christ, it was hot in there. She wished the good Dr. Harrington, whoever he was, would hurry up and get there. She needed to find out about Robert; then she needed to get a couple of hours' sleep. She wondered if eight o'clock would be too early to call Danny. She wondered what he would have to say.

I've found him? That must be it. He told Natalie he had the information Alissa wanted. He knew that was the only information she wanted.

She stared into the hospital room and studied the rhythmic beeping and sharp bounces displayed on the EKG monitor. Robert was forty-six years old. Jay, forty-four. Robert was lying there in who-knew-what kind of a state. The last time she'd seen Jay, he smoked. He took drugs. Not Robert. Never Robert. And yet Robert was the one lying there, in the hospital bed. An eerie thought washed over her. Maybe Jay wasn't sick. Maybe Jay was dead. Just because Danny said he had the information she wanted didn't mean it was what she wanted to hear. *No,* her mind shouted. *Jay can't be dead. You saw him on TV only weeks ago.* Still, Robert had been healthy, Robert had been whole, only weeks ago.

"Mrs. Page?"

His name tag read "Julius Harrington, M.D." Alissa had never heard of him, but he looked too young to have any kind of initials after his name, never mind "M.D."

"Dr. Harrington. How is my husband?"

"He's reasonably stable at the moment. He had us going for a while in the ER."

"Did he have a heart attack?"

"Not that we can tell."

"Then what's the problem?"

The doctor adjusted the stethoscope around his neck. "We want to do an angiogram later this morning. Check for blockages in his coronaries."

Alissa looked back through the window. "Is he conscious?"

"He's sleeping."

"Good."

Natalie grabbed her mother's arm. "He's going to be okay, Mom?"

Alissa turned back to the doctor. "Doctor?"

"We'll know more later. After the angiogram."

Alissa nodded again.

"It would help if you could answer some questions, Mrs. Page."

"Such as?"

"Has your husband been under any stress lately?"

Alissa bit her lip. Stress. Now, there was an interesting word. "I haven't noticed," she said. "Then again, he treats mostly AIDS patients, you know. He doesn't talk to me about his work very often." *Lately, in fact, he doesn't talk to me very often at all.*

"His regular physician is Jacob Stern, is that right?"

Alissa was disgusted. She was standing there, in the middle of the night, with a whimpering daughter on one side and a prepubescent doctor on the other, who was probably intimidated as hell about being on call when Robert Hamilton Page was admitted. "Has Dr. Stern been called?" Alissa asked.

"He's in Zurich," Harrington answered. "At a conference."

"Surely someone is covering for him."

"I am."

She didn't hide her surprise. "You?"

"I'm the group's newest partner."

Alissa sighed and looked back to Robert. At least it wasn't serious, she thought. At least he hadn't had a heart attack. "Then you have his records."

"I'll bring in a specialist in the morning."

"I think that's a good idea," Alissa said, then added, "after, of course, you've checked with Dr. Stern."

"Yes. Of course."

She wondered if Robert's medical records in any way indicated that he was gay. She looked at him. He seemed so vulnerable, so pathetic. It was hard to believe he had once been young, vibrant. It was hard to believe she had once loved him. Or thought she had.

Robert will be fine, she thought, and she was glad. For as much as Alissa wanted to change her life, she didn't want to see him die. She wondered if he would ever believe that.

She put her arm around Natalie. "Come on, Nat. There's nothing we can do here tonight."

Natalie remained rigid. "I'm not going home," she said. "I'm staying here."

"Don't be ridiculous. Your father will be fine."

Natalie shook her head. "I don't care. I'm staying here. The nurse will find me a bed. She likes Daddy. She said he's a fine doctor. One of the best. She told me that when I was here before."

Alissa wanted to tell her daughter to stop acting like a child and come home. But Alissa was too tired to argue; she was too tired to care. She'd come to check on Robert; she'd performed her wifely duty; she'd done what was expected. Now she wanted to go home and go to bed. Besides, if Natalie was not at home, there would be one less person snooping around the house when she placed the call to Danny.

"Hi. This is Danny Gordon. You know what to do."

Alissa was tempted to slam down the receiver.

"If you're there, get your lazy ass out of bed," she barked instead. "This is Alissa Page. Pick up the phone, Danny. I'm paying you enough." She waited a moment. No response. She figured he was rubbing his eyes, fighting being roused from sleep. She wondered if a naked female lay beside him. She wondered if his muscles were sore from a long night of fucking. Was his penis erect, throbbing, ready for more? Would he turn onto his side and slip it into the naked figure lying beside him? And was that figure Meg?

"Danny!" she screamed. "Pick up the phone, you son of a bitch!"

No response.

This time she slammed down the receiver.

There was a knock on her bedroom door. "Mother?" It was Michele.

"Come in."

Michele looked as though she were going to the White House for tea.

"Aren't you a bit overdressed for eight o'clock in the morning?" Alissa asked.

"I was just trying this on. David and I are going to pick out our crystal and china this morning."

"Doesn't he ever work?"

"Mother," Michele groaned as she examined herself in the floor-length, free-standing mirror. "You know he works for his father's investment firm."

"Hard work, I'm sure." Alissa nodded.

Michele adjusted a turquoise silk scarf at her throat. "Do you like this with or without the scarf?"

"Don't you care how your father is?"

Michele removed the scarf and dropped it onto Alissa's bed. "Of course I care, Mother. That's why I came in here." She moved closer to the mirror and studied her eye makeup. "He is okay, isn't he?"

"You say that as if you assume he is." Alissa watched her daughter lift a mascara fleck from her brow.

"Did he have a heart attack?" Michele asked, her eyes never leaving her reflection.

Such a cavalier attitude, Alissa thought. *She's learned so much from me.* Alissa knew that, like her, Michele had definitely mastered the art of maintaining a cool persona—on the surface. But in her daughter's case Alissa wondered how deep below the surface it really went.

"He didn't have a heart attack," Alissa said.

"Oh, that's good," Michele answered, then stepped away from the mirror and smoothed the front of her dress. "He would have hated that. Being restricted. Being an invalid."

Or being dead, Alissa wanted to add, but then decided that perhaps what she was witnessing wasn't so much coldness on Michele's part as it was life in a fantasy world where parents never died until their children were ready for them to die. One thing she did know was that right now she was far too tired to teach her daughter the realities of life.

Michele stood with one hand on her hip. "I thought I'd go to the WFFA luncheon today. It's time I became an active member, don't you think?"

Alissa picked up her daughter's scarf and began folding it.

"You're going, aren't you, Mother?"

Expectations. There was that word again. First Aunt Helma. Then Betty Wentworth, Sue Ellen Jamison. Now her daughter. "No," Alissa answered. "I'll be going to the hospital."

Her private line rang. *Danny*. She looked at Michele. "Would you excuse me, please?"

"You want me to leave?"

The phone rang again.

"Yes. Now."

Michele yanked the scarf from her mother's hand and stomped from the room with her usual overdrama. Alissa grabbed the phone.

"Yes?" she said.

"Alissa, it's Danny Gordon."

She took a breath and tried to sound disinterested. "Oh, yes, Danny. I understand you called. I tried phoning you a few minutes ago."

"I'm not home," he said.

Right, Alissa thought. He's probably in some bimbo's apartment. He probably doesn't even have a home, doesn't need one. His answering machine is probably hooked up to a phone booth in the back of a Forty-second Street bar.

"I'm in Atlanta," he said.

She grasped the receiver. "Here? In Atlanta?"

Danny laughed. "Something told me once you heard I had the information on Jay, you'd demand that I come down, anyway. So I hopped a plane last night. This time I thought I'd call before coming over."

"Don't come here," Alissa said quickly. She didn't want Natalie to come in from the hospital and find Danny Gordon in the library. "Where are you?"

"The Marriott."

The last time Alissa counted, there were half a dozen Marriotts in Atlanta. "Which one?"

"Downtown. The Marquis."

Great. The same place as the WFFA luncheon. It figured. "I'll meet you there," she said, her thoughts racing. "But not right away," she added. "I've had a few problems come up. How about five o'clock?" Five o'clock should be fairly safe. The WFFA women should have disbanded by then.

"In the lounge?"

Should she take a chance?

"No," Alissa replied. "In your room."

"My *room*?" His tone was thick with sarcasm.

"Just give me the number, Danny."

He did.

"And tell me one more thing," she said. "Did you find him?"

"Of course I found him. I told you I'm good at what I do."

She hung up the phone and smiled.

They wanted to do a triple bypass.

"Genetics," Robert said to Alissa as she sat by his bedside. Natalie sat on the other side of the bed, holding her father's hand. "Remember, my father died at fifty-two of a massive coronary."

Alissa nodded. They had been married less than a year when Robert Hamilton Page, Sr., dropped dead on the golf course. *Genetics,* she thought, then wondered if Robert's father had also been gay.

"It's a good thing I've always taken such good care of myself," Robert added. "Otherwise I could have been a goner, too."

"You're only forty-six, Robert."

He tried to smile through the gray pallor of his face. "It's a different era, my dear. Life is a good deal tougher these days."

Only because you've made it tougher, Alissa wanted to say. "When does Dr. Stern come home?" she asked.

"Tomorrow. They'll wait until the day after to do the bypass. They want him around to manage the cardiac medication if my ticker starts acting up after surgery."

"Who's doing it?" She felt as though she needed to ask the right questions. She would support Robert through this. She was, after all, still his wife. And all the world still knew it. But when he recuperated—*if* he recuperated—things were going to be different. Much different.

"Harley Kunze. Jacob is bringing him in from Zurich."

Alissa nodded again. She didn't have to ask if Robert thought Harley Kunze was the top heart surgeon. She assumed he wouldn't let the man near him unless he did. Or maybe, she thought with a grimace, unless he was a good-looking queen, a potential lover.

"How long is the recovery?" she asked.

"A week, ten days, in the hospital. Then a month, maybe six weeks of rehabilitation."

She stood up and looked at her daughter. "Let's go, Natalie. Your father needs his rest."

Natalie looked concerned. "Can we come back tonight?"

"You can if you want," Alissa said. "But I have an engagement I can't cancel."

On the ride home, Alissa made a decision. She still hadn't heard from the "ladies" of the WFFA about her resignation. But as badly as she wanted back in with the gala—as badly as she craved the *control*—Alissa could not admit she'd misjudged their reaction. Now, however, none of that mattered. For Robert had provided the ruse she needed to evoke their sympathy and win the game.

Inside the house Alissa headed straight for the private

phone in her bedroom. In less than a minute Sue Ellen was on the line.

"Sue Ellen..." Alissa gritted her teeth and added, "Darling. How are you?"

Frost coated the wire. "Alissa. What a surprise."

Alissa laughed. "Now, now, Sue Ellen. I'm sure you knew I'd be calling. You've heard about my Robert, haven't you?" When Sue Ellen, of course, replied "No," Alissa was only too pleased to fill her in on the details—how poor Robert had been so sick for so long now, and how, in her martyrlike way, poor Alissa had not wanted to tell anyone and had, instead, sacrificed her own interests to be by his side.

"That's why I resigned, Sue Ellen. What else could I have done? But Robert will be having surgery now, and I'm certain that after a somewhat lengthy recuperation, he'll be fine."

After the expected initial tentativeness, Sue Ellen began to sigh and cluck and say in all the right places how "very sorry" she was to hear that.

"Robert will be fine," Alissa repeated, "but the doctor said I may not be if I don't stop fussing and worrying about my husband and get back to my life. So if I'm forgiven for being so foolish, I'd love to get back to work on the gala. In fact, I have a little plan that's certain to make it a simply stupendous success." She would keep them in suspense for now; then, once she was sure she was back in control, she'd set them all back on their two-inch, sensible heels when she told them Zoe would attend.

And now that Danny had found Jay, maybe Jay Stockwell—not poor, sick, recuperating Robert—would be Alissa's escort to the gala. A shudder tingled in her heart.

"There's a meeting tomorrow," Sue Ellen conceded. "You're welcome to come."

Alissa smirked. The hell with expectations. Once she was back in control, they could all go to hell. Because Alissa Page was going to run the show.

At ten after five Alissa rode the elevator up to Danny's floor. She was smiling. She was happy. She had the gala back. And now ...

Danny knows where he is.

Her stomach lurched as the elevator bumped to a stop.

... Now with the gala she'd have something to keep her busy if Jay didn't want to see her.

The elevator doors opened. Alissa stared at the blank wall of the corridor. She shook her head. Unthinkable. Of course Jay would see her. But what if he was married? Or worse, what if he was happy?

She stepped from the elevator as the doors started to close. She walked down the hall, looking for Danny's room, wondering why she hadn't heard from Meg. Or Zoe. Had they abandoned the plan? Was she the only one with enough courage to see this through? And now that her chance had arrived, *would* she have the courage?

She barely had a chance to knock when Danny opened the door.

"If it isn't my favorite southern belle," he said, stepping aside to allow her to enter.

It wasn't a room. It was a suite. Probably the hotel's most expensive.

"Nice place you have here," Alissa said as she breezed past him.

"First-class expenses, remember?"

She ignored the comment and crossed the room. She took a seat by the window and noticed a bottle of wine chilling in an ice bucket. For her? Was Danny Gordon trying to impress her? To come on to her? The flutter of encouragement died with the realization that the cost of the wine would undoubtedly appear on her bill.

She crossed her legs and let the hem of her white cotton sundress inch up her thighs. Danny was dressed in frayed jean shorts and a T-shirt that declared "Save the Manatee." His boots were gone; he was barefoot. He looked a dozen years younger than the last time she'd seen him. And still incredibly sexy.

"Wine?" he asked.

"I might as well," Alissa said, but didn't add, "After all, I'm paying for it." She was, after all, there for only one reason: to learn about Jay.

Danny spoke as he uncorked the bottle. "I had a real exciting day. Went to the Underground for a while and hung out. Came back here. Watched TV. Yup, the exciting life of a private investigator."

"I couldn't meet you sooner. Something came up."

"I thought this was the most important thing in your life right now. What were you doing? Planning a party?"

Alissa bristled. "You don't like me very much, do you, Danny?"

He handed her a glass of wine, then seated himself in the chair facing her. "I have a problem with ladies of leisure. Especially rich ones. But don't take it personally."

"Oh, I see. Would you like me much if I were poor?"

"That's like asking if Meg Cooper would have any clients if she weren't a redhead. It's an unanswerable question." He swirled his wine around the glass, lightly sniffed the bouquet, then took a sip.

"Is that the big attraction to Meg?" Alissa asked. "Because she's not a lady of leisure?"

He set down his glass. "Meg and I have been friends for years," he said.

"Mmm," Alissa said. So he wasn't going to admit they were lovers. He was being the noble male, the righteous protector of the female reputation. God, sometimes she really hated men. She took a cigarette from her purse. "Do you mind if I smoke?"

"Hell, I don't care if you snort coke. But this is a non-smoking room."

She flickered her lighter. "So tell the management to sue me."

Danny smiled.

"I know. Now, what have you got in that briefcase of yours that pertains to me?" She pointed to the small leather case propped against Danny's chair.

He picked up the briefcase. It caught on the corner of the chair, and a few file folders spilled out. The one on top was clearly labeled "Larson, Bascomb." Beneath that was one marked "Alissa." He grabbed that one and began to tuck the others back into the case. But not before Alissa saw the one marked "Meg."

Was Danny looking for Meg's man, too? Her pulse quickened at the idea. She was dying to know who he was.... Obviously, it wasn't Danny. She'd been wrong about that. But who was it? Maybe it was someone powerful, after all. Someone in the "public eye," Meg had said. *Who the hell was it? And, if not Meg, then who the hell was Danny screwing?*

Danny set the briefcase back down on the floor and took several yellow lined sheets from the file marked "Alissa." She swallowed a big gulp of wine.

"Jay Stockwell," Danny said, reading from one of the sheets. "Age, forty-four."

"I know that."

"Five feet eleven. Sandy hair. Green eyes."

Alissa wouldn't give him the satisfaction of showing her annoyance.

"Broadcast journalist," Danny continued. "With World Press International."

WPI. That was something she didn't know. She sat up straight in her chair.

"Oh, yeah, and you might be interested in knowing this. He's single. Never married."

She hoped the elation wasn't showing on her face.

"He's based out of Los Angeles. Currently working in Djkarta."

"Indonesia?"

He looked up at her. "The last I knew, that's where Djkarta is."

She sank back in the chair. "So what the hell am I supposed to do? Fly to Djkarta?"

"From there he's going on to Singapore." He handed her a piece of paper. "Here's how to get in touch with him when he gets back to the States. He's scheduled to return at the end of July."

She took the paper and stared at it. There was one address for his office, one for his home. "The end of July is six weeks away."

Danny shrugged. "Sounds like it'll give you time to nurse your husband back to health."

She drained her wineglass. "How the hell did you know about my husband?"

Danny smiled.

"Oh, right. You're good at your job."

"More wine?" he asked.

"Don't mind if I do." The alcohol was beginning to fuzz her brain, but Alissa didn't care. Jay would be in L.A. at the end of July. A perfect time to visit Zoe, to lock her in for the gala, to kill two birds with one stone. Her insides began to tingle.

The telephone rang. Danny finished refilling her glass before he answered it.

She drank too quickly. God, why was she thinking about the damn gala? *Danny found him.* Christ, she couldn't believe it. Jay wasn't married. Never married, Danny said. Could it be that he still loved her, that he had loved her all these years, that no other woman could ever measure up to his childhood sweetheart? She took another sip. *Slow down,* she commanded herself. *This means nothing. It doesn't mean he wants to see you. It only means you know where he is.* She stared at the addresses again.

Danny hung up the phone and turned to Alissa. "Would you excuse me a minute? I have to make a call from the bedroom. Private stuff."

"I'd expect nothing less from a private investigator."

He left the room and closed the bedroom door behind him.

She glanced at his briefcase, then looked to the bedroom door. It was firmly closed. Could the call have anything to do with Meg? Alissa could hear his voice on the phone. It was low, indistinct. She slipped from her chair and, keeping her eyes on the bedroom door, bent down and opened the briefcase. She took out the file marked "Meg." She opened the folder. There were a few yellow lined notes, not many. There was a phone number. Beneath that was a newspaper clipping. It was an article about Senator Steven Riley's wife. About the car accident Alissa had heard about.

Her pulse leaped into her throat. Senator Steven Riley? She quickly closed the file, jammed it back into the briefcase, and returned to her chair. Was Senator Steven Riley Meg's lost love? Senator Steven Riley from New York? His party's most rumored about-to-be-presidential candidate? She took another long drink. It all fit. He certainly was in the "public eye." And Meg had said he was married.

And Riley's wife is a drunk, Alissa remembered. Anyone who knew anything knew that.

As she tried to relax in the chair, all Alissa wanted to do was get out of there. Any hopes of getting more information from Danny would be a waste of time. And now Alissa needed to move, she needed to think. For suddenly she was almost as excited about learning that Meg's love might be the golden boy senator with the drunken wife as she was that Danny had at long last found Jay, and that the gala was once again hers.

She shoved the paper with Jay's addresses into her purse and went to the bedroom door. She knocked, then opened it. Danny sat on the bed. He looked up and put his hand over the receiver.

"Gotta go," Alissa whispered.

"Are you sure?" he asked. "I was hoping you'd stick around for a while."

"Sorry," she said. "Next time, okay?" She started to close

the door, then stuck her head back inside. "Oh, and thanks, Danny."

He nodded and she left the room, and the suite, wondering why in the hell he'd hoped she'd stick around. And if he really had meant it.

14

"Well, Zoe, you did it. The part is yours." Tim Danahy leaned back in his office chair, folded his arms across his middle, and smiled as though he'd known all along there was no way Zoe wouldn't get the part of Jan Wexler, super-single-mom of the nineties.

Zoe, however, was speechless. She had done it. She had really done it. "I can understand why you didn't want to tell me this over the phone," she said finally.

"I didn't want to miss seeing that smile on your face. It's still the same, you know. It's a beautiful smile."

Zoe twisted uncomfortably on the chair. She was not used to compliments; it had been too many years. *Better change your attitude, girl,* she said to herself. *You've got the part, and you're gonna be a star again!*

Excitement pumped through her veins. She couldn't wait to tell Marisol. Scott. *And oh, God,* Zoe thought, *I can call that wet-behind-the-ears banker and maybe we can make this work out. Maybe Cedar Bluff will still be mine.*

"Don't you want to know how much?"

How much? Oh. The money. "Okay, Tim. How much?"

He smiled again. "Three hundred thousand."

Zoe nearly jumped from her chair. "Three hundred? You got three hundred? But I thought . . ."

Tim shook his head. "I know I told you less. I didn't want to get your hopes up."

Zoe smiled. "But three hundred thousand?"

Tim laughed. "Would you expect Zoe's agent to settle for less?"

She got up from her chair and walked to the window. Tim's office was on the ground level. There was no magnificent L.A.-smog-coated skyline to view from there, only the pavement and the nonstop string of cars. "I can't believe it," she said quietly. "I really did it."

Tim swiveled in his chair. It squeaked. "*We* did it, my dear."

"Right," she said. "We did it. And thank you, Tim."

"There is one problem, though."

Zoe's heart sank. A problem. Of course there'd be a problem.

"Filming starts in ten days. In New York."

"Ten days?"

He nodded. "This is television, not cinema. You'll find the schedule grueling, and there won't be as many opportunities to make it the best you can, so you'd better be good from the get-go."

Zoe clapped her hands together. "I'll be better than good, Tim. I'll be great. You'll see." She could feel an unfamiliar stiffness creep into her cheeks, into her smile muscles. *Smiling,* Zoe thought. *My God, how long has it been since I've smiled so much?*

Suddenly Tim was by her side. "I think we should celebrate," he said as he put a hand on her shoulder.

Zoe tensed.

"Let's have dinner," he continued. "You pick the restaurant. As long as it's expensive, and maybe romantic."

Zoe pulled away. She smoothed her hair. She bit the edge of a fingernail. "Tim," she said slowly, "I can't. Not tonight."

He stepped forward and rested his hand on her shoulder again. "Not tonight? Or not any night?"

She looked into his eyes. They weren't pleading, but they were hopeful. Tim Danahy had given her her start once, her first big break. Now he had done it again. And again his timing was off. But this time Zoe didn't want to hurt him. This time she was going to be more conscious of other people's feelings, of other people's needs. Especially Tim's. She owed him so much. "It's too soon, Tim. Too soon after William."

He dropped his hand. "Sure, kid. I understand. Another time, right?"

Zoe reached up and kissed his cheek. "It's a date," she said, then quickly asked, "Now, could you leave me alone to make a private phone call?"

His eyebrows raised. "Of course. I'm sure you want to call home."

Zoe nodded without answering.

Tim lumbered from the office and closed the door behind him. Zoe watched him leave, then picked up the phone and dialed the number of First Pacific. She had the part. Now all she needed was to secure the refinancing of Cedar Bluff.

While she waited to be connected to John Burns, she sat down at the squeaky swivel wooden chair behind Tim's desk. The latest issue of *Variety* was spread out across the desktop. She began thumbing through it, knowing that she'd have to start reading it again, she'd have to get a handle on what was happening in Hollywood. She'd have to become visible once more, aggressive. She'd done it once, she could do it again. With or without Eric.

Eric. Why the hell had she thought of him?

"This is John Burns."

She quickly regrouped her thoughts. "Yes, Mr. Burns, this is Zoe Hartmann." She smiled as she heard herself tell him with unwavering confidence that she had landed the part. She could feel his cocky smile through the phone. She wanted to pinch his cheeks and call him Sonny-Boy, then give him a good slap. "I'll be able to give you a hundred thousand against the five," she said. "Then we need to talk about refinancing the balance."

"That would make the balance four hundred thousand," John Burns commented, then paused. "I have an idea," he said. "Would you consider refinancing the entire five hundred thousand?"

His voice had shifted from cocky to condescending. Zoe didn't understand.

"That way you could keep what you're making. It should help your cash flow. I'm sure Cedar Bluff is costly to maintain."

Maintenance. God, Zoe hadn't even considered that. What with nothing much else to do all day, she and Marisol had kept the house going alone, except for the weekly gardener and pool man. Now that she'd be working ...

But why was John Burns suddenly being so cordial?

"Yes," Zoe said hesitantly, "of course, that would be better." She stared down at the phone and wondered if Tim's receptionist was listening in on the line. Or Tim.

"Good. Then I have an idea. I'll draw up some preliminary paperwork. If you could stop by the bank on Friday, say about three o'clock?"

"Three o'clock?"

"Yes. Oh, and by the way, we're having a small reception then in honor of our Grand Reopening. You wouldn't mind helping out First Pacific by having a photo or two taken with the bank officers, would you? As a loyal customer?"

Zoe had to stop herself from laughing out loud. She wondered if they'd have wanted a photo of her if she hadn't landed the role of Jan Wexler. She wondered if they would have repossessed Cedar Bluff. *Hollywood,* she thought. *It'll never change.*

"Of course," she said. "I'd be delighted. I'll see you on Friday." As she hung up the phone Zoe realized he hadn't even mentioned the application he'd given her. Apparently, that would no longer be necessary.

She went into the outer office. Tim was sitting on the corner of the receptionist's desk. The two were talking in low whispers.

"All set," Zoe said. "Thanks."

Tim stood up and straightened his tie. "The contracts should be ready in a couple of days, Zoe. I can run them out to Cedar Bluff if you'd like."

She slung her pocketbook over her shoulder, suspecting that beneath Tim's gesture to be "helpful" was really his intent to be more. "I have to come back into town Friday," she said. "It would be easier if I stopped by here." This was all happening quickly, so quickly. She was excited, she was confused, and she was scared. It would be easy to have Tim Danahy move in on her life to sort things out, to take over the finances the way William had done. She wondered if Tim would make such a mess of things. Probably not. But as she stepped into the parking lot and looked back at the crumbling office building that had been crumbling for the twenty years she'd seen it, she wondered if she'd be better off simply to stand tall, buck up, and figure things out for herself.

The drive home to Cedar Bluff was the nicest Zoe remembered in a long time. Years, maybe. She stopped at her favorite Thai restaurant and picked up chicken-fried rice, spring rolls, and steamed dumplings: a special dinner treat for Scott and Marisol, a fun celebration to tell them the news, a great way for Scott to start off his summer vacation. She hoped he wouldn't be too disappointed when he learned she'd soon be leaving for location in New York.

As she wove her car up the canyon road, Zoe looked up into the clear mid-June sky. *Even the weather is perfect today,* she thought. *Life, after all, may be good.* Then she laughed, confident in the knowledge that even if it had been raining, even if the smog had been so thick it blanketed the area, it wouldn't have mattered. Today was turning into a perfect day, and nothing could ruin it. She didn't need to worry about Cedar Bluff or First Pacific or Tim Danahy. For Zoe was back. And Zoe was going to make it.

She wheeled into the long driveway, then quickly braked when she saw an unfamiliar car parked there. She pulled to the left of it, wondering whose it was. Perhaps a workman Marisol had called. Perhaps the parent of one of Scott's school friends, dropping off the boy for the afternoon. It would be nice if Scott felt he could now have his friends come to visit. Zoe's years of self-exile had virtually sequestered him as much as it had herself. She hadn't wanted Scott to bring his friends home to run through the house, blast stereos, or ogle Zoe. Now she'd welcome the commotion. She turned off the engine and grabbed the bags of food. She hoped there'd be enough for company.

As Zoe crossed the back lawn toward the house, she heard the distinct sound of a basketball bouncing on pavement. It reminded her how long it had been since William had taken the time to play basketball with Scott. He'd been too busy working, too busy, Zoe now knew, trying to hold everything together. But things would be different now. They would begin to lead a normal life. Finally.

She sighed and turned the corner toward the basketball court. Scott was aiming for a long shot; a man moved quickly, blocking him, his back to Zoe. A slow, sick feeling rose in her stomach. Scott threw the ball. The man raced down the court. When he turned, Zoe saw his face clearly.

Eric.

She dropped the bags of food. White cardboard containers split open, and fried rice spilled out onto the ground.

He looked at her. He stopped running.

Zoe was frozen in place.

"Hey, Mom!" Scott called, running toward her, wiping sweat from his neck. "We've got a visitor! He's an old friend of yours...."

"I know who he is," Zoe said, without taking her eyes from Eric. "Where's Marisol?"

Scott shrugged. "Shopping I guess. Hey, is that dinner? Or should I say, was it?"

"Scott," she said firmly, "get in the house."

"Huh?"

"I said get in the house. Now."

"Geez, Mom ..." He looked from Zoe to Eric, then back to Zoe. Then he stooped to the mess on the ground.

"Leave it alone," Zoe said. "I'll get it later."

"Well, I could clean it up...."

"Scott. In the house."

"Geez," he muttered as he headed toward the house.

"You still hang around with Marisol?" Eric asked, scuffing his feet on the ground, his eyes averted from Zoe.

Zoe clenched her fists at her sides. "What the hell are you doing here?"

"Come on, Zoe, I was nicer to you than that when you barged into my life unexpectedly."

She took a deep breath. "What the hell are you doing here?"

He picked up the ball, bounced it twice, then pretended to aim at the basket. "Just stopped by to play a little hoop with my son."

Pain gripped Zoe's stomach. She clutched it, pressed against it. It didn't subside.

Eric kept his eyes on the basket. "He is my son, isn't he, Zoe?"

She stared at him.

He released the ball. It missed the backboard by a foot. "I can't believe you never told me. Christ. He looks just like me. More than my own kids. But, then, he is my own, isn't he?"

She tried to take in a breath of the cool, clear air. But it seemed too thick now, too heavy. The pain in her stomach increased. "Eric ..." was all she could say.

"Is this why you came to find me, Zoe? Were you planning to tell me?"

"I ... no ..."

He started pacing in front of her. "Who else knows? Marisol? What about your husband? Did he know?"

Zoe couldn't speak.

He stopped and turned sharply toward her again. "And what about him? Scott? Does he know?"

She started trembling. "No," she whispered.

He pushed his face close to hers. "When were you planning to tell him? Next year? The year after? Never?"

Tears spilled down her cheeks. "Get out of my house," she said, but her voice cracked, her words sounded broken, syllables snapped by the whip of pain.

He made a sweeping gesture with one arm. "It is quite a house, isn't it? At least you've raised my kid in style." He paced again and shook his head. "More than I could have given him," he muttered. "But I guess you knew that all along."

Zoe still couldn't move, as though there were lead in her legs and quicksand sucking at her feet.

He turned to her suddenly. Tears covered his eyes. Angry tears. Hurting tears. "Why didn't you tell me, Zoe? Were you afraid for your fucking career? Were you afraid of a scandal? Well, you seem to have forgotten one thing. He is my boy. And I want him to know it. I want you to tell him." He turned away again and shoved his hands into the pockets of his jeans. "You tell him, or I'll show you a scandal like you've never seen before."

Scott stepped from the side of the house. "You don't have to tell me anything, Mom. I heard the whole thing."

Zoe bent over and retched, heaving foul bile onto the ground, all over the spilled Chinese food.

Eric didn't move.

Zoe looked up. Scott stared at her. Then he turned and fled down the wooded path toward the cliffs, toward the pool, where he always went to be alone, his safe place, his haven.

She staggered, then stood. "You bastard," she seethed. "You rotten bastard."

She started to take off after Scott, but Eric put out his arm and stopped her.

"You wanted me to know, didn't you, Zoe?"

"Let go of me, you bastard."

He gripped her arm more firmly. "You wanted me to know. That's why you didn't lie about his age. You could have said he was ten. Or twelve. But fourteen, Zoe? Why did you want me to know now? Why? After all this time?"

Zoe looked into his watery eyes. Eric was right. She had wanted him to know about Scott. She had wanted him to suffer, she had wanted him to feel remorse, hurt, pain. Had she really wanted just to see her first love? And once she found him, had she really wanted to thank him? No, Zoe knew now. Never. She had wanted to find him because she really had wanted revenge. She had wanted to watch him squirm. She had wanted to see him hurt.

"Why did you want me to know?" he asked again, his voice lower, his pain exposed.

She spit in his face. "Because I hate you, you bastard," she screamed. "All the years I suffered—it was your fault, all your fault. You left me. I almost died when your son was born. For two years I couldn't even hold him—my own baby. I was too sick. I couldn't hold him or feed him or love him. And where were you? You were nowhere. You left me, you bastard. You left me."

She broke free from his grasp and ran down the wooded path, tripping, stumbling, crying. She climbed down the jagged rocks, praying Scott was all right, praying he wouldn't hate her. Sharp edges tore at her legs, blood stained her flesh. At the base of the cliff was Scott. He sat by the edge of the pool, his face buried in his hands.

She went up behind him and put her arms around him. "Scottie," she whispered. "Oh, God, will you ever forgive me?"

He wrenched himself free. "Then it's true, Mom? That man . . . that man is. . . ?"

"That man is not your father," she said. "He could never be your father. William was." She tried to reach out, tried to touch him. But her hand fell short as though she didn't have the right. "It was William who raised you and took care of you and played ball with you, not that man. William was your father."

"But—?"

"Genetics means nothing. It's love that matters. William loved you."

"Mother, that man—Eric—he said he didn't even know about me!"

Zoe encircled her arms around her waist and rocked back and forth. Her tears would not stop. "No," she said quietly. "No, he didn't."

Scott dived into the pool.

Dear God, Zoe thought, *what have I done? If I had never tried to be an actress again, if I had never gone to that damned spa ...*

But Zoe knew that wasn't fair. It wasn't fair to blame Alissa and Meg for what she had done. Sooner or later Zoe knew she would have gone to find Eric. He was too much an unfinished piece of her life, a piece of which she was painfully reminded with every day that passed, with every bit that Scott grew to look more and more like him. She had needed the closure. Alissa and Meg had merely given her the strength.

As she watched her son slice through the water, Zoe wondered if things between them could ever be the same again.

The next ten days dragged by. Scott barely spoke to Zoe; he spent most of the days by the pool alone. Each time she tried to approach him, he pulled away, into his cavern of pain.

"Give it time," Marisol said. "He'll come around."

Zoe conceded and hoped that by the time she returned from filming in New York, Scott would have forgiven her. But something deep inside her warned Zoe that might not be possible.

She sat in her Manhattan hotel room now, waiting for Meg Cooper to arrive. They had been shooting for three days, and it had taken Zoe that long to feel as though she wanted to call Meg, as though she could handle the news of Meg's happy reunion with her first and, according to Meg, only love.

She stared at the muted litho of a Parisian café that hung on the otherwise barren ocher wall and pondered her future. The filming was not going well. What should have been an exhilarating experience, a rebirth of confidence, had turned into a chore. Zoe knew she was preoccupied, with too much time between takes to think about Scott, think about Eric. She tried not to let it show; she tried to get into character, to develop Jan Wexler into a sympathetic, heartwrenching woman. But staying focused until the end of each scene had become painful, and relief flooded through her every time Zoe heard Cal Baker shout *"Cut!"*

Room service had delivered a bottle of wine and two chef salads. Fortunately, the steamy heat in the city combined with her misery had kept Zoe's appetite in check, for she knew the last thing she needed was to succumb to a Twinkie. In her current dark mood one Twinkie could quickly lead to a dozen.

She gazed out her window at the gray buildings, at the murky sky. She wondered if Meg did, indeed, have happy news to deliver ... she wondered if Meg knew if Alissa had found Jay Stockwell.

There was a knock on the door. Zoe brushed a single tear from her eye: it wasn't until then that she realized she'd been crying. She pressed her hands to her temples and breathed in deeply. Then she smoothed her long robe, padded across the carpet in her bare feet, and opened the door.

Meg was dressed in a straight beige dress that hung loosely from her too-thin frame. Her auburn hair was pulled back from her face; her cheeks were pale and sunken. Zoe was startled. This did not look like a woman who was blissfully in love. Something was wrong. Something was very, very wrong. Zoe quickly smiled.

"Meg!" she exclaimed as she hugged her. "It's so good to

see you." She felt, but did not comment on, the bones that jutted from Meg's spine.

Meg pulled back. "My God, Zoe, let me look at you. You look positively fantastic."

Zoe laughed. "That's right. You haven't seen the 'new me,' have you? Well, come on in. I ordered salads for dinner. You wouldn't believe how hard it is to stay thin for this damn movie."

"And you love every minute of it," Meg said as she followed Zoe into the room.

Zoe didn't reply.

They sat in the chairs by the window and talked about nothing important through the first glass of wine. The spa. Alissa. The relentless hot weather. Finally it seemed there was only one subject left to cover.

"Well," she began slowly, "do you feel like talking about your reunion?"

Meg ran her finger around the rim of her glass. "For one night it was wonderful," she said. "I guess that was all I deserved. Maybe it was more than I deserved."

Zoe carefully set down her glass. Clearly, Meg's pain was as deep as her own. Clearly, her regret was as great. "What happened?"

Meg shook her head. "Nothing, really. I guess he changed his mind."

Zoe could almost feel her heart break for her friend. Was there any worse pain than that of unrequited love? Unrequited love. She had played that role many times, in many movies. She remembered when Eric had "changed his mind." It was a pain you never forgot, not after you denied the hurt, not after you passed through the anger, not even, she knew now, after you learned to hate. It remained with you always, smoldering beneath the surface, aching at will, a mind all its own. "Do you think he still loves you?" she asked quietly.

Meg closed her eyes, then opened them slowly. But her gaze was distant, self-protective. "It seemed that way," she said. "I guess I was wrong. Maybe it would have been better to have kept the dreams intact. Maybe dreams are better than the real thing."

Zoe knew that Meg's dreams had lasted as long as her own, lingering for years in the background, sometimes flickering, sometimes languishing, but never completely disappearing. She put her hand across Meg's. "Oh, Meg, I'm so sorry."

"Yeah," Meg whispered, "me, too." She stared at Zoe's hand a moment, then raised her head and said, "What about you? Tell me about Minnesota."

Zoe picked up her fork and stabbed a tomato wedge, the way she would like to stab Eric, the way he had stabbed her heart. "I'm afraid my reunion, too, was a mistake. One I'll be paying for the rest of my life."

"Oh, Zoe."

Zoe set down her fork and stared into her salad. Suddenly the reality of the last few weeks rushed at her. It had finally happened: all the years of secrets, all the years of lies, had exploded as quickly as a power load of dynamite in a canyon. Exploded, leaving only the craggy, sharp edges of truth.

"Eric figured out that he is my son's father." Zoe looked up at Meg, half expecting to see shock, to see judgment. But Meg's soft eyes only looked sad.

And then Zoe began. She slowly recounted the story she had told Meg and Alissa at the spa—the story of her early years with Eric, their escape to Hollywood, her marriage, her stroke, and her seclusion from the rest of the world. But this time she told Meg about her pregnancy, and that Eric was Scott's father. Then she told her about visiting Eric, about Eric's surprise visit to L.A., and about Scott's withdrawal from Zoe.

"And now here I am, making a comeback. With one half of my life finally coming together again, and the other half completely falling apart."

They sat quietly for a moment. Zoe was surprised she wasn't crying. She felt, instead, numb. Anesthetized. Dead.

"I think we've both learned a major lesson," Meg said. "That the past is better off left alone."

Slowly, Zoe nodded.

As Zoe lay in bed later that night, she admitted to herself that Meg's visit actually had made her feel better. "Misery loves company" was a gruesome thought, but it was the best Zoe could come up with. The big difference was, Meg could walk away from her reunion and the hurt would ease in time. But Zoe's wound was like an abscess: the surface would heal over with superficial skin, but underneath the infection would lie in wait, festering, building, with the constant reminder that Scott had found out the truth about his real father, and that he had found it out the wrong way. And when the pressure became too forceful, too intense, the boil would burst open, poisoning everyone around it again. All because Zoe hadn't left well enough alone.

When the telephone rang, it took Zoe a moment to recognize the eerie, digitized sound. She rolled on her side, reached up, and snapped on the lamp by her bedside. As she grabbed the receiver, she glanced at the clock. Twelve-twenty.

It was Marisol.

"Good God, Marisol, do you know what time it is here?"

"We've got a problem, Zoe."

She sat up in bed. "Scott?"

"He's not hurt or anything," her friend said quickly. "But, girl, he's run away."

Pain seared her heart. She drew her knees to her chest and tried to press it away. "Run away? Oh, God, Marisol, I should have known something like this would happen." She struggled to catch her breath as though Marisol's words had tramped on her lungs and squeezed the air from them. "How long has he been gone? Have you called his friends' houses? He must be at one...."

"He's not."

"Well, of course he is. He wouldn't run away by himself."

"Apparently he didn't."

An ominous sickness rose inside her. She closed her eyes. The darkness swirled.

"He's gone away," Marisol said in a flat, even tone. "To spend time with Eric."

Zoe screamed and threw the phone across the room. The cord ripped from its socket, the eerie bell jangled in mockery as the phone crashed against the wall and thumped to the floor.

She screamed again, then fell onto the bed, racked with loud, mournful sobs, hurt like an animal stabbed in the heart. Then she started shaking: her hands, her shoulders, her legs. She lay on the bed, trembling, crying.

"No," she said aloud. "No. No. No. No." The look of pain on Scott's face when he learned the truth flashed into her mind. Beside it appeared the pain of Eric's. "No," she said again. "No."

She pulled herself from the bed. She had to call Marisol back. She spotted the phone and jammed the plug into its socket. She held out her hand to try to steady it, then slowly punched each number.

"What happened?" Marisol answered before Zoe heard the phone ring. "Are you okay?"

Zoe cried. She couldn't seem to speak.

"Oh, God," Marisol continued, "I wasn't even going to call you."

Zoe's temples throbbed, her throat remained closed. This wasn't possible. This wasn't happening. She heard Marisol's words as though they were blurred, disjointed.

"He left a note...."

She drew her knees to her chest again and hugged them more tightly, trying to regain control, trying to concentrate on what her friend was saying.

"He doesn't want you to come after him. He said they aren't going to Minnesota."

"Like hell," Zoe heard herself scream. Adrenaline surged

and propelled Zoe from the bed. "I'm going to find him. He's fourteen years old! I'm bringing him home."

"Zoe, that's not a good idea."

"Don't tell me it's not a good idea! He's my son, for chrissake. That bastard has no business with him."

"That 'bastard' is his father."

"Don't be an ass, Marisol."

"Calm down. Before you go taking off anywhere, I want you to sit down and take a few deep breaths. Then I'm going to read you the note."

"Marisol . . ."

"Do what I say. Do it now."

Zoe slumped onto the edge of the bed. "Okay, I'm sitting. Read it."

"Take those deep breaths."

She closed her eyes and tried to suck in a long breath. The air quivered around her pain. She tried again. Slowly, her trembling lessened. She opened her eyes. "Read it."

Marisol paused a moment. "Okay," she finally said. "He says, 'I want to get to know my real father. I think I deserve it.'"

Zoe felt the trembling return.

"'Don't worry about me. I'll be fine. He says we can stay together as long as I like.'"

She bit back her tears as Marisol continued reading.

"'Don't try to come after me, Mom.'"

Zoe could stand it no longer. "Don't try to come after him? Is he crazy? Of course I'm going after him. And I'm calling the police. This is kidnapping, Marisol. That bastard has my son, and I'm going to see to it he pays." Her words spilled out and scattered like nonpareils on a hardwood floor. "He didn't go of his own accord, you can be sure of that. Eric probably forced him to write that note. Scott would never do this, never. . . ."

"He wrote the note, Zoe. And Eric wasn't even here. I found an envelope addressed to Scottie in the wastebasket. It was postmarked Minnesota. Eric must have mailed him a ticket."

Her jaw tensed. "To where?"

"Don't know. And there's something else," Marisol said quietly.

Zoe wanted to laugh, a low, primal laugh that would rid her gut of the guilt, of the fear.

"Scottie also says here that if you try to find him, he'll call the newspaper and tell them who he is, and who his father really is."

She no longer wanted to laugh. Now Zoe wanted to die. She reached up and turned off the lamp. "I don't care what he's threatened. I've got to find my son." She hugged her knees again and rocked back and forth.

"You're forgetting one thing, Zoe," Marisol said quietly. "Eric's not a villain. He's mad as hell. But Scottie's his son, too. And you can hate me for saying this, but as long as everything's out in the open now, maybe Scottie's right. Maybe he deserves to know his real father."

Zoe squeezed her arms around herself. "Fuck him," was all she said.

"Cut!"

Zoe glared at Cal Baker and stormed off the makeshift set on the West Side docks. She knew she had screwed up. For about the tenth time this morning she had forgotten her lines. She crossed the pier and marched into the motor home that served as her dressing room. She flung herself onto the sofa. How was she supposed to be a supermom of the nineties when she didn't even know where her own son was? Or if she would ever see him again? *The show must go on. . . . Well,* Zoe thought, *maybe it's been too long.* Maybe she was simply too old to focus when her own son's future was at stake.

The heavy door to the trailer opened. Cal Baker stepped inside. "What's your problem, Zoe?"

She turned away so he wouldn't see her tears. "Nothing, Cal. Just a bad morning."

She heard his heavy boots plod across the pink carpet. He sat down facing her. He wore jeans and a blue T-shirt that read "I'm the Boss, That's Why." The tan that coated his brow pulled white-lined wrinkles together as he scowled. "You walked off my set," he said. "Nobody walks off my set."

She rose from the sofa and walked to the mirror. Her lack of sleep and tearful night were painted on her eyes: they were bloodshot specks, capped with swollen lids and bearded by dark circles. She ran her fingers across them, then down to her mouth. The left side of her lip drooped, the way it always did when she was tired, the way it always had since the stroke, the stroke that had been Eric's fault.

She turned back to the director. "I'm having some personal problems. I just need a few minutes to collect myself."

"We're on a deadline, Zoe. Every minute costs money."

She nodded. "I know that. Please, Cal, I'm doing the best I can."

He stood and headed for the door. "I took a chance when I hired you. If you really want this career of yours back, you'd better keep that in mind." He put his hand on the knob and opened the door. "Don't disappoint me, Zoe," he said, and went out the door.

Zoe clutched her hand to her stomach. She stared at the door as it closed after him, as it closed, perhaps, on the rest of her life. *Maybe this whole thing has been a mistake,* she thought. She still didn't even know if she was any longer good at acting; she didn't even know if she still liked it. For the past few days she had merely been going through the motions.

She looked through the jalousied windows, out at the set. It was a scene on the docks in which Jan Wexler, alone, confronts the gang who is trying to recruit her son.

Her son.
Scott.

Zoe watched the other actors, the grips, the extras, mill around the pier, waiting for her to emerge, waiting for the next take. And then one painful thought crossed her mind: was any job, was any career, worth losing her son?

She turned from the window and went to the phone. In less than a minute she had Meg on the line.

"I need your help," Zoe pleaded. "I have to get off this film. I have to get out of my contract."

They agreed that Zoe would have her agent fax a copy of the contract to Meg; that Meg would meet Zoe on the set as soon as she reviewed it.

"Until then," Meg warned her, "do what you're supposed to do."

Zoe hung up and chewed on a fingernail. Then she took a deep breath, checked her makeup, and returned to the lights, camera, action of the world that, so many years ago, had seemed so right.

The rest of the morning was endless. The sun simmered over the bay and boiled off the pavement of the pier. More than once Zoe felt as though she were going to faint. Nerves were frayed. Faces were tense. The child playing Jan Wexler's youngest threw up; the next to the oldest had a tantrum. Zoe forgot her lines four more times.

During the lunch break Zoe walked to the end of the pier, holding a cool cloth to the back of her neck. She thought about Cedar Bluff. She wondered how Scott would feel if she had to sell the house; she wondered where he was right now, this minute, in what city, what state. She wondered if he would ever come home.

"Zoe?" It was Meg's voice.

"Meg. Thank God you're here."

Meg wiped her forehead. She looked even more drawn, more distressed than she had the night before.

"How can you stand this heat?" she asked.

Zoe shrugged. "That's show biz. Now tell me, what have we got?"

Meg pulled some papers from her briefcase. "What we have here is sealed in stone. If you walk off the set, you'll breach the contract. You'll not only lose your salary but stand to be sued for more than what you're getting paid."

The air grew heavier, hotter. "Is that legal?"

"They probably figure the more they're paying you, the more difficult you'll be to replace. There's an escalating clause, too, which simply means the longer you've been in production, the more they can sue you for."

Zoe leaned against the railing and looked across the Hudson toward the New Jersey skyline. Who was to say that the pressures of tenement life in a gang-riddled city were any worse than those in a two-million-dollar home in a glamorous town? Didn't people simply make a lot of their own pressures themselves? She blinked against the sun, the heat, the dense blanket of haze. "What am I going to do, Meg? I can't afford to make my mortgage payment. How can I risk being sued?"

"You can't. Besides, you're just getting started again, Zoe. If you walk out of here, you'll be jeopardizing your future."

Zoe watched a Circle Line tour boat churn through the gray water. She thought about the tourists on board. Were their lives as complicated as hers?

"Oh, God," she cried. "I can't go through this. I can't take any more." Tears ran down her cheeks, streaking her makeup with stripes of grief.

Meg's arm wrapped around her. "Zoe, what is it? What's happened?"

"It's Scott," Zoe sobbed. "My son has run away." She wiped her eyes and looked up at the sky. "He's gone with Eric. He's run away with his father."

"Oh, Zoe."

"I've got to get him back, Meg."

"Of course. Of course you do," Meg began pacing. "Do you think they're in Minnesota?"

"Maybe. Who knows?"

"We can find out."

"How? Call Eric's house and ask for Scott?" Zoe closed her eyes again. This was so hopeless, she was so helpless.

"No. Remember me mentioning my friend Danny? The private investigator?"

Zoe laughed. "I could probably afford to be sued before I could afford to hire a private investigator."

"I said he's a friend. He'll do this as a favor."

"There will be expenses."

"I'll take care of it."

Zoe cast her a doubtful glance.

"You can pay me back when you're a star again."

Zoe felt the tears well again. "If."

"Okay. If."

"But even if Danny finds Scott, Scott won't listen to a stranger."

"Danny's a pro. He'll know how to handle it."

"Scott will be upset."

"Do you trust me, Zoe?"

Zoe looked across the river once more, at the boats crawling over the calm, soothing water. "I never would have told you everything if I didn't."

"Good. Because I trust Danny. And I know he'll do anything for me—or for a friend of mine."

"And no one will find out?"

Meg shook her head. "Discretion is Danny's middle name."

But discretion or no discretion, Zoe feared that Meg's friend would never find Scott. And she feared that once again—because of Eric Matthews—she had blown her chance at what could have been a wonderful new life.

15

Later that afternoon Meg sat in the visitors' room at the city lockup and listened to the whining excuses of her new client, a woman charged with accessory to murder, whose live-in boyfriend, an Austrian with more titles than money, had been indicted for first-degree murder of his wealthy business partner. The prosecution claimed he'd told the woman about the crime. George Bascomb was defending the Austrian; he reluctantly turned the woman's case over to Meg after Arnold Banks stormed into the office demanding another attorney on the day Meg learned about Candace Riley's accident.

"I swear, he didn't tell me anything." The overdressed woman pouted now. "He would have if he'd killed him, but he didn't. We're both innocent."

"The only person we have to worry about is you," Meg said dryly. Although George maintained the prosecution had little evidence against the Austrian, Meg knew that if his client went down, so would hers. She had to try to keep the two cases separate, if there was any hope at all for her client.

"Can't you get me out of here?" the woman pleaded.

"The bail hearing is scheduled for ten o'clock tomorrow morning."

"Do you mean I have to spend the night here?" She glared at Meg as though this injustice were her fault.

"Afraid so." Meg tried to sound professional but was increasingly aware of her weariness. Weariness over people who took it for granted that things should work the way they wanted. Weariness over spoiled, indulged, always-have-everything-handed-to-them people, the Holly Davidsons of the world, the Arnold Bankses. They were phony and empty and she hated that she had filled her life with them. She stared at the cinder-block wall. "I take it making bail won't be a problem."

The woman shook her head. As Meg suspected, she must be loaded, or she and her boyfriend could not have retained Larson, Bascomb, Smith, Rheinhold, Paxton, and Cooper.

"I'll be here for you at nine forty-five," Meg said. As she stood, the metal chair scraped against the tile floor. She looked into the woman's eyes, searching for sincerity. The woman blinked and looked away. Meg realized now that it had taken seeing Steven again to admit what she'd done with her life, that for years she had been helping people she didn't even know, let alone like. This woman, Meg knew, would be no different.

As she walked down the corridor of the jail, Meg thought about Zoe. Other than Danny, Zoe was the first real friend Meg felt she'd ever had. And it was Zoe—not this whining, spoiled woman—who deserved help now. Maybe she could help by doing more than simply putting Danny on the case. Maybe she could start over, begin a new life for herself. Maybe she could finally do what she'd really wanted—be useful to someone, someone she cared about. Maybe she could finally do something that mattered.

She glanced at her watch. It was two-fifteen. There might still be time to catch Danny having lunch at Schneider's.

Outside, Meg hailed a cab for the ride across town.

She looked out the dirty window at the nameless people scurrying along the sidewalks. For the first time in years Meg felt she had a purpose beyond the drama of the courtroom and the size of her salary. Helping Zoe could make her feel alive again; helping Zoe could take her mind off Steven, and off the fact that he still hadn't called. She'd mustered the courage to read the paper one morning: Candace's condition had been upgraded from critical to fair, and she was being charged on a variety of counts: driving under the influence, driving to endanger, one count of vehicular homicide. No one at the office had mentioned whether Larson, Bascomb had been contacted to represent her. Meg suspected that if they hadn't been, it was because Steven deemed it inappropriate. *God,* she thought, as her eyes skimmed over a street vendor with his wares spread across a blanket on the sidewalk, *wouldn't George Bascomb be pissed if he knew that she was the reason they wouldn't get the case?*

Zoe, she thought. *I must think of Zoe.* Meg tried to characterize her the way she would a potential client, in terms of individual traits and circumstances, rather than as a person, a human being with feelings, a friend. Zoe. Recently widowed, struggling mother of a fourteen-year-old boy, trying to rekindle a career. She focused on the boy. Scott. A boy who had just learned the man he thought was his father, wasn't.

As the cab careened across Fifth Avenue, Meg thought about the child she didn't have. Steven's child. Would it have been a boy? If there had been no abortion, he would have been a little older than Scott. At least Zoe hadn't been a coward. She'd had her baby, even without his real father around. What had given her that strength? Had Zoe loved Eric more than Meg had loved Steven? Meg never would have thought that was possible. And yet Zoe went through with the pregnancy, Zoe kept her son, raised him. Why hadn't Meg been capable of that? Why hadn't she been able to make that choice?

The cab squealed to a stop in front of Schneider's. Meg spotted Danny emerging from the deli, heading in the opposite direction. She thrust a ten-dollar bill in the cabbie's hand and leaped from the cab without waiting for her change.

"Danny!"

He turned. "Yo, counselor!" he said, strolling back to meet her. "If it's a free lunch you want, you're a little late." He reached her and stopped. His eyes roamed over her. "Although it sure as hell looks like you could use some nourishment."

"I need your help."

"Christ, Meg, don't you ever slow down? One of these days I'd just like to hear you say 'screw it.'"

"I need to talk to you, Danny. Now."

"Ah, straight to the point." He took her elbow. "Walk with me, then. I've got a meeting with your boss."

Meg folded her arms across her waist and fell into stride beside Danny. She liked to walk next to him, his hand lightly, protectively, touching her, guiding her through the wavering crowd that seemed to forever fill the midtown streets. She checked her watch. "I haven't much time."

"We'll walk fast," he said, picking up the pace.

She kept her eyes fixed ahead, not looking, never looking, into the eyes of oncoming pedestrians. "I have a friend...," she began slowly.

Danny stopped. Two men behind him collided into his back, then grunted and quickly moved on. Danny shook his head. "You have a friend," he groaned as he resumed walking. "Please. Not another one."

Meg laughed. "This one is different."

"So is Alissa Page. Different."

"That's not what I mean. This one can't pay you."

He stuffed his hands into the pockets of his jeans and smiled. "Something tells me I'm going to regret this walk."

"I doubt it," Meg said. They stopped at the red light on Madison. "You don't know her name yet."

"Oh. Someone with a name. A Larson, Bascomb holdover?"

Meg shook her head. "Remember that day at my place when I told you about the plan I agreed to with Alissa? There was another woman involved. A third woman."

"Yeah, I think you mentioned that."

"I need you to help that third woman, Danny."

"I'm not in the business of finding old lovers, Meg. In this case one was definitely enough."

A yellow cab squealed around the corner. The light turned green. Meg and Danny stepped off the curb.

"It's not her old lover who's missing," Meg shouted against the sound of the traffic. "It's her fourteen-year-old son."

Danny's eyebrows raised. "So why me? Why doesn't your friend call *Unsolved Mysteries*?"

"She can't. She's too well-known." They finished crossing the street in silence.

"Okay," Danny said as they reached the next curb. "I give up. Who is this mystery friend of yours, and how many more do you have in your private little closet?"

Meg tossed back her hair and tried not to reveal that he'd struck a nerve, that he'd reminded her about Steven. Steven. *Push it away. Push it down. He's gone. End of story.*

"She's the last," Meg said. "That's a promise. And I think you'll like her. She's not like Alissa...."

"Praise be to God."

"... Her name is Zoe."

"Zoe who?"

Meg smiled. "Just Zoe."

Danny stopped again, then so did Meg. A woman bumped her pocketbook into Meg's side, then muttered something in what sounded like Yiddish. Danny rolled his eyes. "Holy shit, Meg. You don't mean Zoe, as in *the* Zoe?"

Meg smiled and started walking again.

"Holy shit," Danny repeated, trotting to catch up to her. "You said her name before. That day at your place. But, shit, I had no idea you meant *Zoe*."

"She's only a person, Danny. A really nice person." As they turned onto Park Avenue, Meg told him about Eric, about Scott. About the fact that Scott had run away to be with his father. "I need you to track them down," Meg said.

Danny nodded. "Give me a couple more days. The insider case is almost wrapped up."

"Good. That'll be better for me, too."

"For you?"

"Yeah," Meg said. "I'm going with you."

"What about work?"

Meg smiled and looked up at the entrance to the Larson, Bascomb building. "Screw it," she said.

The next morning Meg convinced the judge to lower her client's bail to fifty thousand, not that it mattered, because the woman could have afforded much more. But it was all part of the game of "beat the government," to show them you were the one in control. She'd be glad when the game was over. Winner take all.

As she went from the courtroom to the office, Meg knew what she had to do. She had to meet with the partners; she was finally going to do something for someone other than herself. She wanted to, she needed to. She had to make something right for a friend, no matter the consequences to herself.

God, having a friend felt good.

They were seated around the conference table, formally reviewing the status of the cases in the house. It didn't escape Meg that they hadn't delayed the meeting until her arrival.

She took a chair and waited until George acknowledged her. "How did the bail hearing go, Meg?"

"Fine. Bail was reduced to fifty thousand."

George scribbled a note on his legal pad. "We'll need to work closely together on this one. Both our clients are innocent."

Ordinarily Meg would have protested his decision to combine the defenses. She would have argued that it wouldn't be fair to her client. But things were different now.

"I won't be working on the case," Meg announced.

All heads turned toward Meg.

George removed his glasses. "Excuse me?"

"I said I won't be working on the case. I'm requesting a leave of absence from the firm."

George flipped the bows of his glasses closed, open, closed. "This is highly irregular. We are overloaded with work...."

Meg sat up straight. "I know. But I've had a personal matter come up. I need some time off."

"How much time?"

"Six months." She said it without blinking. She'd decided that a six-month leave would do more than enable her to find Zoe's son; it would give her time to reassess her life, to rebuild her emotional strength and find the way to start over again, this time the right way.

"A six-month leave? Why not a year? Why not two?" George fired each question at a higher pitch.

"Why not permanently?" came a snicker from the other side of the table.

Meg ignored it.

George returned his glasses to his round, scowling face. "Perhaps we could manage six months. After this case is completed."

"That's not what I had in mind."

"It will go to trial in three or four months."

"I know that. But I plan to leave tomorrow."

The room was swallowed by silence.

"We need you to finish this case, Meg."

She shifted on the imported Italian-leather chair. "I know. I also know you only gave it to me because everyone else was busy."

George sighed. "That's not entirely true."

Meg stood up. "Nothing has been the same around here since Avery died. I know we all haven't always gotten along, and I didn't always agree with Avery. But I do my job, and I do it well. Right now, however, I'd like your indulgence. But if you aren't willing to give me the six months' leave, then I'll have to request a permanent separation. Including my five percent share of the profits."

The partners stared at her.

"I would appreciate your decision by the end of the day," Meg continued. "Until then I'll be in my office cleaning out my desk." She left the room with a euphoric headiness, a catharsis of freedom she hadn't known since the day she moved into her own apartment alone. But this time Meg wasn't going to allow her independence to thrust her into a vortex, into a world that grew smaller and smaller until it was so small, so safe, that no one could enter, no one could escape. She walked toward her office with her chin held high. This time she was going to take the risk. This time, Meg was going to live.

Once at her desk, the first thing Meg did was make two one-way reservations on an early-morning flight to Minneapolis. No sense in planning the return trip: there was a chance Eric and Scott weren't there, and she and Danny would have to fly somewhere else from Minnesota.

She was going through her desk, removing personal things, when she heard a knock on the door. *That didn't take long,* Meg thought. *The partners must be unusually efficient today.*

She took a deep breath, reassuring herself she had made the right decision. First she was going to help Zoe. Then she was going to make some much-needed decisions about her career, her life.

"Come in."

The door opened. Meg glanced up from her work, trying to appear nonchalant. But in the doorway stood neither George Bascomb nor any of the partners. In the doorway stood Steven Riley.

She wasn't certain if her gasp was audible.

He stepped inside and closed the door behind him.

Meg simply stared.

"You're busy," he said. "I should have called."

Steven was standing in front of her. Steven. Her reason for wanting to die these last few weeks.

He walked toward her desk slowly, almost as though he were anticipating she would hurl something at him. There was no chance of that: her entire body had gone numb, and Meg couldn't have picked up a piece of paper, never mind anything of substance, anything big enough or heavy enough or sharp enough to hurt him the way he'd hurt her.

"Meg. I'm so sorry."

Still, she couldn't speak.

He walked to the back of the desk and squatted beside her. He picked up her hands and held them. She was amazed they weren't shaking. "Can you ever forgive me?" he asked.

She looked into his eyes. So blue. So loving. She swayed from love to hate to love, from longing to mistrust, from want, from need to pain. Pain. She looked away, down to his tie. It was pale gray and blue and made of fine silk. She wondered if Candace had bought it for him.

She pulled her hands from his and stood up, nearly knocking him to the floor.

"Forgive you for what? For standing me up on an island in the middle of the Atlantic? Or for making me believe you still cared about me in the first place?" She went to the window and looked down to the street below. She didn't dare face him again. She didn't dare look into those eyes. She never would have believed she'd feel so confused about Steven, about her love for him.

He came up behind her. "Meg, you do know what happened, don't you?"

She laughed. "The whole world knows, Steven. And if you've come to ask if we'll handle your wife's case, I think you'd better find yourself another firm. You see, there could be a small matter of conflict of interest."

"I didn't come here for that." He put his hands on her shoulders. Strong hands. Protective. Comforting. She shook them off and went to the bookcase.

"Then why did you come here? To examine the remnants of what you did to me?" She wished he would leave, wished he'd never come there at all. Not now. Not now that she'd made a decision to change her life, to put the past behind her once and for all, to finally start living. She probably should thank him for that. She squeezed her eyes shut. She didn't think she could stand any more pain.

"Meg," he said calmly. "Please try to understand. I didn't want you to be involved. I didn't want to risk your career...."

"Is that all that matters? Careers? Yours? Now mine? No, Steven, that's not what matters. Life is what's important. Living. I can't believe it's taken me all these years to figure that out."

She stared at the leather spines of the books, aware of his breathing, aware of the heaviness of his presence. Aware of the fact that she wanted nothing more than to run to him, throw her arms around him, and forgive him. To tell him she loved him.

"Candace is going to be fine," he said.

Her spine stiffened.

"Unlike the man she killed," Meg blurted out, then wished she hadn't. Sarcasm wasn't her style. Inflicting misery was something she'd never been comfortable with. "Sorry," she added quietly, "that was uncalled for."

"It was called for. Candace has a serious drinking problem. Perhaps she has finally learned her lesson."

"And the two of you can live happily ever after?"

He crossed the room and stood beside her. This time Steven didn't attempt to touch her. "As soon as she's out of the hospital, I'm telling her I want a divorce." There was a catch in his voice. Meg thought if she looked at him, she would see tears. She remembered the unhappiness Steven once told her he'd endured as a child, as the brilliant little boy whose father demanded perfection. There had been varsity football—Steven was the quarterback, of course—then Yale Law School, a political career that saw only victories, and marriage to the daughter of someone who "mattered." Steven had said he'd never thought much about what he wanted: his father gave him no choices, no options. He'd said he'd never thought much about what he wanted, until he fell in love with her. She squeezed her eyes tightly again.

"Divorce won't bode too well with the voters, Steven. A man deserting his wife in her hour of need."

Steven ignored her comment. "I should have done it years ago. I should have done it back in Boston, when I still had you. I should have just done it, then told you after."

Yes, Meg thought, *you should have. You could have. You would have, if you had known about the baby. Our baby. Instead, I was the one who made the decision. The wrong decision.* God, she had made so many wrong decisions.

"I don't know what you want to do, Meg." His tone was quiet, somber. "Whether you come back to me or not is your decision. But no matter what, I'm divorcing Candace."

Meg heard the words and tried to let them sink in. But they seemed to hang somewhere in the space between the two of them and vanish before reaching her brain.

Steven laughed. "The funny thing is that Candace has always felt as stuck with me as I did with her. If we had stayed together all these years for the sake of the kids, that would have been one thing. An understandable, even commendable thing in some opinions. But no. We stayed together for the sake of the party. The party her father runs so well. If we hadn't stayed together, Candace probably wouldn't have resorted to gin. Maybe that man would still be alive. In a sense, I'm as responsible for his death as she is."

"I'm sure there was more to your marriage than politics," Meg said with dry, choking words.

"There wasn't. The night of her accident Candace wasn't alone. She was with another man. It wasn't the first time."

So. The media didn't always find out everything, after all.

Meg turned and faced him. "And what about you, Steven? Was the night we were together the first time you cheated on her?"

He sifted his fingers through his hair. "You probably won't believe this, but yes. It was. Besides, all these years I felt I was cheating just by being with Candace. I felt I was cheating on you."

She didn't want to believe him, but she did. His eyes told her he was speaking the truth. Solid eyes. Honest eyes. So blue. Meg folded her arms around herself and returned to the window. "Steven, what do you want from me?"

"I want to marry you."

She had asked, and he had said it. She stared out the window to the street below. Park Avenue. Reality. Or was it? Steven's wife was cheating on him, had been cheating on him. A man was dead and Steven's political career was probably finished. Meg didn't know if there was any precedent for a United States senator serving in office while his wife was behind bars.

"I can stay in the city tonight," he said. "I was hoping we could be together."

It was late in the day now, and Meg could see the traffic get thicker, the people on the sidewalks grow in numbers, hurrying more quickly, eager to get home. Meg never walked home quickly. There was no reason to hurry.

She thought about Zoe, spending the night alone in her hotel room, worrying about her son. She thought about her own decision to take a leave from the firm, to try to sort out her life. A prickly sensation inched up her spine. She knew what it was. It was resentment. She resented the fact that Steven had barged in, expecting her to drop everything and be with him. But wasn't this what she'd wanted? She thought about Zoe again, about her pain. *Do any of us ever really get what we want?*

Suddenly everything became so clear. Steven hadn't merely been the reason she'd wanted to die these past few weeks. He'd also been her reason for not really being able to live these many, many years. For so long Meg had blamed herself—her never-born baby, even her long-dead mother. It had been easy to blame her mother; it was always easy to blame mothers. But now Meg knew the truth. Steven—his love, his memory, his absence—was what had crippled her life. Perhaps the reason no man had ever measured up to him was because Meg had never stopped thinking about him ... because she'd been afraid if she stopped thinking about him, he would never come back.

But now, if she was going to go on—if she was truly going to have some sort of real, fulfilling life—she couldn't take the chance of having things continue that way. She might never find the courage to tell him about the abortion—that was her right. But if she never could, if she never could trust enough in Steven's love to tell him, Meg knew she could have no future with him. She also knew the real reason she couldn't tell him: it was the same reason why she'd had the abortion in the first place. Meg was afraid that Steven would abandon her. The way her father had abandoned her mother. Because she was not worthy of love. So Meg had pushed Steven away before he could push her away. Because loneliness was less painful than rejection, and guilt was a burden she could not share.

She turned and faced him. "I'm going out of town early in the morning," she said. "This isn't a good time."

He was quiet. He stood there, staring at her, his eyes growing darker, tiny lines forming around them and across his brow. For a moment Meg thought that Senator Steven K. Riley—admired by his constituents, respected by his peers, and one of the most powerful men in America—was going to break down. Then he opened the door and went out. And Meg was alone again.

Ten minutes later Meg was still standing by the windows, staring out, trying to come to terms with what had just happened. Had she really told Steven "This isn't a good time"? She was so afraid of being hurt by him again, and yet, in reality, she was the one inflicting the hurt now. Just as she had done over fifteen years ago. The only thing Meg knew for certain was that she loved him. And that being alone—even if it meant being without him—was still far safer than being vulnerable to love.

But you don't have to be alone anymore, she reminded herself. *You're changing your life. You're going to free yourself of guilt and of loneliness. You're going to open your heart to friends, to things that matter.*

Yet as determined as she was, Meg wondered if there would ever be room in her heart for a special man, someone whose love she could accept, someone she would love in return. Someone other than Steven.

"Meg?" She turned around quickly. George Bascomb entered her office without knocking.

"We've decided that a six-month leave would be more in the firm's best interest than a permanent separation," he announced flatly. He folded his hands and walked to the window.

In the firm's best interest. The words jolted Meg.

"Of course," George continued, "you'll be expected to be available during that time should any problems arise concerning your cases. Also, we think it's best if we tell the media you're on temporary leave due to an illness in the family."

Meg stared at the little man, at the back of his navy-blue suit. "I don't have any family, George."

He spun around. His face grew red. "Well, invent one, goddammit. You don't seem to want to share with us exactly what this 'personal matter' is that's come up, and we can only imagine it's something the media might use to cast a shadow on the firm. But no one can say anything negative about a family illness."

Meg wrapped her arms around her waist. "That's all you worry about, isn't it, George? The image of the firm." A memory of Avery came creeping back.

George stared at Meg. "The firm pays your salary. The firm matters."

Meg shook her head. "No, George. People matter." Her eyes darted around her office, her photoless office, her mark of success. Suddenly it seemed empty, barren, and very unfriendly. She looked back at George. "Please tell the partners I thank them for their concern, but I've decided to reject the idea of a six-month leave."

The expression on his face was easy to read. It said, "Women are such a pain in the ass."

"I'm leaving today," Meg said. "Permanently." She watched his round face. It still didn't flinch. "You can send my formal severance package to my home."

George straightened his tie. "You're a fool," was all he said as he left her office.

She watched him go, knowing it would only be a matter of days before her name would be deleted from the stencil on the door and the letterhead in the drawers.

It wasn't until they were thirty thousand feet in the air that Meg told Danny she had left the firm. She had slept surprisingly well the night before, eased of life's pressures, her soul set free.

He chewed thoughtfully on the rubber omelette before saying, "Well, I suppose with your credentials you can go anywhere."

"What you're really saying is George was right. That I was a fool to leave. That anywhere after Larson, Bascomb is a step down."

He swigged his coffee. "Yep."

Meg gazed past him out the window of the jet. They were smoothly cruising atop a bed of clouds. "The truth is, I've been thinking of getting out of criminal law."

"To do what?"

Meg shrugged. "Family law, maybe. Something more meaningful."

"There are criminals in families, Meg."

"Fine. They can go to Larson, Bascomb. I'll handle the rest."

Danny whistled. "I can't believe you quit. The tabloids

will hate it. Imagine. No Meg Cooper to chase from the courtroom."

Meg picked at her corn muffin. "The tabloids won't care. I'm sure no one else in the world will either."

Danny reclined against the seat. "This all started with Holly Davidson, didn't it?"

"No, Danny. It started years ago. It's what I've always wanted. Then going to the spa, meeting Zoe and Alissa—even seeing Steven again—it all made me realize how much more there is to life than bullshit."

Danny laughed. "Alissa Page taught you there's more to life than bullshit? Now, that's funny."

"In her own way, she did. I know she seems a little odd, but . . ."

"A little? Babe, that's an understatement."

"Have you seen her?"

"Yeah. Gave her the information she wanted. Case closed."

"I wonder what's happened."

"Who knows? Who cares?"

The attendant came and collected their trays.

"She really got to you, didn't she?"

"Who?"

"Come on, Danny. Alissa. I think you kind of like her."

"She's a lonely, rich, married woman."

"And?"

"And nothing."

"Then I suppose the question should be, why not?"

"Don't know. Losing my touch, I guess. You're changing the subject."

Meg closed her eyes and lay her head back. "I know. So are you."

"Have you heard from your other friend? The one in Washington?"

She kept her eyes closed, aware of the numbness creeping through her once again. She wondered why that still happened whenever she thought of Steven. Then she remembered her new life, her new freedom. The numbness began to fade. "I saw him yesterday," she answered.

"And?"

"And nothing. This morning I got up and showered and dressed and met you at the airport and got on this plane."

"What about the hours in between? The nighttime hours?"

"Raggedy Man kept my feet quite warm, thank you."

"Raggedy Man. Christ. Him again."

They were silent for a while. Meg let the steady rumble of the engines lull her into half sleep and wondered why she felt so content, so happy. It was only yesterday that she had walked away from her megajob, and possibly her career. It was only yesterday that she had walked away from the man she loved. Again.

But right now Meg only knew that she felt comfortable in her jeans and a T-shirt, her hair pulled back in a ponytail, her courtroom demeanor left behind in Manhattan. She was flying toward the unknown, and it was more intriguing, more pressing, more exciting than any job, any case, had ever been. What would happen tomorrow was anyone's guess. As for today, she was going to help find Zoe's son. She was finally going to do something that mattered.

When they landed in Minneapolis, it was raining. Meg confirmed that a car would await them at the Chisholm-Hibbing airport. Then they boarded their connection—a small six-passenger commuter plane. Meg sat behind the pilot and gripped the back of his seat for the entire bouncing, agonizing trip, all the time questioning her decision to seek excitement.

Once they touched down on the tarmac, she turned to Danny. "Remind me never to go up in one of these again."

He laughed. "Never go up in one of these again."

"Very funny."

"Not as funny as it will be watching you walk back to Minneapolis."

Inside the terminal Meg took out the directions Zoe had given her and studied them while Danny got the car. The airport wasn't too far from Eric's diner, which Zoe had indicated was named simply "Lunch."

On their way to the diner Meg asked, "Do you really think they're here?"

"Sure. The guy runs his own business and is married with three other kids. What's he going to do? Take Scott to Mexico? Besides, my guess is he isn't exactly loaded."

Meg studied the rain as it shot across the windshield. "What are you going to say?"

"Just watch me closely. Maybe in your next career you can be a private eye."

Meg laughed. "Now that's *not* funny."

The diner was the picture of Zoe's description. They went inside and ordered sandwiches and coffee from a young waitress. When they finished eating, Danny asked the waitress if he could speak with the owner. Meg couldn't imagine what Danny had in mind.

A tall, fair-haired, yet rugged-looking man appeared from the back. Meg knew it must be Eric. He didn't look like a kidnapper—whatever it was kidnappers looked like. Somehow she'd managed to avoid ever having to defend one. Thank God.

Danny stood up and shook hands with Eric. "Dan Gordon," he said, "from St. Paul."

"Eric Matthews. What can I do for you?"

Meg studied him. She tried to picture him young, filled with enthusiasm for life, filled with love for Zoe. She saw strength in his face, stability. Maybe that was what Zoe had seen.

"The fact is," Danny said, "I'm a marketing rep for Super Saver Markets."

"Super Saver?"

"Based in St. Paul. Looking to grow."

Eric's look grew suspicious. "What's that got to do with me?"

"Not with you, Mr. Matthews. With your diner. This is a nice piece of property you have here. Right on the main road and all."

Meg managed to keep a straight face while Danny convinced Eric that he was interested in buying the property.

"I've built this place up from nothing," Eric protested, shaking his head. "It's my life. My family's life. I'm not about to sell."

"Super Saver Markets is very generous," Danny intimated. "You could retire."

"And do what?" Eric grinned. "Move to Florida?" He offered Danny his hand. "Thanks, anyway, but tell the folks in St. Paul I'm not interested."

Danny shook his hand. "No harm in asking."

Eric nodded; then Danny asked if there was a phone he could use.

Back in the car Meg laughed. "You're a very convincing liar, Mr. Gordon."

"Hey, all that matters is that now we know who he is. And we know that he's here. Which means, so is Zoe's son."

"What about the phone? Who did you call?"

"No one. I looked up Eric Matthews in the book. Got his home address. See if you can find Ten Mile Road on that map of yours."

She found it.

Within minutes they were parked in front of Eric's small clapboard house. The yard was big, a cluttered graveyard of snowplows and old tires. But there were brightly colored flower boxes on the porch of the house, and a calico wreath that read "Welcome" hung on the shiny red door.

"Now what?" Meg asked.

"Now we wait."

"For what?"

"We'll know that when it happens."

They didn't have to wait long. Two boys rode up on bicycles. They were wearing long green rain ponchos, but Meg could tell that one was young, about seven or eight. The other, a teenager. The teenager rode a girl's bike.

Danny quickly got out of the car and approached them.

"Hey, boys!" he called. The boys stopped.

Meg rolled down her window in order to hear. She ignored the rain that pelted her shoulder.

"What, mister?" the young boy asked.

"Not you," Danny said. "I want to talk to Scott."

The younger boy looked at the older boy. The older boy looked at Danny. "What about?" he asked.

"We're friends of your Mom's," Danny said. "We just want to talk to you a minute, that's all."

Scott looked to the car. Meg got out so he could see her. She didn't want him to think it was Zoe sitting in the car; she didn't want him to run.

"Hello, Scott," she said. "I'm Meg. This is Danny." She pointed to Danny, then walked toward them.

Scott turned to the younger boy. "Take off," he said. "I'll be in the house in a minute."

"You sure?"

"Yeah."

After the boy had left, Scott said, "I told my mother not to try and find me."

"She didn't," Danny said. "We did. We're concerned about her, because she's concerned about you."

"I'm okay."

"She'll be glad to know that," Meg said.

"I'm not going home."

Meg backed off and decided it would be best to let Danny speak. "We didn't say you had to," he said. "We only wanted to be sure you were okay."

Scott wheeled the bike back and forth in the mud. "She didn't say I had to go home?"

"Not if you don't want to," Danny said.

"I don't. Eric is my father."

"Yeah. We know. What's he like? Is he a pretty cool guy?"

Scott shuffled his feet. "Yeah, He's okay."

"Your mother misses you."

"My mother's in New York. Working. I'm sure she doesn't have time to miss me. Besides, she lied to me."

"About your father?"

"Yeah."

"Yeah, well mothers do those kinds of things. They think they're protecting their kids when all they're really doing is screwing up. Bet you didn't think your mother could ever screw up, did you?"

Scott didn't answer.

"The trouble is, she really loves you, Scott. She wants you to go home."

He stared at the ground. "I gotta go in the house," he said. "Eric's wife made chowder for lunch. She cooks. You know, real food. Not like my mother."

"Any message for her? Your mother?" Danny asked.

Scott mounted the bike. "Nope." He started down the driveway. Meg and Danny walked back toward the car. Scott wheeled the bike around and pedaled up next to them. "I guess," he said quietly, "I guess you could tell her I'm okay." His voice cracked a little. Meg thought she saw tears in his eyes. Then he turned again and biked toward the house.

As they got into the car, Danny looked at Meg. "He'll go back to L.A.," he said. "Once he thinks he's proved his point."

16

"What if something happens to Daddy while you're gone?" Natalie cried as she stood in Alissa's bedroom watching her pack.

"Stop sniveling," Alissa said. "It's been almost six weeks since his surgery." What it really had been was six of the most frantic weeks of her life. Plans for the gala, of course, had been a mess. She'd fired the two caterers—one of whom refused to return the WFFA deposit until Alissa reminded him that "One word from Alissa Page to the right people would assure he'd never again work in this town." She argued with printers, rearranged the seating a dozen times, fought with the women to select a band that played music more contemporary than the forties, and convinced the decorations committee to start over. As always Alissa got her way, this time by tantalizing everyone with the alluring promise of her "little surprise." And now the gala was only a month and a half away.

On this trip to L.A. Alissa would have to work quickly. She'd have to close in on Zoe and get her to commit to come.

And ... she'd finally get to see Jay.

She wrapped a silk shirt in tissue paper. As she carefully folded the fabric, she wondered why the threads of her life had never been woven so smoothly. It seemed she was always trying. Trying for bigger, trying for better, probably trying too hard.

She lay the shirt inside the suitcase and wished she could pack her negative thoughts away so neatly. "Nothing's going to happen to your father," she told Natalie. "Besides, you have Dr. Stern's phone number."

"Mom, are you forgetting I'm the one who found him before? Do you really want me to go through that again?"

"I told you, your father is fine. Dolores and Howard will be here. And Michele."

"Big deal. Two crotchety old people who can't get out of their own way and a sister who's too busy playing bride games to be bothered with her father."

"Natalie . . ."

"How long will you be gone?"

If I'm lucky, forever, Alissa wanted to say. *If I'm lucky, Jay will sweep me into his arms and take me away to far-off, romantic places, and this time I won't come back.* Unless, of course, Zoe agreed to the gala. "I don't know," she answered. "A few days."

"Are you going to leave a phone number?"

"So you can bother me every time your father sneezes? I don't think so."

"Mom. Get serious. What if something happens?"

If something happens, I don't want to know. She tossed in another satin and lace nightgown. She wondered if Natalie noticed. "All right. I'll give you a phone number. But only for a real emergency. Got that?" She took out her small notebook and jotted Zoe's number on a pad beside her bed. "Your father's napping now. Tell him I said good-bye, then ring for Howard to get me to the airport."

Natalie eyed her mother, then her mother's suitcase. "Do it yourself," she said, and left the room.

The Los Angeles headquarters of World Press International wasn't nearly as impressive as the name implied. Alissa stood in the middle of a large room and looked around. Tables that ran along one wall were smothered by piles of newspapers scattered every which way; on the opposite wall was a row of computers, only three of which were being used by intense, bespectacled, horrendously dressed young people. The only other time Alissa had had this kind of up-close-and-personal view of a press office was years ago at Stockwell Media Group, but the only discernible differences now were the flickering computer screens in place of thumping typewriter keys and the clear air instead of a permanent cloud of thick gray smoke. The employees still had the same left-wing look, only they were younger. Young enough to be her kids. Her anxiety over being there eased until she suddenly remembered that these were Jay's co-workers. This was his life.

She checked the string of clocks on the wall and searched for the one with L.A. time: it was after two o'clock; she hoped he wasn't out to lunch. She played with the guard chain on her gold bracelet and wondered what she had expected. Had she thought Jay would be sitting there, waiting for her reemergence after twenty-four years? Had she expected he'd have somehow guessed that she was coming?

One of the bespectacled young men finally stopped typing and acknowledged Alissa.

She stared at him a moment, as though she'd forgotten why she was there. Then she said, "I'd like to see Jay Stockwell. Has he returned from abroad?" Abroad? She couldn't believe she'd used that word. Did anyone say that anymore?

"Yeah," the young man answered. "He's back, but he's not here. He'll be here tomorrow."

"Tomorrow?" She questioned him as though he were lying to her.

"Yeah. Tomorrow." The young man turned back to his computer and resumed his typing.

"Excuse me," Alissa said loudly.

He stopped and looked back at her.

"What time tomorrow?"

He shrugged. "You never know with Jay. Maybe nine o'clock. Maybe three. You want to leave a message?"

Alissa looked around the room once again. Maybe nine o'clock. Maybe three. She was reminded of Jay's free spirit. Once it had made her crazy with lust. Then it had simply made her crazy.

"No," she said. "No message."

Outside again, she sat in the rented Mercedes and considered her next move. She couldn't possibly wait until tomorrow. Could she? She took out the notes Danny had given her. Jay's home address was there: 730 Mesa Linda Drive. Did she dare?

She started the car. Yes, she dared. Alissa Page would always dare when it was something she wanted badly. And she'd never wanted anything as badly as this. She fumbled through the papers the rental agency had included in the car. Stapled to a location guide to the homes of the stars was a street map of the city. She checked it; she found Mesa Linda Drive. She wheeled out of the parking lot and headed in that direction.

Fifteen minutes later Alissa stopped in front of 730 Mesa Linda Drive. She stared at the house. It was a sad little ranch, beige stucco in need of a paint job with a faded red-tile roof. It was nearly identical to number 728 on one side and 732 on the other. There were a couple of palm trees in what must have been considered the front yard. Underneath a carport sat a dark-green Chevy Blazer.

Of course he wouldn't live in a decent place, Alissa reminded herself. *He's never here. He's single, and he's never here.*

Still, it was pretty tacky. She'd have hoped that over the years Jay had developed more taste than this. But he was a man. Alone. She wondered how much taste Robert would have if it weren't for her.

Robert? Why the hell was she thinking of that faggot husband of hers now?

She shook her head and grasped the steering wheel.
She should get out of the car.
She should go up to the front door.
She should ring the bell.
What was stopping her?
Her heart started banging against the walls of her chest.
It wasn't as though she were afraid. What the hell should she be afraid of? She could tell him she was in L.A. on business. She could tell him ... what? That by some fluke she just happened to find out he lived there? That she just happened to know where he worked?

"Hi," she could say. "Remember me? I know I left you twenty-four years ago, but I've decided to give you another chance."

There were drapes at a large picture window. The living room, probably. The drapes were closed. Was he in there sleeping? Maybe he had jet lag. Or maybe he was fucking someone.

God, she thought, *I hope it's a female.*

She sat, intently, and stared at the drapes, half waiting for them to move. She didn't see the front door open until the movement of a man on the steps distracted her. Alissa caught her breath. *It must be him,* she thought. *My God, it must be him.*

With the lightning reaction of a thief caught in the act, her trembling hand threw the shift into gear, and she sped off down the street.

The house was fairly impressive: not bad for a backwoods girl from Montana or Minnesota or wherever the hell Zoe was from. As Alissa climbed the winding stone path that appeared to lead to the front door, she suddenly remembered the news stories. She shuddered. They'd said Zoe's husband had killed himself at home. Here. The house she was about to enter. Regardless of their differences, Alissa truly hoped that Robert would never do something so gruesome. And if he did, she hoped to God he wouldn't do it at home. She would absolutely, positively, have to move.

She stepped up to the door and rang the bell. She hadn't bothered to call ahead: hell, in a place this size someone must be around. Cooks, maids, gardeners, someone. She wondered if Zoe had got the movie deal, if she'd managed to keep off the weight. She wondered if Zoe would agree to the gala, and she wondered why in the hell she'd let herself get so wrapped up in the plans that she hadn't stayed in touch. At least called Zoe once. At least acted as though she really cared.

Zoe opened the door.

"Hi, stranger," Alissa said.

Zoe stepped back in surprise. "Alissa! My God, I was just talking about you. What are you doing here? Oh, come in. Come in."

Alissa went into the huge stone foyer. It was light and airy and didn't at all seem like a house where someone had died such a short time ago. Not a bad place to be a recluse. "So you were talking about me. Only in the best terms, I'm sure."

Zoe laughed. "Of course. I had breakfast with Meg before I left New York this morning."

"Meg as in Cooper? What were you doing in New York? And how on earth did you and Meg manage without me?"

"Come on into the family room," Zoe said. "Gosh, what a surprise." She led Alissa past a string of suitcases in the hall.

As Alissa settled onto one of the three sofas, she quickly surveyed the room. Nice. California casual, but nice, nonetheless. Even the gauche old movie posters seemed to look good in there. "So you didn't expect it to be me at your door?"

"Hardly!" Zoe brushed back her thick black curls. Her smile radiated.

"You look terrific," Alissa said, and meant it. The Golden Key Spa had come out victorious once again. Zoe would be a huge hit at the gala.

"Thanks. But it's really hard to keep the weight down. You look wonderful, too. But what brings you here?"

Alissa smiled. "You mean you don't believe I've come out to L.A. solely to see you?"

"Something tells me that drop-in visits from over two thousand miles away aren't exactly your style."

"Well, you're right," Alissa said. She wanted to light a cigarette but remembered that Zoe didn't smoke. No one did anymore. She played with the fringe on the giant pillow beside her. It was too soon to talk about the gala. She didn't want Zoe to think she was using her. "I've come to meet him."

Zoe's dark eyes widened. "Jay Stockwell? He's here? In L.A.?"

"In the flesh."

"My God. You haven't seen him yet?"

"I tried. He won't be in his office until tomorrow." There was no way Alissa was going to tell Zoe about sitting in front of Jay's house, stalking the property as though she were some kind of low-life Danny Gordon. There was no way she was going to tell her she thought she had already seen Jay. From a distance.

"Well. Where are you staying?"

"I haven't thought about it yet." Hadn't thought about it? Of course she had. Alissa had planned to stay with Zoe. If not Jay. "I'll run back into town when I leave here and get a room at the Wilshire or somewhere."

"You'll do no such thing. You'll stay right here."

Alissa smiled. It amazed her that Zoe had ever made it to the big time. She was too open, too nice. Not the way successful people tended to be. But, then, Hollywood and the film industry were different from the real world and, Alissa suspected, played by their own set of rules.

"I wouldn't want to put you out," Alissa said, "but, you know, maybe it would be easier ... if you have the space...."

"Space? This place has eight bedrooms and six baths. My

friend Marisol has gone to a crafts show in Monterey for a few days, and my son is . . ." She paused and looked away from Alissa. "Out of town."

"Perfect," Alissa said. "Actually, I did leave your number with my family in case of emergency."

"Good. Now, tell me, how did you find Jay?"

Alissa nodded as she kicked off her heels and pulled her feet underneath her on the sofa. She was beginning to feel curiously comfortable there. "Not until you tell me what you were doing in New York with Meg."

Zoe laughed. "I wasn't exactly with Meg. But I saw her a few times. I went there to shoot the movie."

"The movie? You got the part? I knew you would." So Zoe was on her way back to stardom. And Alissa would reap the benefits. She tried not to smile too broadly. "How did it go?"

Zoe waved a hand in the air. "Okay. Fine. Now tell me how you found Jay."

Alissa sighed with a smile, filling her lungs with girlish excitement, suddenly eager to share her news. "I didn't find him. Meg's friend Danny did."

"Oh, yes. Danny Gordon." Again Zoe looked away.

Alissa thought she could see Zoe's eyes glaze over. *Christ,* she thought, *did Danny get to her, too?* She watched as Zoe stretched her feet in front of her and examined her shoeless toes.

"Are you sure you're ready to meet Jay?" Zoe asked.

"Of course I'm ready. I've been ready since we made the decision in April."

"It may not go as you hoped. I think you should be prepared."

The caution in Zoe's voice told Alissa something had happened, something had gone wrong. Alissa wanted to sound concerned and then realized that she was. "Did something go wrong?"

Zoe shuffled her feet back and forth across the alpaca rug. "I saw Eric. I talked with him."

"And?"

"And I'm only telling you to be prepared. People change. Or maybe it's that they're not as you remember them."

Well, Alissa thought, *life can certainly be a bitch.* First Zoe's husband blew himself away, then the one guy she'd probably figured still loved her blew her off. Again, apparently. But that was Zoe. And Alissa was Alissa. She folded her hands in her lap. "I'm sorry things didn't work out for you, Zoe. But it won't be that way with Jay and me. I know it won't: Jay Stockwell isn't like Eric at all."

Zoe suggested they get Chinese take-out for dinner. Alissa loathed Chinese food.

"It's hard for me to go out in public and try to enjoy a meal," Zoe explained. "Too many people recognize me since I lost weight and look like a star again." She laughed. "So it's your own fault, Alissa. If you hadn't forced me to diet, we could go to Chasen's for a delectable dinner."

"Never mind," Alissa conceded, "Chinese will be fine." She couldn't imagine sitting in a restaurant where other patrons would be whispering and pointing not at her, but at the woman with her. It would be a humiliating experience, not unlike being the scrawny twelve-year-old wallflower all dressed up for the cotillion her aunt had made her attend, where Alissa had spent the night shrouded in embarrassment, her eyes glued to the older, glamorous debs, the girls everyone was making such an all-fired fuss over. All eyes would be on Zoe at the gala too, of course, but that was different. On her own turf Alissa would be well-known.

Their dinner was delivered in white cardboard containers that made everything taste like paper. Salted paper. They sat at the kitchen table, though there was a perfectly lovely dining room that appeared never to be used.

Throughout the ghastly meal Zoe chattered about the film and New York and how she couldn't understand how anyone, let alone level-headed Meg, could stand to live in that dirty, noisy city. "It does have its advantages—the ultimate in theater and unmatchable concert halls," she went on, "even though Meg doesn't seem to take advantage of them."

Alissa didn't much care. She barely listened. She was too busy thinking of the gala, thinking of Jay. Would he really be her escort? She had decided not to mention the gala to Zoe that evening, not wanting to rush it. There would be plenty of time later. She poked at the questionable innards of a steamed dumpling and finally saw an opportunity to interrupt. "I'd like to use your phone to make a call tonight," she said.

"Of course," Zoe said. "There's one in your room."

"I'm going to call Jay."

Zoe took a forkful of something wet and stringy looking that Alissa had declined. "Oh," she said, then quickly changed the subject. "Shall I make tea?"

Alissa set down her fork. "Look, Zoe, I'm sorry if things haven't worked out for you and Eric. But I've waited a long time and I've come a long way to see Jay. Please don't spoil it for me."

"I'm sorry," Zoe said. "I just don't want to see you get hurt."

Wow, Alissa thought, *things with the old Minnesota Viking must have really exploded in Zoe's face.* But Alissa and Jay were different. They had loved each other. *Really* loved each other.

Alissa got up from the table. "I think I'll make that call now. I'll have tea after." She walked down the wing toward her room and realized Zoe hadn't wished her luck.

But once in her room, Alissa wondered if she really did have the courage to go through with her plans. She told herself that Jay wouldn't be home: after all, hadn't she seen him leave the house earlier? She told herself it would be better to talk with him in person, to have him see how good she still looked: wouldn't that serve as justification for all the pain and suffering she'd undergone with her nips and tucks?

But the truth, Alissa knew, was that if she went to his office, she was afraid he would snub her, make her feel like a fool in front of those left-wing young people, make her feel as if she were someone who didn't matter.

She sat at the built-in desk in the guest room and picked up the receiver. Then, slowly, she punched in the numbers, telling herself that everything would be fine, because Jay wouldn't be home anyway.

"Hello?" a male voice answered.

She froze.

"Hello? Anybody there?"

It was Jay. She'd know his voice anywhere, anytime, anytime from twenty-four years ago, anytime from now.

"Jay?" The word came out in a whisper.

"Who?"

Maybe it wasn't him. Maybe she had a wrong number.

"Jay?"

"Yeah, it's me. Who's this?"

How could it be that she recognized his voice, but he didn't recognize hers? Didn't he ever think about her? Did he even remember her?

She cleared her throat. "Jay, this is Alissa."

There was silence a moment, then, "Alissa?"

"Yes, Jay," she said, her voice growing stronger. "Alissa."

"Hey," he said, "well, God. What a surprise."

Alissa laughed. "A blast from the past, huh?"

"God, I can't believe it's you. Where are you?"

"I'm in L.A. I thought we could get together."

"You're here? In L.A.? Why?"

There it was. The big question. *Why.*

"Business," she lied, and hoped he didn't ask what kind. But she could always tell him Zoe was working on a benefit for her.... "Could we?" she repeated. "Get together?"

"Christ, Alissa, I'd love to, but the truth is I just got back from being on the road for a few months...."

I know that, she wanted to scream into the phone.

"... and I'm way behind in my work."

"I thought perhaps cocktails," she said. "Tomorrow evening?"

"I don't drink anymore. Can you believe it? I'm as straight as they come now."

"I understand the Perrier in the lounge at the Wilshire is extraordinary," she said. "Will seven o'clock be too early?" Her heart fluttered in her throat. Would he reject her? No. *She'd* been the one who'd rejected him.

Jay laughed. "Do you still insist on always getting your own way?"

Yes. God, he was going to say yes. "I only want my way when it's something worthwhile."

"Okay, you win. Seven o'clock. At the Wilshire."

"Don't be late," she said with a giggle as she hung up the phone.

She sat at the desk, trembling, quivering, euphoric. Tomorrow night she had a date to see Jay. The one man in the world who had ever loved her, the one man she had ever loved. Twenty-four years. And now she was going to see him again.

A small ache formed inside her. Was Jay as excited about seeing her? *The opposite of love is not hate. The opposite of love is indifference.* She'd read that somewhere. Had Jay sounded ... indifferent? *"Okay, you win,"* Jay had said. Not exactly a hotbed of enthusiasm.

She stared at a woven mat that hung on the wall. It couldn't be, she thought. Jay had merely been caught off guard, that's all. It was surprise, not indifference, that she'd heard in his voice.

She went back to the kitchen and forced a smile.

"I talked to him," she told Zoe. "He sounds wonderful."

"That's good," Zoe said as she poured hot water into two mugs.

"We have a date for tomorrow. He was so excited, though, he wanted to see me tonight. I thought it was better to wait. Give him a little time to think about me, you know? She had no idea why she was lying.

"Sure," Zoe answered as she set a steamy mug in front of Alissa. "And I'm sorry if I didn't sound excited earlier." She placed her hand over Alissa's. "But you're my friend. I don't want you to be hurt. Forgive me?"

Alissa smiled. She was going to see Jay. And Zoe had called her a friend. It looked as though she was going to get the two things she needed most right now in her life.

She arrived at the Wilshire at quarter to seven, her palms sweaty, her stomach in knots. She pulled into a parking space away from the valet service, but close enough to the front door that she could see anyone coming or going. She glanced around the lot: no dark-green Chevy Blazer. She turned off the ignition. She waited. She lit a cigarette and rolled down the windows so she wouldn't smell like smoke, then remembered she'd read somewhere that the powers-that-be in L.A. had talked about an ordinance to ban smoking citywide. Had it happened yet? Could it ever? She took a deep drag. *Fuck it.*

She tapped her fingers on the steering wheel. She checked and rechecked her eye makeup in the rearview mirror. She took out her lipstick, ready to apply as soon as she was done with her cigarette. She knew she looked great in the pink linen dress—hell, she almost looked angelic. She tried to think about what she was going to say, but she couldn't seem to think about anything beyond what kind of car was coming into the parking lot, what type of person was walking through the hotel door.

Then she saw the dark-green Chevy Blazer.

She glanced at her watch. Five minutes to seven. Alissa smiled. He was on time. A good sign.

She watched him park, watched him get out, watched him stride across the pavement. His hair was thin on top—she hadn't noticed that on TV—and it was bleached out, probably from the strong sun in those godforsaken near-to-the-equator countries. His clothes were loose: jeans and a cotton khaki jacket with the sleeves turned up. She was surprised to see that he wore glasses. She knew he hadn't worn them in that clip a few weeks ago. Nor had he worn them when they were young. But, then, Alissa remembered, forty-four was a long way from twenty.

Jay disappeared inside. Alissa took a deep breath. And waited.

At ten minutes past seven she got out of the car and slowly walked toward the entrance, not so much for effect as to be sure her legs would remain steady. She stopped outside the lounge: he was there, by the door, seated on a bar stool, watching the television that hung from the ceiling and hovered over the lineup of bottles below. Alissa walked up behind him. She studied his back, the thick muscles that strained through the thin fabric. He was larger than she remembered, broader. She wondered if he'd ever grown hair on his chest. Finally she leaned toward him.

"Jay?" she asked.

He turned and hesitated only a brief second—one of those moments-just-before-recognition seconds—then smiled.

"Alissa," he said, and moved to kiss her cheek. She felt the heat rise and hoped she was blushing. A slight blush would look fabulous with the pink linen dress. "You look terrific."

She smiled. "So do you." She knew her voice sounded timid, but she didn't know what to do about it. And then Alissa got scared. Before her sat her future. Until now it had been only a dream. But Jay was no longer a dream: he was there, flesh, blood, mind. And she had been right, he looked softer. Maybe not softer. Maybe content. Then she realized if she couldn't make this work, she would have nothing. No more hopes, no more dreams. Even the gala wouldn't matter. She tried to take a deep breath, but the air didn't seem to get past her throat.

He slid off the bar stool. "Let's get a table," he said.

She obediently followed him across the room, too nervous to speak. Jay was in front of her, a touch away. Jay was there, and ... Jay was walking with a limp.

They sat down. Jay pulled a wrinkled matchbook from his

pocket and lit the small candle in the center of the table. His green eyes were lighter than Alissa had remembered, or maybe they looked lighter through the tortoise-framed glasses. But his mouth was the same. Still full, still inviting.

"You still look like a girl, Alissa," he said. "I don't know how you do it."

A little thing called plastic surgery, she wanted to say, but instead responded by smiling. She wanted to ask him why he was limping. Had he been in a car accident? A war? *God,* she thought, *the last time I saw him, Vietnam was still raging.* "You have a limp," she blurted out.

Jay smiled. "Not from anything heroic," he said. "I was doing a live shot during the Gulf War. It was at night. I was walking backward, talking to the camera. I tripped over a tripod and fell off the roof of the building. Broke my leg."

"You fell off a building?"

He laughed. He had a warm laugh, beautiful. The same as ever. "It was only one story. The photog went to black. The world thought we'd been hit by a scud."

"It must have hurt." She couldn't believe she'd said that. She couldn't believe that Alissa Page, the ultimate in captivating society hostesses, had said anything so stupid. *It must have hurt. God.*

Jay shrugged. "Yeah. It was a couple of days before it was set. That's why the limp."

She pictured him lying on the ground. She remembered when he'd been thrown from a horse and broken his collarbone. He had refused to let an ambulance come and, instead, had Alissa drive him to the hospital. Even in pain, Jay didn't want a fuss made over him.

A waiter appeared. Jay ordered a club soda for himself, Perrier for Alissa. She'd have given anything for a glass of wine, but what the hell good was wine without a cigarette, and she was getting the distinct impression that Jay didn't smoke anymore either. A quick glance around the room told her that neither did anyone else in the place. Ordinance or not.

"God," he said, "You really do look terrific." And then he laughed again. The warmth radiated from his lips, across the table, into her breasts. "Pink. That's always been a good color on you. Remember the country-club dance? You wore pink that night."

She remembered. The dress had been pink organdy. The orchids he'd bought for her wrist had been white, tied with pink ribbon. Alissa had been sixteen. They'd made love in the car after the dance. He'd pulled out quickly—teenage birth control of the sixties. His semen had spilled onto her dress. She'd thrown the dress away, too afraid Aunt Helma would see.

"I can't believe you remember that night," she said quietly.

"Sure. It was the first time my old man let me drive the Rolls. I'd just turned eighteen, remember?"

No. Alissa didn't remember that part. "I was thinking of something else," she said.

"I know," Jay answered. "I remember."

The waiter brought their drinks. Jay leaned back in his chair and smiled. "God, can you believe we ever lived that way? We were kids, for chrissakes. I wore black tie more than I wore jeans."

"I always loved you in black tie."

"I always hated it. Remember Fred Carter? He had that flask with the loop that locked onto his cummerbund?" He pulled back his jacket and imitated the way Fred Carter's flask hung from his cummerbund. But all Alissa could see was Jay's waist—trim, hard, and so damn sexy. She didn't want to talk about the past. She wanted to talk about today. Tonight. Tomorrow.

"Fred Carter was killed a few years ago," Alissa said. "DUI."

Jay sat straight again. "Shit. I didn't know. I guess it's no surprise."

"Not to anyone in Atlanta."

"Man," Jay said as he took a big drink of soda. "Atlanta.

It's been years since I was there. Not since my mother died." Jay's parents had been older than most: his father had been well into his seventies when he died not long after they'd run away to San Francisco. His mother, Alissa knew, had died more than a dozen years ago. The eulogy had been delivered by a past president of the WFFA. "Hey," he interrupted her thoughts, "whatever happened to Hank Benson? Remember the night he rode into town on one of his father's prized polo ponies?"

Hank had dated LuAnn Palmer—one of the girls Aunt Helma felt wasn't good enough for Alissa. "Hank Benson is a judge," she said. "He married LuAnn." She wanted to ask why Jay had never married.

"No kidding. Old Hank. A judge." He laughed. "God, I never thought he'd buy into the establishment."

Alissa laughed because she thought she was supposed to. What she really wanted to do was talk about him. About her. About them. She didn't want to dwell on the past, but somehow she couldn't steer the subject away from it.

For nearly three hours Jay reminisced. Alissa nodded, smiled, and added a few words here and there. *The important thing is,* she reassured herself, *he's having a good time. He likes being with me again.*

They talked about Atlanta. About old friends. About their high-pressure families. They did not talk about when they'd gone to San Francisco. They did not talk about their lives since then.

Finally the lounge was emptying, the evening was drawing to a close. Jay looked around, as though back from another place in time.

"It's been wonderful to see you, Alissa," he said. "Give me a call if you're in L.A. again."

The muscles in her jaw tightened. Was this it? *It's been wonderful to see you?* Was he telling her to leave?

"I was hoping we could continue our conversation," she said.

He stood up. "I'm afraid I've got an early flight." He smiled. "To San Francisco."

Her thoughts raced. "San Francisco? I have nothing pressing to do tomorrow. I'd love to come along." She smiled, trying to quell her pounding pulse. "Besides, I think San Francisco would be rather appropriate."

He laughed. "You're right about that." He tucked his thumbs into the waist of his jeans. From where Alissa sat, if she slowly leaned over, she could press her mouth against his fly. She could blow hot breath onto the fabric. Her heart skipped a beat when she suddenly pictured the strawberry-shaped mole buried within his pubic hair, just above his testicles—those wonderful, tender balls she had loved to hold, to lick, to suck. He'd always told her he never thought he'd let a girl touch him there. She supposed he had again, but she'd been the first. That had to count for something.

"But I'm afraid it's not a good time," Jay was saying. "I'm just running up there for a day-long conference."

She blinked back to the present. "You'll be back tomorrow? How about dinner?"

He studied her, as if trying to determine what she wanted. She wondered if he had picked up her scent.

"Sure," he said, "why not? Eight o'clock? There's a great Italian place over on Sunset. DiNardo's."

"Great. I'll see you there."

"I'll walk you to your car."

"No," Alissa said, "I need to stop in the ladies' room. You go ahead. I'll see you tomorrow night."

He gave her a kiss on the cheek and left the lounge.

Alissa stayed in her chair, numb with disappointment. This had not gone as she'd hoped. She couldn't be sure if the magnetism was still there—God, he was nearly bald. But his body, well, that was something else. She drained the ice from her fourth Perrier. Why hadn't they talked about themselves? The years between the then and the now of their lives? But what had she planned to tell him? That she'd spent the last twenty-four years planning parties and having parties and attending parties and having her picture taken with the right people? Oh, yes, and raising two kids along the way? And keeping the servants in line? Her life, she knew, had been all the things Jay hated, all the things he'd mocked tonight.

She leaned back in her chair and signaled the waiter. She needed a glass of wine—no, make that a whiskey.

It was after two when Alissa returned to Zoe's. The lights were still burning: Zoe must have waited up for her. Alissa toyed with the idea of what she would tell her. For some reason Zoe was one of the few people she'd met who was difficult to lie to—the type who you just knew, knew. The type Alissa usually avoided. She would love to be able to tell Zoe that she and Jay had slept together and made mad, passionate love; that he had told her he'd waited all those years for her, only for her. It certainly would change Zoe's tune about things not being the way people remembered them. But, *after* she told her about the gala, about what a great career-rebuilding opportunity Alissa would be giving her.

Alissa let herself in with the key Zoe had given her. She had barely stepped into the foyer when she heard Zoe's voice.

"Alissa? I'm in the family room."

Alissa hesitated a minute. Damn. She'd have to decide fast what to tell Zoe about Jay. Maybe she'd just let Zoe guess, come to her own conclusion. Yeah, that would be fun. She sighed and started down the hall. The gala could wait until tomorrow. "You needn't have waited up, Zoe. But I'm glad you did." She went into the family room where Zoe was seated, twirling a lock of hair around her finger.

"You had a phone call," Zoe said quickly.

Alissa groaned and flopped onto the sofa. "I can't believe Natalie actually called. The most important night of my life and my daughter is tracking me down like I've never left the house overnight before."

"It wasn't your daughter," Zoe said. "It was your husband."

Alissa sat up. "Robert? Why the hell would Robert be calling?"

"He said it was urgent."

Fuck him, she thought. *He can wait.* Besides, now that she'd decided what she would, and would not, share with Zoe, her eyes had begun to sparkle, her head had started to reel with the urgency of a teenager needing to share the dizziness of her first date, even if it meant stretching the truth a little. Just a little—enough to make the tale more exciting than the date itself. Yes, Robert could wait.

"Aren't you going to ask how my evening was?" Alissa asked.

"I thought it was more important that you call home first. He really sounded upset, Alissa."

Shit. The last thing she wanted was for some idiotic family crisis to step on her mood. "All right, all right. I'll call. But first I've got to tell you about Jay. He's absolutely divine. Better than I remembered. Zoe, I can't explain it, but I feel like my life is going to turn around. I feel like finding Jay again is the best thing that's ever happened to me." Maybe she hadn't slept with Jay tonight, but tomorrow ... tomorrow night ...

"That's wonderful. I'm happy for you."

"Are you? I hope so. Because it's only going to get better. I'm seeing him tomorrow night. Oh, Zoe, it was wonderful." She lounged back on the sofa and draped her legs over the arm. "We talked about everyone we used to know, all the things we used to do—our little adventures." The more she spoke, the more Alissa herself began to believe she'd actually had a good time.

"I never got the idea you were one for adventure."

"Oh, Zoe, I was a much different person when I was with Jay. I was so much happier." But even as Alissa said the words, she wondered if they were entirely true. It was so difficult to remember, so long ago.

"That's nice, Alissa. But don't you think you should call your husband?"

Alissa sat up again. "Jesus, Zoe, I said I'd call him. It's only five o'clock in the goddamn morning in Atlanta." *Easy, Alissa,* she reminded herself. *Don't alienate her.* She softened her tone. "I'm afraid if I call now, I'll wake up the whole house."

"He said it was urgent," Zoe repeated. "He said it didn't matter what time it was."

She didn't want to talk to Robert. She wanted to talk about Jay. She wanted to hear the sound of his name, she wanted to think only thoughts of him. Positive thoughts, and possibilities. Well, maybe they weren't possibilities—yet. Maybe for now they were just fantasies. But what the hell. She deserved a little fantasy, didn't she? It's not as though it could hurt anyone.

Alissa smiled. She wanted to tell Zoe that Jay had wanted her to go to San Francisco with him tomorrow. She opened her mouth to speak, then was stopped by the motherly look on Zoe's face. It was apparent there would be no more talk of Jay until after Alissa called Robert. Alissa's smile faded into resignation. "All right, all right. Where's the damn phone?"

"There's one over there," Zoe said, pointing to a corner table. "I'll leave if you want."

Alissa got up and walked to the phone. "If I needed privacy to talk to my husband, I'd go to my room. Believe me; stay. This won't take long."

She hesitated a moment, then picked up the phone and put the call through to Atlanta, her elation, her dreams, deflating with each number she pushed.

Robert answered on the first ring.

"What's the big emergency?" she asked, forgoing the word "hello."

"Thank God you called."

Alissa looked over at Zoe and rolled her eyes. Zoe looked away.

"It's Natalie."

Alissa stiffened and quickly sat in the high-backed chair beside the table. "What about her? What happened?"

"She's okay. But there's been a problem."

"What kind of problem?"

"She being questioned," Robert said. "By the police."

Alissa bolted from the chair. "*The police?* Why, for chrissakes?" Natalie had finally done it. Natalie. Natalie. Natalie. Her rebellious, renegade daughter. She'd finally done something really stupid, and now she'd been caught. Visions of things like fucking in public shot through Alissa's mind.

"I told them it was an accident. That it wasn't her fault." His tone was flat, robotic.

"Exactly *what* wasn't her fault?"

"Well ... ah ... I ..." Robert stammered. Then she heard what sounded like a sob.

"Robert! What has she done?"

The sob slowed, then stopped. "Derek was here."

"Who the hell is Derek?" What was he talking about? Was Derek Natalie's latest lay?

"Derek is, ah ..." There was silence again. Then Robert cleared his throat. "Derek is my friend."

Derek. Oh, yes. A sickening feeling in her stomach told Alissa that Derek wasn't her daughter's latest lay, that he was Robert's. Derek. So that was his name. The man who was pinned under Robert that night at the lab. The man who was fucking Robert's brains out, or whose brains Robert was fucking out, or however those same-sex people managed to do things.

"What the hell does Natalie have to do with Derek?" She dropped her voice and turned her head toward the wall, as though Zoe might know about Robert, might guess about Derek.

"I was resting. In my room. Derek was, ah, Derek was visiting me."

"Oh, Christ."

"Natalie walked in. Without knocking."

The nightmare image of Robert's white ass pumping up and down on the floor of his office flashed before her. *I should have told the girls,* she thought. *God, I should have told them. Natalie should never have found out this way.*

"Alissa? Are you all right?" Robert strained to ask.

She felt her body go rigid. *"Why are the police questioning my daughter?"*

Silence. One. Two. Three seconds.

Then Robert tried to speak. "Derek ... he ... she ..."

Dread flooded through Alissa. "Robert. Where is Derek now?"

There was silence again; then Robert let out a small cry, and Alissa knew she didn't want to know the rest of the story.

Finally Robert spoke. "It was an accident," he repeated.

"Where is he? Where is Derek?"

"Derek," Robert said quietly, "is in the morgue."

Her body went numb. A tiny ache formed in her heart and spread, slowly, oozing up to her head, out to her limbs. The pieces began coming together. Robert and Derek. Fucking. Natalie. Interrupting. Derek. In the morgue.

Alissa gripped the phone with all the strength she could find. Through clenched teeth she asked, *"What happened?"*

Robert tried to speak. "Natalie," he said, then paused. The crack in his voice made him sound like a child. A little boy. He cleared his throat again. "Natalie shot him."

"Natalie?" Alissa screamed. Her vision blurred, the room tipped, and she slid from the chair to the floor.

17

Alissa left on the first morning flight to Atlanta. After she had gone, Zoe went down to the pool and sat on the edge, stirring the warm aqua water with her toes. She watched the quiet ripples; she listened to the wakening song of a rousing bird. Zoe gazed at the sun's mirrored image on the water and thought how unfair life could be, how lonely. Alissa lived on the surface, yet, like the water in the pool, underneath there lay depth, different sensations from those visible to the world.

Alissa had told her that Robert was gay.

Alissa had told her her sixteen-year-old daughter had shot Robert's lover.

Alissa had begged her to meet Jay Stockwell that night; to explain that she'd had no choice but to return home. Then she had started to ask Zoe something—started to tell her something else that was "really important." When she hesitated, Zoe reassured her that Alissa could ask her anything. But Alissa had looked at her blankly a moment, then lowered her head, shrugged, and said, "Never mind."

When Zoe hugged her good-bye, Alissa's tears were real. And the aggressive, fiery, energetic society lady had crumbled. "My life," Alissa had said, "is unbelievably fucked up."

Is anyone's not? Zoe wondered now.

She dug her feet deeper into the water and felt the calmer water, cooler. Like so many women, Zoe thought, Alissa spent her days trying to convince everyone around her that her life was perfect. *What's going to happen to Alissa when everyone finds out that it's not?* She lifted her gaze and stared off into the canyon. *And why,* she wondered, *should it matter what other people think?*

As she sat there, at Scott's special place, Zoe's thoughts drifted to him, and to Eric. Her motivation for finding Eric, she realized, had not been the right motivation. She had, indeed, wanted revenge. She had wanted him to feel pain. Instead, she was the one with the aching heart. She was the one who had lost her son.

She pulled her feet from the water and tucked them under her on the stone deck. She had spent so many hours there, so many days, months, years. Sitting in solitude, shutting out the world, fearful of the hurt she would feel if she became a part of life again. Using first her stroke as an excuse for her seclusion; then hiding behind the weight she'd gained, using each layer of fat to construct another wall of protection from the world, to save her from being abandoned again by someone like Eric, to keep her from feeling love.

It hadn't been fair to William. But he had known from the beginning that she didn't love him. Still, Zoe thought now, it hadn't been fair.

She looked out to the canyon below and wondered—as she had wondered so many times, so many years ago as she sat there in solitude—if she screamed, would it echo? Would her pain resonate among the cliffs? Would everyone find out?

She had asked herself those questions so many times so long ago, and yet now, as Zoe again thought of Alissa, she asked the one question that pertained to them both: if everyone found out ... did it matter?

"Is this a private party?" Tim Danahy hoisted the cuffs of his trousers and squatted beside Zoe at the pool.

She shielded her eyes from the sun. "Tim. I didn't expect to see you today."

"I have a surprise for you," he said. He stood and extended his hand. "Come with me. It's up at the house."

Zoe couldn't imagine what his "surprise" could be, but she grasped his hand and let him pull her upright. She bent to shake the water from her feet. Then she realized that Tim was still holding her hand. She looked into his somber eyes. In the bright sunlight the lines that skittered around them cast a well-defined web of age.

"You looked very lonely sitting here by yourself," he said. "I hate to think that you're sad."

Zoe gently removed her hand from his. "Not sad," she said. "Reflective, perhaps."

"About William?"

She shook her head. "About life."

"Your life is going to be just fine."

"You must know something I don't."

"I do. The surprise is another script."

Zoe smiled. She leaned down and picked up her sandals. "Another script?"

"Cal Baker again."

Zoe dropped the shoes. "Cal Baker?" she asked.

"It's a feature. No made-for-TV crap this time."

Zoe looked back over the water. Cal Baker wanted her for another film? Cal Baker? She'd barely made it through the final two weeks of shooting *Close Ties*. She'd hardly spoken to Cal—or he to her—since the incident on the pier. She'd tried to do her best, tried to get through each day, tried to glean hope about Scott after Meg's return from Minnesota. Still, she hadn't been immersed in the film. When they finally wrapped, they were four days past deadline—her fault, she'd heard Cal remark to the producer.

She squatted down and swished her hand across the water. "I didn't think he liked me," she said.

"He saw the dailies. He told me you were great."

Great? Cal Baker thought she was great?

"And besides," Tim continued, "he liked you enough to offer eight hundred thousand for the feature."

Zoe closed her eyes. The sun warmed her skin, the glow warmed her heart. But it didn't filter into the hole that was there, the hole left vacant by Scott. "Eight hundred thousand?" she asked. Could she go through it again? Could she pretend to be cool, calm, in control, when there was such a void in her life?

Tim laughed. "Don't worry. I told him we wouldn't consider anything less than a million."

A million dollars?

"He hesitated the required three minutes, then he agreed."

A million dollars? Zoe was certain she'd stopped breathing.

"Then he said something I've known for years," Tim said.

Zoe shuddered, unable to speak.

"He said you've got the makings of a star."

By the time Zoe stepped inside DiNardo's restaurant that evening, she still hadn't grasped what was happening. She knew that she had been offered a million dollars to do a Cal Baker film. It had taken only a quick read through the script that afternoon for Zoe to know she was going to accept. Cedar Bluff would be hers now, forever. She would have her career back, she would have a life.

But what would life be worth without Scott?

She was glad for the diversion of having to meet Jay Stockwell. She was relieved to have to think of Alissa—instead of herself—if only for a few moments.

She stood in the foyer and surveyed the atmosphere. It was a small restaurant decorated in red, white, and green; the wood floors were crammed with tables occupied by numerous families with noisy children. Straw-basketed wine bottles hung randomly from wooden beams; a long white plastic sign announced the specials of the day in black stick-on letters. Alissa, Zoe thought, would have hated it.

A broad-hipped hostess approached her with a smile. If she recognized Zoe, she discreetly gave no indication. On Sunset Strip, Zoe remembered, stars weren't a big deal. Not to the natives.

Zoe explained that she had to meet someone she didn't know. "He's about five eleven, sandy hair, glasses." She omitted the part that Alissa said about his having a hot body. "His name is Jay Stockwell."

"Jay? Sure," the hostess said. "He's over there, in the bar." She pointed toward a room off the dining room.

Zoe nodded her thanks and went into the bar. There was only one person there, a man. He was, however, not seated on a stool. He stood behind the bar, wearing a white apron, washing glasses.

She went in and sat on a stool. "You wouldn't be Jay, would you?" she asked.

"That's me," he answered brightly. "What's your pleasure?"

Zoe fought back a laugh. This was Alissa's Jay Stockwell, man of the world? Zoe was sure Alissa had no idea he would be tending bar. If she had, chances were she never would have wanted Zoe to meet him. "Are you really Jay Stockwell?" Zoe asked. Though he was quite good-looking in a laid-back, liberal sort of way, Zoe couldn't quite picture Alissa loving a man who didn't have a starched collar and gray at his temples. Zoe wished she'd paid more attention when she'd seen him on television.

"Actually," he said as he swished a glass in rinse water and held it up to the light, checking for spots, "my Christian name is James Ellis Stockwell the Fourth." He peered over at Zoe. "Kind of makes you gag, doesn't it?"

Zoe laughed. "Are you really Jay Stockwell, the television journalist?"

He set down the glass and smiled. "I'm flattered that you recognize me," he said. Zoe was instantly taken with his warmth. "We media types aren't usually too popular with movie stars like Zoe."

Zoe felt herself blush. "My secret's out," she said quietly.

"And mine," he laughed as he leaned against the bar. "You've discovered how I keep myself sane when I'm in this lousy town, land of the plastic people."

Now, more than before, Zoe couldn't imagine Alissa with this down-to-earth guy. Not twenty-four years ago. Not ever. But the thought of Alissa roused her sympathy again, and she wondered what was going on in Atlanta.

"What brings you to our humble eatery?" he asked.

"Better still," Zoe said, looking around, "what brings your 'humble eatery' to Sunset Strip?" She hoped he wasn't offended, but DiNardo's hardly resembled the awning-entranced, thickly carpeted, fine dining establishments of the world-famous avenue.

"It's a joke on the tourists," Jay said with a wink. "Believe it or not, they don't care about the accoutrements. But because we're on the Strip, they think our little restaurant must be loaded with stars. Which isn't true. Or, rather, wasn't until tonight."

"Did you say 'our' little restaurant? Do you own this?"

"Partly," he answered. "The DiNardos are old pals. Mama DiNardo makes the best sauce this side of Napoli. I encouraged her to open it."

And probably helped foot the bill, Zoe thought.

"Are you dining with us tonight?" he asked with a friendly flourish of a white cotton dish towel.

He has a wonderful smile, Zoe thought. *Maybe that's what Alissa loves about him.* Alissa. She realized she'd been taken off guard a moment, captured by Jay's charm. She cleared her throat. "I came to see you," she said. "To give you a message."

"You? Came to give me a message? Don't tell me. Warner Brothers thinks I'm the next Tom Cruise."

Zoe laughed.

"Okay, okay, so I'm a little old to be Tom."

She grinned and noticed that through the lenses of his glasses Jay's eyes were remarkably green. Alissa hadn't mentioned that. *Alissa. That's why I'm here.* Alissa, Atlanta, homosexuals, and murder. The muscles in her cheeks relaxed, her smile disappeared. "Actually," she said, "I'm a friend of Alissa's."

"You? You're a friend of Alissa's?"

If that surprised him, Zoe couldn't tell by his expression. "She asked me to do her a favor, so here I am."

"Don't tell me," Jay said, rinsing another glass, "she's not coming."

"She didn't want you to think it was because she didn't want to."

Jay shook his head and set the glass in the drainer. Zoe noticed that the beautiful smile had vanished from his face. "Alissa does what Alissa wants. She always has. She probably always will."

"Honestly," Zoe said, feeling the need to defend her friend. "She wanted to come. But there was a family crisis. She had to fly back to Atlanta today. She didn't want to leave a phone message, so I offered to explain it in person."

Jay set the glass in the drainer. "Message delivered. Thank you," he said without looking up.

Zoe sensed he was angry. Or was he hurt? Whatever it was, Jay obviously didn't believe her. "It really is true," she said. "I was there when the phone call came." Alissa would be devastated if Zoe couldn't convince Jay. And devastation over Jay Stockwell was the last thing her friend needed right now.

Jay shrugged. "I don't think she would have liked it here, anyway."

"Oh, I think she might have. It's quite"—she paused, trying to come up with the right word—"charming." And so, Zoe decided, was Jay. No wonder Alissa wanted to find him again. No wonder she had never stopped loving him.

"Charming, yes. But Alissa always preferred elegant. Oysters Rockefeller, not ziti and meatballs."

"Maybe she's changed."

"Maybe," Jay said, then smiled again, "and maybe not."

"You hadn't seen each other for a long time."

He turned off the water and wiped his hands. "But some things you never forget."

It wasn't anger, Zoe knew now. What Jay Stockwell was feeling was hurt. Probably an old hurt. Uncovered, unearthed, when it shouldn't have been.

Eric.

She tried to make the pain go away.

"Anyway," Jay was saying, "DiNardo's is strictly for people who appreciate good food served by your basic, fun-loving Italians. Are you interested?"

Zoe wasn't quite sure what he meant.

"You haven't lived until you've had Mama's linguine marinara."

"Is that an invitation?" she asked.

"Absolutely," he answered as he untied the apron. "Besides, it's rather humiliating for a grown man to be stood up, especially when this date was her idea."

Alissa's idea?

Zoe wondered if she should stay. This was Alissa's man, the love of her life. But, then, it was only linguine marinara, and Jay Stockwell, Zoe was certain, was only being friendly.

He hung his apron on a peg and moved from behind the bar. "Dinner?" he asked again.

She was still trying to make up her mind as he walked toward her. And then Zoe noticed his limp. And she knew that this man had gone through pain, and that he probably didn't need Alissa to cause him any more.

There were three courses even before the linguine marinara appeared. Soup. Salad. Antipasto. Zoe was glad she'd worn a long cotton-gauze elastic-waist skirt with matching overblouse. The gold chain belt was designed to hang loosely from her waist: it was a good thing, or there would have been positively no room for Mama DiNardo's pasta.

"Tell me about Alissa," he said as the waiter delivered two heaping platters.

Zoe stared at her plate. "I can tell you Alissa would not be pleased if she could see what I'm about to stuff into myself."

Jay laughed. "Don't worry about it. You look terrific."

Zoe felt a tingle in her heart. "You wouldn't say that if you'd seen me four months ago."

Jay picked up his fork and dug in. "I don't agree."

Zoe tentatively followed his lead and plunged her fork into the mound of calories. "Actually, I have Alissa to thank for the way I look now. She's a great makeover artist."

"Great makeover artist or not, she's missing out on one terrific meal."

"I agree," Zoe said. She smiled as she watched Jay twirl the pasta around his fork. She wondered why he limped; something told her it would make him laugh if he knew that she, too, had limped for years. Too many years.

"So what happened in Atlanta?" Jay asked. "Why is Alissa missing this meal, anyway?

Zoe set down her fork and took a sip of wine. "A family emergency."

"I hope it's not serious." He, too, set down his fork. Then he shook his head. "God," he said, "I got so wrapped up in talking about the past last night I never even asked what she's been doing. Is she married? Does she have kids?"

Zoe hesitated. "Yes," she said finally. "She has a husband. And two daughters."

Jay nodded. "That's good. Alissa needed a solid home life. She didn't need to be wandering all over the globe." But as he reached for his wineglass, Zoe thought she saw that look of hurt again on his face.

"It's odd," Zoe said, "that the person you thought you wanted to spend the rest of your life with, you suddenly realize would have been so wrong for you." She hadn't meant to sound so direct; she had only wanted to make Jay feel better. She crossed her ankles under the table and hoped she hadn't said anything wrong.

"We go back a long way, Alissa and me," Jay said. "Since we were kids. Our families' estates were near each other. Not to mention the fact that we were both spoiled, overindulged kids."

"I can't relate to that," Zoe said. "My parents never had enough to overindulge me with."

"You were better off. Too much money for a kid means too many problems."

They ate silently for a moment. Zoe wondered if she should tell Jay the details of what had happened with Alissa—of the phone call, of her daughter's arrest. Surely it would be in all the newspapers. Then Zoe remembered this man was a journalist. If he had been in his office today and not up in San Francisco at that meeting, he might have seen it come over the wire services.

"Alissa has a rather serious problem herself right now."

Jay set down his fork again. "So. It is serious."

"Actually, it's her daughter who has the problem," she said quickly.

"What happened?"

Zoe dabbed the red-and-white checked napkin to the corners of her mouth. She wondered if the left side was drooping. "There was some sort of accident," she said.

He leaned forward. "An accident?"

"It's apparently all a mistake. Her daughter accidently killed a man."

"Car accident?"

"No. She shot him."

Jay took off his glasses and set them on the table. Then he rubbed his eyes. "Jesus," he said, "Alissa must be frantic."

"Yes. But that's all I really know." She didn't want to tell him the details; she didn't want to tell him about Robert. "Does this mean you'll forgive her for not coming tonight?"

Jay smiled that wonderful smile. "I'm sorry for Alissa's problems. I'm sorry for her. But to be honest with you, I forgave her the moment you agreed to have dinner with me."

Zoe returned his smile. Their eyes lingered a moment, their voices didn't speak. Then Zoe remembered the sparkle in Alissa's eyes when she'd said to Zoe: *I feel like finding Jay again is the best thing that's ever happened to me.* Zoe quickly flicked her gaze away from Jay. She picked up her fork, then set it down again.

"Are you married, Zoe? Do you have children?"

"I'm recently widowed," she said. "I have a fourteen-year-old son. What about you?"

Jay laughed. "Not me. After Alissa dumped me, I decided to remain a bachelor for the rest of my life. By the time I realized that was a fairly stupid thing to do, I was too busy globe-trotting to get tied down, or worse, to tie a woman down. Not that I haven't regretted it . . ." His sentence ended somewhere in the air.

So Jay had been the one who'd been hurt. As Zoe had been. As Meg. "We all have regrets," Zoe said. *Eric.* Damn.

"But let's talk about you," Jay said, brightening again. "I feel like I've known you for years."

She stared at the tablecloth, then looked back into his eyes. Is that a compliment?"

He shrugged playfully. "Nope. Just an observation. Probably because I've seen every movie you've ever made."

She smiled. "Well, I've seen you, too. On the news. So we're even."

"No, we're not. I've seen your movies all over the world. You have no idea how intriguing you are with Japanese coming out of your lips."

She laughed. It was so nice to be with a man she could laugh with. Sit across the dinner table from, and talk, and laugh. "Do people recognize you wherever you go?" she asked.

"No. But I do get recognized a lot."

"It's difficult, isn't it?"

"Yeah. But I don't let it get to me." He twirled his pasta again. "But, hey," he added, "I could be somebody nobody knows tomorrow, and that would be okay, too."

Zoe took another sip of wine. She liked it that Jay wasn't impressed with who she was, or who she'd been, or who she might be again. He didn't seem to be. But, then, Jay had to deal with the perils of celebritydom in his own right. It was wonderful to feel on equal ground with a man.

Alissa. This was Alissa's man.

She took her napkin from her lap and set it beside her plate. "This has been a wonderful dinner," she said, "and a nice surprise for an evening. But I should be getting home."

"Really?"

Before Zoe was sure what had happened, Jay's hand reached across the table and rested on top of hers. Without much resistance she looked back into his eyes. He was smiling again, not the somber, lovesick smile of Tim Danahy, but the warm, genuine smile of a man who, though very much comfortable as his own person, was clearly enjoying her company.

"You can't have a proper meal at DiNardo's without a bit of zabaglione. And a cup of espresso."

Zoe didn't speak.

Jay motioned to a waiter. "Peter," he called, "two espressos and one zabaglione with two spoons." He looked back at Zoe. "See? Now you can't leave. Your dessert has already been ordered, and leaving now would be a very un-Italian thing to do."

Zoe laughed. "I'm not Italian. I'm Jewish."

"So? I'm not Italian either. I'm English. With garlic in my bones."

She wished he would take his hand off hers; she hoped he wouldn't.

When the waiter delivered the tiny espresso cups, Jay removed his hand. Zoe watched as he rubbed the rind of a lemon around the rim of the cup; then she followed suit. She took a sip of the thick, dark liquid and immediately felt the inside of her mouth squirm. She quickly set down the cup.

Jay laughed. "You don't have to drink it if you don't like it."

Zoe smiled. "It's been a long time since I've had any."

A dish of desert arrived: the waiter put it in the center of the table.

"You must try this," Jay said as he handed her a spoon. "It's not bitter. I promise."

Zoe raised her spoon and took a small bit from the plate. It was foamy and smooth, and in her mouth it tasted like sweet custard, still warm from the stove.

"Oooh," she said, "you're right. This is wonderful." She returned her spoon to the plate they now shared. Their spoons touched, and Zoe felt a tiny thrill of arousal. They looked at each other again. Jay smiled.

"I'm glad you like it," he said. "Now tell me what else you like."

Zoe smiled back and took another spoonful of custard.

"Let me guess," he said. "How do you feel about driving up the coast?"

The custard melted on her tongue. *Driving up the coast.* She and Eric had done that when they'd first come to L.A. With his busboy tips they'd put a down payment on an old Volkswagen convertible and explored the breathtaking coastline, their dreams full of hope, their hearts full of innocence. It was, Zoe knew, a wonderful memory. But it was just that: a memory. The past. "It's been a long time," she answered Jay now.

"Then how about tomorrow? It's my day off, and I can't think of anything I'd rather do."

She folded her hands in her lap. Things were happening so fast. Too fast. Still . . .

Alissa, she thought. *Scott. Eric.* The million-dollar script that sat in her study.

"I'd love that, Jay. But . . ."

He groaned. "Why did I sense there was going to be a 'but'?"

Zoe laughed. "But I've got an awful lot going on in my life right now."

"All the more reason for a drive up the coast. Clear the

cobwebs, and all that." He winked at her with confidence, yet not arrogance; friendship, yet not pressure.

Still, he was the man Alissa loved. Had loved. Maybe still did love. And didn't Alissa have enough problems right now?

"Jay," she said, wishing that the sounds of other people in the restaurant hadn't grown so quiet. "I had a lovely time tonight. You'll never know how nice this has been for me." She took a sip of her water. "And as much as I'd love to see you again, I just wouldn't feel right."

He put his napkin on the table and studied it, as if reading a script. "Because of Alissa?"

Zoe nodded.

He folded the napkin into a triangle, then opened it again. "Look, Zoe, I don't know how to say this. You know that Alissa and I have a history together. But, honestly, that's what it is. History. In some strange way I probably still care for her—no, not care *for* her, care *about* her. But only as a growing-up memory."

A growing-up memory. Like Eric. "What if Alissa doesn't feel that way?"

Jay smiled. "I'm sure she will, if she really thinks about it." He refolded his napkin into a triangle.

"You know something," Zoe heard herself say, "I think you might be right. And I think that a drive up the coast tomorrow would be terrific."

He nodded and smiled. And in that instant Zoe knew that Alissa had been right about one thing: Jay Stockwell wasn't like Eric Matthews at all.

The next morning Zoe knew what she had to do. Before Jay came to pick her up, before Marisol returned home from Monterey, before anyone could influence her in any way, Zoe had to take control of her life.

She sat on the deck, sipping her morning tea. There was something about Jay that made her feel comfortable within herself. And yet, she reminded herself, there was something about Jay that could be a problem: Alissa. Yet for all the closeness between Alissa and Jay when they were young, Zoe believed Jay had recovered from the relationship long ago. He had been hurt, he had fond memories, that was apparent. But, then, Zoe had fond memories of Eric, too. Fond memories. And not so fond.

But Zoe knew it was now time to take control of her life, to stop blaming others in her heart for what could have or should have or did or did not happen.

Before she could give it another thought, Zoe set down her mug, went inside the house, and picked up the phone.

It rang twice, then Eric answered.

"Let me speak to my son," Zoe demanded. "Now."

"He's outside playing with the kids."

"Get him."

There was a pause, then Zoe heard Eric put down the phone. While she waited, Zoe realized her heart wasn't thudding, her pulse wasn't racing. *I am,* she thought, *really in control. Finally. I am in control of my own life.*

"Mom?"

"Scott," she said, hearing her voice waver just a little. She quickly cleared her throat. "Scott, enough is enough. I want you home. Today. I'll reserve you a seat on the six-thirty flight out of Minneapolis. You can pick up your ticket at the airport."

He didn't say anything.

"Did you hear me?"

"Yes, Mom, I heard."

She couldn't tell by his voice if he was about to start crying or screaming at her, or if he was about to slam down the receiver.

"The six-thirty flight, Scott. I'll make sure Eric gets you to the airport. Now, put him back on the line."

There was another pause; then Scott said, "Mom?"

"What?" Her heart began to lightly thud.

"Thanks."

She heard the receiver set down. A lump came into her throat. Tears came to her eyes. *Thanks.* He'd said *thanks.*

"What is it Zoe?" It was Eric again. Her heart calmed.

"You're to get Scott to the airport for the six-thirty flight that will get him back to L.A. Do you understand?"

"I told you before, Zoe. I'm not stupid. But you're forgetting one thing. Your son told you in his note that if you made him go home, he would notify the media about me. About us."

"I think if you talk to Scott, you'll see that he's changed his mind." She stared out the glass doors onto the deck. Marisol sat there, her back to the door. But Zoe knew she could hear every word she as saying. And Zoe knew Marisol was proud of her.

"Maybe he changed his mind," Eric said. "But I haven't."

Her jaw tightened. "What are you talking about?"

"Just what I said. Maybe Scott won't notify the media, but I will. He's my son as much as he is yours. You seem to keep forgetting that."

"You bastard," she said, her voice rising. "Even if you'd known I was pregnant, you probably would have left anyway."

Eric paused for a moment, then sighed. "I did know you were pregnant, Zoe."

Somewhere in his words Zoe thought she'd stopped breathing.

"I knew it would ruin your career," he continued, then stopped, then started again. "I thought if I was out of the picture, you'd get an abortion. I never dreamed you'd marry William. Or anybody. And I sure never dreamed you'd have the baby."

Zoe sucked in a breath. "You thought I'd get an abortion?" She couldn't believe what she'd heard. "You thought I'd kill our baby?"

"I knew how much you wanted your career. I knew how good you were. But what was I?" His voice cracked. "I couldn't have been Mr. Zoe Hartmann. I would have been miserable. And so would you. I did what I thought was best."

She closed her eyes and took a deep breath, a deep,

steady breath, a steadying breath. "If you never knew that Scott had been born, why do you want him now?"

Silence hung heavily. "Because he is my son, Zoe. Our son. And because you owe me this."

She took another breath, then thought about Jay, about his easy, comforting manner. Then she opened her eyes and carefully spoke the words that had been taking shape for years—words that were fraught with retribution, with truth; words that were waiting to be delivered to one person, and one person only. "That's what this is really about, isn't it, Eric? It has nothing to do with the baby—with Scott. It has to do with you and me. Because the truth is, you never forgave me for being the one to make it. You never forgave me for being the star."

Tension hung over the line.

"Zoe, it's ancient history now. But I swear," Eric said finally, his voice growing low, almost angry, "if you try to make Scott leave here, I'll call the press."

A vision came into her mind of when she sat by the pool, thinking of Alissa, thinking of Scott. Did it really matter what anyone thought anymore? Was Zoe going to go on living her life in fear of what everyone thought? And who the hell was "everyone" anyway? And did they really give a shit about her?

Eric said the past was ancient history. He was right. And she was tired of letting the past rule her life.

"Then call the media, Eric," she said. "I don't care what you do. Just get Scott on that plane tonight, or I'll have the FBI crawling all over your house like ticks on your dog. The last time I heard, kidnapping was a capital offense."

18

*M*eg stood in the middle of her huge closet, sorting through clothes. One pile for the Salvation Army; one pile for the trash. She still hadn't made a decision about how she'd spend the rest of her life. Or, at least, the next stage. In the meantime sorting through old clothes was a way to purge herself of the past, a way to begin what she was afraid would be a long process of detaching herself from her material possessions—possessions she had hoarded in lieu of love. She still had thoughts of Steven—not as often as she'd once had, but, nonetheless, the thoughts were still there. It was different now, though, for when he came into her mind, it was as though he had been only a dream, an apparition of hope, a ghost of love. She did not know if there would be any more Stevens in her life; she only hoped there would be no more Roger Barretts, or any other unfulfilling, empty relationships.

Raggedy Man sauntered into the closet, climbed over one pile onto the other, then stretched out his front paws, arched his hind end, and yawned.

"Do you find this as boring as I do?" Meg asked as she bent to rub his fur. "Does it bother you that I don't go off to work every day? Have I invaded your space?" She scratched his ears and waited for the purr that she knew wouldn't come. Raggedy Man was too self-assured, too confident in her love for him to indicate that he needed or wanted any affection. *Leave it to me to get a male cat,* Meg thought as she heard the ringing of chimes. It took her a moment to realize it was the doorbell, an unfamiliar, infrequent sound here in her private domain.

The chimes rang again. She sighed and kicked aside a stack of clothes. It had to be someone looking for someone she didn't know or selling something she didn't need.

It was Danny.

"Hey, stranger," he said brightly, and stepped inside the door. "I happened to be in the neighborhood...."

"At least you rang the bell this time." Meg smiled and closed the door behind him. She wondered if, wherever she ended up, she'd ever find as good a friend as Danny.

He made himself at home it the study, amid the piles of papers and cartons of books that Meg had begun weeding out, organizing, packing—memories of a life's chapter completed, making room for a new one to begin. Danny was, Meg knew, never one to spend much time in living rooms. He claimed that living rooms were too formal, too uninviting, too much a reminder of too many years lived in stifled silence being seen and not heard at his overbearing grandmother's. He never offered any other information about his family, and Meg never pried, preferring instead to maintain mutual unspoken bounds on the subject of their personal lives.

Meg sat on the floor in front of him and straightened papers as he spoke.

"I still can't believe you've done this."

"All I've done is quit my job, Danny. A career change as one nears forty is hardly anything new. Or shocking."

"Not if one has a plan."

"All I know now is that whatever I do, it will be on my terms, handling cases I want, not those dictated to me by senior partners." She moved a stack of papers to one side. "I want a peaceful life now, Danny. A quiet life."

"Seems to me your life has been fairly quiet right here, doing what you've been doing."

The telephone rang.

Meg smiled. "It was until today." She reached for the phone.

"Meg." It wasn't a question, it was a statement. "God, Meg, I called your office. They said you don't work there anymore."

It was a female voice, but Meg couldn't place it. "Who is this?"

"It's me, Meg. Alissa."

"Oh." She looked over at Danny and rolled her eyes. "Alissa. How are you?"

"How am I? Do you really have to ask how I am? Don't you read the papers?"

Meg laughed. "I try not to."

"Well, if you'd read them this morning, you'd know. There's been an accident. A man is dead."

"What kind of accident?" Visions of Candace Riley sprang to Meg's mind. Danny put his elbows on his knees and leaned forward. "And who's dead?"

She listened carefully as Alissa spilled her story. Fortunately, it had nothing to do with Candace. It had nothing to do with Steven. Alissa's daughter Natalie had come home from a date. She had surprised an intruder in the library. She had grabbed for the gun they kept in the desk drawer. The intruder had picked up the fireplace poker. Natalie had been frightened and the gun mistakenly had gone off.

"Was anyone else in the house?"

"My husband. He was upstairs, asleep. He's still recuperating from surgery. My other daughter wasn't home, and Dolores and Howard didn't hear anything. They never do."

Meg watched Danny as she carefully asked the next question. "Are you certain this is what happened?"

"What kind of a question is that? Of course I'm certain.

My daughter may be a lot of things, but she's not a liar, and she's not a murderer."

Murder? Meg bit her lip. "Does she have a good lawyer?" Meg asked. She'd learned long ago that it was best to stay objective, not to offer advice on a case she knew nothing about.

"She will have."

"That's good," Meg said, but thought, *She's going to need a good one.* No witnesses. Nothing more than Natalie's word against the prosecution.

"She's going to have you," Alissa said.

Meg thought she must have heard her wrong. "Excuse me?"

"I want you to defend my daughter."

Meg looked at Danny and scowled. He stood up and began pacing the room. He was, she knew, itching to find out what she was hearing. "Alissa," she said slowly, "has your daughter been charged with anything?"

"Not yet. But with these overeager police it won't be long."

"She should have an attorney present if they're questioning her."

"I remember *Perry Mason*, Meg. I'm not exactly stupid."

"Then you'd better get a lawyer. Fast."

"As I recall, Atlanta is only a two-hour flight from New York."

"Alissa." Meg cautiously chose her next words. "You already know I'm no longer at the firm. What you don't know is that I'm no longer practicing criminal law."

"Don't tell me that. I won't listen."

"Alissa, it's true. But I'm sure I can recommend someone in your area ..."

"I don't want anyone in my goddamn area! I know them all. They're all assholes who only care about their reputations and how much publicity they can get for themselves."

Meg smiled at the irony in Alissa's words. She was glad they were having this conversation on the phone and not face-to-face. Danny stopped beside her and sat on the edge of the desk. Meg didn't want to look at him; she was afraid she would laugh out loud.

"Alissa," she said, "I'd love to help you. But as I said, I've given up criminal law."

"I think you'll change your mind."

"I don't."

"Even if it means the media finding out about you?"

Meg felt a cold wave crawl up her spine. The smile vanished from her face. "What are you talking about?"

"I'm talking about you, Meg. Would it make a difference to you if the media found out about you ... and Senator Steven Riley?"

Meg reached out and grabbed Danny's forearm. "Alissa, you don't know ..."

"That's where you're wrong, Meg. I do know. I know all about you and the senator. He was married when you had your affair and he still is." She laughed a tight, sneering laugh. "His wife is having a few problems of her own right now, too, isn't she? It seems to me the press would have a real field day between the both of them."

"Alissa," Meg said, "this is blackmail."

Danny bolted off the desk and tried to grab the phone from Meg. She moved back and gripped it firmly.

"Call it what you will, darling, but that's the deal. You help my daughter, or you and your precious lover will be smeared all over the world."

It took two glasses of wine to get Meg to stop shaking.

"She's serious, Danny," Meg said. "That bitch will do it."

"She's not serious, Meg. She's scared. It was the only way she could think of to get what she wanted. That's Alissa's way."

"Jesus, Danny. Whose side are you on?"

He shook his head. "Not hers. But I do understand Alissa. I understand where she's coming from, and I'm telling you, she's scared."

Meg rubbed the back of her neck. It was hard to believe that only an hour ago she was calmly sorting through clothes, speculating on the possibilities of her new life. Now, because the daughter of a friend who wasn't even really a friend was in trouble, pessimism for her own future was seeping in. "She said the 'accident' was reported in the morning papers. Didn't you see them?" Meg asked.

"Yeah. There was nothing I noticed. It probably won't hit New York until tomorrow. Besides, if it was self-defense, it won't cause much of a ripple."

Meg chewed her lip and thought about what Danny had just said. "There's something that doesn't feel right. Alissa said her daughter wasn't a murderer. Why would she even have mentioned the word if everything was so simple?"

Danny shrugged. "My guess is your friend tends to over-react."

"I know. But you didn't hear the intensity in her voice when she said it." She poured another glass of wine, hoping it would numb her the way the first two hadn't. "And why blackmail? Self-defense would hardly warrant that." She took a slow sip of wine. "And why me?"

"What are you going to do?"

Meg started trembling again. "I've got to call Steven. I've got to warn him."

"Does that mean you're not going to help her?"

"Even if I did, what makes you think Alissa won't use what she knows against me someday? It's blackmail, Danny. Blackmailers save their information for when they need it."

"And I'm telling you, she's not thinking of blackmail here. She's just damned scared."

"I wish I could believe you."

Danny paced the study once again. "If you want to help her, count me in."

"What are you talking about?"

"I said count me in. Maybe we should at least go down there. See what it's about. Dig up some facts."

Meg laughed. "Is it that you want to help me, or that you want to see Alissa again?"

Danny leaned against the bookcase and folded his arms. "I said I'll help. I mean it."

Meg took a deep breath and let it out quickly. "I've got to call Steven." She shook her head. "For the life of me, I can't imagine how she found out."

"People like Alissa have a way of finding out things. But maybe this isn't so bad."

"What do you mean?"

"At least she's given you a good excuse to contact lover boy again."

"You know, Danny, I think that deep down, you really like Alissa."

"Let's just say I understand her."

"That's all?"

"Yeah. Besides, she isn't interested in me. The last time I saw her, she couldn't get away fast enough." He started toward the door, then stopped. "Oh, shit," he said aloud.

"Shit?"

He turned back to Meg. "My hotel room. In Atlanta. I had to make a call." He returned to the study and sat down. "Shit. My grandmother ..."

"Your *grandmother*?"

Danny nodded and ran his hands through his hair. "She broke her hip."

"God, Danny, I didn't even know she was alive."

Danny frowned. "She's tucked away in her manor, upstate on the Hudson. She raised me."

Meg was confused. "What's your grandmother got to do with Alissa?"

He stood up again. He paced. "She's got nothing to do with Alissa. It's with you. And Steven. When I met with Alissa in Atlanta, I went into the bedroom to make the call to the hospital. To check on her. My briefcase was in the other room. With Alissa."

"And?"

"And inside I had the file with the clippings on the senator's wife. The car accident. I must have had notes with your name on them."

Meg set down her wineglass and watched the pale-yellow liquid sway from the impact. "And Alissa helped herself to the file and put two and two together."

Danny nodded. "So it appears."

She stared at the glass until the liquid settled. "Then it's true," she said. "She really does know."

Danny sat down again. "God, Meg. I'm so sorry. I was only trying to help you."

The senator, his assistant told Meg, was out to lunch. She left a message that this was an emergency, then hung up the phone and told Danny she would be in touch. After Danny left, Meg slouched on the sofa in the study, her thoughts whirring, her eyes glued to the phone. *Ring, dammit.*

When it rang an hour and a half later, Meg jumped as though she'd been shot by sniper fire. His voice was tentative, on guard, as though she were an associate, as though they'd never been intimate.

Slowly, Meg told him the story.

When she was finished, there was silence for a moment. Then Steven said, "How did she find out?"

Meg thought about Danny. Her friend. He'd only been trying to help. "I've no idea how she found out," she said.

"Well, it doesn't matter. She knows, and there's no sense denying it."

"But, Steven, if the press finds out ..."

"If they do, they do. I've got nothing to hide."

"What are you talking about?"

"Listen, Meg, I've done a lot of thinking since I saw you." He paused a moment. She heard a half laugh. "Actually, I've done more than think. I've left Candace. I've filed for divorce."

Meg sat perfectly still, trying to digest his words. But

something about them wasn't getting through, as though she was afraid to believe them.

"Public sympathy probably won't be with me, so I may be through in politics," Steven continued, "but maybe going back to practicing law won't be such a bad idea."

Meg pressed her temple. Her breathing had grown short, shallow.

"If you want to defend your friend," Steven continued, "then you should do it because you want to help her. Don't do it to protect me."

Protect him? Is that what she was trying to do? Of course it was, Meg realized. The same way she'd tried to protect him by having the abortion, the same way she'd tried to protect him from herself ... and from the misery she could have caused in his life. Protection. But at what cost?

She took a deep breath. "My friend says he doesn't think she'll do anything. That she's just scared."

Steven paused, then said, "I was going to ask how well you know her, but I've realized lately that no matter how well we think we know someone, we never really do."

He was, she knew, speaking of her. He was trying to tell her he didn't understand why she'd left him—twice. But what he didn't realize was that Meg hadn't really known Steven either, for in her heart she had never believed that Steven would leave his wife, she had never believed that he had the courage to jeopardize his career. She'd never believed it, because she'd been so afraid of being hurt. She'd been afraid; she'd been scared. She thought about Alissa. Maybe Danny was right. Maybe she was just scared, too. Damned scared. "I have to think about this some more," Meg said. "I've quit the firm, you know. I've decided to get out of criminal law."

"No," he said quietly. "I didn't know." He didn't say it, but she could hear surprise in his voice. "What are you planning to do?"

Meg suddenly realized the fact that she had no concrete

plans was foolish. Had she made an immature decision? Had she made it too quickly? She felt as though she were going to cry. She felt as though she were lost in the darkness with no light to show her the way out. "I'm not sure," she said. "Family law, maybe. Women's issues."

Steven paused. "That's good, Meg. I always thought you were meant to be a crusader instead of a barracuda."

Meg made no comment; she was too amazed that Steven had, after all, understood her so well.

"Will you let me know what happens?" he asked. "Not just with your friend, but with yourself? Will you let me know how you're doing?"

Meg bit her lip. "Yes," she said quietly, "of course."

When she hung up the phone, Meg lay on the sofa and felt the tears come. She'd never felt so alone. She had no one to love her, no work to occupy her. All her life she'd been afraid of being abandoned. Now she had been. She wondered if it was a self-fulfilling prophecy, fate, self-induced. More than anything in the world, Meg wanted to rush down to Washington and into Steven's arms. More than anything, she wanted someone to care about her. *Scared.* Yes. Alissa was scared. But so was Meg. She was lost, empty, and truly alone. A painful ache throbbed in her head, then crept through her body. And for the first time in her life Meg allowed herself to feel the fear. Fear that couldn't be masked by studying or reading or by working on all the legal cases in the world. For she knew that if she didn't finally feel it, she would never face it. And facing it was something that was long overdue.

Two thousand miles away Zoe and Jay stood on the deck of Cedar Bluff, looking out at the morning sun. They had slept together last night; they had made love until dawn. When Zoe protested they were "too old to behave like this," Jay had smiled that wonderful smile and said, "Lady, we've got a lot of years to make up for."

He put his arm around her now. "You're really something,

Zoe. Keeping this magnificent house. Diving back into your career. You're very much a woman of the nineties, aren't you?

Zoe smiled. "Hardly. I'm more like a woman of the seventies, just trying to catch up."

Jay hugged her. "Well, I think it's great what you're doing. Most women wouldn't even attempt it. Especially alone." He rested his chin on her shoulder. "But there's one thing I'd like to know. How flexible are you?"

Zoe pulled away from him and looked through his glasses into his green eyes, the eyes she trusted without hesitation, though she'd known him only a few days. His hair was blowing every which way, the sun melted into his smile. "What kind of a question is that?"

He reached across and took her hand. "I've got to be gone for a couple of weeks. South Korea."

"What's that got to do with my being flexible?"

Jay shrugged, then looked back over the canyon. "I guess I want to be sure you'll still be here when I get back."

Zoe leaned closer to him. "I'll be here, Jay. Well, maybe not here. I may be off shooting the new film, but I'll be back."

"You won't find another guy in the meantime, will you?"

Zoe laughed. She buried herself in his khaki jacket, smelling the sweet scent of the man. "Are you kidding? I'll be too busy studying my lines."

"Ah. Now you're making yourself too available. Don't you know that's not how you play the game?"

"What game?"

"The boy-meets-girl game. The game of love."

Love. It was the first time Jay had mentioned the word. Zoe stood back, her hand still in his, her eyes locked on him. "Is that what this is?" she asked. "Love?"

He smiled that warm, wonderful smile, that little-boy smile. "Damned if I know. But something's happening here. Yesterday I went to work *smiling*, for chrissake. Me. The one who specializes in tugging at the hearts of viewers, in being somber, in exposing doom and gloom. I smile now. And what's worse, I've started whistling."

Zoe couldn't help but laugh.

Just then, from inside the family room, came the sound of whistling. They looked at each other and laughed together, as Scott appeared on the deck.

"What's so funny?" he asked.

"You're whistling," Jay said.

"Yeah, well, why not?"

Zoe felt a glow as she looked at her son. It was so wonderful to have him home. So right. And like herself, he'd taken to Jay right away.

"Scott!" Marisol's voice called from the kitchen. "Get yourself in here and leave your mother alone."

Scott rolled his eyes and ducked back into the house. Zoe leaned against Jay's shoulder again.

"Happy?" he asked.

She closed her eyes and listened to the steady sound of Jay breathing, the morning song of the birds. She wondered how it was possible that she felt she'd known this man all her life—that, without realizing it, she'd waited for him forever. She opened her eyes and looked into his again. She did not know what their future would bring, but right now, right here, Jay Stockwell was making her feel like more of a total woman—spiritually, emotionally, and physically—than any man had ever done. She could not be certain that they'd be together for a long, long time, but she would capture this moment, these feelings, into a velvet box of memory in her mind. And when the craziness of stardom began once again, as Tim Danahy and Cal Baker assured her it would soon do, Zoe would always remember this morning of peace, this very special time of loving so much, of feeling so loved. She closed her eyes again, savoring his arm around her, surrendering to his heart. "Yes," she said quietly, "I am very happy."

As the plane banked its descent into the Atlanta airport, Meg took Danny's hand in hers. "You really are my guardian angel, you know that?"

Danny laughed. "I've been called worse, I suppose. What amazes me right now is that we're coming to the aid of a woman who both of us basically feel is more than a little bit out of her mind."

Meg removed her hand and tucked the magazine on her lap into the pocket behind the seat in front of her. "You said she's scared, Danny. I think you're right. And being scared is a very lonely place to be."

"Are you scared, Meg?"

"Not about Alissa. I have nothing to lose."

"But you do. You have Steven. If you want him."

"Steven is changing his life. So am I. Maybe one day we'll get together again, when we're both clearheaded and no longer afraid." She heard herself say the words, but she didn't believe them.

Danny leaned back on the seat. "Everybody's afraid, Meg."

She laughed. "Surely not you?"

He smiled and took her hand. "I'm glad you're my friend," he said. "I'm glad we never got involved."

Meg looked out the window. "It would have been over by now."

He squeezed her hand, then let it go. "I know."

Meg turned her head back to him. "Tell me about your family," she said, crossing the boundary of privacy, yet, after all these years, now curious about Danny's life. Maybe it was because she, at last, felt comfortable in sharing her own secrets. Some of them. "You were raised by your grandparents?"

Danny nodded. "My grandfather traveled a lot. He was in the wine business. A distributor. When he had to be home, he spent all his time in his greenhouses. With his orchids."

"Orchids. So that's where your passion began."

"I figured my grandfather spent so much time with them

because it was the only way he could stand staying married to my grandmother. I couldn't stand her either."

"Why not?"

The seat-belt sign lit up. Danny pushed a button and his seat moved upright. "She was a bitch. Still is. I guess she's always thought her money gives her that privilege."

"She's wealthy?"

"Very. Even more so after my grandfather died a few years ago, although he did leave a chunky trust fund to me."

"To you? My God. You're one of those independently wealthy trust-fund types?" She put her face in her hands. "Oh, no. I'm so disappointed in you!"

Danny laughed. "I've always had one, Meg. My mother left me one, too."

Meg stopped joking. She took her hands from her face and toyed with the metal ashtray, now soldered closed, on the armrest between them. "What about your parents?"

Danny was quiet a moment. "My father was killed in Korea. I never knew him. My mother died when I was seven."

She rested her hand on his. "How awful for you. Do you remember her?"

"Sure. She was beautiful and busy, always busy. A real socialite, the way my grandmother demanded. But she smoked too much and drank too much champagne. Even though she was her mother's daughter, I don't think she was ever comfortable in that role."

Meg leaned back on the seat. "So that's why you have no patience with rich women."

Danny shrugged.

"What about Alissa? Do you think she's uncomfortable in her role?"

Danny thought for a moment. "Let's just say I think there's more to Alissa than we see. And, yeah, I think that maybe she was never given a chance to be the kind of person she could have become."

"But apparently she did once. With Jay Stockwell."

"She was too young. Too scared."

"And now she's scared again." Meg looked out the window and watched the streets and buildings grow larger. "What happened to your mother, Danny?"

The plane dipped toward the runway.

"She was scared, too," he said quietly. "So she killed herself."

"I thought you'd never get here," Alissa said as she opened the front door to them.

Meg ignored Alissa's gesture to follow her. "Before we come in," Meg said, "there's something we have to discuss."

Alissa turned around. "Money? That will hardly be a problem."

"Not money. Blackmail. As an attorney I am an officer of the court. I could arrest you."

Alissa looked at Danny, then back to Meg. "You're serious, aren't you?"

"Quite."

Alissa pursed her lips and nodded. "Is it an apology you're looking for? Well, okay, then, I'm sorry." She sighed and put her hand to her forehead. "Jesus, Meg, I'm desperate. Can't you see that?"

"And I'm going to tell you something, Alissa. I will speak with your daughter. I will see if I can help. *If* I want to help. But if you ever so much as mention the name Steven Riley around me again, you'll be the one with the legal problems."

Alissa stared at her a moment, then nodded. "I understand," she said quietly.

As Meg and Danny stepped through the doorway, Danny touched Meg's elbow. "Nice going, counselor." He winked.

Natalie had not been arrested, though the possibility loomed. Meg and Danny sat on winged-back Queen Anne chairs in Alissa's living room, a long, museumlike room filled with dark-cherry furniture, nineteenth-century landscape paintings, and small bronze sculptures. Robert and Natalie were seated across from them on a Victorian sofa; Alissa moved to the large marble fireplace, where she positioned herself, poised, the unflinching matriarch. Michele, according to Alissa, was far too humiliated over the entire incident to be present.

"Before I agree to get involved, Natalie, there are a few questions I need to ask," Meg said.

"I told you what happened," Alissa said sharply. "It was an accident. But even if it weren't, the worst it could be called is self-defense."

Meg didn't acknowledge Alissa. "Natalie?" she asked.

Natalie twisted her hands in her lap. She was a beautiful girl, Meg noted, dark-haired like her father, but with her mother's fair complexion and piercing blue eyes. But she was too heavily made up for the witness stand and wore her skirts too tight and too short to garner any sympathy from a jury. Meg made a mental note to change these things if it came to trial.

"It's like my mother told you," Natalie finally said. She spoke in a small, frightened tone that belied her tough-looking facade. "I grabbed the gun to scare him. When he picked up the poker, I was the one who got scared. The gun went off." She dropped her gaze to the navy-and-maroon Oriental carpet. "I never shot a gun before. I never even held one."

Robert leaned his head against the back of the sofa and stared at the ceiling.

Danny crossed his legs and rubbed a scuff mark from his boot.

Alissa began drumming her fingernails on the ornately carved mantle.

"Does anyone have any idea how the victim got into the house? Was there forced entry?"

"Yes," Robert said quickly. "Derek came in through the French doors in the library. He broke the glass, then apparently reached inside and unlocked the dead bolt."

"Didn't you hear any noise, Doctor?"

"I was asleep."

Alissa spoke sharply. "Why are you asking all these questions? It sounds like you don't believe us."

Meg paid no attention to her and continued. "There's no alarm on the house?"

"No," Robert answered. "This house was built in the fifties. We've never have had a system installed."

Meg made a note and concealed her surprise. A house this size? With all these expensive things? Maybe Atlanta was safer than New York. Maybe the people down here weren't as paranoid.

Danny uncrossed his legs and moved forward on his chair. His next move, Meg assumed, would be to go into the library and check out the claim of "forced entry."

Meg looked over at Alissa. "You weren't at home?"

Alissa fixed her gaze on Danny, then turned to Meg. "No. I was in Los Angeles."

From the corner of her eye Meg could feel Danny's gaze penetrate Alissa's. Obviously he knew something about this. *What on earth,* Meg wondered, *was Alissa doing in Los Angeles?* Did Danny know something about it? Danny, Meg thought. Alissa. There was, as far as she knew, only one connection: Jay Stockwell. Hadn't Danny said he'd located Jay in L.A.? It had to be, Meg thought. Alissa had been with Jay Stockwell while her daughter was shooting a man.

The doorbell rang. The eyes in the living room darted around to one another. Low, muffled sounds came from the foyer; then Alissa's housekeeper escorted two men into the living room. They flashed opened, flat wallets and introduced themselves as police detectives.

"We'd like to look around if you don't mind."

Meg stood. "Excuse me, gentlemen, I'm Meg Cooper. An attorney. What is it you're looking for?"

One of the men sighed, reached into his breast pocket, and pulled out a piece of paper. "Yes, counselor," he said tiredly, "we have a search warrant." The other man browsed the room with his eyes.

"What are you looking for now?" Alissa barked as she folded her arms across herself. "I've had just about all I can take of you people swarming all over my house."

"Evidence, ma'am," the man who seemed to be in charge replied. "The preliminary autopsy report came back, and there are a few discrepancies we need to clear up."

Meg quickly noticed that all three Pages—Alissa, Robert, and Natalie—seemed to freeze in the moment, like statues, their heads, their arms, suddenly stone. They didn't even seem to blink.

"What discrepancies?" Meg asked.

"First of all, the victim's body has an exit wound through the lungs. Our officers didn't locate a bullet in the library. We need to double-check."

Danny hauled himself to his feet and shook his jeans over the tops of his ankle-high boots. Meg knew if there was any evidence left to uncover, he would want to watch the police firsthand. He followed the men from the room, leaving Meg alone with the three distraught family members who undoubtedly had something they were covering up.

Alissa crossed the room and tugged at a bellpull. "I don't know about anyone else, but I could use a drink," she announced.

It was almost an hour before Danny and the detectives returned to the living room. As they stepped in, Danny shot Meg a look that told her something was wrong. The detective in charge walked over to Natalie and stood in front of her.

"I think it's time for a trip downtown," he said.

Alissa moved between them. "This is preposterous," she said. "My daughter isn't going anywhere."

The detective reached into his pants pocket and produced a set of keys. He gave them a quick toss into the air, then caught them. "We may not know exactly what happened here yet," he said calmly, "but there's one thing we now know for certain." He tossed his keys again; the jangle broke

Alissa's silent, icy stare. "We now know that everyone here is lying. And it's time to get at the truth."

"Are you arresting my daughter?" Alissa asked, her face so close to the detective's that Meg was sure he would wince at the whiskey on her breath. He didn't.

"We're just bringing her in for formal questioning," he said, then added coolly, "You're welcome to come, ma'am. And," he turned his face to Meg, "her attorney, too, of course."

They sat at a long wooden table in the interrogation room—Meg, Danny, Natalie, Alissa, and Robert—waiting for the detectives to join them.

"You have to tell me the truth," Meg tried to convince them, although what little she knew of Alissa, she wondered if this would be at all possible. People like Alissa lived in the gray areas of life, a little bit vague, not always who or what they appeared. With people like Alissa, sometimes the truth was convenient, sometimes it was not. No matter how much compassion Danny had for Alissa, or how much understanding he had for her unhappy lifestyle, Meg cursed herself for having gotten involved. Chances were, there would be lies upon more lies. And if Natalie was arrested, there would be publicity upon more publicity. But ultimately, the rich would survive. This was exactly the reason Meg had escaped to the spa in the first place; this was exactly the reason she'd decided to give up law. She folded her hands on the table and looked directly at Alissa. "Sooner or later," she said wearily, "they'll figure it out, and it will only be harder on Natalie."

Robert's and Natalie's eyes quickly flicked back and forth to each other, then to Alissa.

"It was an accident," Alissa said. "That's the truth, and that's all that matters."

Meg sighed and sat back in her chair. Whatever they were hiding would come out eventually. She wondered if she'd have the patience to see it through to the end.

Danny stood up. "I'm going to see if I can get a look at the autopsy report."

Meg didn't ask why. She knew Danny must have his reasons.

She spent an exasperating half hour watching mother and daughter shoot knives of tension between them, watching Robert sit quietly with his hands folded, his head bent. World-renowned research physician, Meg thought, helpless when overpowered by aggressive females. Maybe he was so famous for his work because it was the one facet of his life that he could control.

The door to the room opened and Danny stuck his head inside. "Meg. Could you come out here, please?"

Meg was relieved to escape the dynamics of the Page family. Once in the hall Danny closed the door behind her. The two detectives were with him and another, older man. Danny introduced him as the captain.

"We've got a couple of problems," Danny said. "Back at the house we found the bullet that killed the victim."

Meg nodded.

"But it wasn't in the library. It was in the wall of a bedroom, next to the bed."

Meg frowned.

The captain spoke next. "Apparently it was the bedroom used by Dr. Page. His clothes and personal belongings were in the closet."

Meg looked back at Danny. The intruder was killed in Robert's bedroom? She wanted to ask Danny what he thought that meant, but she knew not to ask—or offer—anything in front of the police. It was not in her client's best interest. She silently sighed, accepting for the first time that Natalie was, indeed, her client now.

"There's more," the captain continued. "Your friend here, Mr. Gordon, asked how the victim had been dressed. He wasn't, like we'd expect, dressed in jeans and a T-shirt or some other clothing that might suggest robbery by someone in need—a druggie or something." The captain's eyes narrowed as he spoke; the lines of his high forehead deepened to furrows. "The victim was dressed in a suit. Italian. An expensive job. Plus, traces of aftershave were still discernible. It appeared as though he'd been going out for a night on the town, not an evening of B and E. We'd already done a background check on him. He had no priors. Mr. Gordon here urged us to prod further. That's when we discovered that two years ago the victim worked as a technician in Dr. Page's lab."

Meg could no longer hold back. "A disgruntled ex-employee?"

The detectives snickered. The captain looked at Danny. "You tell her," he said.

Danny cleared his throat and held up a piece of paper for Meg to see. "The autopsy. According to this, the victim had recently"—he paused and looked at the three men, then back to Meg— "ejaculated. We both know that bodily fluids sometimes secrete at the time of death, but the tests indicate the victim had the orgasm *before* death."

Meg stared at him.

"Obviously, he'd had a fine time for himself before he was killed."

"He and Natalie had sex?" Meg asked.

Danny shook his head. "Not he and Natalie," he said. "More than likely, it was he and Robert."

The captain shook his head. "No matter how many times I hear about queers, it's still sickening."

Meg shifted her weight onto one foot. "Danny? Are you sure?"

"Fairly sure." He looked at the paper. "It also answers a lot of other questions."

Without having to ask Meg knew he wasn't referring to the crime; he was referring to Alissa—her unhappiness, her desperation to find Jay Stockwell.

Meg took the autopsy report from Danny while he explained the rest. Then she and Danny returned to the interrogation room.

She tossed the report onto the table. "Okay, people, I want the truth. Robert, was Derek Lyons your lover?"

Robert's mouth gaped open. Natalie looked at the floor. Alissa went white.

"Two years ago," Meg continued, "Derek Lyons was tested for the HIV virus. You ran the test, Robert. You knew that Derek Lyons was HIV positive."

Alissa gasped.

Robert buried his face in his hands. "How did they find out?" he asked.

"The guard at the lab," Danny said.

"Dickson," Alissa muttered. "I knew he was an asshole."

Silence loomed; then Robert sighed. "Bring in the police," he said quietly. "I want to talk."

Meg winced. "I can't advise you to do that."

Robert waved his hand. "I don't need advice. I need to get this over with."

Meg nodded at Danny, who opened the door and signaled the captain and the detectives to join them.

When the door was closed behind them, Robert fixed his eyes on Danny. "How did Dickson find out?" he asked.

Danny glanced at one of the detectives. The detective glanced at the captain. The captain nodded once. The detective looked back at Robert. "He recognized Derek's picture from when he worked there. Derek told him you were running the test. Later Derek told him the results."

The only sound in the room was the captain's raspy breathing.

"You bastard," Alissa hissed. "I cannot believe you were screwing a guy who had AIDS."

"We were careful," he said. "It may surprise you to know that I'm not altogether irresponsible."

The captain walked to the window. The others stood still, not looking at Alissa or Robert, not looking at one another. Meg rubbed the back of her neck and wondered if the officers, like herself, felt awkward at having to witness this family crisis.

The captain coughed. "The guard also told us that Derek left your employ around the same time he tested positive, but that he came around once in a while."

Robert nodded. "He came in for treatment."

"The guard said that Derek was driving a new car. That he'd moved to a new condo." He turned from the window and looked at Robert. "Did you buy them for him, Dr. Page? Were you supporting Derek Lyons?"

Robert didn't answer.

"Jesus Christ," Alissa said as she bolted from her chair and left the room. Danny slowly got up and followed her.

The captain moved to the end of the table. He placed his hands on the edge and leaned forward, his shirtsleeves rolled up, his jaw firm. "Now tell us, Dr. Page, what really happened that night."

Meg listened as Robert Hamilton Page quietly told the story. It wasn't complicated; it was really very sad. Derek and Robert had been lovers for three years. When Derek had tested positive, he'd had nowhere to turn. Robert was the only friend he'd had, and Robert had wanted the time left for Derek to be comfortable, financially secure. Robert did, after all, love Derek.

Meg studied Alissa's husband as he spoke and marveled at his composure. He was a strong man, she guessed, who had survived a great deal of pain.

After Robert's surgery, Robert continued, he and Derek hadn't been able to get together until Alissa had gone to Los Angeles. Derek had come to the house; Natalie was out on a date. She'd arrived home early and went to check on her father. Outside Robert's room—Robert paused to take a deep breath as he said this—Natalie had heard strange sounds.

At this point Meg looked over at Natalie. Mascara-stained tears silently streamed down the girl's face.

"She panicked," Robert said. "She thought something was wrong."

Natalie raised her head. "I heard someone else's voice. I thought he was hurting you, Daddy."

Robert nodded, his face grim. "I know, honey."

The captain turned to Natalie. "I'd like to hear what happened next in your own words, miss. The truth."

Natalie wiped her tears. "I went down to the library and looked for the gun. Then I went back to Daddy's room. It all happened so fast. They were in bed—together." Natalie paused and chewed a fingernail. "Derek saw me. He jumped up and tried to take the gun away. It went off."

Meg studied Natalie's eyes. They were distant, trancelike, as though her words had been rehearsed.

"Nice try," the captain said.

Natalie stared at her finger without looking up.

"They weren't in bed, were they?"

Natalie didn't answer.

"If they had been," the captain continued, "Derek Lyons wouldn't have been fully dressed. In his Italian suit. The bullet went through his clothes."

Natalie wept into her hand.

"Captain," Robert spoke up, "I can explain." He took a long breath, then slowly let it out. "Derek was on the edge of the bed, I was"—he paused again, this time closing his eyes—"I was kneeling on the floor in front of him."

The captain frowned. Clearly, Meg thought, he didn't understand. But she did. She looked over at Natalie. The girl's chin was tucked into her chest. Her hair covered her face. *My God,* Meg thought, *how will this child ever be the same?*

"It's called fellatio," Robert said, then opened his eyes and with an uncharacteristic snap to his voice he added, "If you don't understand the meaning of the word, look it up."

The captain turned away from them and went back to the window.

"My back was to the door," Robert continued. "Natalie saw Derek before she saw me. Derek had his hands on my head. I guess my daughter thought he was trying to strangle me."

Natalie began to cry loudly.

"That's when she lunged for him. That's when they struggled. That's when the gun went off."

The captain studied whatever it was outside the window. "And after she shot him, the two of you moved his body downstairs. To the library. To make it look as though he were an intruder."

"It was foolish, I know," Robert said.

"But still," the captain went on, "you expect us to believe it. All of it."

Meg watched Robert, saw the agony on his face as his gaze moved from the captain to his daughter. For what seemed like a very long time, no one spoke. Then, slowly, Natalie lifted her head.

"I have a scratch," the girl said, holding out her arm, "from where he tried to stop me."

The captain hesitated a moment, then turned and walked to where Natalie sat. He lifted her arm and examined the scratch.

An accident, Meg thought. It had definitely happened the way they'd said. The way they'd finally said. Meg also knew that at some point Natalie would have to be tested for HIV. It was a very long shot that Derek could have infected her, but it was something that would need to be checked.

The captain scowled. "If this is all true, then why all the lies?"

Robert sat straight in his chair. "The lies were my idea," he said. "I wanted to protect Alissa. And the girls. Protect them from the scandal that their father is nothing more than"—he paused—"than a fucking queer."

Natalie pushed back her chair, stood up, and went to Robert. She stooped down and put her arms around him. Together, they cried.

And Meg realized that trying to protect anyone—wives, husbands, children, even lovers—from problems, or from pain, only causes greater hurt in the end. She picked up her briefcase and turned to the captain. "I think we have some paperwork to do," she said.

19

"I cannot believe you people have done this to me."

Michele stood in front of Alissa and Danny, hands on her hips, eyes wild with rage. Alissa knew that the only time Michele would have expected to see the inside of a police station was if she was organizing their charity ball.

"We people," Alissa said as she glared back at the mirror image of herself twenty-four years ago, the way she must have looked when she'd left Jay, "have not done anything to you."

"You've ruined my life. Positively ruined it. You don't honestly think David will want to marry me now, do you? Even if he does, his family will never let him."

"Good. He's an ass anyway."

"Mother! How could you?" she cried. "David is the best catch in this city, and you know it."

Alissa turned her head away. "So was your father."

Michele sniffed. "That's not fair, Mother. None of this is fair. I don't even know why I have to be here. *I* haven't done anything."

"It's just routine," Danny said. "They need to question everyone who might have been in the house."

"I told them I wasn't there! Don't they believe me? God, this is so humiliating!"

Alissa sighed. "It's no picnic for any of us."

Michele snorted and adjusted the sash tied around her hair. "But *they* were involved, Mother. Natalie shot the man—Father's—whatever you call him. *They* were involved for godsake, not me. God, how are we ever going to show our faces at the homeless gala?"

Before Alissa could answer, an officer appeared. "Michele Page? We're ready for you."

Michele shot a hateful glance at her mother, then sniffed and marched off with the policemen.

Alissa turned to Danny. "Children are so fucking selfish. It's a pity you never had any."

Danny laughed.

"The worst part is," Alissa added, "Michele is just like me." She sat still on the hard wooden bench, staring down the hallway after her daughter. "I used to be like that. I liked it that I could dress her up and show her off, that she adored the attention and the parties, and that she could spot a fake anything, anytime, no matter if it was a fake diamond or fake French perfume. I liked that she cared about knowing who the best caterer in town was, and that she'd learned what kind of hors d'oeuvres are acceptable for cocktail parties or for dinner. I *liked* it, Danny. I liked having a little Alissa clone."

She wrapped her arms around herself and rubbed them. "But in these past few weeks I've realized how shallow she is. Shallow, and even worse, insensitive. I guess I've really done a good job of making her just like me."

Danny rested one foot atop the other knee and ran his hand across his boot. "I don't think you're giving yourself enough credit. You're a strong woman, Alissa. There's nothing wrong with that."

Alissa stood up and walked to a bulletin board. She studied the grainy black-and-white notices of codes and regulations and the country's most wanted, trying to dispel the vulnerability she felt whenever she and Danny were in the same room. She turned back to him, this tousle-haired, blue-jeaned, sensitive guy.

"You're wrong, Danny," she said. "I'm not strong. If I were, I'd have left Robert years ago. And none of this would be happening. A man would still be alive, and my family wouldn't be in this mess. Even though I didn't know Robert was gay all these years, I knew he was fooling around. And whether he was with a man or another woman, the truth is, our marriage was glued together by appearances and infidelities. His, then mine."

She walked back to the bench and sat down. "It didn't take strength to stay married to a man with so much money, so much power. It took fear. Of independence."

Danny formed a tent with his fingers. Alissa wondered if his calluses would feel rough against her skin.

"I thought you had money of your own," he said.

"Only half as much as he and I put together." She couldn't believe she was saying this out loud, that she had stayed with Robert only for the money, for the prestige of being Mrs. Robert Hamilton Page. But it was true, and Alissa suspected that Danny knew it anyway.

"What are you going to do now?"

Alissa shrugged and pulled a pack of cigarettes from her purse. She shook one out and lit it. "A lot depends on what happens with Natalie." She looked around for an ashtray. A No Smoking sign caught her eye.

"Natalie will be okay," Danny said. "My guess is it will be ruled accidental and there won't even be a trial. They'll check under the victim's fingernails for skin tissue. If it matches Natalie's, it would indicate a struggle. Her story and Robert's verification will hold up then."

Alissa shivered and took a deep drag on her cigarette. "I hope you're right. I hope it's as easy and painless for Natalie as possible. But we can't be sure of that. Especially since your girlfriend, Meg, will probably bail out on me."

"She's not my girlfriend, Alissa. We're close friends, that's all. But, Jesus, you did try to blackmail her."

Alissa ignored the sergeant behind the desk who was flipping his gaze back and forth from the No Smoking sign to the small curl of smoke at the tip of her cigarette. She smiled. "Yes, I thought that was rather brilliant of me." She took another drag, then ground the butt on the gray tile under her feet.

"Well, I thought it sucked."

Alissa folded her hands in her lap and stared at the floor. "You're right," she said quietly, "it did suck."

Danny leaned back and stretched his arm across the back of the bench. "What are you going to do now? No matter what happens with Natalie, you can't go on living like this."

Alissa hesitated, then nodded, without words.

"And what about the homeless gala? Are you going through with it?"

Alissa laughed. "You heard my daughter. 'How are we going to show our faces there?'"

"That's ridiculous. You're not the first family to have problems."

"I think 'scandal' is a more appropriate word here."

Danny shook his head. "No, Alissa, you're wrong. Besides, I've seen a lot of people weather a lot of scandals, and I've learned that the ones who save face are the ones who face them."

Meg saw Alissa and Danny sitting head to head, talking in inaudible whispers. Danny had his arm around Alissa. A sting of envy shot through her, followed quickly by slow anger. Danny—her friend—was comforting the woman who had only yesterday threatened to destroy her life.

As she walked toward them, they stopped talking.

"You knew all along, didn't you, Alissa?" Meg asked.

Alissa didn't answer.

"Meg," Danny said, "it's over. Leave her alone."

Leave her alone? Danny's words burned into her. *Just who is your friend here?* she wanted to shout. *Leave her alone? The woman who tried to blackmail me? The bitch who put together these lies to save her precious reputation among the rich and famous?* She tried to swallow her rage.

"Robert is in there confessing," she said coldly. "He's telling the truth. I hope."

"It's the truth," Alissa said. "All of it. I'm sure you'll find it's consistent with what I've just told Danny."

Meg tucked her briefcase under her arm. She looked at Alissa, so fragile looking, so injured. She wondered which woman was the real Alissa—the sympathetic one, or the blackmailer.

Alissa put a small jeweled hand on Meg's arm. "Will you stay?" she asked with watery eyes. "Until this is over?"

Meg thought about Holly Davidson, about Arnold Banks. Surely the trial of Dr. Robert Hamilton Page's daughter, who had admitted to killing her father's gay lover, would command as much publicity, probably more. It was the stuff Larson, Bascomb would wet their pants over. In its own infamous way this case would be certain to draw many other married men out of their proverbial closets. Only in America, Meg thought, would anyone be arrogant enough to turn the issue of homosexuality into scandal in the first place. And now the tabloid-tantalized public would most likely throw all its support toward Natalie. The cause would be ruled accidental; it would never make it to trial. *Sorry, Avery. Sorry, George Bascomb.*

"I feel badly for you, Alissa," Meg said quietly, her anger calmed, her voice low. "I feel badly for Robert, and for the ordeal your family is going through. It probably isn't fair. But, then, what's equally unfair is that Robert didn't have the freedom to be who he was all along. I'm sure Derek's family would agree."

"Robert told me that Derek's family disowned him when he told them he was gay," Alissa answered.

"Then it's even more sad. Now they've lost him forever, and so has Robert."

Alissa ran her hand through her hair. "You have to help me," she begged. "There's no one else I trust."

"I hope you're not threatening me again."

Alissa stood up. "No, Meg. No threats, no strings. But . . ." She looked at the floor, then raised her chin to Meg. She blinked back tears. "But I need you, Meg. I have no one else."

Meg studied Alissa's pale, drawn face. Alissa was, obviously, tired. Probably so tired of being scared, so tired of feeling alone, that she no longer cared if her weaknesses showed. Meg thought of her own friendless years, and of the many ways in which she had shut love out. How different was she from Alissa?

Before Meg realized what she was doing, she'd set down her briefcase and wrapped her arms around her friend—her tiny, fragile, very vulnerable friend.

"I'll help you, Alissa," she said quietly. "Now, let's get out of this hellhole. Let's get you home." Alissa clung to her a moment longer, and as Meg glanced over Alissa's shoulder, she saw Danny. He was smiling.

When they pulled into the circular driveway, Alissa groaned. "Oh, shit. Whose car is that?" She pointed to a white Eldorado parked by the front door.

"It can't be the media," Meg said as Danny stopped the car and they got out. "They aren't paid well enough to drive Cadillacs."

"It's probably Sue Ellen, who's come to tell me my services for the homeless gala are no longer needed."

"Bullshit," Danny said as he put his arm behind Alissa and they went up the stairs. "They need you more than you need them, and don't ever forget that."

Inside the foyer all was quiet. Alissa shrugged as she led Danny and Meg into the library. Then she stopped. On the sofa, her back to them, sat a woman. Her hair was thick, and very dark. The woman stood and turned around.

"Zoe!" Alissa and Meg cried out together.

"Zoe," Alissa repeated. "What the hell are you doing here?"

Zoe stepped forward. She smiled and took Alissa's hands. "I've come to see you," she said. "I thought you could use another friend."

Alissa looked at Zoe, then back to Meg, then back to Zoe. "I can't believe this."

Danny approached Zoe and extended his hand. "I can't speak for the girls, but I for one am very glad you're here. Danny Gordon," he said as he shook Zoe's hand.

Zoe studied him. "Danny Gordon," she said. "It's nice to meet you. I believe you're the man who saved my life."

"Long story," he said in response to Alissa's look of confusion. He turned back to Zoe. "How's Scott?"

"He's fine," she nodded. "He's home."

"Great," Danny answered. "That's great."

Zoe smiled and nodded again. "I hope you don't mind, Alissa. Your housekeeper let me in."

"Mind? I'm thrilled. Please, everybody sit down. I'll get us a drink," she said, and headed for the door.

"Why don't you ring for Dolores?" Danny asked.

Alissa shook her head. "I'll be right back."

In the foyer Alissa slouched against the wall and took a deep breath. She couldn't believe Zoe was there. She couldn't believe everything that was happening. Zoe had come to Atlanta. She was a few weeks early, and Alissa's present situation wasn't exactly the gala she was hoping for, but Zoe was there. *God,* Alissa thought, *talk about twists and turns.* Danny was there. Meg was there. And now Zoe. Maybe Alissa Page had some friends, after all. She briefly wondered if Aunt Helma would think they were good enough. Then she laughed sharply and walked down the hall toward the kitchen, eager to be a good hostess and to get her guests something to drink.

"Are you going to tell her about Jay?" Meg asked.

Zoe rubbed the arm of the sofa. "I don't know. I think Alissa's going through enough right now."

"She can handle it," Danny said. "Alissa is stronger than you think. Stronger than *she* thinks."

But Zoe wasn't convinced. It had seemed like the right thing to do, when she had thought about it that morning after Jay had left for work. For beneath her growing feelings for him lay an edge of guilt, deepened by the lessons she'd learned about avoiding truth. But now, seeing Alissa, the pain on her face, the marks of sleeplessness under her eyes, Zoe didn't want to cause any more hurt. Still, Alissa had to know. And if Zoe didn't tell her now, Alissa might hop onto the next flight to L.A. after this mess was over and find out in an even more hurtful way.

"Lemonade, anyone?" Alissa called as she walked into the library, toting a wide silver tray laden with glasses and a pitcher. "It's very southern and even tastier with a dash of vodka." She set drinks in front of Meg and Danny and handed one to Zoe. "I'm sure Meg and Danny have filled you in on what's going on," she said.

Zoe nodded. "How are you doing?"

Alissa took her glass and walked behind the desk. She sat down, straightened a pile of letters, then folded her hands. "I'm doing lousy," she said. "But thanks for asking."

Zoe's heart sank.

Danny sat up straight in the chair behind the desk. "Alissa will be fine once she gets back to work," he said.

"Work?" Zoe asked.

"She's got a charity ball coming up. She needs to get cranking."

Alissa rolled her eyes. "I'm quite sure the homeless will survive without Alissa Page."

Zoe sipped her lemonade. Even with the vodka it was tart, tangy, and, like Alissa, very southern. "You're holding a charity ball for the homeless? I think that's wonderful."

Alissa tapped her fingernails on the desk. "It was supposed to be." She laughed, then got up and walked to the window. "It was supposed to be my 'coming out' party, if you'll excuse the pun under the circumstances. At one point I actually dreamed I'd be going with Jay."

"Jay?" Zoe asked weakly.

Alissa nodded and pushed back the long, heavy drapes. "I wanted to have you here, too, Zoe. You were going to be my trump card. My way of making Atlanta sit up and take notice. My way of showing the world that Alissa Page still has it. But now"—she shrugged and walked back to the desk—"none of it matters."

Danny cleared his throat. "Meg, what do you say we go in the other room and look over Natalie's statement?"

Meg stood up. "Good idea."

"I guess they're tired of hearing me bitch," Alissa said after they had left.

Zoe shook her head. "I think they wanted to give us some time alone." She took another drink, hoping the vodka would warm her, calm her. "Alissa," she said slowly, "tell me about Jay. Aren't you planning to see him again?"

"I don't think he'll miss me. The truth is, Zoe, I pushed myself on him. I may be an idiot sometimes, but I'm not a total fool. Jay was glad to see me, for old times' sake. Beyond that, I really don't think he was interested."

Zoe rubbed the arm of the sofa again. "But how did you feel? How do you feel? About him?"

Alissa laughed. "I haven't even thought of him these past couple of days. So much for true love." She reached over and plucked a magazine from the rack, then began thumbing through it, looking at the pictures. "But that's right. You met him. He's going bald, Zoe. And I'm sure you noticed that he and I have nothing in common except the past."

"The past can be a lot to have in common."

"It's not enough. The man hates black tie, for godsake. I guess I never opened my eyes long enough to realize he always did."

"There must be more on your mind than black tie, Alissa."

She closed the magazine. "There is. He would detest my life. And I, quite frankly, would be more than mildly annoyed at his."

Zoe smiled. Alissa seemed to be over Jay, really over him. "No regrets?" she asked.

Alissa shook her head. "No time," she said. "The rest of my life is so fucked up, I have no time for regrets over Jay Stockwell."

Zoe set down her glass and twisted her hands together. "I thought he was very nice," she said.

"Nice? Yeah, Jay's one of the good guys. Which is why he deserves more than me."

Zoe closed her eyes, then opened them again. "I, ah ..." She spoke slowly, carefully. "I've seen him since the other night," she said.

Alissa raised her eyebrows. "You've seen him?"

"Yes."

"On a date?"

Zoe nodded.

"Jesus Christ," Alissa said, and pushed the magazine off the desk. Her face flared crimson. "You're dating Jay?"

"I didn't mean to, Zoe. He didn't mean to. It's just that we ... we have so much in common."

Alissa stared at Zoe for a few seconds, then began to cackle. "This is unbelievable. You. Dating my Jay. Un-fucking-believable."

"I hoped you'd understand," Zoe said weakly.

Alissa kept laughing. "Understand? Sure, why not?" She raised her glass to take another drink. Zoe noticed her hand was trembling. "Here's to love. Here's to true love."

"Come on, Alissa, it's a little soon for that. We've really only just met."

"It only takes a minute to fall in love," Alissa said. "At least that's what I've heard."

"Alissa," Zoe interrupted, "you mentioned the charity

ball. That you'd wanted to ask me to come. When is it? I'd like to do that for you."

"Because you feel sorry for me? Because you feel guilty for stealing the man I once loved, who I've now discovered I don't love anymore anyway?"

"No. Because I'd like to do it for you. Because you're my friend."

Alissa got up and walked to the bookcase. She ran her fingers across the leather spines. "I don't even know if I can go through with this gala. Danny is trying to convince me to, but I don't think it's possible."

"Even if I were here?"

Alissa pulled a book from the shelf, moved three others to the left, then tucked it back into place. "If you were here, it would certainly take the spotlight off me. Off Robert. Off this whole ordeal." She shrugged. "Not that Robert will go. I don't think I could allow that."

Zoe stood up and went to Alissa. She put a hand on her shoulder. "Then it's a deal. I'm coming. Just tell me when and where. I'll be here, Alissa. I promise."

Alissa turned and faced her. "You are, of course, welcome to bring an escort." Then she broke into a smile. "If you think you can stuff him into black tie for the night."

In the living room Danny and Meg sat on the stiff settee. Meg had her head on Danny's shoulder. "This has been exhausting," she said.

Danny laughed and stroked her hair. "Alissa has a way of doing that to people."

"She's a good person, though, isn't she, Danny?"

"Yup."

"She is," Meg confirmed to herself. "Deep down, Alissa Page is a good person. You recognized that."

"I told you before. I think she's been a victim of her life, her wealth."

"Like your mother."

"Maybe."

Meg sat up straight. "Maybe in some way we're all victims of our lives. Maybe we make ourselves victims."

"It sounds like your next comment is going to be 'Life is too short for that,'" Danny said.

Meg nodded. "It is. And it's too short to spend being miserable simply because we think we don't deserve happiness."

"You're not talking about Alissa anymore, are you?"

"No."

She picked up the pages of Natalie's statement from the floor and put them in her briefcase. "This should be wrapped up in a few days," she said. "Then I'm leaving."

"Back to New York?"

Meg shook her head. "No. Washington."

Later, as Meg left for her hotel room, Zoe offered to drive her. She said she wanted to get back to L.A., to get back to her son. Alissa suspected she wanted to see Jay, to tell him that she had told Alissa everything, and that Alissa was all right. The odd thing was, she was.

Alissa stood in the doorway and waved as Zoe and Meg drove away. Danny moved beside her.

"So Zoe will be coming to the gala," he said.

Alissa nodded. "With Jay."

He put his arm around her. "Will you be okay with that?"

"Sure," Alissa answered wryly. "A double coup. It'll be a triumph."

"Well, you won't have to do it alone, you know."

She turned to him.

He tightened his arm around her. "I'm going to be here, too," he said. "For you."

She leaned against his chest. Tears fell from her eyes. "I'm too old for you, Danny. You need someone young. I'm not young anymore."

She felt the gentle strength of his arm around her, then felt his lips softly brush her hair.

"What the hell would I do with anyone young? At my

age? Besides," he laughed, "they'd only want me for my money."

She shook her head. "You'll probably regret getting involved with me," she said quietly.

"I don't think so," Danny answered. "I don't think so at all."

20

The flowers were late. The caterer was short of praline mousse. The *A* of "WFFA" on the ten-foot ice sculpture had broken in half during transit. And the guests would begin to arrive in forty-five minutes. But all things considered, Alissa thought as she surveyed the ballroom, it was no ordinary gala. "Another Day in Paradise" was beyond even Alissa's wildest dreams.

When Zoe had agreed to come, Alissa had immediately called the printer and had him boost the ticket prices to a thousand dollars a couple. Sales soared. Renowned corporate heads scrambled for tickets. Senators, congressmen, ambassadors. There would even be eleven people whose photos had appeared on the cover of *Time* or *Newsweek* in the previous six months. Alissa had initially anticipated twelve hundred people: at the last minute she had begged the hotel to squeeze in tables for an additional four hundred. They could have used more.

There had hardly been time to handle the delicate task of arranging the seating. But something told Alissa that, for once, it wouldn't matter if corporate competitors or conflicting politicians or even ex-spouses wound up sitting together, for they would know they were privileged just to be there at the most magnificent gala—the most *politically correct* social event—of their generation. It was incredible how a small splash of Hollywood suddenly brought out the cause-consciousness in so many.

And it was going to be worth it. After expenses they would net well over a million dollars for the homeless. Her friends in the Underground would be ecstatic.

She wove through the tables, randomly checking linens, silver. There was no Baccarat stemware; there would be no Cristal champagne. And no goody bags. Only a small white tent card at each place setting with a gold inscription that read: "In lieu of favors, Hobart Pharmaceuticals, Inc. is pleased to donate a supply of antibiotics to the 'Health Care for the Homeless' programs throughout Greater Atlanta."

Alissa wondered if the media would credit her as the trend-setting woman who changed society's fluff into substance.

She stopped at a ficus tree and adjusted the tiny white lights strung through the leaves. *Chances are,* she thought, *the press won't see anything beyond Zoe. Zoe and Jay. And Meg. God, Meg will hate that.*

"Hey, lady," she heard Danny call. She looked across the room and watched him approach her. He was smiling. "You come here often?" he asked. He bent and kissed her cheek. "God, you look gorgeous."

Alissa smiled. She knew the white, crystal-covered sheath that she wore was as striking and as beautiful as she felt. She was glad Danny noticed. "And you," she said, "look at you, all dressed up in black tie."

Danny leaned against a chair and struck a model's pose. "Quite dashing, don't you think?"

Alissa laughed, then looked down. On his feet Danny wore boots. They were black, they were shined, but they were boots. Of course. And on him they were perfect. "Very dashing," she said, "my Prince Charming. Have you heard from Meg?"

Danny nodded. "She got into town this afternoon. Zoe's here, too. Upstairs, in her suite."

Alissa nodded.

"And by the way," Danny went on, "there are about a million people lined up in front of the hotel, not to mention cameras and lights and tons of reporters with steno pads flipped open. Christ, it's like Oscar night in Atlanta."

Alissa felt warmth surge through her, warmth over the familiarity of it all, another success, another grand event, this time the grandest of them all. "The people want to see who's here," she said. "They want to see the faces and the gowns and who's-with-whom."

"In other words," Danny said, "they want to gawk. Well, I suppose everyone who will be here will expect that. In fact, being seen is probably the reason most of them are coming at all. Tomorrow they'll run for the papers and turn on their TVs, hoping to catch a glimpse of themselves."

Alissa looked at Danny. *Of course,* she thought. *Of course that's what they'll do. It's what I would have done before . . . before I wasn't the only one who mattered.* She thought about Zoe again, about Jay, and about Meg. Zoe, who, though two weeks ago had sent TV ratings soaring with her performance in *Close Ties,* was really more comfortable out of the limelight, curled up on her "off-camera time" on her livingroom sofa. Jay, who never liked "social bullshit." Meg, who, visible as she was, detested the press and their power to destroy. And then there was the business of Meg and Senator Riley. . . .

"Danny, will you excuse me a minute?" Alissa asked.

"Need any help?"

She started to say no, then changed her mind. It was time to stop thinking she was the only person in the world, the majordomo, the queen bee. "Yes, I'd like that. I'd like you to witness what I'm about to do. Then later you can tell me I was out of my mind."

They went into the grand foyer, a huge, crystal-chandeliered and mirror-walled hall, which had already been cordoned off by security with brass stanchions and red velvet ropes.

"Where are we going?" Robert asked.

"Outside."

"Are you nuts? I told you there are about a million people out there."

Alissa smiled at him and kept walking, headed for the tall, sculpted wood doors. "Tell me that later. Not now."

The two guards posted at the doors stepped aside for Alissa and Danny. She thought for a moment that one of them bowed. A doorman appeared. "May I help you, Mrs. Page?"

"Yes. Open the doors, please. I have an announcement to make to the crowd."

The doorman hesitated only a moment, then unlocked the doors. As he swung them open, Alissa gasped. A cacophony of shouts and cheers rose in the air from the sea of faces that covered the stairs, the street, the parking lot. *A sea of faces.* She had read that somewhere. She was seeing it now. The press releases had been sent out, and for once it appeared as though everyone had shown up. Everyone, and more.

Danny leaned down and whispered in her ear, "I told you so."

She smiled and raised her hands to quiet the crowd. "Ladies and gentlemen," she said as loudly as she could. But her voice was drowned out by the sounds.

The doorman reappeared and handed her a cordless microphone. Alissa turned it on and began again. "Ladies and gentlemen," she repeated. This time the crowd began to quiet. "May I have your attention, please?" The noise dropped some more. She waited until it was still.

"Ladies and gentlemen. My name is Alissa Page. I'd like to say what a pleasure it is to see so many people interested in our gala."

Cheers roared again.

She waved her arms. They silenced. "Unfortunately, our

tickets have been sold out. If you would like to stay outside and watch our guests arrive, please be courteous."

There were a few jeers; then they ceased.

"However, there is something I would like to address directly to members of the media."

More jeers.

"Thank you for coming tonight. However, as chairperson of this event, I must ask you to remain outside. The media will not be allowed inside the foyer, or in the ballroom tonight."

Angry shouts arose.

"Hey, lady, I've come all the way from Washington."

"Yeah, give us a break."

Alissa spoke into the mike again. "I'm sorry, but the decision is final. You'll have plenty of opportunity to take your pictures out here. Again, I ask you to be courteous."

"But what about interviews?" came another shout as Alissa led Danny back inside. The doorman locked the doors behind them.

Danny whistled. "No press inside? But I thought you wanted publicity."

Alissa shrugged. "My friends won't be comfortable with it."

"But what about the people who paid a thousand bucks to see their picture on the front page of tomorrow's edition?"

"They'll survive. And maybe they'll learn there are more important things in the world than what other people think. It's something I learned too late. And Robert learned too late."

They walked back into the ballroom.

Danny shook his head and glanced around the room. "Does it seem strange not having Robert here?"

"A little, I guess," she answered honestly.

Danny smiled and touched her cheek. "I'm proud of you. For what you just did," he said. "Now I think I'll go check on the birds."

Alissa laughed and wondered if Danny had any idea in

how many ways he had saved her sanity, and saved her life. She watched as he strolled toward the bandstand. It was draped in white chiffon and adorned on either side by fifteen-foot-high white-and-gold bird cages filled with cooing white doves—the birds that would have presided over Michele's wedding, had there been a wedding. Yes, she thought, it was strange to be there without Robert. But she had been so busy during the past weeks, so crazed with last-minute preparations, that she'd barely had time to put her life in perspective. No charges had been brought against Natalie. As Danny had predicted, tissue samples under Derek's fingernails matched Natalie's. The case was declared accidental. The following day Robert had flown off to Switzerland; their attorneys were drawing up the preliminary settlement for the divorce. Alissa knew they would see each other from time to time: the bond of twenty years was too strong for them not to remain friends. And besides, they had their daughters, though Michele had currently elected to forget that. She had flown off to Dallas without David and had made some noise about starting a new life. With the five-million-dollar trust fund Michele would inherit on her twenty-first birthday, Alissa knew her daughter would have no trouble finding a "new life." She only hoped she'd learned something from her mother's mistakes.

And then there was Natalie. Alissa sighed now as she straightened a napkin on a table. Since the "accident," Natalie had sequestered herself in her room, drapes pulled, remote control in hand, though she often watched television without turning up the volume. After several days Alissa had convinced Natalie to see Lou Gentile, a prominent psychologist who specialized in depression and who had agreed to come to the house four times a week. Surprisingly, money did not seem to be his motive. And he had come highly recommended as someone who actually cared.

"What if the birds shit on somebody's head?" Danny cried from the front of the room.

Alissa laughed. She could think of a few people she would

love to see that happen to. Grant Wentworth. Betty. Sue Ellen Jamison. She smiled and headed for the doors leading out of the ballroom. "I'll be right back," she called to Danny. "I need a last minute makeup check." Then she walked down the hall toward the ladies' lounge, hoping the concierge had remembered to station three attendants there and remove from the marble vanity counters those godawful, tacky, shell-like bowls used for tips.

"It's a freaking monkey suit," Jay said as he tried to adjust the black silk tie. His hair hung down, his shirt was overstarched, and he did, indeed, look out of his element.

Zoe laughed. "You look marvelous. Come on, now, chin up. We're doing this for Alissa, remember?"

"I've only ever worn these damn things for Alissa," he said. "I thought I paid my penance years ago. Besides, this all seems rather ridiculous. Alissa Page putting on a benefit for the homeless. You don't suppose old age has finally turned her into a liberal, do you?"

Zoe smiled and turned back to the mirror. "People change, Jay. I have." She clipped on her large onyx-and-diamond earrings, then slipped the matching pendant around her throat. Jay stepped up behind her and fastened the clasp. He put his hands on her shoulders.

Zoe looked at their reflections. It seemed so right to have Jay standing behind her; it seemed so natural. They were a picture with balance, a picture that fit together in every way. Then she touched the corner of her mouth and, for the first time, noticed that it no longer drooped. She smiled as another thought came into her mind: It had been weeks since she'd craved a Twinkie.

"God," Jay said, "you look radiant. It's worth putting on this monkey suit just to see you so beautiful." He reached around and slid his hands over the bare tops of her breasts, where they swelled from her low-cut black gown. She sighed.

"Better move those hands," she said softly, "or we'll never make it downstairs."

"In which case," he said as he turned her around and kissed her throat. "It would probably be an understatement to say that Princess Alissa would be royally pissed."

"I'd better get dressed, or Alissa will never speak to me again," Meg said as she traced her finger down the narrow strip of soft hair on Steven's stomach.

"Senators and their wives are allowed to be fashionably late," he whispered. He reached down and moved his hand between her legs.

"I'm not your wife," Meg answered.

"You will be. As soon as my divorce is final. I want us to have a life together. I want us to have children."

Meg closed her eyes and felt his touch, so warm, so loving. This was the man who wanted to spend the rest of his life with her. And yet...

When she'd left Atlanta three weeks ago, she'd gone to him. She'd told him she still loved him, had never stopped loving him. He'd moved into her hotel room for a week. While he'd worked each day, Meg had scouted the area for office space—a place where she could set up a practice, specializing in family law. When she had returned to New York to check on Raggedy Man, Steven had gone with her. And yet she still hadn't told him.

"Steven," she said quietly now, "there's something you don't know." The room was still, its silence painted only with the soft sounds of their breath, breathing together, life as one. "When we were at Harvard, I had an abortion, Steven," Meg said. "I killed our child." The words, at last, were out. And yet, surprisingly, they hadn't been difficult to say. *Maybe,* she thought, *it's because I finally trust him. Maybe it's because I finally trust myself.* She closed her eyes and wondered what had taken her so long.

Steven watched her for a moment, a long, slow, aching

moment. Then he took her hand in his. "How hard that must have been for you."

She wanted to keep her eyes closed. She didn't want to see if the hurt was there, if there was pain. She didn't want to feel the guilt. Yet this time she opened her eyes. She made herself look at his face, into his cobalt eyes. And this time what she saw was love.

"I love you, Meg," he said. "I want to make this up to you. Today is a new day. Everything else is in the past."

And then his lips met hers. Lightly, gently, fully. And Meg knew that from the past, at last, had come her future.

There was hardly any room on the dance floor, which gave Alissa all the more reason to hold Danny as tightly as she possibly could. Tonight, she knew, she would go to his room. Tonight they would make love for the first time. *The first time,* she thought, *and it will be magical.*

She rested her head against his shoulder and looked around. Grant Wentworth was dancing with a woman Alissa didn't recognize—probably his new Tuesday-afternoon tryst; at the opposite end of the room Betty, dressed in dowdy beige organdy, was holding court at the bar. Sue Ellen sat at a table with her bored husband. Alissa wondered how long, and why, that marriage had lasted. Money, most likely. Hers. His. Theirs. She knew the story well.

She looked back to the crowded dance floor. There were, though, smiling couples, happy couples, like her and Danny: women in sequins and chiffons and silks, adorned with their safe-deposit-box jewels, gliding over the dance floor with glittering ease; men with power-made postures and manicured nails, as impressed with the evening as the women they held. And then there were Meg and Steven, so in love, dancing slowly, their eyes lost in one another's. Not far from them danced Zoe and ... Jay. *God,* Alissa thought, *they're laughing. He's making faces, but they're having a good time.* She noticed his limp, then wondered if his leg was bothering him, or if Jay Stockwell simply still hated to dance.

"It's a wonderful evening," Danny whispered in her ear. "No one even seems to miss the media."

Alissa nodded. "Especially my friends."

He hugged her and pulled her closer. "You've changed, Alissa. Or maybe you're just becoming who you really always were."

"Well, I've learned something in these past few months, that's for sure."

"Like ... ?" Danny stopped dancing and followed her gaze across the dance floor, toward Zoe and Jay.

"I've learned that our first loves," Alissa said with a smile, "may not always be our best."

Danny nodded toward Meg and Steven. "Sometimes they are."

"I think it's rare," Alissa answered.

Danny touched her chin and turned her face toward him. "I've learned something, too," he said.

"Like ... ?"

"I've learned that Atlanta is a wonderful climate for growing orchids."

Alissa smiled and started dancing again, being careful not to step on his boots.

About the Author

JEAN STONE ran her own award-winning advertising agency for fifteen years before becoming a full-time writer. Her first novel was *Sins of Innocence*, inspired by the baby she had in 1968 whom she gave up for adoption. Jean Stone lives in West Springfield, Massachusetts, where she is at work on her next novel.